PRAISE FOR
GREER MACALLISTER

THE THIRTEENTH HUSBAND

"A whirlwind tour of the life and loves of incomparable Aimée Crocker. Macallister deftly captures the raucous, devil-may-care attitude of a woman who wasn't afraid of scandal, while also beautifully depicting her more vulnerable side— especially when it came to matters of the heart. A truly wonderful read."
—Fiona Davis, *New York Times* bestselling
author of *The Spectacular*

"An absorbing portrait of a fascinating woman, *The Thirteenth Husband* explores the raucous life of Aimée Crocker: millionaire, mystic, and iconoclast. In Macallister's skillful hands, Crocker comes to vibrant, sensational life. I couldn't look away!"
—Heather Webb, *USA Today* bestselling
author of *Queens of London*

"In a story as captivating as the real-life heiress Aimée Crocker who inspires it, *The Thirteenth Husband* takes its readers on a journey across cultures and continents, through fortunes, and, of course, husbands. Utterly gripping."
—Marie Benedict, New York Times bestselling author
of *The Mystery of Mrs. Christie* and *The First Ladies*

"An , *The Thirteenth Husband* is respl   ;ic, and yearning. Macallister elega   spectacular and complicated woman living life to the very fullest, and Aimée Crocker is a flawed heroine to be celebrated."

—Noelle Salazar, *USA Today* bestselling author of *The Flight Girls*

"Greer Macallister's Aimée Crocker is exactly the kind of sassy, strong heroine you want to stay up late into the night gabbing with—and soaking up every detail of her epic life. I loved adventuring with Aimée from San Francisco to India and Japan, walking in the shoes of a woman who lived and loved life to the fullest. This is compulsively readable historical fiction!"

—Kerri Maher, *USA Today* bestselling author of *All You Have to Do Is Call*

THE ARCTIC FURY

"Equal parts courtroom drama and literary thriller, *The Arctic Fury* bears all the twists and turns of a runaway train, barreling through an expedition as harsh and unrelenting as the Arctic north itself. A remarkably unique and mesmerizing tale."

—Kristina McMorris, *New York Times* bestselling author of *Sold on a Monday*

"An unforgiving, snow-dazzling landscape, a cast of extraordinary, fierce women, and a nail-biting courtroom drama that wrecked my nails make this historical gem unputdownable!"

—Kim Michele Richardson, *New York Times* bestselling author of *The Book Woman of Troublesome Creek*

"In her novel *The Arctic Fury*, Greer Macallister plunges readers into a wild, frozen landscape as beautiful and awesome as it is punishing and lethal. This is a story of thirteen intrepid women, each with her own reasons for setting out on an ill-fated expedition, as well as a story of the secrets we carry, the pasts we try to outrun, and the bonds of friendship that save and inspire us to carry on."

—Allison Pataki, *New York Times* bestselling author of *The Queen's Fortune*

"A captivating look at the manner in which the 'truth' is formed by the lens through which it is perceived, a lens formed by time, place, and views on women."

—Marie Benedict, *New York Times* bestselling author of *The Only Woman in the Room* and *The Mystery of Mrs. Christie*

WOMAN 99

"A gripping story that exposes the Gilded Age's tarnished veneer, when women who didn't acquiesce to the standards of the day were locked away. Powerful and electrifying, Macallister is at the top of her game."

—Fiona Davis, bestselling author of *The Masterpiece* and *The Address*

"A gorgeous ode to the power of female courage… Greer Macallister pens a nail-biter that makes you want to stand up and cheer."

—Kate Quinn, *New York Times* bestselling author of *The Alice Network*

"Readers will become engrossed in Charlotte's journey of self-discovery as she fights to free herself and her sister from a rigged system."

—*Library Journal*

"It's impossible not to root for the sisters as they work to combat that mistreatment on behalf of themselves and others. *Woman 99* is a fast-paced historical thriller perfect for book club discussions."

—*Shelf Awareness*

"Macallister sensitively and adroitly portrays mental illness in an era when it was just beginning to be understood, while weaving a riveting tale of loyalty, love, and sacrifice."

—*Publishers Weekly*

GIRL IN DISGUISE

"Greer Macallister brings the original Miss Pinkerton roaring back to life in this electrifying tale. *Girl in Disguise* is a rollicking nineteenth-century thrill ride, complete with clever disguises and coded messages, foiled plots and hidden agendas, lies, indiscretion, and forbidden love. Kate Warne is a scrappy, tough-as-nails detective who did a man's job for the first time in American history. She lives and breathes again in this riveting novel."

—Amy Stewart, *New York Times* bestselling author of *Girl Waits with Gun*

"Inspired by a real-life story, Greer Macallister has created a fast-paced, lively tale of intrigue and deception, with a heroine at its center so appealingly complicated that she leaps off the page."

—Christina Baker Kline, #1 *New York Times* bestselling author of *Orphan Train*

"*Girl in Disguise* cleverly unearths the story of Kate Warne, the first female Pinkerton detective. Fast-paced, subversive, and with rich prose, it's everything a historical mystery should be. In the end, it will leave you stunned. And then you will want to read everything else Greer Macallister has ever written."

—Ariel Lawhon,
author of *Flight of Dreams*

"Macallister (*The Magician's Lie*) pens an exciting, well-crafted historical novel featuring Kate Warne, the first female Pinkerton detective in 1856 Chicago. Loaded with suspense and action, this is a well-told, superb story."

—*Publishers Weekly*, Starred Review

THE MAGICIAN'S LIE

"Smart, intricately plotted…a richly imagined thriller."

—*People*

"More bewitching than a crackling fire…The battle of wits that plays out between these covers is best read curled up under the covers."

—Oprah.com

"It's a captivating yarn… Macallister, like the Amazing Arden, mesmerizes her audience. No sleight of hand is necessary. An ambitious heroine and a captivating tale are all the magic she needs."

—*Washington Post*

"[A] well-paced, evocative, and adventurous historical novel… top-notch."

—*Publishers Weekly*, Starred Review

"Macallister is as much of a magician as her subject, misdirecting and enchanting while ultimately leaving her audience satisfied with a grand finale."

—*Dallas Morning News*

"In her historical fiction debut, Macallister…has created a captivating world of enchantment and mystery that readers will be loath to leave."

—*Library Journal*

Also by Greer Macallister

The Magician's Lie
Girl in Disguise
Woman 99
The Arctic Fury

the
THIRTEENTH
HUSBAND

GREER MACALLISTER

sourcebooks
landmark

Copyright © 2024 by Greer Macallister
Cover and internal design © 2024 by Sourcebooks
Cover design by Chelsea McGuckin
Cover images © Lee Avison/Arcangel, Yakov Oskanov/Shutterstock

Sourcebooks and the colophon are registered trademarks of Sourcebooks.

The characters and events portrayed in this book are fictitious or are used
fictitiously. Apart from well-known historical figures, any similarity to real persons,
living or dead, is purely coincidental and not intended by the author.

Published by Sourcebooks Landmark, an imprint of Sourcebooks
P.O. Box 4410, Naperville, Illinois 60567-4410
(630) 961-3900
sourcebooks.com

Cataloging-in-Publication Data is on file with the Library of Congress.

Printed and bound in the United States of America.
LSC 10 9 8 7 6 5 4 3 2 1

For Jonathan,
who first found Aimée for me
and is worth more than all her husbands put together

That's about all we get out of life, rich or poor, isn't it, a few hours of enjoyment here and there? I think it is folly to allow a single chance for pleasure to slip past you.

—**Aimée Crocker, 1911**

You know, don't you, that I've been fighting this nearly my entire life?

I don't expect sympathy, of course, from you or anyone. There's been precious little of that. Certainly none from the tabloid press. People think the rich don't struggle. And I understand why. Money solves so many problems, opens so many doors. That's why I held on to mine instead of giving it away: it was the only power I could count on. Because I was so very rich, at almost any point in my life when I wanted to go somewhere, I went. For a woman in these times, that was no small thing.

But with the tabloids dogging my steps, painting me with their scarlet brush in my very girlhood, I had my own struggles. The press called me wild, among other things. They were outraged by the notion of a woman determined to make her own choices. They labeled me an adventuress, a hussy, a known menace. Even when the *Philadelphia Inquirer* loudly proclaimed me the queen of Bohemia, it wasn't entirely a compliment. And when I'm dead, they'll trumpet my husbands' names in the headlines, as if my marriages were all that mattered. I am more than gold bands and paperwork.

Of course there are men in my story. Some would say an unseemly number. There's love and scandal, heartbreak and poison, passion and deceit. It takes place in courtrooms and orphanages, palaces and temples, in Hawaii and Tokyo and the world around. And in my story, there are also questions. So many questions. One of which you are the answer to.

The three things that have haunted me all these decades are simple enough to name: the tabloids, the Spanish fortune teller's prophecy, and the woman in white.

Where to begin? Not at the beginning. That would be expected, and you know as well as anyone, doing the expected was never my style. Let's start, instead, in the middle.

CHAPTER ONE

All my life I have been drawn to that which I cannot clearly define.

—AC

I arrived in Spain fresh off the boat from Hawaii, twenty-three years old and reeling from my first divorce, in search of a woman I didn't know was already dead.

What had happened in Hawaii had scared me badly, made me think about a reckoning. Not that I believed in the musty Christian vision of heaven and hell, but if I were to find myself at those much-written-about pearly gates, where would I fall short? What did I regret leaving undone? So when the captain of my chartered vessel asked me for our next destination, I thought about the contessa, who had once been kind to me at a low moment, and I said, "Madrid."

Captain Judd knew me well. He knew the contents of my passbook even better. So rather than deride me for naming a landlocked city, he said, "Would you prefer to go via Lisbon, Bilbao, or Barcelona?"

I pictured the map of Europe I recalled so clearly, rugged brown coastlines nudging up against the blue of oceans and seas. "Bilbao, I think."

"A good choice."

Even with no interest in the captain beyond the professional, I flirted a bit. "Would you tell me if you thought it was a poor choice?"

His smile was genuine. "I would not."

We cabled ahead to Bilbao to have arrangements made for docking the *Tropic Star* and my travel beyond. With so many messages flying back and forth, so much to manage, I got on the train before realizing my letter to the contessa had gone unanswered. At the Burgos stop, I sent telegrams to make other inquiries. When I arrived in Madrid, the bad news was waiting for me: the contessa had passed away the previous year.

Another traveler might have cursed herself for coming all this way without arranging things more firmly beforehand, but I've never been that kind of traveler. In my view, why not go? I needed to be somewhere. Madrid was as good as any other place and better than most. Besides, most women of that age—this was back in 1888, remember—never traveled without husbands or households in tow. A woman alone was viewed with suspicion. Society's rules defined the ideal woman of those days as one who made her family her entire purpose for being, their care her highest calling.

Is it any wonder I never fit in?

So after settling my things in an elegant, comfortable chamber at the Gran Hotel Inglés, I thought about what I most wanted to do. In a foreign country where I knew no one, with time and money no object, what should be my first step?

I changed into my plainest gown, secured my valuables in the hotel safe, and went in search of a local fortune teller. Spiritualism was still all the rage, the debunking crusades of the 1920s not yet a glimmer in a cynical Houdini's eye. In the 1880s, if a divorced woman and a medium sat in a room together, the medium was the less suspect of the two.

The palm reader I found on that day in Madrid was of the mysterious and handsome school, which I'd found only slightly less common worldwide than the toothless and disreputable type. His skin and hair were dark, his fingers long and delicate, his receiving room full of fragrant flowers with waxy leaves that transported me straight back to that night in the orangery with the doomed, beautiful Miguel. I was journeying straight into the memories I'd once fled from. I thought I was being brave. I have found out since that bravery and foolishness are easy to mistake for one another.

Once I sat down across the table from him and paid his fee—modest, considering—the handsome Spanish fortune teller asked me, "Very well. What is your name?"

"Why do you need to know that?" I shot back, perhaps a little more aggressively than needed. "Shouldn't we remain strangers? The less you know, the more impressive I'll find it when you tell my future."

He shook his head. "I have few questions. But I need something to call you. Any name will do."

I made a snap decision. "You may call me Miss Crocker."

"Very well, Miss Crocker. Your hand?"

I presented it, and he drew the palm toward him, lowering his face almost close enough to kiss it. I felt his breath in my hand as he looked, following lines, turning the entire hand to examine it from every angle.

Finally, I said, "Enough looking. What do you see?"

In a steady voice, nothing too dramatic, he said to me, "Ah, you need to be careful about getting married."

My response was quick and sharp, my pain still fresh. "Tell me something I don't know."

Perhaps my sarcasm was lost in translation. He may not have been familiar with the American phrase. In any case, his eyes met mine, and the next words out of his mouth were surprising indeed.

Teeth bared in a tight, threatening smile, the palm reader said, "Miss Crocker, you will have thirteen husbands. The thirteenth will bury you."

A sharp, icy shiver went up the back of my neck. I held myself still so he wouldn't see it. And I said, sounding like I could take a joke, "Well, I didn't know *that*."

CHAPTER TWO

The vision came to me first before I had reached my teens.

—AC

Further back. Before the prophecy that second time in Spain, before I was even in Spain the first time, meeting the matador. Before the German prince, before the king of the Sandwich Islands, before the songwriter and the commodore and the men who bet my future on a hand of cards, I was just a girl like any other, and the most important man in my life was E. B. Crocker.

My father was a brilliant man, self-made, a passionate student of the law his whole life long. He made his name and his money as legal counsel for my uncle's railroad, though thanks to a short term on the California Supreme Court, people often called him Judge. In his later years, he dedicated himself to amassing a glorious art collection, which I loved to hear him explain to me, though I never found collecting art of much interest. Acquiring a thing made by someone else never interested me as much as doing the thing myself.

I called him Papa and he called me Princess. I adored the sound of his voice, a low rumble, soothing in its consistency. I sat through hours of descriptions of what art he'd found and where he found it—and who he'd outmaneuvered to get it at a reasonable price—as well as more esoteric subjects. He even occasionally recounted to me particular lectures of interest from his days as a civil engineering student at the Rensselaer Institute. My sister Jennie, more interested in Mama-approved pastimes like flower arranging and the selection of appropriate hats, never had much patience for such tales. But me, I was rapt. A girl of three to nine years who can remain awake as her father explains the fundamentals of suspension bridge design is truly a devotee.

The woman in white entered my life the same night my father left it.

Midsummer, a warm June night, 1875. I was ten years old. Was it in a dream that she appeared? Or a vision? Something else, perhaps. A premonition, a rip in time. I didn't have the words for her then. I'd led only one small life, a life of tactile luxury I took entirely for granted, one that made no space for the mystical.

This is how it happened.

I never liked the dark, so I kept a lamp burning low in my room during the night, a privilege my mother only reluctantly granted. I woke that midsummer night smelling the faint smoke of an extinguished wick. Swimming up from sleep rapidly, I opened my eyes to darkness, realizing the lamp had likely been snuffed by a stray draft from the window. We sometimes kept it open a crack in the heat of summer. Staring into the uninterrupted dark scared me—I hated not being able to see even the outlines of familiar things—so I shut my eyes tight again.

My heart quickly began to speed. I could feel unease clawing its way slowly up my throat. I knew I was safe, knew it absolutely, but I also knew that if I screamed, someone would come to help me. So I was only thinking about screaming. Before I made up my mind to do it, I sensed a curious light through my closed eyelids. Perhaps I had already screamed, I reasoned, and someone was coming to light my lamp again.

"Hello?" I said softly and opened my eyes.

The wrongness was clear right away. The light wasn't coming from the doorway or the hall. The light was in the bed next to me.

At first, I saw only a large white shape, so bright and sharp against the dark it blinded me. I blinked, then forced my eyes open to let the light in, trying to see.

Then I made out her shape: a woman, silhouetted by shadow. She lay next to me as if she belonged there, arms resting at her sides, almost like a dropped doll.

"Who are you?" I whispered. She didn't answer.

I tried to peer into her face but couldn't. In fact, the more closely I looked, the less I could see.

The woman's gown was only the suggestion of clothing, with no clear lines or edges. The clearest thing about her was the line between her pale shape and the dark shadow surrounding her. And as I watched, I realized the shadow was growing.

My curiosity curdled into fear. *It's imagination,* I told myself. *You're imagining this.* But the growing shadow put fear in me. I pulled my knees up and shrank back to the very edge of the bed.

Then I heard her voice—unfamiliar, her words borne on a long, low exhale—speak three words.

"*Die like this,*" said the woman, and her shadow reached for me.

Half leaping, half falling, I tumbled off the side of the bed and thumped to the floor. I landed hard on my hip and felt a sharp, radiating pain. It couldn't be a dream, could it? The pain felt too real. The scream I had been holding back worked its way out, exploding into the dark of the night.

Shouting louder than I ever had, I screamed, "Help!"

In the long moment afterward, sprawled on the floor, tangled up in my disheveled nightdress, I expected to hear footsteps rushing toward me. Nurse, from the next room over, or maybe my older sister, Jennie, whose room was only one more door away. Mama, even, perhaps.

But the only answer that came out of the darkness was another scream, high and mad like my own, an uncanny echo.

"Help!" Then it came again. "Help me!"

Not an echo, I realized. It couldn't be. And not a dream.

A third time, louder, with a desperate edge. A woman's voice. "Help us!"

Then I heard footfalls running down the hall outside my room, steady thumps, the fainter sound of panting. Except the footfalls got softer instead of louder. Whoever was running, they were headed not toward me but away.

Terrified, no company but my own breath, I shrank. I curled into a ball, feeling the pain in my hip subside into an ache. I tucked my knees to my chest and pressed my cheek against the carpet, eyes shut tight against both the darkness and the possibility of that other-worldly light.

More sounds floated my way, but they seemed far off. The only thing that terrified me more than not knowing what was happening down the hall was the idea of going to investigate. So I would simply decide that everything would be all right. It always had been. My parents had always put things to rights, and they would do so again tonight, I was sure.

And as I lay there, I made my decision. I decided against believing in the uncertain, in the ambiguous. I had simply seen a shape in a dream, that was all. Nothing to be afraid of. The longer I lay there, the easier it was to believe it had all been imagined. The smoke from the blown-out lamp, the vague shape on the bed, even the sounds of footfalls and shouts from the hallway. None of it had to be real.

The next thing I felt was Nurse's hand shaking my shoulder. First light streamed in the window, along with a cool breeze. She was often the person I saw first in the morning, but I always called her. I called and she came. Today I hadn't called, or I didn't remember calling. Dread bloomed in me even before I saw the expression on her face.

"What is it?" I blurted, then regretted asking, as if not asking could have staved off what was coming.

Nurse's face was grave. She had been with us since I was a baby; I knew her every mood, and she was struggling to contain herself. Her fingers stretched toward mine on the coverlet, then stilled.

In a halting, tentative voice, she said, "I'm so sorry, Amy. There's bad news."

Even as a child, I could see that she didn't want to tell me. I didn't ask again. She would say what she came to say in time. So I relished the last moment before knowing.

"It's your father," she said. "In the night, he…" She paused, swallowed, tried again. "He's no longer with us."

Half my mind denied it, refused to understand, and I protested. "He's left in the night many times before. You didn't need to wake me for…" But I trailed off. The other half of my mind knew exactly what she meant, even if she struggled to say it outright.

Nurse reached out for my hand again and this time wrapped her fingers around mine, holding on. In a firmer voice, mastering herself, she said, "Amy. His heart, it stopped. Death came for him. Do you understand?"

I couldn't respond. The image of the woman in white roared back up at me from the depths of memory, her shadow, her words. *Die like this.*

"I'm so sorry," Nurse said again and then drew me into her warm embrace. She wrapped her arms around me and held on even as I sagged, as if I were a limp-bodied doll. My head felt like hollow porcelain, ready to break.

It was just a dream, I told myself. A coincidence. I dreamed of a woman speaking words of death, and I imagined voices in the hallway, and my father had died in the night. But there was no connection between these things. Nothing true. Nothing real.

Then grief took me, and I sobbed in Nurse's arms. Because the grief, that was all too real. Death was real. Papa was gone, and my loss would always be bottomless. I would never have a father again.

Are you still following? That's the story of the prophecy told and the woman in white, although only the first time I saw her and well before I understood.

The third thing that shaped my life was the attention of the tabloid press. Before my father's death, I don't think I'd ever given them a single thought. But as soon as he passed and the contents of his will were read, they gave me plenty.

CHAPTER THREE

I have nothing to be ashamed of, in spite of the scandalous press reports that hopeful reporters managed to use to amuse a scandal-loving public.

—AC

No one cared how badly my father's sudden death had broken me, but they cared very much that his will bestowed me with the unthinkable, almost monstrous sum of ten million dollars.

The newspapers were aghast, their editorial pages full of scandalized disapproval. If theirs were the only opinions I knew, I might have leapt into the Pacific before I even came of age. Mama and Jennie were old enough to handle such largesse, said the papers. They were women grown, and as it was legal, if unusual, to give women their own money, a man's decisions about his fortune should and must be his own. But I, a mere child, was sure to be ruined. They had no quibble with my father's good intentions, wrote the *Call* and the *Herald* and the *Chronicle* in prose sweet as syrup. All the same, they said, a young girl couldn't possibly handle the demands of such a fortune. The world would roll over me like a boulder.

Early on, my mother gave a few terse comments to the press, assuring reporters that she would hold tight to the reins of the Crocker dynasty, that her girls would never be given more than they could handle. But once a *Chronicle* writer compared her to the witch that kept Rapunzel in a tower, casting me as an imprisoned innocent in the grip of a selfish, wicked crone, Mama gave no more interviews.

I began to see the dark outlines of reporters everywhere I looked, lurking in doorways or even in the shadow of a tree across from our front door. Mama said to ignore them. I did my best. And for a while, I was able to pretend they didn't exist. I developed a thicker skin, or thought I had. What did some silly reporter's opinion matter anyway?

Because the vast majority of people in my life, anyone I might greet in the course of a day, treated me like a queen. No one likes to say no to a pretty girl with ten million dollars. I found that the answer to almost any question I could ask would be yes. Could I have the finest things on offer at any dressmaker's, the silks and laces and ornaments, just by saying I wanted them? Yes. Once I turned fifteen and began to attend social events, did every young man in the room want to dance with me? Yes. When we took our box at the opera, would the finest families of San Francisco send their tidings and wave their fans in my direction? Yes. When we traveled abroad and I craved a cup of chocolate *mit schlag* before dawn because my body knew it was not yet midnight in California, would a butler wake someone from the hotel kitchen to bring me what I asked for? Yes.

It would have taken an uncommonly strong young woman not to have her head turned by such opportunity. I was not yet that strong. And if the papers had decided to label me "wild" anyway, what reason did I have not to be?

That was how I found myself in a San Francisco hotel room late one night in 1882, seventeen years old, unchaperoned and draining my second glass of fine champagne as I watched five young men in shirtsleeves play poker for the right to marry me.

"Three of a kind," crowed the dark-haired one, whose name I didn't know. In Sacramento, I knew everyone—it was essentially a small town—but San Francisco gatherings attracted a larger crowd. And Marjorie Stanford's wedding, the social event of the season, had brought society from all over California and beyond. We'd taken over the top two floors of the Palace Hotel. And while official wedding events filled our days, everyone knows young people will find more amusing ways to spend their nights.

As guests left their tables after the wedding banquet, a group of cheeky young men had invited myself and two other girls of my acquaintance, Christine Porter and Dorothy Blake, to watch their midnight poker game. All three of us girls had agreed, giggling at our own daring. I was the only one who actually showed up.

Well after dark, I'd snuck out of the hotel room I shared with my mother, knowing she would never come looking for me, even on the slim chance she awoke to find me gone. It would be too scandalous for her to admit she didn't know where I was. Besides, I'd be back before dawn, and she always took laudanum when we stayed in hotels, claiming she could never get comfortable in a strange bed. More than once, she suggested I try it too, given how tired I often seemed to be when we traveled. This might have been my first midnight poker game, but it was far from my first sleepless night.

While gambling ridiculous sums of their parents' money kept the rich boys' attention for a while, they eventually decided their bets should be more interesting. One bet his racehorse, another his dog, a third the rights to name his firstborn son. I was distracted at the moment when someone suggested a lady's hand in marriage be added to the pot, but I did hear someone say "There's only one lady present."

I quickly answered, "Or none, depending on who you ask." Their laughter was as delicious to me as the bubbles in my drink.

When the conversation caught me up on what I was agreeing to, it was too late to demur without losing face, and whether or not any of these boys remembered these events in the morning, it seemed important to stay in their good graces tonight.

The blond one, who I thought was named either Daniel or David, swore mildly and tossed his cards down. "I fold. Sorry, sweetheart, I'm out of the running."

"Sorry for you," I said, the bubbles in the champagne fizzing up through the crown of my head. I thought I might float away. I felt commanding, adored. "Only one can win."

There was more swearing, mild and otherwise, and the game continued, knocking out the dark-haired one along with Daniel or David. Another round of bets, another round of drinks. Then another competitor folded. This left only two young men remaining in the game. They were, I noted happily through my champagne haze, my two favorites of the bunch.

Henry Mansfield Gillig, known to his friends as Harry, had a head of black hair as sleek as a seal's and a baritone singing voice to make the angels weep. We'd met several years before and often bumped into each other at events, always conversing politely. I flirted with him—I flirted with everyone—but Harry rarely flirted back, which of course intrigued me. Over the course of tonight's poker game, he'd played somewhat conservatively. His bets were modest. His pile of chips steadily grew. He took his time, considering his cards at length and letting his gaze drift up to his opponent, down to his cards, and back up again. This seemed to unnerve all the young men playing against him, except one.

Porter Ashe was a newer arrival in San Francisco society. His family hailed from the other coast, having founded a city in North Carolina that they named for themselves, and his uncle had apparently been a navy officer of some renown during the war. Porter had stick-straight eyebrows and a slightly overlarge nose above soft, full lips that gave him a hedonistic air. His playing style was indifferent, occasionally wild. His fortunes over the course of the game had ebbed and flowed. But he'd made it to the final round against Harry, and the copious amount of brandy he'd been swigging from his own personal bottle didn't seem to go to his head. He'd become more serious as the kitty grew. Including my hand in marriage among the winnings had been his suggestion.

The room grew quiet as cards were dealt, picked up, put down. I took another drink of champagne to ease the tension.

"Now, you boys remember," I said with more confidence than I felt, "I'm not some chip to be traded. Women aren't chattel anymore, not in modern America. Winner gets the right to ask for my hand in marriage. There's no guarantee I'll say yes."

I was surprised when it was Porter who nodded soberly and Harry who said, "Ah, Amy, you'll say yes all right." The opposite was what I expected. But when Harry saw annoyance cross my face, he said, "If you want to! If you want to. Of course."

"You're a dear," I said and finished my champagne.

I already knew I would say yes. Yes had become a habit.

Besides, I was desperate for change, and what better way to change than to throw caution to the wind? Girls I knew complained that marriage only meant trading one master for another. But with my father dead, my mother was the one holding the reins. I was more than ready to trade her in. Either of these boys would be a great deal more permissive than she, and besides, I liked them both well enough. In my opinion, people who were unhappy with marriage had expected too much from the institution. I knew how to lower my expectations.

The spectators roared, and I looked down. The cards came into focus, but only briefly. The young men were leaping to their feet, and I had only glimpsed smears of red and black. But it was clear from their reactions who had won.

"Ashe, Ashe, Ashe," chanted the tipsy young men, clapping and laughing.

Porter raised both fists in the air, triumphant. His laugh was easy and long, his handsome face radiant with his victory grin. He looked at me, not Harry, as if once Porter had won, his opponent ceased to exist.

His eyes were not the only ones on me. They all were. I felt a pulse in the air, reminding me that I was alone with half a dozen drunk boys, who weren't really boys but men, and if a friend of mine had described herself in this situation, I would have been aghast. When I'd decided to attend, I knew I was risking an absolute shellacking in the press if this escapade came out. But reckless as always, I hadn't thought about what else I was risking.

"Well, that's that, isn't it?" I said cheerfully, as if I hadn't a care in the world, brandishing my empty glass. "Now, who's going to pour me more champagne?"

Then I caught sight of Harry's face, his downcast eyes. The deep disappointment I saw there surprised me. I hadn't thought he liked me that much, but he looked devastated.

"Here, Harry," I said, thrusting my flute in his direction. "Would you mind?"

Without a trace of apparent resentment, Harry swiped the champagne bottle from the table and began to fill my champagne flute. He wasn't smiling as he slowly poured the drink, but he covered the glimpse of true emotion I'd seen. His voice was amiable, mild. "Happy to. I suppose you'll have Ashe to pour for you for the rest of your lives."

I raised my glass. "Who knows?"

Harry drained his own glass, then met my eyes, and the melancholy in his eyes sobered me. He said, "No one."

The next morning, hundreds of wedding guests gathered on the balconies surrounding the Grand Court to watch the bride and groom climb into their carriage and ride away. The hotel at that time had seven stories of white columned balconies, stacked like tiers of lace on a petticoat, overlooking a grand carriage entrance. It was the perfect place to wish the couple well.

There was much jockeying for position, of course. Much of the point of these things was to see and be seen by the right people in society. Who knew what Marjorie Stanford even wanted? This event was only a little bit about her. Thinking about the night's events, I wondered what my own wedding would look like. Marriage in our class had little to do with love, I knew, but I at least hoped for affection. All I knew was that I wouldn't be allowed to remain unmarried indefinitely. I remembered my father telling me that undeployed assets were basically a sin.

"Don't forget, Amy," he'd told me. "Money under the mattress can burn in a fire. You bank what you have, and it grows."

At the time, I thought he was speaking literally of money and fire, but as I got older, I realized he meant more.

Anyway, the wedding. Meek and obedient in a high-collared dress of lilac satin, I trailed my mother wherever she wanted to go. I was determined to play the part of the perfect daughter this morning so she wouldn't suspect what I'd been up to during the night. My stomach was still a little queasy from overindulgence.

"The bride looks so lovely," I said to Mama as we took our position in one of the uppermost balconies, an excellent vantage for looking down on the other guests. I had guessed she'd want to.

"You'll make an even lovelier bride than Marjorie," my mother said, "when you calm yourself enough to settle down."

I looked up to see if anyone was eavesdropping. Mama had positioned us at the outer edges, so the balcony she chose hadn't yet filled. No more than half a dozen people were close enough to hear our voices, let alone our words.

"I'm calm enough," I said. "Don't I seem calm?"

"You're too young yet in any case," she said musingly, as if I hadn't spoken.

"Am I? Girls of seventeen marry all the time."

I'd spoken too forcefully, and now she was curious. Her head swiveled smoothly in my direction. "Are you considering it, then? Did you have someone in mind?"

"Oh no," I hastened to say, pretending nonchalance. I barely stopped short of wide-eyed innocence. "Nothing could interest me less. It's only that attending a wedding naturally makes one think of marriage."

"It's never too early to start thinking about candidates, though," she said, peering down over the balcony, taking in the familiar and unfamiliar faces arranged below us in neat rows. "There are plenty here. Do you see any you like?"

I waved a hand dismissively and kept my eyes on her. I was afraid I might give too much away. "I'm hardly going to pick my future husband at random out of a standing-room crowd. Aren't you always telling me I need to be careful who I associate with? That most boys don't want me, just my money?"

"That isn't quite how I put it."

"Isn't it?" I stopped myself there, realizing my tone was too aggressive. More pleasantly, I said, "Though I suppose one could do worse than start with the boys here. At least we know they're all from good families. And I'm sure that's one of your criteria."

"My criteria? They hardly matter. The choice will be yours, not mine," she said.

That was a trap. I waited for her to continue.

"But what I hope for you," she said, still surveying the crowd, "is a boy from a good family with enough money of his own that we know he's not a fortune hunter, who will adore you and give you handsome children."

"A good boy, good-looking, from a good family. An easy find."

"Not a hard one. There are several I can see from here. You see that dark-haired young man on the third balcony down from us, for example?"

I followed her pointing finger, which she kept discreetly on the balcony rail so it wasn't obvious to anyone who might catch sight of us. Her finger had happened to land on a poker player from the night before. My breath caught, but I held in any further reaction, waiting to hear what she'd have to say.

"That's Harry Gillig," she said. "You know him?"

"I'm not sure," I said, because I couldn't remember whether I was supposed to.

"Twenty years old," she told me. "His father's in silver. His mother grows the most beautiful azaleas. You could do much worse."

"I could." I pretended to muse, scouting the crowd. I saw another familiar, uncommonly handsome face, only one balcony up from the Gilligs. I smothered a smile. "Like that one," I said and pointed to Porter Ashe.

The young man who'd won me at the poker table was chatting with an older lady in sage green I assumed to be his mother. As we watched, he beamed toward her, sporting his handsome grin.

To my own mother, I said, "Disreputable, isn't he?" I suppose I thought I was being clever, thinking she would talk him up to be contrary.

But my mother surprised me. She frowned and considered, then answered, "A bit. I'm talking about the younger Ashe boy, if that's who you mean?"

I nodded.

She'd folded her pointing fingers back in, her hand resting lightly on the rail in a loose fist. "Yes, you'd better stay away from that one."

"Really? What in the world is wrong with him?" I strove to keep my tone mild.

She gave the subtlest of shrugs. "One hears things."

"Mama," I said, a bit aggrieved, "it doesn't do to traffic in idle gossip."

"Who's idle?" she said. "And I'm agreeing with you! You had it right. Porter Ashe isn't marriage material."

I rubbed my finger along the railing of the balcony, trying to figure out what to say. Certainly telling my mother I expected Porter Ashe would shortly ask for my hand in marriage and I had every inclination to give it to him was not on the table. Perhaps the best answer was to keep silent.

After examining my glove—I'd rubbed a little dirt off the railing—I looked back at my mother, and I caught a light in her eye that I did not at all like. She was watching me too closely, too critically.

In a measured, careful tone, she said, "But as I said earlier. You're too young to be thinking of marriage anyway."

"Yes," I agreed, murmuring downward, forcing myself not to look at Porter, afraid of what his expression or mine might reveal to my mother's watchful eye. "Too young."

Whether I would have done better in marriage if I'd waited longer to embark on my first one, I don't know. Mama may or may not have had my number. About Porter, she turned out to be right in the end, though I still maintain that was at least half luck.

———

The week after the Stanford wedding, Porter and I began to meet in secret, under assumed names. We were the Worthingtons or the Meriwethers, the Olsens or the Chadwicks, as the occasion called for. I can barely stand to recount it now, though at the time, it all seemed so daring, romantic, adult. Suffice it to say I was completely swept away. His attention was intoxicating, his kisses even more so. His lush-looking mouth, I found, delivered on its promise. When I told him breathlessly there were things we shouldn't do until we were married, he said evenly, "We can march down to city hall any day as far as I'm concerned. Would now do?"

I answered him, "Is this you finally asking me to marry you?"

"Are you saying yes if it is?"

To needle him, I shrugged. "Maybe."

But we did marry, and shortly after, we did what married people do. We both found our new status very satisfying.

Since we married in secret, without our families' approval, nothing changed for a while. We continued to meet furtively, picking a last name at random from our handful of identities when names were required, stealing precious, passionate moments.

Could we have kept our secret forever? No, not forever. But we would've kept it longer if an enterprising reporter named Sheffield, chatting up a desk clerk at the Baldwin Hotel on Market Street, hadn't looked up just as I was crossing the lobby to mount the stairs. Sheffield had written about me before. He knew my face on sight.

He gestured to the nearest attendant. "Excuse me. Did I just spot Miss Crocker?"

The clerk looked up and watched me. Not knowing any better, the clerk answered, "No, sir, that's Mrs. Meriwether."

The next day, Porter and I found our trysts, then our elopement, exposed in the pages of the *Tribune*.

Our mothers were furious, but since the damage was already done, they agreed to make the best of it. They sent announcements on impeccable stationery and funded an immediate honeymoon, giving the marriage a public start that they hoped would overshadow the private one.

It certainly succeeded, but not in a way anyone would have wanted.

The night before Porter and I were to leave on our honeymoon to Los Angeles, I slept alone. Married or not, said my mother, she wanted me under her roof one last time. There was a small dinner, just the Ashe family and our family, and my mother toasted to our good health as if she meant it.

Afterward, I went up to sleep in my childhood bedchamber one last time before my time as Amy Isabella Crocker ended and life as Mrs. Porter Ashe officially began. After the night my father died, I was always sure to place my lamp as far as possible from the window, even though I pretended to myself that the extinguished lamp that night, along with everything else I'd seen and heard, was only part of a dream.

I closed my eyes, drifted off to sleep, and woke well after midnight with the feeling I wasn't alone.

I first felt the soft breeze from the window and wondered if perhaps Porter, unable to resist the challenge, had come to visit me in my bedroom for the first time. But when I opened my eyes, it wasn't his shape I saw.

This time, the woman in white stood by the window. She was no less clear for it, though her white shape was easier to see against the patterned curtains than it had been against the white counterpane seven years earlier. Her face was still turned away, unreadable, unrecognizable. She still wore shadow that hugged her shoulders and spilled downward behind her like a fine silken cape.

"Be gone," I said to her, though quietly; I didn't want anyone else to hear. I was only talking to myself after all.

When she spoke, it was hard to hear, but I heard clearly. Three words rippled between us in the dimly lit bedroom.

"*Not to go,*" she said.

Was that her entire message or just a fragment? I wondered for a moment and decided not to care. She couldn't be real, I told myself, so she wasn't. If she didn't exist, neither did her warning.

So I only repeated, "Be gone," once more, then rolled over, turning my back on the shadow woman as if to show she couldn't do me any harm. I was so young.

When I woke in the morning, there was no sign she'd ever been there. I took that as an indication that I'd been right.

It was the first day of my honeymoon, and the weather was cloudless, and I was starting my official life as Mrs. Porter Ashe in style. Our trunks were packed and transported. We lingered over a delicious luncheon of cold lobster on buttered toast. And in the late afternoon,

I stood arm in arm with my husband on the familiar platform to take the Southern Pacific railway to Los Angeles.

The woman in white only crossed my mind again the moment I took my first step onto the train.

Not to go, she'd whispered. She was a dream, I'd told myself, with no more meaning than a squawking dream bird or hissing dream snake. Until that moment, I didn't realize I should have asked myself the question, *Go where?*

Those who believe in ill omens, which I didn't then but certainly do now, won't miss the obvious when I say that my honeymoon began with a train wreck.

The first few hours of the journey toward Los Angeles were uneventful, the remainder tragic.

As we slept, the locomotive labored up steep tracks clinging to the mountainside through Tehachapi Pass. It delivered seven cars to the mountaintop—including a mail car, a baggage car, a car of Chinese railroad workers, and a sleeper car identical to ours that happened to contain the former governor of California—without incident. Having made its miles, the train was braked for an hour of rest.

However, instead of remaining safely braked at the top, the entire train began to roll backward, slowly at first and then quickly, down the steep track. When the rails curved sharply four miles later, the train was going too fast to make the curve. Several cars plunged to the valley below.

At first, I thought I was dreaming: I had a sense of weightlessness, of soaring, and when I opened my eyes in the darkness, I thought, *How pleasant to fly*, but that only lasted until we hit rock.

The noise of the first crash was horrific, unbelievably loud, all around me. On instinct, I tried to clutch the bedclothes in both fists, but the force of the crash threw me from my berth. I heard Porter cry out, but I couldn't answer him before the next jolt—our sleeper car had begun to roll down the mountainside. We were flung in one direction after another, smashing against a wall or floor or window every few feet. Everything went dark.

When I next opened my eyes, I was relieved to see color, but it only took a moment to realize the flickering orange and red meant fire. Faint smoke hit my nose next, then the scent of blood. Everything hurt to move. I raised my face to look about me. I caught faint movement at the far end of the car. My maid, Sophie, stared at me with wide eyes. I didn't breathe until she blinked.

"Are you hurt?" My voice came out too soft, barely a whisper in the madness.

"Miss Amy," she yelled back. "We need to get out."

But I wasn't listening. I was searching the car for my husband. Before I even took stock of where we were and what was happening, I wanted to reassure myself that he too had survived.

"Porter?" I called. "Porter!"

No response.

I began to twist this way and that, searching. I saw unmoving forms, but none of them wore his clothes. I looked to the last place I'd seen him. His sleeping berth had been smashed as the car rolled and, I realized, so had mine. Sharp slats of broken wood draped with twisted bedsheets littered the remains of what had been our compartment. I was standing on the actual ground, framed by a large square of hollow metal that had once held a grand window. Bits of glass sparkled in the dirt around my bare feet. My hands were clean, but my feet were bloodied. That was the blood I smelled, or at least some of it.

"Porter!" I shouted again. Still no answer.

"Miss Amy," called Sophie again.

Her voice snapped me back to attention. At the far end of the car, behind her, flames licked the space where the door to the dining car had been. But the smoke wasn't filling the sleeper car. It was rising. I followed its thin gray plumes upward and saw that the other side of the overturned car had also lost all its window glass, leaving the side overhead open to the night sky. That was our only way out.

I pointed. "There. Let's go."

Sophie nodded, a sob catching in her throat, and hurried over to meet me below the only exit to the outside. She gestured for me to go first, but I shook my head, boosting her onto the lowest wrecked berth until her feet disappeared through the opening.

Bracing my bloodied feet on the wreckage of one berth after another, I climbed.

Once I lifted my head into the fresh air, I could hear voices. Quickly I identified three kinds, all heartbreaking: shouting their desperation, sobbing their terror, and screaming their pain.

We were told later that the heating stoves in each car had smashed on the way down, letting the fire free. Hungrily the flames made their way through fuel. All those fine carpets and soft bedsheets would burn until there was nothing left.

Sophie and I stood side by side, wordless, staring down. I didn't want to leap from the top of the car, but it might come to that. At least we had time to consider the choice. I felt strangely calm atop the wreckage of the sleeper car, watching from a god's vantage, and I took in the scene.

Perhaps twenty men—some dressed in the finery of first-class passengers, others the uniforms of Southern Pacific employees, but moving as one—urgently rushed from car to car. They searched for survivors, called out to locate the trapped, pulled people free of the wreckage. A smaller group of figures seemed to move with less urgency, and I realized they were moving dead bodies, those who no hurry would help. I looked away.

"Here! I'm here!" came a hoarse shout from somewhere unknown, and I saw a man in the bottom half of a postal clerk's uniform stop still alongside the wreckage of the baggage car, looking around for the source of the shout.

"Call again!" the clerk barked in response. Nothing. He turned and turned, searching wildly, unsure. "Where are you? Call again!"

Closer to me, near the wreckage of the other sleeper car, I caught sight of a lone man in a bloodied nightshirt. He scooped up a white-haired man I recognized as the former governor as if he weighed no more than a newborn. The governor was motionless, and it was impossible to tell whether he'd survived. I watched to see which direction they went in. When the man set the governor down among a knot of wailing survivors, not in the motionless heap of dead, I felt a wash of relief, my first since we'd crashed.

The governor's rescuer seemed, at first, faceless. I realized as I watched that he wore a handkerchief over his nose and mouth, no doubt to block the thick smoke roiling from the other sleeper car. Soot and ash smeared his hair, his forehead, the handkerchief. His nightshirt was streaked with gray and black along with the red. After he set the governor down gently, he squared his shoulders with resolve and turned back in the direction of the wreckage. As he did so, I must have made some kind of noise or movement that caught his attention; he raised his featureless face to me.

I shuddered. It was like a spirit was looking through me, into my soul.

The man without his face was still watching me, motionless, still staring where I perched atop the slowly burning car. I felt I'd been standing there an eternity. I calculated later it couldn't have been more than two minutes.

Then the stranger blinked hard—I could see his eyes if I focused—and he shouted up toward me.

"Amy?" came his voice, hoarse with smoke.

With great shock and relief, I realized this man, this stranger, was my husband.

"Porter!" I called to him, and almost before I finished saying his name, he was already running in my direction.

As soon as he reached the sleeper, Porter scrambled halfway up in what felt like an instant. The ladder that should have led from the ground to the roof of the car, now hanging sideways, provided him enough purchase to bring his head level with our feet.

"I can't quite reach," he said, his voice still raspy with smoke. "Lower yourself to sit, then slide down. I'll catch you. One at a time."

"Sophie, you first," I told her in a voice of sharp command.

She followed our instructions. From a seated position, she lowered herself into Porter's waiting arms. I wanted to breathe a sigh of relief, but my mind swam with other emotions as I swung my glass-stabbed feet over the side of the train car and prepared myself to let go.

Joy at knowing Porter was alive sang through my veins, but something troubling bubbled there too.

In that first moment he'd called to me, I hadn't known my own husband. He'd been an utter stranger. How had I married a man I couldn't recognize? I'd fallen in love with Porter Ashe, loved him enough to defy our families and elope in secret, but was it possible that I didn't truly know him?

After lowering Sophie safely to the ground, Porter turned back, climbed to his perch again, and turned his face up to me.

Seated on the edge of the wrecked car, feet dangling, I looked down at Porter Ashe, the man I'd chosen, the one I'd sworn to love and cherish until parted by death. This half of our sleeper car was still untouched by flame, but behind him I could see the fire consuming the crushed sleeper car the governor had been traveling in, red tongues of flame roaring against the black backdrop of the night. Though Porter was only a few feet away from me now, with a trick of the light, his face was lost again. He'd become a silhouette, the shape of his body outlined by the fire behind him, everything else shadow. I realized that if I jumped with too much force, I might knock him from the crooked ladder toward the ground, toward the hungry, waiting fire.

If I'd known then what Porter would do to me, how our story would end, I would have fed him to the flames and never looked back.

But instead, I lowered myself carefully toward my new husband. He reached out for me. He steadied my waist as I trusted my weight to him, then curled my body to his with one arm as we both slowly descended the ladder. Our right feet moved down, then our left feet, then our right feet again. Wordlessly we moved as one. When our feet touched solid ground, we let out identical sighs. And the both of us emerged safely, bloodied but whole, from the wreck of Tehachapi Pass.

Fifteen souls perished that night, most of them in the sleeper cars, which had hit the mountain first and hardest. Governor Downey survived with three broken ribs, but his wife, who hated newfangled trains and had only taken the trip under great protest, died in the flames. A retired railroad man named McKenzie, quick-thinking when the train began to roll out of control, managed to throw a brake and save two of the cars midway down the slope, including the entire car of Chinese railroad laborers. The remaining five cars had leapt the tracks. Honorably discharged soldiers from the Presidio, an army captain, an express messenger, three porters, two society ladies, and several others never drew breath again.

And I blamed myself.

Those deaths are on my conscience still. They aren't the only ones—anyone who's read the papers knows how death and tragedy have dogged my every step for decades—but through the years, the losses at Tehachapi Pass have somehow stayed painfully fresh. Perhaps because I was so young when it happened, old enough to know better but not wise enough, not yet. Perhaps because I feel guilty it took such a cost in human lives to make me pay attention.

I should have done something. Gone to the papers, perhaps. They wouldn't have listened to the average person, but they might have listened to me. I could have used the attention of the reporters for good for a change: if I'd demanded the train be canceled because of a premonition, the papers would certainly have said nasty things about me, but I was used to that. Instead I let things go on. And I wasn't the one who paid the price.

When the sun dawned after that awful night of fire and death, we waited in the January cold for the relief train to come, all numb and exhausted. It arrived around ten in the morning. Doctors had come from Tulare and Sumner to tend to the most gravely injured. Once that was done, they bandaged the wounds on my feet and scratches that had marked up Porter's uncommonly handsome face. Then it was time to go. Porter and I rode the special on to Los Angeles, but our honeymoon would never be what we'd hoped.

We moved through our Los Angeles itinerary—the hotel, the dinners, the opera, the excursions—like poorly made facsimiles of ourselves. Not that we didn't try. We did our best to recapture the magic of our early days, hungry for each other, indifferent to the world, but it was impossible. We were new people, fresh, easily bruised. We found ourselves on edge with each other during what was supposed to be a sweet new beginning.

Perhaps our marriage would have ended as it did regardless of how it began. But during those days and nights in Los Angeles, it didn't help that my injured feet ached every time I forced them into my fanciest shoes, never letting me forget how I'd hurt them. It didn't help that when Porter looked in the mirror in the morning, lifting his razor to shave, his eyes would go vacant as he caught sight of the long red cuts where broken window glass had left its mark on him. It certainly didn't help that when the waiter set down a roasted lamb shank in front of me at dinner, I gagged from the smell, too much like what I remembered of burning flesh.

It might have ended anyway. There might still have been desertion and deceit, infidelity and kidnapping, court cases and lies. But such an ill-starred disaster was surely the worst way to start out, seeding the end of my marriage before my wedding bouquet had even had the chance to wilt.

It turned out that no matter how low my expectations of marriage, I expected too much.

CHAPTER FOUR

Even the mistakes that I made were worth the making.
I would make them again too.

—AC

Despite our marriage's false starts, once we settled in, Porter and I were happy. My mother commissioned an enormous house to be built for us on Van Ness Avenue as a wedding gift. It wouldn't be ready to live in for several years, of course, but it was still very generous. Of more immediate benefit, she also gave us a second honeymoon, different in every way from the first.

Porter and I spent months roaming Europe, taking well-worn paths to well-known sights. We rode down the canals of Venice and walked the streets of London; we feasted like kings in Rome and wept at the opera in Salzburg. I only asked that we avoid Spain, and Porter was so agreeable that he never even asked why.

Looking back from my current vantage, I wouldn't say those were the very happiest months of my life, not exactly. But at the time, I had everything I thought happiness was supposed to be. My new husband was my constant companion. Every time we reached a new destination, I found myself relishing the chorus of "Welcome, Mr. and Mrs. Ashe."

The only marriage I'd spent much time observing, my mother's and father's, had seemed businesslike at best—a cordial partnership between two people who had completely different strengths and weaknesses, who carved up household roles between them with the precision of a swordsmith. He earned the money, and she spent it; she ruled the house, and he ruled the world. He would no more express an opinion on a dinner menu than she would report to his office and take the chair behind his desk for her own. They spent more time apart than together. I can't recall ever seeing them kiss on the lips.

So when Porter and I caroused around Europe in each other's company almost every single hour of the day and night, I delighted in how different we were. I thought we were forging a newer marriage, a better marriage, perfectly aligned. Not just partners but lovers, two people born for this union.

And the way we saw Europe was an extravagant, delicious experience. I'd traveled before, from the time I was very young, but my mother made practical choices. Porter was the opposite: renting suites in the finest hotels that were far more room than we needed, ordering meals at the fanciest restaurants that two people alone absolutely could not eat. We did everything to excess. I knew I liked champagne, but in Porter's company, I found I was equally fond of whiskey, gin, vodka, and rum, as long as they were of good quality.

But as a wife of six months, I found that my favorite new intoxicant was anticipation. With my earlier flirtations, I'd never been sure what reaction to expect. A kind word to a charming young man at a party might cause him to throw himself at me with disturbing efficacy, to blush and run, or to run his eyes up and down my body in a lascivious manner that, depending on who he was, I might or might not relish. Every night, every man, was a mystery. That had its place in my youth, but there was something I liked better about certainty. I knew exactly how Porter would respond to me when we were alone, and I knew exactly how much I would like it.

As we toured Europe, we might go most of the day touching each other in ways that would be appropriate even to a maiden aunt or at least seemed so. In company, Porter knew how to position himself so that he could run his fingertips along my arm in a way that looked perfectly decent…while his palm and the pad of his thumb lingered on my breast, indecently brushing the nipple through the thin fabric of my bodice and driving me absolutely wild with want. It was knowing that the want he conjured would later be fully satisfied that addicted me.

When we strolled under the soaring arches of Notre-Dame Cathedral, my hair covered and our eyes downcast, we moved as solemnly as any procession. The music soared above us. I lingered, examining a particularly lovely color of stone beneath my feet.

Leaning close without touching me, Porter whispered in my ear, "When I get you alone tonight, I'm going to lick that freckle off your thigh."

That night, I suggested skipping dinner and retiring to our hotel room early. Porter readily agreed. The door had barely clicked shut behind us before his lips were bruising mine, and I had to hold him off, giggling, to make sure we'd locked the door. Even then, he was hoisting my skirts up as I fastened the chain. If the stubborn freckle was still on my thigh come the next morning, it wasn't for lack of trying.

Porter encouraged me to do the same, to toy with his lust in public in ways no one else would see. At first, I was too shy to make the attempt. I know it sounds odd now. I developed such a reputation for flouting rules, for seeking sensual pleasures anywhere and everywhere, later on. But I was still quite young—not yet twenty—and my earlier flirtations had culminated in nothing more than a kiss. Perhaps some rubbing up against each other's tender parts. The matador's lips had made it as far as my collarbone, but that was our limit, afraid of discovery. Nothing could be meaningfully loosened or unbuttoned when chaperones lingered just out of sight. Suitable garments for young women of my station were complicated, structured affairs, surely not a coincidence. So the idea that sexual congress was not just allowed, not just encouraged, but *expected* in my situation hadn't fully sunk in.

But soon I proved game. The right combination of courage and circumstances presented themselves in Venice. We climbed into one of the long, streamlined gondolas. The pilot with his long pole stood at the far end. I saw my chance.

I signaled to Porter and pointed to the end of the bench. "You sit there," I said, "and I'll sit in front of you. That way, we'll have the same view."

"But if we're next to each other…"

"Husband," I said sweetly. "Please indulge me."

Whether or not he had an inkling of what I intended, he immediately nodded and followed my direction. He turned around, settling himself with his back against the very end of the boat. It may or may not have been comfortable, but comfort wasn't what I had in mind.

"Open your legs," I said.

His eyebrows shot up.

"One foot on each side of the bench," I said, indicating the right position by pointing again. He cooperated.

Then I climbed onto the bench and leaned my back against his chest. "Ah," I said. "Best seat in the house."

Our pilot asked in Italian if we were ready to begin; if he thought our seating choice was odd, he knew better than to criticize paying customers.

"Andiamo," I said merrily, and we were underway.

We'd chosen an evening cruise, so the sun had begun to set. As we drifted along the water past elegant townhomes and palazzos, the life of the early evening buzzing in the nearby bridges and squares, I could feel Porter's heartbeat behind my shoulder blades.

"This is lovely," he said.

His mouth was next to my ear, and that was the only challenge of the position I'd chosen, that it was easy for me to hear him but harder for him to hear me. But for my first attempt to inflame him, I didn't intend to use words.

I'd rested my elbows on his knees, and I left the arm nearest the gondolier showing. The gondolier himself didn't look in our direction a single time, as busy as he was steering and piloting the craft, but I still wanted to be as subtle as possible. It was the far arm that I shifted and dropped behind me, placing the back of my hand on the small of my own back, which put my palm directly between Porter's legs.

Gently, I stroked downward once, then twice. I felt the changes in his body instantly: he came to attention not just where my hand touched but in his legs, his chest, all over. I stroked a few more times and was rewarded with a deep, lustful, wordless groan.

Then I felt his face come forward, next to mine, his breath hot on my cheek.

"I love you, you wicked, wicked girl," he breathed into my ear. His voice was the most sensual I'd ever heard.

By the time we finished our cruise and climbed out of the gondola, I was sure that my husband was happy that full dark had descended. He kept me walking in front of him for the first little while just in case. Our bed in the Venice hotel room was a fragile antique, so we spent ourselves in the confines of the vast bathtub, making such a mess sloshing water out of the tub onto the tile that it was still slippery in the morning. We threw down all the towels we could find and wore ourselves out laughing, even as his lips found my neck again and we missed the hours for hotel breakfast. I regretted missing our last chance for *sfogliatelle* only a little.

You might expect that our bliss ended when our second honeymoon did, but that wasn't immediately the case.

Back in San Francisco, as 1883 turned into 1884, I found myself very much enjoying married life. What I'd heard whispered—that husbands weren't the same as beaus, that they took their attention elsewhere and snapped the purse strings tighter than piano wire—seemed like it had just been idle talk. In my marriage, at least so far, none of it was true. The purse strings stayed as loose as ever. Porter remained attentive, in public and private, though of course I often gave him permission to do things on his own. It was equally difficult to fathom either going with him to the dog track or forbidding him from going. I was only being practical.

The newspapers loved to write about both of us, but they did so differently. Their tone was friendlier toward me than it had been, which I viewed as a temporary but welcome reprieve. Their mentions of Porter were always positive, sometimes gushingly so, as they held him up as the new Californian ideal. Between the two of us, we could count on seeing the name Ashe in the *Chronicle* once a week or so. It became a sort of game, paging through the paper to see which of us they'd mention and how. My name came up most frequently in updates on the construction of the Van Ness mansion, which the *Call* was following breathlessly.

One morning, Porter raised his eyebrows at me from across the table and said, "A whole column here on the construction today, Mrs. Ashe."

"Anything exciting?"

"The usual blather. The mistress of the house has chosen the finest of everything, solid oak for the front doors, art glass in the windows, granite steps, let's see."

"That sounds mostly right. The granite steps were an economy, actually. We could have asked for marble." I popped the last bite of buttered toast in my mouth, then washed it down with a sip of tea.

"Is this true?" Porter said, pointing to a column of type too far away for me to read for myself. "Did you really ask for the Turkish bath on the second floor?"

"Yes. Why?"

"Water's usually on the ground floor if possible. Especially with a pool this large. Construction's a lot more complicated this way."

"Well, how was I supposed to know that?" I grumbled, plucking another piece of toast from the rack. "I was thinking that I'd like to have fewer stairs to climb after I bathed."

"When you think of it your way, it's reasonable."

"Most things are."

He smiled at me and turned to the next page.

Two weeks later, after Porter had gone to the coast for a few days with some friends and I'd stayed home due to the secret brewing in my belly, we paged through the Sunday paper over breakfast again. But this time, the news was quite different. My eyebrows shot up to the ceiling at the truly outrageous headline.

"Porter!" I exclaimed. "A shark?"

He flushed almost like a schoolboy, pink rising to his cheeks. Clearly he hadn't expected this. "What about the shark?"

I was laughing as I said, "The fact that you met one at Santa Cruz, for starters."

"What do they say about it?"

"I almost want to make you guess," I teased.

"Please don't," he said, his cheeks turning even pinker. "Mrs. Ashe, if you would be so kind, please let me know what the *Chronicle* has to say about my encounter with a shark in Santa Cruz."

I decided to put him out of his misery. "It says, Mr. Ashe, that you killed the shark with a champagne bottle."

"I mean, I did hit it. I don't know that I killed it."

"This is terrific stuff!" I crowed, smacking the paper with the backs of my fingers. "You can't make it up! And what else aren't you telling me? Maybe you cut the head off a snake with garden shears? Smothered a tiger to death with a pillowcase?"

He waved a half-eaten pastry in my direction. I could see its soft red jammy center, threatening to drip. "You were ill, remember? I didn't want to make the trip sound too exciting, like you'd missed out."

He was right. I had definitely been feeling unwell all that week.

It had been an easy decision not to join the group at Santa Cruz. "It was kind of you not to torture me with descriptions of all the fun I'm not having."

"You'll be back to full strength soon enough, I hope, poor thing," he said. "But I'm sure all they've written is embroidery and foofaraw. You needn't waste your time reading it."

Well. All I needed to push me to do something was to be told not to do it. With great relish, I fully extended the paper and began to quote. "'Mr. Ashe's heroism knows no bounds! Only months after shooting a bear between the eyes at Lake Tahoe, he has battled again with one of Nature's most deadly predators and emerged victorious.'"

The Tahoe story, at least, was true; vacationing with friends in the pine woods, Porter had been attacked by a brown bear and shot it, which was only reasonable. My first instinct had been to feel sorry for the bear, but if only one of the two were to survive the confrontation, I knew I should cheer for the one I was married to.

I went on. "'This past week, yet another luxurious leisure trip turned potentially deadly—a powerful reminder that California is still mostly wilderness!—and in particular one young lady must feel grateful that our local paragon Mr. Ashe is here to stand strong against the wild beasts of the native territory.'"

As I read aloud, I didn't look over at Porter's face to see how he was receiving the details of the story. Perhaps I should have.

I read out, "'Only this time, when no regular weapon was at hand, Mr. Ashe needed to use what he could find—to remarkable effect. When at swim with friends off Santa Cruz, he was escorting...'" My brow creased. "You were escorting a Miss Dawsett?"

He took a deliberate bite of the pastry and chewed it thoroughly before swallowing it down. Then he said, "It's an exaggeration. You know how these things are. Ten people in the ocean is a recipe for disaster. They paired us off for the swimming so we'd have someone to keep an eye on. Can't have nine pals making it to the float and no one knowing what happened to the tenth."

He wasn't wrong, but I wasn't convinced that was the whole explanation. "I don't think I know this Miss Dawsett. What's she like?"

"I barely remember!" he protested. "Nice enough, I suppose. One of those silly debutantes the East Coast mothers send here for the marriage market."

"So why didn't she get paired with a bachelor if she's here to find one?"

"I don't know," he said. "I wasn't the one who did the pairing."

I sensed a dangerous prickle in the air that I wasn't used to. I could almost physically feel Porter's irritation, see him struggling to rein it in.

"Luckily for Miss Dawsett," I said, shaking the paper, "you were the one who did the saving! Shall I quote further?"

"If you like," he said in a tone that I knew meant he didn't want me to. I pushed on.

In an announcer's voice, I read out, "'As a strong swimmer, Mr. Ashe had been selected for one of the party's most important duties: carrying the champagne. He secured it around his waist with a twist of rope and began to swim.'" My eyebrows went up again. "That part's true, at least?"

"We planned a picnic on the float," he explained. The pastry now gone, he didn't seem to know what to do with his hands. He reached for his coffee cup. "They put the basket on a kind of raft, and George and David guided it with one hand while they swam with the other, but one of the Smith boys brought extra champagne, and there wasn't room."

"Well, I know no one would want to leave the drinks behind," I confirmed.

"Priorities," he said firmly.

I skimmed the next few sentences to make sure I wasn't about to read something aloud—like some physical expression of gratitude on this marriageable young woman's part—that might lead to further disagreement. I'd decided we were going to be happy. At least that day.

Satisfying myself that I could keep the rest of the story a mildly outrageous joke about the newspapers and nothing else, I summarized, "And it says here that upon spotting a shark headed for your companion, you clouted it heavily about the head with the bottom of the bottle of champagne, which broke. And then, desperate to ensure that the dazed shark would pose no further threat, you drove the broken end of the bottle into its brain? Porter! Really?"

He laughed. "Not really. But it makes a great story, doesn't it?"

"Perhaps we should send a correction."

"They'll print what they want to print," he said, his voice warm and familiar again. "Now turn the page. I want to know if there's anything in the business pages about that new development going up over by the track. Seems people wouldn't want to be able to hear the bells of horse races all day and night, but they didn't ask my opinion before planning a whole bank of houses there, did they? Let's have it."

I obliged. And though the press's tall tales were funny to us that day—Porter Ashe as a modern-day Ivanhoe or the Finn MacCool of legend—that wouldn't last. The fact that they could print whatever fictions they wanted turned out to be the only truth we could count on.

In November 1884, that same newspaper, the *Chronicle*, printed that our household had recently welcomed a beautiful baby girl, who we named Gladys. This was true enough. But a few short sentences on how welcome she was, how proud we were, only made it clear to me that the facts of a printed story could be correct but wholly misleading. The real story could be in everything that the reporters and publishers left out.

What the *Chronicle* didn't print was how the pain of childbirth nearly drove me out of my mind. How it rendered me helpless, like no part of my body was my own, from limbs to core to breath. How unprepared I was for the waves of pain, crashing on me again and again, with no sense of how long it might continue until I was finally and utterly destroyed. For once, money was no insulation, no refuge. I became nothing but my pain.

During all those hours of labor, I was certain I wouldn't be ending the day as a mother. I believed, as fully as I ever believed anything in my life, that it would kill me.

When the baby was out, I couldn't even feel glad. I was angry—imagine that, angry!—that I hadn't died. After hours where the pain would ebb away and then crash back over me like a relentless, angry tide, I would have welcomed oblivion. I wanted it. In those worst moments, the ones where pain blotted out everything good in the world, I'd embraced the thought of death. When that possibility faded, it left an empty darkness in its wake.

For once in my life, I thought of the woman in white, the shadow woman, and wished she had been with me. I would have felt less alone then. As it was, there was no one in the world who understood or valued me, not my husband or mother or anyone. Is it any wonder, with my mind so dark, that I looked down at my fresh-born girl and thought, *She won't love me either?*

"Congratulations, Mrs. Ashe! You're a mother," said the midwife, patting the child in my arms and stepping away.

I certainly didn't feel like one. And I try not to blame myself for that now. Thousands of mothers, maybe even most of us, feel the same way just after birth. We're exhausted by a process that, even though it takes place within the confines of our body, is completely beyond our control. We transform so quickly that nearly every aspect of our lives remains unchanged—our history, our surroundings, our core identity—yet we've gone through something remarkable. The process of birth itself is impossible to understand until you're in the midst of it and still feels like a mystery as you come out the other side. In those first minutes and hours after birth, what woman is really able to make the transition instantly, to say to herself, *Yes, I am ready for motherhood. I am a mother. I am changed forever?*

So it wasn't those doubts in the first moments after birth that led to what happened later. It's not my fault, I firmly tell myself now, that I would never really be a mother the way that giving birth to a child would normally imply.

When did I ever do anything normally?

CHAPTER FIVE

But there was a jinx on us, despite the birth of my daughter
and despite all that Husband Number One and I could do to
make it go; it did not and could not last.

—AC

At the same time as I struggled to see myself as a mother, as my daughter cried every time I held her and turned her tiny face away rather than nurse at my breast, Porter seemed to see me as nothing but. The first time he saw me after I gave birth, he pressed his lips briefly to my forehead and said, "Excellent work, Mama," when I wanted him to kiss my mouth and call me by my name.

I'd been a fool to think our marriage was more solid than anyone else's. I was seduced by the way he'd romanced me on our second honeymoon, how he'd catered to me while I was expecting. He'd rarely left me in those months, except for those trips to Tahoe and Santa Cruz and of course some visits to the horse track and evenings out with his friends. But I had encouraged him to do all that. I wanted him to enjoy himself even if I couldn't.

After the baby, though, that changed. Some of what changed was his actual behavior: staying out until long after I'd retired for the night, leaving the house without saying a word. Some of it was just the same things he'd always done—betting heavy on the horses, coming home reeking of cigars—that were starting to bother me more.

And when he called me Mama over the breakfast table, when he hadn't resumed his visits to my bedroom, I started to feel desperation bubbling inside me. I wasn't mother enough to please my daughter, but I was too much mother to please my husband. So I began visiting the nursery less often, keeping the late-morning hours free for Porter in case he wanted to see me, making sure he didn't have occasion to think I was choosing Gladys over him. I was careful never to talk about her in his presence unless he mentioned her first.

Yet he left more often. Stayed out later. Seemed to view me as a completely different person than the one he'd known.

I saw us quickly slipping, not just toward the separate lives that my mother and father had led but even worse: a marriage where Porter was living his best life and I was boxed out, left behind. I'd wanted to be a partner. I was starting to feel like an anchor instead.

I was unwilling, however, to simply watch my marriage fall into cliché. I was young, yes, but I'd always been accustomed to getting my way. It was just a matter of strategy. I decided to keep a light tone and hope that Porter could hear the real concern under the quips and make the decision for himself to change his behavior.

So I teased him about the stink of his cigars and asked if he'd brought one home for me to smoke. He played along, patting his pockets and pretending to have forgotten, exclaiming, "Oh no, so sorry! I swear it was right here!" I pressed my nose against his shoulder and inhaled the smell deeply, then declared it was the same as if I'd been there, and perhaps I'd join him next time and compare.

I also played at making staying at home more like leaving it. Even as my soft middle stubbornly continued to spread, not flattening out right away to the prebaby figure of which I had been rightly proud, I dolled myself up in Chinese robes that flattered me. My favorite was yellow flowers on a scarlet background, so visible from a distance that any ship in the harbor could've run it up the flagpole to signal distress. I bought a robe for Porter too, a brightly patterned confection of blue birds and green leaves, for us to wear at home together.

This worked a few times: I welcomed him to our front parlor as if it were a high-end club in a foreign land, pressing Mr. Jenkins into service as a bartender and then dismissing him so my husband and I could be alone. Once Porter and I were good and soused on gimlets, our hands started roaming, and we resumed at least some of what had made our marriage work so well. One of the advantages of Chinese robes is how quickly they can be nudged aside, worked under, or removed completely. With a sliver of my attention during these seductions, I enjoyed how, once discarded, thin silk almost seems to slither to the floor. The motion always put me in mind of a snake shedding its skin. Three or four times we did this, over the course of a few months, and it gave me hope. But after that, when I invited him to the "Crocker Bar," he always had other plans already in place. He'd kiss me on the forehead, saying, "Good night, Mama," before heading out the door. After that, all Porter's Chinese robe did was hang in his closet, empty, making me secretly furious every time it caught my eye.

The nanny had stopped even asking if I'd come to see Gladys in the morning. If I secretly hoped my absence would make my daughter's heart grow fonder, it did not. Our visits were rarer but just as fraught. Feeling both neglectful and neglected drove me into an angrier, darker mood. If I couldn't reclaim my husband with grins and gimlets, I'd try another way.

The newspaper, our uncomplicated source of amusement in those early months, now became something more ambiguous. I was unsure whether it was ally or enemy. Perhaps a little of both. It was the *Chronicle* that alerted me to just how out of control Porter's behavior had become. The newspaper didn't find it alarming, of course. It was all presented as more of his previous behavior: tales of the dashing man about town, full of derring-do, pure entertainment.

On this particular morning, Porter hadn't appeared at the break-fast table, which usually meant he'd been out too late and his head and stomach were suffering too much from the previous night's antics. Having been in that position myself more than once, I knew it was best not to add food to that brew. But after I read the latest tale of what Porter had been up to, empathy wasn't foremost in my mind.

Even though I wasn't particularly hungry for luncheon—I'd eaten a good breakfast at a reasonable hour, not having set foot outside the home the night before—I decided that was the best time to make my stand. I made sure the maids let him know that only cold meats would be served and he would probably be alone at table. I perched on a chair in the nearby parlor, listening for the sound of his footsteps, which I knew as well as my own. Eventually, I was rewarded with the sound of Porter approaching, in no hurry. The door to the dining room swung open and closed. I gave him a few minutes to settle himself. I spent the time settling myself in a different way.

Then I came to the table, all innocence, and casually reached for the newspaper on the sideboard as if I weren't already familiar with every word, every nuance it contained.

"It won't be a very exciting luncheon," I said, "but I suppose you've had plenty of excitement lately and could use a bit of time to recover. Coffee?" I offered to pour.

He signaled that his cup was already full.

"Shall we quote from the *Chronicle*? You always used to find it amusing."

He probably would have looked wary if he hadn't already looked so miserable. His handsome face rarely had capacity for more than one expression at a time.

I spread the paper wide like an albatross's wings and said, "Here you are already, on page two! Score for you this week, I suppose. They haven't written about me since the beginning of the month. And that was just some little puff, you know the 'motherhood suits her' sort of business, about a turn I took in the park with Gladys."

Letting our daughter's name hang in the air for a long moment, I squinted down at the page, pretending to read it for the first time. My heart was hammering at my own boldness; it might have been the first time I mentioned our daughter to him without prompting. Out of the corner of my eye, I could see Porter sipping his coffee with no apparent alarm. If he knew what was in the newspaper, he wasn't going to give it away.

"Any guesses what they wrote about you?" I asked, still innocent.

"None," he said, his voice without inflection.

"Really? Not a single guess?"

"You're the one with the paper. You know what they said. So share it already if you want me to know. Or don't. You know they make up whatever they want to."

"Well, they do have an arm's-length relationship with the truth," I agreed. "But there's usually a kernel."

He stared down at his coffee. "Well, tell me what they said, and I'll tell you if there's a kernel this time around."

I cleared my throat and began to read out loud, word for word. "'Our San Francisco elite are certainly enthusiastic patrons of the arts. After a recent opera performance successfully concluded with its usual curtain call, not everyone was ready for the night to end. A half-dozen music lovers convened at the apartment of the lead diva at her invitation. An unusual choice for a celebration, but what was even more unusual was how late the party went on. Have we become a West Coast New York City? These aficionados stayed late, late into the night playing music and toasting the diva's success. Whether it was her beauty, her talent, or the contents of her liquor cabinet that kept them so enthralled, no one saw fit to report. But enthralled they certainly must have been. A particular local light, a certain man whose passions flame high before they burn out, was observed leaving the apartment after the next day had dawned.'" I lowered the paper just enough to give him a significant look over its top.

Porter sipped his coffee again, then scoffed. "What?"

"Porter."

Casting about for the right emotion, he settled on mild outrage. "Amy! 'A man whose passions flame high before they burn out'? That's what you're attaching to? They could mean anyone."

"They mean you. Ashe. It's a pun."

He still looked blank, but it was impossible to tell whether he really didn't understand or was just pretending.

"It's obvious," I pushed. "Not even a clever pun at that."

His expression shifted from emptiness to shimmering resentment, and I knew I had pressed exactly enough. Even in the midst of my anger, there was room for a bit of grim satisfaction.

His tone was tight as he said, "All right, say they mean me. Are you asking me if it's true? If I spent the night at the opera singer's apartment?"

I let the newspaper fall, now that it had done its work. "Yes, I suppose that's what I'm asking."

"It wasn't what you think."

I cocked my head. "What do I think?"

"I stayed there overnight, yes. We'd all had so much to drink. I was in no fit state." Now that he'd begun telling his story, the words spilled out. "And I'd sent the carriage home around midnight in case you needed it this morning. So at three o'clock, I couldn't have come home even if I wanted to. They're making it out to be something scandalous when I was really just acting responsibly!" His voice was authoritative and clear, very impressive for as drink-sick as he was, up until the last few words. Then there was a faint note of hysteria. He was genuinely offended, I think, even though he was in the wrong.

"But you did stay all night. That's the kernel of truth."

"Yes."

"Porter," I said in a neutral tone, "do you expect me to believe that you spent the entire night at an opera singer's apartment and nothing happened between the two of you?"

"That's what I said happened. Now you're accusing me of lying?"

"I'm not accusing you of anything. I just wonder what you think of me. I used to think you respected my mind. Now I'm not so sure."

I could see the gears whirring in his head as he scrambled for an answer. "I love you as much as ever. Nothing has changed."

"Everything has changed," I said. I could hear myself whining, nagging, and I hated it, but I couldn't stop. "You stay out all night and live your life, and I'm trapped in this house like a prison."

Something in his gaze had shut down. His voice was still animated, but his eyes were cold. "You want to come out next time and drink whiskey all night at a diva's apartment? Please, you'd be welcome."

"Even I can't do that." I could get away with more than most women because of my money, but even for me, there were limits. "The scandal would make the front page!"

"Then something else. Something less scandalous. But I'm not trapping you here, Amy. You're trapping yourself."

He almost had me there for a moment. Was I? Was it my own fault that I didn't kick up my heels at parties anymore, the way I had in our early days of marriage? Had I been turning down invitations to have fun, scared about what the papers would say, now that I was a married woman and a mother?

Not even a good mother, said a voice in my head, and I nearly clapped my hands over my ears to silence it. I couldn't think about that now. I was failing in so many ways at once.

Then I remembered how many times I'd held up an invitation and asked Porter if we should go. How many times he'd told me he wasn't up to it, it was too soon, what if Gladys needed me? So I'd decline, then find myself alone at the dinner table on that evening, asking the help if they knew when Porter would be down, then hear that he'd gone out for the night without me.

I wanted to snare him, to keep the upper hand. But suddenly, I was sick of the game. I would tell him how I felt. It was his turn to feel pain.

"If you think this is my fault, Porter," I told him, "I don't think we should be married anymore."

That stopped him short. I saw the panic flare, just for a moment.

It was a ridiculous thing to threaten—divorce—and I knew it. Women's purpose was marriage and a family. A divorced woman had turned her back on both. Our circle of society shunned divorcées, somehow feared them, as if the desire to abandon these standards might be contagious. Perhaps it was. Divorced men suffered a lesser portion of society's derision, but there were still whispers about them, hints that somehow, somewhere, the man had been measured and come up short.

But I knew it wasn't the idea of society's disapproval that worried Porter. It was losing access to the money that funded his lavish lifestyle. His family had money, but not like mine. That day at the luncheon table, seeing that flash of panic in his eyes, made me wonder for the first time if my money had played a bigger role in our romance than I'd ever suspected.

After that initial moment, Porter managed to recover himself quickly, cloaking his worry with his usual suave charm.

"Amy," he purred in his softest voice, reaching for my hand across the table. "I can see how hurt you're feeling. But to—that would be so rash. Foolish even. To throw away all the good we have, our sweet, wonderful family, over little disagreements. Let's not even speak of it."

I thought back to that moment several times over the next few months. The category of what he had called *little disagreements* expanded to cover things that, to me, didn't seem so little. Money disappearing from my accounts even faster than it had before.

Rumors that grew ever louder, ever stronger, about him carousing with actresses, in groups and otherwise. His ever-expanding stable of thoroughbred horses, a stunningly expensive habit, which I felt must be funded at least in part by my disappearing funds.

Whenever Porter thought of it, he tried to do better, and my social life improved slightly for a while. Then he got distracted with horses and gambling again, and I was alone in the house, and my mind drifted back to exactly where it had been that moment I blurted the truth over a luncheon of cold meats: I didn't want to be married to this man anymore.

Thousands of women have had similar thoughts, I'm certain. Women in every era, every nation. If there's anything universal in the world, it's the experience of waking up one day and realizing that you've gotten the short end of the stick.

But I had money, and I had status, and that set me apart from the thousands of others who might have wanted to turn their back on their no-good husbands and make a new life without them. We all felt cheated. I was in a position to do something about it. If I was going to fail at both marriage and motherhood, I could at least take action to make ending the former my own choice.

Did I want to be a divorcée, to wear that word like a scarlet flower in my hat? Of course not. But it was the lesser evil. Caring more for what others thought than for my own freedom was a trap. I didn't have to put up with this treatment, and I wouldn't.

So one night in the fall of 1886, rather than creating another luncheon ambush, I simply waited on Porter's bed for him to return from his night's carousing. I wrapped myself in the bright yellow-and-red Chinese robe, but for my own pleasure, not his. It was a long wait, but I was rewarded at three in the morning by a stinking drunk Porter, hair and tie askew, stumbling into his bedroom exactly like a cartoon illustration of a philandering husband. He even had a smear of pink on his collar that might have been lipstick. The universe had orchestrated for me exactly what I most and least wanted: evidence no one could ignore or deny. Porter was a cad and a louse. And my husband. He would always be two of those, but I hoped it was in my power to disqualify him as the third.

"I'm divorcing you," I announced, then swanned out of the room in my trailing robe. Fewer sounds in my life have been more satisfying than his helpless, nonsensical sputter and the slam of the door behind me as I left.

Of course, at that time, in California, wanting a divorce and getting a divorce were two very different enterprises. The state's laws were very clear. Men could divorce for any reason; women had to prove neglect, adultery, or cruelty. I leapt before I looked, hoping that with lawyers and money, I would be able to sort it out.

Our new home on Van Ness Street, the one my mother had ordered built for Porter and myself to celebrate our marriage, was finally ready. Gladys and I moved into it; my mother came to stay with us for a while.

Gladys's nanny carried her over the threshold of the Van Ness house as we reestablished our fractured household there. If I had a shred of hope that the change of scenery might cement our affections at last, it faded quickly. My daughter could hate me in the new house as easily as the old one. I tried harder, and it only seemed to scare her more.

Exploring the house itself brought me no joy. It felt a cruel twist of fate that the marriage had barely lasted long enough for the house to be built. It felt like the entirety of my life had been sped up somehow, as if ten years had passed in a blink and I'd missed something important. But I was there for the whole thing, I knew. It had simply been a swift descent.

My mother was opposed to the separation and even more firmly against divorce. "The entire family's reputation is entwined with yours, Amy," she told me. I thought fleetingly of Jennie, now married and far away. Were she here, she would be glaring daggers at me. To her, reputation was all.

"Porter is the one ruining our reputation, not me."

"Who's going to see it that way?"

"The people who matter, I hope," I said.

She answered, "Amy, hope isn't a plan."

But when I invited my lawyer to the house to explore how a divorce might proceed, Mama surprised me by joining the meeting. I assumed she wanted to be there to try to talk me out of it, but I was the one paying the lawyer, so I didn't think she could do too much harm.

We received Mr. Everleigh at our house in the enormous front parlor. He carried a beautiful leather briefcase that reminded me of the Italian leather goods I'd fallen in love with on my second honeymoon. I wondered where he'd gotten it but decided that this wasn't that kind of conversation. I put on a sober face, folded my hands in my lap, and let him speak first.

"I understand your interest in divorce, Mrs. Ashe," Everleigh began. "But before we proceed, I need to share new information that's come to light since we last spoke."

"New information?" I asked. I felt a twinge of dread.

He said, "I happen to be familiar with the opposition's representation, and I had a quick conversation with them, just to hear their plans."

"Is that allowed?" my mother asked.

He gave her a shrug and a half smile. "Whether it's allowed or not, it's the most helpful thing we can do for your daughter at this point in the process. We need to know what she's up against. It makes a big difference to how we proceed."

"We proceed by me divorcing the bastard," I said, partly to shock my mother and partly to give the lawyer an idea who he was dealing with. Big words and long odds weren't going to scare me. He should know that up front.

My mother glared daggers at me, as I expected. The lawyer chose not to react at all. Which, when I thought about it, was probably the right choice.

"Well. You'll want to know what I've found out," said Everleigh, "and I think discussing it is the best first step. I have here a list." He produced a sheaf of documents from his briefcase and lowered his spectacles to take a closer look at the words on the first page.

"A list of what?" I asked, a queasy feeling beginning to gather in my gut.

Without looking up, Everleigh clarified, "Stories his lawyers collected. Things they plan to bring up. Either at the trial itself—"

"Trial!" my mother broke in, aghast. "This cannot go to trial. Amy cannot appear in a courtroom. It'll be the end of us all."

"You're exaggerating, Mama," I said. But I looked to my lawyer for backup, and he provided none.

Instead, he said, "One of the reasons I made sure to procure this list—don't ask my source, I won't tell you—is so we can make that decision. To a certain degree, it isn't up to us. But if you have a preference…it will be good to know that. And in order for us all to go in with our eyes open, I may need to ask you some uncomfortable questions."

I said merrily, "I'll be happy to answer anything as long as it's about sex and not money." The poor man's face turned red as a beet.

"Amy," my mother growled warningly.

I waved her off and gestured to indicate the privacy of the parlor. "He wants me to tell the truth in here. There's no one else to know. If you're not comfortable hearing, Mama, that's quite all right. I promise not to think any less of you if you leave."

It was the grandest speech I'd given since the whole disaster began, and I quite liked it. But it didn't get the response I wanted. Mama didn't get up and storm out. Nor did she give an immense sigh and settle herself to stay.

Instead, she fixed me with a glare and said, in a stern tone, "Amy, I'm not a selfish woman."

She was right about that, although I thought it irrelevant, but I did her the courtesy of keeping my mouth shut and listening for more.

My mother went on, "I'd like to spare myself this experience. But what you do affects the whole family. Let's proceed."

Without further debate and without looking my way, Everleigh did. Settling down to business, he checked the sheet in front of him, tapping it with a pen. "Mrs. Ashe. You were sent to finishing school in Dresden, Germany, at sixteen."

"Oh goodness, I was taught to curtsy by a foreigner!" I said. "Is that what qualifies as a scandal?"

He continued as if I hadn't interrupted. "While there, your houseful of girls lived unchaperoned for several weeks, running up bills your families were then forced to pay. You became secretly engaged to a German prince but then broke it off. You romanced a young Spanish matador who died."

Each mention hurt like a blade. He reduced the most painful heartbreak of my teenage years to a few clipped, terse sentences.

I put on haughtiness like a shield. "Our chaperone ran off and abandoned us; that's hardly my fault. Mrs. Burridge was a grown woman and made her own poor decisions. And matadors are gored in the ring every day without my involvement. It's an unfortunate occupational hazard. If you know the whole story, you'll know I wasn't even there to see it happen."

In a stiffer voice, Everleigh said, "Mrs. Ashe. I'm not asking for explanations."

"Oh?" I blinked my eyes, feigning innocence. "Then what are you asking for?"

"We must be prepared," he explained. "If these stories come up in court, you won't be provided an opportunity to add color."

Mama said, "That's why we can't go to court."

I glared at her. "If it's the only way I can stop being married to Porter, I intend to do just that."

Everleigh said, "If, and this is only if, you go to court, and these stories are brought into the open air—Mrs. Ashe, you can't quibble with the details."

I opened my mouth to protest that explanations were not the same as quibbling, then realized that such a protest might itself be considered a quibble. I closed my mouth and listened.

The attorney went on. "This is all that matters: Are these stories true or false? Can they be proven one way or the other? That's what we need to know."

If those were the terms, I would play his game. I could see that there was no value in debating the nature of the court—we weren't going to change it. "Very well."

"Thank you." He nodded with satisfaction. "So let's take them one by one. The houseful of unchaperoned teenage girls in Dresden?"

"True."

"The German prince?"

Deep down, I still felt Alexander's soft, hesitant, first kiss in the courtyard, saw his look of utter dismay when I later told him we couldn't marry after all. I hadn't been careful enough with his heart, it was true, but to be punished for it now? That didn't seem fair. I let none of it show. "True."

"And you fell in love with a matador?"

"True."

He asked, "What was the extent of your—"

"Excuse me," interrupted my mother, rising. "I need to have a word with the cook about dinner. Please continue without me."

Before she left, I caught a glimpse of her face, and her cheeks showed just a hint of pink. I realized she was badly embarrassed, even with no details, even in front of a friendly audience. She had thought she could listen to my misdeeds, but it appeared she had changed her mind.

Once she was gone, I turned back to Everleigh. "You heard her. Continue."

"Thank you for your candor," he said, as if I had a choice in the matter. "I know it must be hard for you."

"It isn't," I lied in a clipped voice. "What's next?"

"I was asking about the extent of your relationship with the matador."

"What does the list say was the extent? You told me I only needed to confirm or deny."

"You're correct," he said, though it didn't sound like that realization made him happy. "We can move on to the next."

"Let's."

He consulted the paper in front of him. "You then secretly married a man who won you in a poker game."

"He did not *win* me," I said with great disdain.

Everleigh lifted his pen as if to mark the place, then paused before the tip of the pen touched paper. He looked up at me, scrutinizing. "Is there truth to the story?"

"There was a poker game," I admitted, glad that my mother wasn't there to hear. Misbehaving in Europe was one thing, but if she knew I'd snuck out right under her nose at Marjorie Stanford's wedding to go wild, it might break her. "Several young men, including Porter Ashe, thought it would be fun to wager for the right to ask me to marry them. You can tell who took home the victory."

"So," the lawyer said slowly, "Ashe didn't win you in a poker game. He won the right to ask you to marry him in a poker game?"

"Yes."

"That distinction will be lost on the judge." He made a mark on his paper.

As right as Everleigh was this time, I couldn't completely suppress my irritation. I said, "And doesn't that story reflect poorly on a man who gambles so much of his family's money away that he leaps at the chance to put something else at stake?"

"It does, but…"

I knew the answer. "But it doesn't matter. It isn't the same."

The lawyer said, "I'm sorry it's so, but yes."

"I suppose there's nothing to be done about it," I said, resigning myself. I could see this going on for hours. "Tell the next story."

The lawyer checked his list. I wanted to tear it from his hands and rip it in half, but I knew when I was beaten. "There's one about a cockfight at the St. Elmo. Not a lot of detail."

"The details don't matter. It's true."

From the doorway, my mother's voice said, "Amy! A *cockfight?*" She'd apparently forced herself to come back and listen, her hand pressed to the doorframe as if she needed support to hold her up.

"Which *Porter* took me to!" I protested, struggling not to throw my hands in the air. I couldn't help the edge in my voice. "I was in the company of my husband! I never would have gone on my own. It was a miserable spectacle, so disgusting."

"But you were there," the lawyer said. This one, I felt, he was rubbing in.

"Yes."

"Were you the only woman?" my mother asked. I couldn't tell whether she was probing to find out just how badly I'd misbehaved or hoping that the presence of other women from our circle might excuse my own.

Not knowing what answer she truly wanted, I decided honesty was easiest, if I could recall the evening clearly enough. "Maybe? Or no, there was an actress I recognized. Mellie something."

My mother simply gave me a stunned look as she sat back down, but I could hear the word in her voice as clearly as if she'd said it aloud. An *actress*. Not better than a roomful of men, but worse.

The lawyer presented more stories, and I confirmed them. Something scandalous at the opera. True. Whiskey at Levi's. True. The death and destruction that had rained on our first honeymoon, though of course I was not responsible for any of that and assumed they only included the story to emphasize Porter's heroic turn. That was all true.

Finally Everleigh reached the end of his list. He set down his pen, opened his briefcase, then placed both document and pen inside. It took him a long time to speak. When he did, he said, "I can't recommend pursuing this in court."

He'd disappointed me, but he wasn't the first, and he wouldn't be the last. I pushed him. "What if I do it against your recommendation? Will you represent me?"

Before he could answer, my mother hastened to step in. "Thank you for your candor, Mr. Everleigh. We will discuss this privately. We hope to have no further need of your services, but if you will maintain the file on this matter and treat everything we've said here with utter discretion, I'll have the retainer money sent over."

Not caring if Everleigh heard me, even if discussing such matters was uncouth in front of the hired help, I said, "Mama, I can pay for my own lawyer."

"You can," she said, "but if it comes out, it will look better if I was the one."

I threw up my hands but gave up objecting. At least she cared, I told myself. Things could always be worse.

CHAPTER SIX

And "Finis" was marked indelibly upon the first entry in my book of matrimony.

—AC

Midway through 1887, we had an agreement. It was all very civil, none of it face-to-face between myself and my husband, only my lawyers to his lawyers. When my mother offered him an allowance, he agreed to a trial separation, which was plenty convincing enough to me that his heart and other body parts were no longer in the marriage.

Despite pursuing me from the beginning, despite giving every appearance of loving me as much as a person could, Porter had turned against me with remarkable speed. I couldn't help but think that had somehow been my fault. If he was the person who knew me best in the world and he couldn't stand me, what did that mean for my future? What about my daughter? When she grew old enough to know me, would she hate me too?

The daughter in question, a round-cheeked toddler not yet three years old, kept reminding me how much I fell short as a mother. We'd started off so badly, but I still tried. I kept visiting Gladys in the nursery, trying to hold her, speaking in a purr to her and giving her what she wanted, hoping that would help her love me. On the rare occasions I made her smile, my heart nearly exploded with joy. But then she turned dark as a storm cloud, rubbing my face in my failure, and I went to my room and wept. It always took me a few days to gin up my courage again.

Gladys's nanny was still with us, and the young woman was an absolute saint. Every day, I feared she'd quit. That was the worst thing I could imagine happening. How thoroughly my imagination failed me.

My mother seemed ever-present, and while I knew she meant well, I began to avoid her. I didn't want to have yet another conversation about why Porter and I should try to reconcile. The Van Ness house was large enough that I could manage not to see her for a full day if I really worked at it. I preferred to be alone, stewing in my discontent, spending long stretches wandering alone until it was time to go to the nursery and fail again at mothering my daughter.

But later that month, I got my days mixed up. Mama and I ended up both sitting down to the breakfast table at the same time. I made a show of buttering my toast and sipping my tea in silence, hoping to avoid a conversation, but it was not to be.

"I have a proposal for you. Let's get away," my mother said. She was wearing a colorful gown, a blue so bright I felt it was attacking my eyes. She stirred her tea in slow circles. "There's a wedding in New York City. Remember Darlene Messerschmidt?"

I absolutely did; she'd been my favorite of the other girls on the ill-fated Dresden excursion, and I'd always regretted losing touch with her. I didn't want to tell my mother why we hadn't kept in contact. I kept my response vague. "I do. It's been forever."

"Her parents invited me to the wedding, and I think we should both go."

"Mama, I'm not sure—"

She cut me off, brandishing her teaspoon in my direction. "It's been six months since you and Porter began living apart. It'll be an excellent way to show society that you're not broken."

"I am broken," I answered.

"Pish," she responded, returning the spoon to her tea. "The gossips think you're getting a divorce. We can tell them it's not so."

"If I were a man, I'd have the divorce already. They make it so much harder for women. Like everything else." I dropped another cube of sugar in my tea, letting the tongs fall with a clatter for emphasis.

"Your generation," she said dismissively. "You think everything's so hard for women. You complain about it nonstop."

"Well, there's a reason for that."

"Yes?"

"Because it is," I said with satisfaction.

"Women today have so much freedom!" said my mother. "It's not like you were traded to a stranger for camels or cows. Honestly, I can't fathom what you are all complaining about."

"Not being able to cast a vote? Or own our homes? Being so at our husbands' mercy that we could be clapped into an institution for insanity even if our brains are as sound as bedrock? And most of us unable to pursue any career men would rather have, from journalism to the law?"

Sniffing, my mother said, "All that was true of my generation too. And you didn't hear us whine."

"Maybe we're not the ones who are wrong to object," I said, more sharply than I intended. "Maybe you're the ones who were wrong not to."

My mother wasn't the type to roll her eyes, but disapproval practically rolled off her in waves. "Amy. I want to go to a lovely event and have a lovely time. Can we just do that, please? Can you just say yes to that?"

I paused before replying. I made an effort to keep my tone even. Still, I wouldn't just knuckle under. She had to realize what she was proposing we undertake. "Won't appearing at this lovely event with a screaming child make the event somewhat less lovely? With a long unlovely train trip all the way there and back for bonus?"

My mother had her answer ready. "Gladys can stay here. My second cousin Mrs. Bender is helpful in situations like this. She'd be happy to watch her. And the nanny will stay, of course. Then you and I can both have a little break."

When she put it that way, a break sounded like exactly what I needed. I would force myself into a spirit of optimism, take the opportunity to begin again.

So I made myself ask brightly, "When do we leave?"

Even now, I'm tempted to describe the wedding. So much of what the papers said about me was describing every little detail of my life so people could picture themselves there. They wanted to imagine themselves at the social occasions I'd been at, living the life I led. They wanted giddy excess, luxury. The papers gave them those things in spades. They got their quotes from maids and porters and "unnamed sources close to the family" that may or may not have existed at all. People who claimed to have been present on nights that I attended cockfights or disappeared into the bushes with married men or wept my sadness into a tumbler of whiskey and then drank it all down.

So when I say it was a lovely wedding, I don't intend to be evasive. It had all the flourishes one would expect at this level of society, fresh, heavy-headed flowers lining every pew, candles on the banquet tables plentiful enough to rival the stars in the sky. The details simply made no difference, then or now. Especially not now. I only spoke with Darlene in the receiving line, giving her my brief congratulations. I could see her mother eyeing me, and I knew nothing had been forgotten. So I told myself I'd write a letter to Darlene once she and her husband were settled at their new address and tried to communicate everything else with my eyes.

But as far as the wedding goes, loveliness is what my mother had promised me, and it did feel, as she'd said, like a respite.

Until the telegram arrived from Mrs. Bender telling us Porter had attempted to kidnap Gladys.

Writing as few words as possible, as if money mattered at a moment like this, Mrs. Bender let us know that Mr. Ashe had appeared at the house in our absence. He pretended that I had asked him to take the child for the day. Mrs. Bender, a stolid and reliable poor widow who also happened to be terrified of my mother, wisely refused. In that, at least, she'd done the right thing.

The wedding events continued, but I couldn't attend. I could only pace our hotel room, fretting. My heart seemed to twist in my chest, worrying about my daughter, though I hoped she barely even perceived the danger. My mind zigzagged from certainty that all was well to equal certainty that the worst possible thing had happened and I just hadn't been informed yet. Mama, for her part, seemed confident. When she found me hollow-eyed and wakeful at three in the morning, standing by the window staring out at nothing, she assured me that next we heard, the news would be good.

We received another telegram. Porter's next kidnap attempt had succeeded.

For a treat, Mrs. Bender had taken the child to Wollweber's Drug Store. Mr. Ashe, accompanied by his brother, intercepted their party and repeated the lie about having my permission to take the girl. Mrs. Bender again refused.

Mr. Ashe ordered his brother to shoot anyone who stood in their way, lifted the child from Mrs. Bender's arms, stepped into a waiting carriage, and was gone.

When Mama heard the news, she did two things. First, she blanched so pale I thought she was sure to faint. But fainting was not Mama's way, not even when she had gotten something so dreadfully wrong.

Second, she chartered a special train from New York City to Los Angeles. An hour later, we were both on it. I wanted to point out to her that the power to summon a cross-country train was why it was good not to give too much of one's money away, but I knew it wasn't the time to grind that axe. We didn't speak at all, really. There was nothing to say.

Even a fast train feels slow when there are thousands of miles to cross. Time crawls. Every moment stretches out like torture. If you dare to look out the window, the landscape stretches out, flat and forbidding, for a nearly infinite distance. America has never seemed as large as it does when you wish it already crossed.

But the journey takes the time it takes. Your physical needs roll forward and back like the miles. Sleep seems impossible until it falls on you like a heavy curtain. What feels like only half a heartbeat later, you're rattled awake. Day and night lose meaning. Your own skin turns against you, feeling too loose or too tight. Your throat feels parched even while you're drinking. Add that to the constant rattle and coal stench, and if one squints, it can be hard to tell the difference between a cross-continental express train and the antechambers of hell itself.

Of course we received no news in transit, so on top of the other tortures of the journey, I had no idea what had happened to my daughter. I had no idea what Porter was trying to do. He had rarely ever seemed to be aware that the girl existed; she was an extension of me in his eyes, and he hated me. Good God, what could he intend?

Ill thoughts multiplied in the absence of anything to counter them. I arrived in Los Angeles an utter mess: sleepless, grimy, desperate.

Storming past the doorman, I yanked open the front door of the house on Van Ness Street with my own hands, desperate. Mrs. Bender stood before me. With no politeness to soften what I thought, I said, "Tell me. Good or bad. Tell me."

"He sent a note," Mrs. Bender said and handed it to me.

The paper felt rough under my fingers. I hesitated to open it. Once known, what was inside could never be unknown.

So even with the answer in my hands, I looked to my distant relative's face. "Did you read it?"

She didn't nod yes or no, which I figured meant that she had but might be afraid to say so.

"It's all right," I said. "Please. If you read it. Tell me what it says."

"You're summoned to the court," Mrs. Bender said.

"Court? What court?"

"The Third District. Mr. Ashe is suing you for custody."

"He wants Gladys?" I said incredulously. After the initial fuss, he'd seemed to see the baby only as an inconvenience, an appendage of mine that made me less attractive. After we separated, as far as I knew, he hadn't seen her once. He hadn't even asked to. Now, in my absence, he'd attempted to steal her for himself? It made no sense. "A baby he wouldn't even recognize on the street?"

The answering shrug was unsatisfying.

"And he's bringing suit against me. But he could have done that without the kidnapping," I said.

"Possession is nine-tenths of the law," my mother broke in.

"I hope Gladys vomits down his neck," I said, feeling I might vomit myself.

"Amy!" my mother chastised.

I whirled on her. "I can't even wish him ill? Don't you? When he's tortured us in this ridiculous, public way? What if he hurts her?"

"He won't hurt her. He's trying to hurt you."

"He's succeeding," I said, unable to keep the strain from my voice. I felt so tired, wrung out, but I couldn't rest. I rubbed the backs of my grubby hands across my wet face. "All right. Call the carriage. Let's go to court."

"No," said my mother. She reached for the bellpull. The ring, so loud, jangled my nerves. "First, you'll take a bath."

It was such a ridiculous interjection, I could only parrot it back. "A bath?"

Mama's voice was as sharp as I'd ever heard it as she said, "Amy, you look like an absolute savage. What will the judge think?"

I wanted to rant that I didn't care what the judge thought, he could go hang, but I wasn't too far gone to understand. She was right. What this judge thought mattered more than anything else right now. As much as I hated putting on appearances, that was exactly what I had to do.

But wearing a fresh gown and a smile didn't get the judge on my side, that day or any day. It turned out that the assigned judge was named Baskin, a friend of the Ashe family. Unfortunately, I'd met the man often enough to know his nature: punctilious, detailed, a petty tyrant who enjoyed using his power to benefit those he liked and punish those he didn't. No doubt Porter's lawyers had somehow gotten him assigned to the case. More than likely, it was already too late.

In the short term, temporary custody of Gladys was awarded to the sheriff, of all people, with both Porter and myself having rights to visit her on particular days at particular times.

So a new pattern began. A new way of living, one that would have seemed impossible only a week before, now became as regular as a heartbeat. Whenever it was my appointed time to visit Gladys, I always went. I dressed to the nines, dragged myself there, pasted on a smile. I could practically feel my mother breathing down my neck on those days, waiting to pounce, waiting for me to disappoint her. But I knew what was at stake. I did what was expected.

I reached out for Gladys, held her even as she wailed, sang sweet songs to her she didn't seem to enjoy. If anything, it was worse than it had been when we'd lived in the same house; I was even more of a stranger to her. I frightened her, I realized. But I couldn't help myself, so tense and overly bright, feeling like so much depended on every moment of my interaction with my daughter. I wanted to prove she belonged to me. She was a baby; I don't blame her. But I tried so hard to hold on to her, and I terrified her, and in the end, I frightened her so badly she began to cry the moment I appeared in the room.

Still, I came. I would be there even if she didn't want me there. If we could weather this storm, everything might still be repaired eventually. In the short term, the baby wasn't the one making the decisions. The judge alone would decide our fate.

Perhaps, despite his friendship with the Ashe family, Judge Baskin could be reasoned with. Porter was facing kidnapping and weapons charges for what he'd done to take Gladys in my absence; that had to count for something. I hoped it did.

And what had I ever done wrong, really? Had a bit too much fun here and there? I'd been given money I hadn't earned, but heaven knew that was true of most rich people. I had never endangered my child, never been so drunk in public I couldn't see straight, never stayed out all night unaccompanied and not returned until after dawn the next day. Unlike my own husband, I had never been known to gamble and lose thousands of dollars on a single race.

But as the weeks went on, the fight began to feel more and more futile. Porter's attorneys knew what they were about. The most scandalous of the stories they'd gathered—the ones my lawyer had asked me to confirm as we considered the divorce case—were presented like gift-wrapped baubles for the judge's enjoyment. They weren't public, not yet. I suppose I should have been grateful for that. But hearing thirdhand from my lawyer that my character and not Porter's was being used to influence the judge infuriated me.

Once Mr. Everleigh left, I still burned with anger, and I couldn't help but rise and stomp around the parlor. I'd chosen every touch in the room when Porter and I had still been in love; it all irritated me now, because I had everything and nothing I wanted.

My mother attempted to calm me. "Amy. Sit down."

"No! This isn't over. I'll fight forever. He has to know we can afford it."

"That's what you want to do with your money?" she asked, returning to her familiar melody. "You didn't contribute at all during the last charity drive for the art museum, and now you want to squander thousands, tens of thousands, on fighting a battle you can't win?"

My anger burned brighter than my fear of her disapproval. "I have to win. Because I can't let *him* win."

"And because you love your daughter?"

"Of course!" I said. I wasn't sure I was convincing, but it was the correct answer.

She tried a soothing voice again. "But you have to take the long view. This particular battle, this particular case, you're not going to win. Stop fighting."

"I'll fight forever," I said, then repeated, "I can't let him win."

"Well, he won't let you win either. So where does that leave us?"

"I don't know!" I shouted in frustration. "But I know I can't give up."

She put her hand on my arm, but I kept moving, letting it fall. Her voice was part soothing, part irritated as she said, "You don't want to. I understand that. But you have to."

"Why?"

"Because he doesn't really want custody. Think about what he loves in life. His nighttime activities. His freedom."

I cut in, sneering. "His right to stay out all night with divas and actresses."

"Exactly. He doesn't want to be responsible for a baby, Amy! Days and nights, for months, then years? No. He just wants to win."

I had to admit what she was saying made sense. "So if he doesn't want her—we let him have her? And then what happens?"

"He'll keep her a little while. Hire a nanny or two to do all the work. But even that will feel like too much."

I was starting to understand her logic. "And he'll have no choice but to give her back to me."

She said, "It's the only thing that makes sense."

For once, I did as my mother said. In May, we settled out of court so that the custody question wouldn't go to trial. I let Porter have our daughter, even though he had been less of a father to her than I had been a mother. His vision of fatherhood was to have a child to boast about at the club. He had already handed out those cigars. Surely, as Mama said, he would grow bored.

The headlines, of course, proclaimed their joy. "Porter Ashe Victorious in Custody Suit," screamed the *Chronicle*, even though that was not at all what had happened. On its front page—below the fold, but still—the *Call* printed a sweet little story about Porter taking Gladys to the beach and dipping her little toes in the ocean for the first time, calling him "a father for the ages."

I was doing nothing, going nowhere, and still the papers found a way to feature me. One of Porter's lawyers, I suspect, slipped a friend in the press part of the file they'd compiled on my young adventures. One morning at breakfast, when I sat down, my mother stood up and left the table without speaking to me. I had no idea why until I looked at the paper she'd been reading before I came in: "Crocker-Ashe Marriage Resulted From a Wild Gamble," shouted the headline. The whole story of the midnight poker game was there in black and white. The wedding, the drinking, the late hour, the hotel room. No detail was spared.

The rest of May was a frosty month. Mama and I never discussed what the papers were saying about me, and she continued to stay at my house instead of moving back to her own, but I knew she was both ashamed and hurt. I realized I should have told her before the truth came out another way. But I'd hoped she'd never know. Now there was no going back.

June brought fresh pain. My petition for divorce had of course been denied, but Porter had filed his own. His expert lawyers, who I resented and grudgingly admired in equal measure, had even gotten the case moved up the docket with lightning speed. Through my lawyer, I learned that the money would be divided in unsurprising ways, with both of us keeping what we'd brought in. On the question of Gladys's custody, though, things were less certain.

"That's up to the judge," Mr. Everleigh kept saying. "He could award her to Porter or to you, or maybe split the time between you both. We're advocating behind the scenes, but I just can't make you any promises."

"I suppose I wouldn't believe you if you did," I said and meant it.

The day the divorce judgment came in, I dressed as if my finery were armor, closing my eyes as my maid buckled and strapped and laced me in, pretending I was Joan of Arc. I met my mother downstairs to share a carriage. We said not a word to each other. There was no comfort she could give me even if she were inclined to, and I could tell she hadn't gotten over my bad behavior dominating the headlines. I felt lucky she was accompanying me at all.

In the plainest terms, the judge granted Porter's petition for divorce. It was that simple. With a few words, I instantly became the scarlet divorcée I both longed and feared to be. On the matter of custody, however, the judge beat around the bush.

"I think we can all agree that no one has covered themselves with glory in this proceeding," Judge Baskin said, glaring down at both me and Porter like a stern headmaster.

I felt a pang of joy that someone was finally saying something negative about Porter, but it didn't last.

Then, the judge turned his disapproval entirely on me. "Mrs. Ashe, your youthful indiscretions are well-known. It is clear from Mr. Ashe's petition that you failed to mature into a model wife, and there is little evidence you reformed yourself into a fit mother."

Joan of Arc, I chanted to myself, refusing to burst into tears. *Joan of Arc.*

He turned to Porter. "But the way in which you went about securing your child's safety, stealing her away without permission, was not appropriate. And your income is less steady than that of your former wife's family, raising some uncertainty on whether you're best prepared financially to care for the child."

My heart lifted. Was it possible? Could my daughter be mine again?

The judge looked past me, over my right shoulder, to my mother.

"Mrs. Margaret Crocker," he began. "You are a paragon of the community. It is well-known that you share a great deal of your husband's bequest with the less fortunate but without compromising your financial stability. It is the court's belief that you are best suited to care for the child. We award you full custody of Gladys Ashe. The parental rights of Mr. Porter Ashe and Mrs. Amy Crocker Ashe are terminated. Mrs. Crocker, we highly recommend that within the next year, you legally adopt the child to ensure that your rights are protected."

I swiveled to look back at Mama. Her eyes were still on the judge. I realized, with a sinking, stunning horror, that she didn't look surprised.

The judge's gavel came down, dismissing us all.

First, the reporters in the back of the room hustled out to file their stories. The judge turned and vanished through a door behind his bench. Then, Porter and his army of lawyers strode out, and while I couldn't see their faces, I assume they were congratulating themselves on a job well done. Behind me, I heard slippered footsteps as my mother turned away. Without a word, Mr. Everleigh followed her.

I stood there, numb. It took a while to gather myself. When I did, I was the last one to leave the court.

In the hallway, a groom awaited me. "Mrs. Ashe," he said. "I have a carriage for you."

My mother had thoughtfully arranged for me to be taken out a side entrance, saving me exposure to the reporters who were no doubt thronging the courthouse steps, hoping to get more details on my misery. I climbed into the carriage. I wanted to tell myself again that I was Joan of Arc, and in a way, I was. That's what we sometimes forget about Joan. In the end, she burns.

The carriage took me to the Van Ness house. When I entered, it was eerily quiet. It didn't take me long to discover what had changed.

It turned out that my mother's arrangements went far beyond taking me out the side door of the courthouse. Though she had indeed been thoughtful, it wasn't my comfort she was most focused on preserving.

Mama's things were gone. So were Gladys's. My mother had known about this long enough to plan.

For the first time in my life, I was truly alone. I would live by myself in the Van Ness house while my mother and Gladys took up residence in my childhood home. I could visit, but I would only ever be a visitor.

Porter and I had both claimed we were ready to fight to the death for our daughter, made such a hue and cry over it, locked in vicious battle. With a stroke of the judge's pen, we'd both been thwarted.

The newspapers found that detail especially delightful. Not only were Porter Ashe and Amy Crocker Ashe no longer husband and wife, neither were we parents. That had all been stripped away. The tabloids found a hundred different ways to trumpet it on their pages, sneak it into other stories, point it up again and again.

I finally stopped reading the newspapers.

CHAPTER SEVEN

Circumstances favored me. They favored my traveling by hurting my heart.

—**AC**

At the young age of seventeen, I'd become a wife, and at nineteen, a mother. But per the law, at twenty-three, I was no longer either. Gladys had no more affinity for me than her nannies—indeed, much less. I remembered back to the day of her birth, when I stared at the squirming red bundle in my arms and thought *I don't feel like a mother,* a premotion that had now come true. Alone in the Van Ness house where Porter and I had intended to raise a family, I was surrounded every day by reminders of the future I'd dreamed of but never lived.

Is it any wonder I began to dream of escape?

I paid regular visits to my mother's house, hoping to stay in my daughter's life, but I was constantly frustrated. Every time we spoke, my mother pushed me to rejoin the circuit of balls and dances. To become the society lady she'd always wanted me to be, the one Jennie had happily become. To spend my days organizing charity drives, to donate vast swaths of my money for the good of the poor. To follow her excellent example, since paying attention to my own wants and needs had gotten me nowhere quickly.

Instead, I made arrangements to charter a ship for an entire year, well into 1888, and selected Hawaii as my first destination.

I chose to stop by my mother's house to tell her on the way to the pier. I asked the doorman to send her to speak with me under the portico, highly unconventional, but I wanted her to see my packed trunks piled high on the coach. She spotted them immediately.

"Making a trip, Amy?" she asked. Her voice was innocent, but I knew better.

"Yes. I leave today." I smoothed my gloves as we spoke. Nonchalance was my armor.

"Am I allowed to know your destination?"

I considered it. "Allowed, yes, but does it matter? You can neither approve the trip nor forbid it. Given that, would you like to know?"

She looked affronted, though I wasn't sure whether that was genuine or she just felt like taking offense was the most motherly thing to do in the situation. I couldn't read her expression in full, though there were certainly elements of disappointment and annoyance and something that looked a bit like longing.

We stood there in silence so long I finally repeated myself. "Would you like to know?"

She squared her shoulders. "Yes. I think I would."

"Hawaii. The Sandwich Islands, they're sometimes called. Remember meeting King Kalakaua?" He'd been a memorable figure on the London scene, speaking passionately about his culture and the opportunities awaiting those willing to emigrate to those sunny, sweet isles. Mama and I had both enjoyed conversation with him, though my mother had moved on to other guests while I remained with the king, fascinated. "He told me I had an open invitation to visit any time I liked."

"So you chose now."

"Yes."

"And how much will this cost?"

I almost laughed. "Does that matter?"

"Our money is a gift, Amy. We choose how to use it."

I'd heard her sing from this sheet of music often enough, and I moved to cut off what came next. "There's still plenty left for the less fortunate. I promise. When I get back, I'll host a tea to raise funds for the Marguerite Home. Or the Bell Conservatory if you'd rather. And I'll serve on one of your committees, all right?"

She still looked skeptical.

"Two," I bargained.

She somehow gave the impression of giving a sigh without sighing. "This deserves a longer conversation."

"Please." I hadn't intended to let the desperation creep into my voice, but when I heard myself speak, I realized there was no hiding it. "I can't be here. I can't do this." Then I repeated, though there was no sense in doing so, "Please."

Then she finally seemed to hear me, thank goodness, both what I said and didn't say.

Mama took one step back from me, closer to her own door. "Go," she said. "Only take care."

I wanted to scoff, to tell her that care wasn't required. But she had been sincere with me, and I returned the favor. "I'll take the best care I know how."

Without further warnings or requirements, without even asking me to write, she turned her back and mounted the stairs. She didn't suggest I come in to say goodbye to Gladys. I think we both knew there was no point. I wanted to go to my daughter; of course I did. But she would cry, and then I would, and nothing would change except we'd have red eyes and wet faces. I was angry at my mother for the situation we were in, but not nearly as angry as I was at Porter. Even though he hadn't exactly succeeded in stealing our daughter, I'd still lost her.

Now I could only hope not to lose myself, I thought as I sailed for Hawaii. I might lose myself there or find myself there or both or neither, but at least I would be thousands of miles away. At least whatever happened would be *new*.

Sailing into the bay of Hawaii, in an odd way, felt like coming home.

It was the most foreign place I'd ever been, of course, so my reaction struck me as dissonant. I felt the doubleness of it even as the observation occurred to me. Not a single thing about this world was familiar, not the longboats in the bay nor the thatched huts that lined the black sand beaches nor the people whose skin came in far more shades than I'd ever seen in California.

But there was a rightness to the place, one that flooded my veins and sank into my bones as we arrived, from the first moment I saw a stranger's welcoming smile. I breathed easier than I had since catching Porter stumbling into his bedroom at three in the morning smeared with lipstick and booze. I truly felt I had left all the bad in my life behind and now there was this new life, this new world, I could inhabit. Perhaps it was that the king had described it to me so precisely that I knew what to expect; perhaps it was just that it was all in such great harmony, every piece belonging to the whole, when I had felt off-kilter for so long.

The king himself was on the pier waiting for me, though I hadn't let him know I was coming; the word seemed to have passed to him somehow.

"The wondrous Miss Crocker!" he said. "It is my distinct pleasure to welcome you to my homeland, Hawaii. Thank you for accepting my invitation."

A bit off balance, I answered with the first thing that came to mind. "Not Miss Crocker anymore, I'm afraid."

"Yes, yes." He waved a hand. "You married. But then you unmarried."

If only everyone saw it so clearly, I wanted to tell him. But to speak of divorce at all felt like it would break some sort of spell.

He went on. "To me, you are Miss Crocker, and that is what we will call you here, until you gain your title. But I get ahead of myself. Step on land?" And then he extended a hand to me, all formality. I took it and set foot on his island nation for the first time.

The freshness of Hawaii—no one here called it the Sandwich Islands, I quickly found—was exactly what I needed. Clear air, quiet nature, the slow pace of life. All the formality of San Francisco was absent; I could almost believe I was a whole new person, a younger, more innocent Amy.

And the feeling of rightness, the one that had filled me the moment we sailed in, it only grew with time. It felt right as I took my first bites of their local specialties, the poi and poke and that delicious roast pork called kalua, and filled my wanting belly with exotic fruits only minutes off the tree. It felt right as I heard their words wash over me, even when I didn't understand them, losing myself in the music of their language. It felt right as I breathed in the refreshing salt air, so different from the salt air of San Francisco that it was impossible to believe the same ocean nudged against both shores.

I found that the king had been rather lavish with the sort of invitation he'd extended to me at our first meeting. I'd thought myself special before I came. Now I saw that I wasn't special at all, that he'd invited every sort of visitor from con artists to cardinals. The pale faces and sunburnt limbs of Americans and Europeans were everywhere. But I didn't take offense. Instead, I found myself relishing the feeling. How wondrous, to be someone no one cared about.

Once a week in those days, the king threw his gates wide to welcome all comers to a celebration of Hawaiian culture, the traditions he was helping his people reclaim. We feasted, bathed in music and dancing. I was so fascinated by the motions of the local dance, the hula, that I asked to begin taking lessons. The young woman who agreed to teach me, Mahina, was one of the star performers at these weekly feasts.

I was watching Mahina, trying to keep myself from moving my hips in concert with hers, when I overheard a woman's sharp voice nearby. "Don't even look. No, Mr. Abernathy. I said no! Turn this way. Let's all turn this way."

Shifting my position so I could look in the direction of the voice, I identified the speaker immediately: a prim woman in midlife, dressed in navy blue from head to toe, her mouth set in a disapproving line. Around her were a gaggle of others, mostly younger, all wearing the same color. A young man with flushed cheeks stole a look past me, and I guessed he must be the unfortunate Mr. Abernathy, chastised for watching the dancers' swaying hips.

I tapped the older woman on the shoulder and greeted her with a broad smile. "Hello! Are you fellow Americans?"

"We are the Society of Cousins," she said, not an answer. I could see her sizing me up as a potential friend or foe. "My name is Miss Medford."

I did my best to remain positive. "Pleased to meet you, Miss Medford. I'm Miss Crocker. What brings you to Hawaii?"

Gesturing to the group, who had begun to cluster around her like ducklings, she said, "We are on mission. Here to save the natives from their ignorance and encourage them to embrace Jesus."

I liked Jesus just fine, but I didn't see any reason the Hawaiians should choose him over their own gods. I was still trying to figure out how to diplomatically say so when the head missionary spoke again.

Indicating the dancers with a shake of her chin, she said, "This kind of immodest display is exactly what we must help them realize is not appropriate. Uncovered bodies." She suppressed a shiver.

I said, "They dance like this because it's their tradition. What could be more appropriate? It's not their concern whether it makes you uncomfortable."

"It isn't a matter of comfort. It's what the Lord says is right and wrong. You must agree, Miss Crocker," said Miss Medford, "that so many people of the world fail to follow the holy word of the Christian god only because they've never heard it."

"Actually, I don't agree," I answered cheerfully. "People of the world believe what they are raised to believe."

"That sounds like you agree to me," she snapped back.

"Then you aren't listening." I had tried my best, but I realized quickly that there was no point in further conversation. There was no changing her mind, and I knew there was no changing mine, so why waste time? "Please excuse me. My drink has run dry." I didn't look back as I left her.

I ended up sitting next to an elderly man who strummed his guitar so beautifully I nearly wept. There was something about the music that spoke to my soul better than words ever could. My time in Hawaii was full of these moments, beauty around every corner if I was only willing to open myself up.

But the Society of Cousins didn't see it that way, and over the next couple of weeks, they became a nuisance. Not just to me. I saw Miss Medford and her flock at the market, on the beach, and on the hiking paths, even near the children's school as I passed it on my way to my hula lessons with Mahina. Each time, the missionaries were accosting local after local, communicating their disapproval, haranguing them until even the most polite Hawaiian had no choice but to walk away.

Matters came to a head at another of the king's weekly banquets, another evening so beautiful I wished I could bottle the feeling and wear it like a scent. Guests strolled the lanes in feathers and furs, some a great deal and some almost none; scents of pineapple and pork, taro and sea vegetables wafted through the air. Lights blazed high from torches, the open flames roaring so high it seemed wise to keep one's distance.

I was watching the dancers, Mahina leading them in a complex and beautiful hula, when an unpleasantly familiar voice behind me said, "I'm disappointed in you, Mrs. Ashe."

Without looking at Miss Medford, I answered, "I'm disappointed in you too." Then her form of address sank in, and I turned.

Even with a downturned mouth, the navy-clad missionary radiated satisfaction. "You lied to me on our meeting. Gave a false name."

"Not intentionally. Amy Crocker is who I am."

"No," she said with mock patience, "Mrs. Porter Ashe is who you were, and as a divorcée, Mrs. Ashe is who you remain."

"You have no idea who I really am."

"I know you're not fit for society anymore, with your appalling behavior. No wonder you enjoy this sort of shameful display." She gestured toward the dancers without looking at them.

Her argument was so absurd I couldn't even be insulted by it, but I came close. I wasn't sure whether I was more outraged on the dancers' behalf or my own. "This dance is beautiful."

"This dance, as you call it, is appalling. This is what separates us from the natives, Mrs. Ashe. They put themselves on display. It's barely human."

My temper almost boiled over, but instead, I took her hand in mine. She was surprised but didn't pull away.

"Miss Medford," I said, forcing myself to sound sweet. "I see exactly what you're saying. Could you stay here for a few minutes, please? I want to speak with them, and we'll see what comes of it. Would you indulge me?"

"All—all right," she stammered.

At the next pause in the dancing, I took Mahina aside and quickly explained the situation. She insisted on sending a runner to bring King Kalakaua. He grinned when he heard our plan. With the time that it took to discuss and change clothing, I was worried that Miss Medford would lose patience and wander off. But when I peeked out from behind the curtain, I saw her group's blue habits standing out from the crowd like a cluster of uncomfortable jays.

The drums started up, kicking like an insistent heartbeat, louder than one could imagine. Then after the drums, a flute. After the flute, the dancers, led forward by two ornately costumed figures whose hips swung wildly in grass skirts.

Leading the men was the king himself, his headdress enormous and his eyes dancing in merriment; leading the women was yours truly, my arms gesticulating in the precise patterns I'd spent weeks learning, my costume leaving precious little to the imagination.

I tried not to look at the missionaries, but the temptation proved irresistible. Swaying my hips in careful circles, undulating my arms in time to the music, I let my gaze drift over the five of them. Four, including the dour Miss Medford, took enormous care to avoid meeting my eyes. The fifth, Mr. Abernathy, was gazing at me so lasciviously I feared he might leap up and fling himself upon me at any moment. That wasn't what we had in mind, so I broke the gaze quickly and turned my attention to the next phase of our plan: showing them exactly how little the people of the islands cared for the missionaries' opinion. My participation wasn't necessary, of course—the king's people would and could have handled it admirably—but it added a particular insult to injury. The Cousins had expected any reasonable white person to side with them, and here was a white person who had chosen to throw in her lot with what they perceived as the other side.

And my word, was it satisfying.

———————

Afterward, I saw a white man, a stranger, looking closely at me from afar. He had been watching me earlier. I felt a sense of dread when I looked at him, and it took me several hiccupping starts to name the feeling.

He looked like a reporter.

His clothing was a little too formal for the islands, the amount of brilliantine in his hair excessive for the heat. I didn't see a notepad in his hands, but I could easily imagine one. He might be the enemy I feared most: a journalist.

I moved to speak with him, but he melted back into the crowd.

My suspicions seemed to be confirmed when, several days later, I spotted my name in the local paper. I was no longer as anonymous here as I had been. The stunt at the feast had, however good it felt in the moment, caught some attention. My feud with the missionaries, my decision to dance in scant native dress, it was printed there for all to see. At least the overall tone of the piece was approving—the writer clearly didn't care for the Society of Cousins any more than I had—but I saw how easily that could have been different. Per the article, the missionaries had been so appalled by my actions that when the sun came up the following morning, they were already gone. I was impressed with their industry. I wouldn't have thought they could get off the island so quickly without prior arrangement.

By a stroke of luck, or what I took for it, I spotted the man in the street the same day I read the newspaper article.

The wise thing to do would have been to track him from a distance and find out more about him, but I lacked the patience for that. Instead, I stormed up to him and said, "How dare you?"

His eyes sparkled, which only made me more sure I was right. "And what crime am I accused of?"

"You're a reporter," I said. "You wrote about me."

"You have me wrong. Let's clear up the misunderstanding." He thrust out a hand, all bonhomie. "I'm Washington Irving Bishop. I'm not a reporter at all. I'm an entertainer."

I shook his hand, feeling relieved, though in the end, he would do more long-lasting harm to me than a single reporter ever had.

CHAPTER EIGHT

*The fact that I could be brought out of myself and could drift,
through his influence, into another sort of existence, was
like the realization of a dream. And even the man himself
bewildered me and fascinated me beyond my control.*

—**AC**

When most people say they fell under a man's spell, it's an expression. In my case, with Washington Irving Bishop, it was literally true.

Vacillating between fearing the power of the woman in white and telling myself she'd been a mere flight of fancy, I had become more curious about the supernatural during my first marriage. The popularity of spiritualism made it easy to indulge my curiosity. Attempts to reach across the chasm separating us from the spirit world were everywhere: séances and spirit walking, automatic writing and crystal balls. In certain circles, people loved to test themselves against these practices and prove themselves immune. I'd learned too much about the world to think myself untouchable. I knew anyone who told themselves they couldn't be hurt was a liar or a fool. I walked into every new situation with a healthy skepticism.

Did my skepticism save me? Not this time.

After my brief first meeting with Bishop, I noticed him more frequently in passing, but we only nodded to each other. I couldn't tell whether he was playing coy or whether he wasn't interested in becoming acquainted. He obviously knew who I was, which might be a point either for or against me, depending.

The next time we actually spoke, I'd chosen to attend one of the expatriate evening entertainments at the hotel. Several acts in, I was regretting my choice. First came an opera singer, not top-notch but solid, followed by an older gentleman who declaimed some Shakespeare in a very classical style. I suspected he was imagining himself onstage at the Globe, projecting his voice to the groundlings and beyond. His Caesar was excellent, his Titus Andronicus passable. I can find nothing positive to say about his Prospero. The woman next to me in the second row was a passing acquaintance, but I didn't know her well enough to make a cutting observation. Not everyone appreciates those.

Then the master of ceremonies, a native woman elegantly dressed in a gleaming white gown and matching top hat, announced that the evening's final act would be an American spiritualist of great renown. She tilted her hat to a jaunty angle and called out, "And now, please welcome Washington Irving Bishop!"

I recognized the name only because he'd given it himself at our previous meeting; I hadn't heard of him. I learned later he had made his reputation by working for years as the assistant of Anna Eva Fay, then publishing a book debunking her spiritualism act in detail. He gave away all her secrets. He may not have been a journalist, but he showed a pressman's willingness to make his name on the backs of others without their cooperation or consent.

"Good evening, ladies and gentlemen!" Bishop was formally dressed, wearing a somewhat standard mentalist's garb of a black tuxedo, a matching tie, and a white shirt with a pointed collar. His dark hair was slicked back with brilliantine. "Let me introduce myself. I am the great mentalist Washington Irving Bishop, sometimes known as Wellington."

If he was expecting recognition, none was visible on the audience's faces.

Undeterred, he continued, "But I have another name as well. The wonderful King Kalakaua himself gave it to me. He has honored me with a rare title, which means 'the favorite child of the heavens.' It is a name I rarely use outside the islands, knowing no one will understand its meaning. But I can share it with you here tonight. I am deeply honored to be known here in Hawaii as Kamilimilianalani."

His pronunciation was surprisingly good. A smattering of applause greeted his competence.

Now he could build up a head of steam. "My parents were both on the stage, and I took in all their secrets with my mother's milk. What I have learned, first and foremost, is that this"—he gestured with an expansive arm—"is all a game. But while we're playing, let's have fun, shall we?"

He set about turning the makeshift stage into the scene of a séance, calling on assistants to lay a table, to dim the gaslights. Once the room was transformed, he turned to the audience.

"Who here wants to help me call upon the spirits? How about you, young man?" He pointed to a ruddy young man in the front row, who'd come on the arm of a sea captain's wife.

There were murmurs, and the young man said, "Sir, I apologize. This sort of thing just isn't my cup of tea."

Bishop took the rejection in stride. "Who else, then? Who here is brave enough to reach across the border of the spirit world? Who lives without fear?"

The sea captain's wife, hands in her lap like the most proper of churchgoing ladies, looked away. The French couple in the front row on her other side, who'd been paying more attention to each other than the performances all evening, also declined. The Frenchwoman murmured in halting English that probably couldn't be heard two more rows away, "No thank you. I fear too much."

Bishop nodded and raised his eyes to those of us in the next row. When his gaze met mine over the Frenchwoman's head, I knew he'd intended to make me his volunteer all along.

He extended a hand toward me, calling me toward him silently. I went with a smile on my face. Some might have thought it unseemly, public participation in a séance for entertainment's sake, but no one of that ilk was here. The missionaries were gone. The Frenchwoman's fears notwithstanding, no one came all the way to Hawaii merely to toe the line.

When I mounted the stage, before he could get out a question or instruction, I waved to the audience. "Good evening, fellow travelers! Are we all ready for a new adventure?"

The crowd knew me. They saluted my enthusiasm with a ripple of applause.

When I turned back to Bishop, satisfied, I could tell he was already a little annoyed with me. I didn't mind that. Keeping a stranger happy was rarely on my list of aims. It was not inconsistent that I had chosen not to give away my money to philanthropic causes as my mother had done. I was similarly stingy with my attention and approval, which I was happy to give if there was a reason. I didn't bestow them automatically. They should be earned.

In his showman's voice, he said, "Welcome to the stage, Miss…"

"Crocker," I supplied. He knew my name, but he was giving me a chance not to use it, which I appreciated.

"Miss Crocker! We are so lucky to have your company tonight."

"Yes," I agreed in a loud voice, playing to the crowd. "You are."

I was rewarded with a ripple of laughter. When I turned toward Bishop, my smile was broad with genuine pleasure.

"Now, Miss Crocker. Are you interested in the spirit world?"

"Not to get there too soon!" I exclaimed.

"True, true," he said, pretending to laugh along, though I was certain I'd irked him. He was used to being in charge, and I was unbalancing him, or at least that was how it seemed to me. "None of us would wish that. But are you prepared to assist me as I reach across the border between the living and the dead?"

"Well, what do I have to do?" I asked brightly.

He became serious, affixing his gaze firmly to my face. I had the oddest sensation, as if everything and everyone else in the room had disappeared. "Simply, you must put yourself completely in my hands."

Bishop was not a physically fearsome man. And nothing I had seen of him so far gave me cause to fear his intellect. So I said gamely, "Of course! Let's begin."

With satisfaction, he nodded. Almost instantly, I saw the transformation in him, his utter focus. He seated me in a chair and asked me to sit straight up, facing him, with my hands flat on the table. I complied.

He hummed a tune under his breath as he sat in the other chair, facing me. Then in the gentlest, softest tones, he said, "Do I have your attention, Miss Crocker?"

"Yes," I answered.

"You needn't speak words," he said, still gentle, as if calming a skittish horse. "You need only think your answers."

Yes, I thought.

He nodded, eyes locked with mine. "Good girl."

I didn't realize he was hypnotizing me. I thought hypnosis was all swinging watches and incantations. This was just a gaze, just words. Yet the room around us was gone; only we two existed in the world. As I think back and try to reconstruct the evening, so much of what followed remains hazy. But I remember one moment clearly: still holding my gaze, the depths of his brown eyes offering mystery, he touched me for the first time.

Bishop raised his right hand and reached across the table to touch my breastbone, two fingers landing high above my décolletage with a dancer's grace. Then he moved his fingers together, almost like a pinch, though he pinched nothing between them but air.

"Ouch," I blurted inadvertently. Somehow, even though his fingertips were barely grazing me, I had felt him grab hold of something. But what?

"You feel no pain," he said, soothing. He was right. I didn't.

Then he drew his hand back toward his own chest, still with those fingers pinched, and hunched over the table protectively. He cupped his palms and turned them inward, as if he held a lightning bug between them, not wanting the creature to escape. I was told later by a friend that in this moment, I had appeared like a marionette with the strings cut, my body half-limp, my gaze vacant.

Then Bishop's face broke into a smile, and he leaned eagerly across the table with a great flourish, turning his cupped hands upward as if bearing something between them.

"Miss Crocker, look," he said. "I have your soul in my hands."

Without question, I saw it. A glow, one like I'd never seen, a kind of smoke lit from within.

I believed him utterly and completely. He held my soul with complete tenderness. It was so lovely, so precious. Tears began to streak down my face.

"This is mine," he said.

I didn't hesitate. I wanted him to know. I replied, "It's yours."

The rest of the night, as I've said, was hazy. Apparently I became the vessel for a departed spirit dear to someone in the audience, providing consolation from the great beyond. When the evening's entertainment concluded, I was not under my own power as I followed Bishop from the stage.

When we walked out of the hotel together, it was the beginning of something new.

More than anything else I'd experienced at that point in my young life, even more than my vision of the woman in white, Washington

Irving Bishop's power over me made me conclude that supernatural forces exist in the world. Because without them, I would never have done the things that man made me do.

Our first public performance was not our last. I was trotted out again the next night, in front of a smaller group handpicked by Bishop. Again, he commanded me; again, I followed his command without hesitation, his will replacing my own. I sang "What Shall We Do with the Drunken Sailor?" a song I despised, in front of a crowd of acquaintances and strangers who watched me like a trained monkey. Two men in the front row who kept refilling their empty whiskey glasses from a shared flask were laughing fit to bust a gut.

Somewhere in the depths, my conscious mind struggled to warn me of the danger. Bishop could make me do whatever he wanted. What if there were reporters in the audience? What if my antics made the papers? The headlines would be ten feet high. If things got bad enough, if newspapers that had already predicted my fall got this evidence that proved their predictions true, if I were declared mad in front of all and sundry, my fortune might even be taken away.

But even with those thoughts, I couldn't break free. I still did the things Bishop wanted me to do, whether or not I wanted to do them. It was the most powerless I've ever felt, hollowed out and refilled with something that was no longer me.

Every day, he began the day by reading my tarot, an activity I had enjoyed on occasion before I met him but that had not yet become widespread. Such decks were rarely seen in American hands in those days, being more of a Continental fashion. Bishop had commissioned a one-of-a-kind deck for his own private use, based on the Marseille deck available in Italy and France, translated into English. The backs were decorated with a swarm of line-drawn bees, a pun on his last initial. When he read the cards for me, he did it the simplest way: one card for the past, one for the present, and one for the future. I knew the basics—the Death card rarely means literal death, dealing a card upside down changes its meaning, that sort of thing—but not the nuances, so I listened carefully as he told me what my readings meant.

"Ah, in your future, the five of swords," he'd purr, his low voice a mellow baritone. "Now, this is interesting. It does concern me a bit. Someone in your life isn't being aboveboard. It isn't clear what they're trying to get away with, but you need to be on your guard... They might succeed."

From the vantage point of decades on, I can see what he was doing. Nearly every day, my reading showed some sort of threat, according to Bishop, and the universe was signaling that I needed to keep a protector close. Of course he was that protector.

At the time, though, I missed the pattern. So when he'd tell me that the cards showed danger, I'd cling closer to him. He'd reach out and lay his fingers against my breastbone the way he'd done that first night, and I would feel a surge of warmth and connection that smoothed any fears and doubts away.

Over the course of our weeks together, even when my readings were fraught with warnings and omens of peril, I came to find it soothing. In those moments, I could fully relax. Whatever Bishop saw in my past, present, and future, he would ask nothing of me in those few minutes. If only the same had been true the other hours of the day.

I prefer not to go into more detail about where he took me and what I did there, as none of it matters much. I count myself lucky he didn't humiliate me in truly irrecoverable ways. The only crucial story to tell of my entanglement with Bishop was how it ended.

Some weeks into our entanglement—the English language truly lacks words for what we were to each other—I found myself in a horse-drawn cart with him. We both sat on the driver's seat, but the reins were in his hands. I had no idea what our destination was. That wasn't my role, to know.

We rode for a while in silence. Then, in the tone he got when he was ready to amuse himself, Bishop said, "Why don't you whip the horses, Amy?"

I put out my hand automatically, and he placed the handle of the whip across my palm. The seat lurched underneath us. I knew horses well from my early days in Sacramento, and if he'd handed me the reins, I would have happily driven, but he didn't. He gave me only the whip.

When I didn't act, Bishop said, "Now whip the horses, Amy," in a clear voice of command.

"Are you sure they need the whip?" I ventured, my voice tentative. A whip was a tool to get a result, but what result could he need? We were trotting along at good speed already.

Instead of answering my question, Bishop used his voice of command again, saying, "I should like to see you whip them."

Almost everything in me insisted I obey him, but underneath, there was the old Amy, who knew this was wrong. I lashed out with a half-hearted motion, too softly for the whip even to snap above the horses' backs, let alone cause them pain.

Bishop was displeased. I could see his hands tighten on the reins, his knuckles going white. "Now, now, Amy," he said. "You need to try harder."

I raised the whip again. My hand hovered in the air. But I found that if I concentrated hard enough, if I fought my urges, I could lower it again.

Bishop grunted, almost a growl, low and threatening. "This won't do."

He shifted the reins to his left hand, freeing his right, and reached out toward my chest. But we were awkwardly placed, and without meaning to, I blocked his hand with the whip before he could touch me.

To my astonishment, my mind got clearer. I didn't want to whip the horses. I wouldn't whip the horses. I didn't have to. He couldn't make me. There was a growing pain in my chest, a feeling of tearing, but I fought past it.

Bishop reached for me again, and I blocked him again, this time deliberately, keeping those extended fingers away from the spot on my breastbone he had touched so many times. The pain grew, but I wouldn't yield.

Warring with myself for every inch, I raised the whip, brandishing it toward him instead of the horses. "You will stop telling me what to do," I said in the calmest voice I could muster.

He had the gall to laugh at my threat. "Put it down, Princess." He knew my father had used it as an endearment, knew the king had given me the honorary title, but somehow, Bishop made it sound like the worst slur a man could call a woman.

"Stop telling me what to do," I repeated, whip held high, less calmly this time.

As I threatened him, the pain increased, but it couldn't stop me, not now that I knew what was possible.

Bishop's eyes narrowed. "You wouldn't dare."

I dared.

He was too close to whip properly, so I simply hit him in the face as hard as I could. The handle of the horsewhip caught Bishop high on the cheekbone, splitting the skin. The sound he made was half howl, half screech.

For good measure, I hissed, "Will you stop now?"

Bishop's eyes seemed more wounded than his person, even though the injury on his cheek was already streaking blood down his cheek and onto the point of his sharp collar. "But…you…you're under my thrall!"

"Not anymore," I said, and when I raised the whip again to make my point, he finally took me at my word.

"Put it down, please," he said, his voice pleading. He held his hands up to block me, the reins still dangling awkwardly from his left hand.

The horses, good-natured, had slowed without direction and were plodding along amiably. I thanked my lucky stars they weren't more spirited, or Bishop and I might both have been thrown and trampled during our tussle.

"No," I said.

With more confidence than I felt, I reached out for the reins and took them. I clucked my tongue softly at the obliging horses and watched their ears perk up. Then, I turned the cart around.

I drove us back in absolute silence. The horses were perfect angels, sure-footed and steady-paced. The pain in my chest subsided. I was almost able to enjoy the sight of gently swaying green palms as I breathed in the salt-baked, sun-laced air.

When we arrived at the residence area, the sun still high in the cloudless sky, Bishop scuttled down from the seat like a crab. He walked off in a rush, not even turning around to look at my face.

I never saw Washington Irving Bishop in the flesh again. The rest of my time in Hawaii, he didn't appear in any room where I found myself. Like the missionaries, he might have found a way to disappear in the night, though there were no facts on the record either way. I remained on the island for another week, purely to regain my equilibrium and satisfy myself that I hadn't been permanently harmed. I didn't want to leave before I had at least tried to reclaim the islands for myself.

Once I left Hawaii, sailing on the craft still under my command, I didn't stay in one place for long. The East continued to call to me, but I was unready to settle anywhere, preferring to hop from island to island and then sail off into the sunset without a goodbye.

Though I would carry the unpleasant memory of Washington Irving Bishop with me for the rest of my life, I refused to write off mysticism entirely because of his chicanery. I hadn't refused to ever travel by train again after the honeymoon wreck at Tehachapi Pass, nor did I swear off marriage forever because Porter Ashe had made such a hash of our first go at the institution. I still sought answers about the world in general and the woman in white in specific, and I wasn't going to let a toad ruin that for me. The only thing I avoided because of him was tarot; though I had enjoyed having my cards read before Bishop and I met, his daily repetition of tarot reading had associated him forever with the deck in my mind. I would never again see a tarot deck without thinking of Washington Irving Bishop.

Given how large he loomed in my memory, I was not in the least sorry to hear about Bishop's gruesome death a few years later.

But you know all about that, don't you?

CHAPTER NINE

Flirtation, as I mean it, is or can be the most fascinating pastime in the world. It can employ more wit than political intrigue, more comprehension of your fellow humans than applied psychology, and more intuition than gambling in Wall Street.

—AC

To explain why I went to Spain after Hawaii, I need to tell the story of my first experience in Madrid. And Madrid makes no sense without Dresden. My stories are all intertwined, all my thoughts and actions linked, inextricable.

During the divorce proceedings, my first husband's lawyers had trotted out certain stories from my early days in Europe: the German prince, the matador, the vanished chaperone. In truth, these episodes only scratched the surface.

At the age of sixteen, I had been sent by my mother to finishing school in Dresden, the most beautiful city in Germany. Despite its location, Dresden is an Italian city at its heart, the Florence on the Elbe. I wondered if my mother had known that, thinking she was sending me to a place of great discipline and precision instead of one whose lush beauty and passion ran all through its streets.

Six of us girls lived in a household under the care of Mrs. Burridge, a married woman probably a decade younger than my mother, slim in build, her eyes the cool gray-blue of the Pacific Ocean on a cloudless June day. I could see why the matrons of California entrusted Mrs. Burridge with their daughters. She could pass for an older sister or cousin, could look like one of us, putting us at our ease. Then, when we were comfortable enough to misbehave in her presence, she'd mete out punishments and threaten us into submission. It was as if she'd been created for the purpose.

It was a happy time. My friendship with Darlene Messerschmidt, with whom I shared a room on the ground floor, was a new thing: almost instantly, she felt more like a sister than my own sister ever had. Hers was the first face I saw in the morning when I woke up and the last one at night before I closed my eyes. We shared a room, cosmetics, secrets. It was thrilling and comforting at the same time.

The weeks in Dresden quickly began to blur together. During the day, we would undergo lessons in comportment, etiquette, flower decorating and needlepoint, all the things young ladies must know to catch a husband who will keep them in style as they gradually become old ladies. In the evenings, we'd dine under the watchful eye of Mrs. Burridge, who would keep us guessing by correcting our fork grip one night and regaling us with off-color gossip the next. And after we all retired to our bedchambers and the house was dark, Darlene and I would take turns sneaking out to social engagements that we'd arranged in stolen whispers during the day. I never went far. Our neighbors on the Schulstrasse were fabulously wealthy Austrians who kept a large household. In just a few months, I managed to hold hands with a stable boy in an empty coach, sip schnapps behind the pantry door with a dashing Italian footman, and stroll side by side in the darkened garden with the valet.

I asked Darlene once, after the maids had plaited our hair and said good night, if there was a risk of us romancing the same servants next door. "There are some things it's better not to share with a friend," I told her. "So if you want to lay claim to one man or another, let me know, so I don't overstep."

I couldn't see the look on her face in the dim light, but it took her a long moment to respond. When she did, she said, "Don't worry at all about that, Amy."

At the time, I was merely grateful, but years later, when I learned more about the world, I finally realized what Darlene had been up to those nights in Dresden. Perhaps if we'd stayed the whole year as intended, I might have figured it out sooner, or perhaps she would even have trusted me with her secret. Circumstance made that impossible.

I could tell all about our formal presentation at the German court, how we were drilled in advance as rigorously as any cadets, repetition turning our lessons into reflexes. I could go on and on about the first time I saw Prince Alexander of Saxe-Weimar-Eisenach, who wore a uniform in dashing royal blue with a gilded collar and buttons, his light blond hair slicked back, his eyebrows so pale they almost disappeared against his skin. I could explain how, when we stole a moment on a secluded balcony, he whispered, "I cannot kiss you unless we are engaged to be married," and I responded softly, "Then we are engaged," and shocked us both by leaning in to close the space between us, pressing my mouth to his.

None of my past flirtations had involved kissing on the lips, but mere seconds after kissing the young Prince Alexander of Saxe-Weimar-Eisenach, I vowed I would have no future flirtations without it.

The next morning, I slept in. We'd returned to the house well after midnight, and the process of unmaking us was time-consuming as well. After the maids divested us of our elaborate white gowns and many-layered undergarments, Mrs. Burridge came to collect our jewelry for safekeeping. We'd worn our absolute best for the court. Our chaperone took my emerald necklace and bracelet and Darlene's sapphire choker and earbobs and folded them into black velvet so the hard gems wouldn't scratch each other. I kept stifling yawns as we readied ourselves for bed, but as soon as the room was dark, I felt wide awake, reliving the feeling of Prince Alexander's lips against mine, the way we yielded to each other, giving, taking. Having not fallen asleep until the wee hours, I slept like the dead until after the sun came up.

So I missed the morning of discovery and the worst kind of excitement. But in time, the news brought itself to me in the form of the three other girls standing at the foot of my bed, discussing whether to wake me.

"I'm awake," I said groggily. "What is it that you can't leave me in peace?"

"Mrs. Burridge," said Adelaide. Even in my sleepy haze, I could see her face was creased with worry. "She's gone."

"Gone?" I sat upright.

Darlene and Kate came into focus behind her, Kate's face as worried as Adelaide's but Darlene radiating something like delight.

"Gone," confirmed Adelaide. "Her clothing, everything from her bedchamber, every last bit and bauble."

My stomach dropped. "Including our jewels from the safe." It wasn't a question.

Darlene said, "And the passbook for our household account."

I put my head in my hands. The absconding Mrs. Burridge had left us not just without guidance but without funds.

The story of that time could fill a book I never had time to write. To tell it simply, we all agreed to conceal the truth from our families, living on credit, running up house accounts all over Dresden as girls of good families are generally known to do. All was well, more or less, until three weeks later, when I opened the front door to a grim-faced dowager in emerald silk, her skin an enviable satin, and I realized one of our own had betrayed us.

My mother arrived the next morning, showing up in the company of two other mothers and a half-dozen maids and porters. The first thing Mother did was look me up and down with a disapproving glare I felt down to my bones; the second was to issue commands to the servants, who sprang into action. Everything I'd brought was gone inside an hour, everything personal stripped away and packed into trunks, leaving the shelves and wardrobes hauntingly bare. With every possession that vanished, I felt like my life itself was being erased.

Darlene and I sat on the settee, holding hands to comfort each other, staring numbly at the scene unfolding before our eyes. Darlene's mother was the only one who hadn't come. But during that exhausting hour, her surrogate arrived. The hubbub was enough that neither of us noticed her until a woman's low voice rasped, "Darlene," and then again, louder, "Miss *Darlene*."

Her attention finally caught, Darlene turned toward the door. When she saw who stood there, her whole body went tense. Sharply, she withdrew her fingers from mine, curled them into a fist in her lap. She went so still she didn't even appear to be breathing.

The woman in the doorway was older than my mother, the shape of her eyes enough like Darlene's to hint they were some sort of relation. Those eyes were gazing down at Darlene's hand, which had only a moment before been holding mine, and the set of her mouth was grim.

"Mrs. Wolf," said Darlene, a pleading note in her voice, "I wasn't—we didn't—"

The woman's mouth twisted in something worse than disapproval, more like disgust, and she snapped, "Don't. Not here. When we return to the States, you may explain yourself to your mother."

"No, you can't tell her. Amy isn't—"

"Don't!" snapped Mrs. Wolf, more loudly. "You've embarrassed us enough."

I don't remember how we said goodbye. I know there were tears. I suspect the pain of the moment was so sharp my mind refuses to return to its memory. My life has been filled with men, shaped by men, from my gone-too-soon father and several not-gone-soon-enough husbands, legally recognized and otherwise. Darlene was the only woman I ever considered a true friend.

When we boarded the train leaving Dresden, I kept my eyes on the swaying hem of Mama's day dress, a very proper dark gray with lavender trim, as we mounted the stairs and strode down the aisle. Even as we found our seats, I kept my eyes down, looking only at her boots, her gloves, never her face. Sadness settled on my shoulders like a cape. I dreaded undergoing the whole long voyage that had brought me to Europe, only in reverse: the train from Dresden to Hamburg, ship from Hamburg to New York, transcontinental train all those thousands of miles across the United States back to California. It had been trying enough when I was full of excitement, moving toward something new and unknown. All those hours and days and weeks with my old, constrained life at the end seemed a terrible prospect.

But when the conductor came through and asked for our tickets, Mama handed them over, and he nodded and said, "Very good, ma'am. Two for Prague."

I turned to her in obvious surprise, brimming with questions. She quieted me with a look. Only after the conductor had moved two rows down, out of earshot, did she quietly say, "Well, I've come all this way to fetch you. For my sake, at least, we may see the sights before we go."

Three more times in the next three weeks, my mother and I boarded a train. Each time, I was certain this was it, we were finally bound for a port, and from there, home. But each time, she surprised me. After Prague, it was Munich, then Paris. After Paris, Madrid. All too far inland for ships, I knew. So with each city, though Mama never spoke to it directly, I knew my European adventure hadn't yet ended. Each time felt like a pardon, a reprieve.

Each of those beautiful cities was striking in its own way. The long streets of Munich, the music flowing through it like lifeblood, so like Dresden but so different. Then Paris, all elegance, the glorious opera, its upper-crust ladies in proud finery every bit as haute as I'd ever imagined.

But Madrid, ah, Madrid. That was something else entirely. My mother had a friend there from her old school days, a dark-haired beauty née Mary Forshall who was now the Contessa of Salvatierra. When we disembarked at the train station, the contessa was waiting for us with arms widespread. After Dresden, I had trailed my mother around Europe like a well-behaved duckling. Mama, always commanding, had scheduled every event, arranged every hotel, dictated our itinerary without asking or wanting anyone else's opinion. But from the moment we set foot on Spanish soil—the grinning contessa surging forward in a swirl of copper-colored lace to embrace my mother so heartily I actually saw Mama's slippers lift off the ground—it was obvious things here would be different. The contessa took charge from the beginning, whisking us into her gilded carriage, presenting us with a rich midday meal of broiled fish and roasted potatoes in a red sauce, prattling away to my mother about all the wonderful things she couldn't wait to show us. Interesting, though, that during that first meal, she didn't mention the one thing that would change my life, the unforgettable event that made Madrid's adventure unlike all the others.

That afternoon, we attended a bullfight.

We sat close to the action, the sunlight winking off the matadors' sequins in our wide-open eyes. It was so warm the contessa removed her gloves, and I decided that if our hostess deemed it appropriate to do so, I could follow suit. My mother, of course, kept hers on.

The contessa merrily narrated what was happening, describing to us the purpose of everything from the parade of the toreros— banderilleros on foot, picadors on horseback, and of course the matadors—to the three acts of the fight itself. At first, she addressed her comments to both of us, but as the scene grew bloodier, my mother's face progressively paled, and the contessa realized that only I was truly interested in what was going on. So when the final matador came out to address the weakening bull, she whispered into my ear, "His name is Miguel de Rivas," and I knew exactly who I was looking at.

About the final stage of the bullfight, the *tercio de muerte*, the less said the better; in the moment, it thrills, but recounting the details strips the process of its beauty and leaves only grim brutality. My interest was not the death of the bull. I had eyes only for the young bullfighter, Miguel de Rivas. The contessa had explained to me that over the course of a day of bullfights, the least experienced of the matadors goes last, so perhaps the rest of the crowd found him less remarkable than his predecessors, but that was not the case for me. It seemed I had never seen a more graceful person in my life. He swiveled his hips and arced his arms as nimbly as any ballerina. His lean body was everywhere and nowhere. Certain death plummeted toward him, roaring and bellowing, and he danced away at the last moment, his cape flowing, soaring. Toward the end, it seemed to me he was no longer even a man but a god.

Once the bull lay bleeding on the ground and a cheer went up from the crowd, though, I blinked, and Miguel de Rivas was a young man again. Human, beautiful, desired.

The contessa handed me a red rose to throw to him, and I stood to fling it forward but then hesitated. Everyone else was flinging roses, the air thick with their scent. I'm not sure whether I intentionally waited or whether I was just frozen, staring at him, at the sweat and blood and his beautiful face, cheekbones so high the sun cast small shadows in their hollows that changed shape as he turned to acknowledge the applause from the right, from the left, and then with an inevitability that made my throat and cheeks prickle with excitement, turned to face right toward me.

I held out the rose in his direction. I meant to fling it, I think, but was still so disconcerted by him that my fingers held tight to the stem.

Finally I forced myself to release the rose, and as I did, a thorn pricked my thumb. I gave a small gasp of pain.

His deep brown eyes shifted, taking on an obvious note of concern. Before I knew what was happening, he had shifted the rose to his other hand and taken my hand in his, inspecting the spot on the pad of my thumb where blood was welling up in a small ruby bubble.

Murmuring in Spanish too softly for me to hear, the matador wiped the blood away with the edge of his cape. Then he bent to kiss the injury. I nearly swooned on the spot.

I heard the contessa whisper behind me, "You'll see him again."

And I did. My mother retired early that evening, fatigued from a day in the sun and quite possibly trying to make a point about the inappropriateness of the contessa's chosen activities. The contessa didn't remind her that guests were coming over for a small soiree; I didn't ask my mother whether I would be allowed to attend. A lack of a no was as good as a yes.

The party didn't start until well after ten o'clock. The cool of the evening provided some relief from the day's heat, but the tiles were still warm under our feet. Instead of an outdoor garden at the back of the house, as I was used to in Dresden, the contessa's garden was inside the house itself. Several rooms of atriums and orangeries framed a central courtyard in which the largest fountain I'd ever seen cascaded water high into the air.

I strolled from room to room, feeling entirely unfettered. No one here knew me. In Dresden, I had found some measure of freedom, but as the eventual arrival of our mothers there had proved, we were not far enough from California to escape where we'd come from. Tonight, in Madrid, felt different. My mother upstairs might as well have been a world away.

The contessa found me raptly watching the fountain about an hour after the party began, tapping me gently on the shoulder from behind.

"Miss Amy Crocker of California," she said, "I'm delighted to introduce you to tonight's guest of honor."

I put a polite smile on my face as I turned, prepared to indifferently greet a stranger, but the contessa had brought me something else entirely: the young bullfighter Miguel de Rivas, just as dashing in a black tuxedo as he had been hours before, sweaty and bloody, in the ring.

Momentarily struck dumb, I could think of nothing to do but extend my hand, which he bowed over. We grinned at each other wordlessly. Finally, the contessa murmured something in Spanish, to which the young bullfighter nodded. To me, she said, "There's dancing in the back parlor. Why don't the two of you follow the music?"

Soberly, Miguel offered me one of the lean arms I'd so admired during that day's bullfight. Tentatively, I slipped my arm into his. Once we arrived in the room where the musicians were playing a waltz, we moved into position. He held me rather closer than the American rules dictated, but we weren't in America.

If the first kiss I shared with Prince Alexander of Saxe-Weimar-Eisenach lit a fire within me, feeling the warmth of Miguel de Rivas's body against mine—brushing, rubbing, shifting—fanned that flame into a conflagration.

We danced and danced. We barely spoke; my Spanish was rudimentary, his English equally so. But we were drawn together like magnets, unable to release each other for more than a moment as the music changed, even as we were too shy to look in each other's faces.

Hours passed in what felt both like the haze of a dream and the most awake I'd ever been, every feeling heightened, every sensation sharp. Between dances, we strolled the gardens, finding ourselves on the edge of the crowd, experimenting with how we could touch. He pressed his hand over mine, gently stroking my hand from wrist to fingertips. I leaned my head on his shoulder, feeling his warm breath stir my hair.

The crowd thinned but did not dissipate. Long tables were

brought out, then topped with what looked like a delicious breakfast. I relaxed then, knowing we at least had a little more time together. I saw the contessa directing the arrangement of the breakfast, and she caught my eye, beaming. That was when I realized she had played matchmaker. She had put Miguel in my path and me in his. Her reasons for doing so, whatever they might have been, didn't enter my mind. All I felt was gratitude.

As a hint of dawn lightened the sky, we took a seat in the eastern-most orangery to watch the sunrise. I could feel the warmth of his hip, thigh, knee all touching mine. The entire world shrank to that sensation. Then I felt his fingertip gently turning my chin.

Miguel stole a kiss as if it were his own idea, lowering his lips to mine with a swiftness a less eager girl might have found frightening. I returned it with my full enthusiasm.

It was one of the purest moments of my life, all joy, all pleasure.

And when I opened my eyes again and saw my mother standing in the doorway—feet anchored, face stone—I knew it was over.

We left Madrid on a Tuesday, which seemed wrong somehow, too prosaic for such a heartbreaking departure. In my head, I was in love. The one person who was perfect for me, whose body sang to mine, whose voice was pure music, I would never see again. Our future was torn away. I was sure that I was losing something irreplaceable, that I could never feel this way again.

Of course, I was sure of many things in those days, things I now see as foolish. But I was sixteen years old. I've learned to forgive myself for not knowing better.

When I boarded the train with my mother, I held my breath. Three times, I'd feared a port city as our destination; three times, I'd received what felt like a stay of execution. This time, there was to be no more reprieve.

Once the conductor had moved on, I repeated the city's name he'd spoken, the question implied. "Barcelona?"

"I'd planned for us to go on to Italy." She sighed, staring away from me, out the window. "But after Spain, I think you've had enough adventure, haven't you?"

Italy would have been lovely. If I'd known, would I have done what I did? Would I have let myself get swept away by the young bullfighter? I asked myself the question many times, and every time, I reached the same answer. I'd had no choice in the matter. Love's arrow had struck, and I was helpless against it, pierced to the core.

My dreams seemed to agree. I dreamed of the woman in white for the first time since my father's death. The last night we stayed in Barcelona, as we waited for our ship, rain poured down outside as if the weather knew my mood and chose to match it. My bed was near the window, and the patter of raindrops against the glass was so loud it kept me awake. My wakefulness in the dark dragged on so long that when I saw the woman in white, I assumed I was still awake, assumed I was only seeing my mother dressed in a white robe moving through the room.

It was the shadow around her that made me realize who it was. That and the fact that I couldn't make out her face. It was the same woman who had brought death into our house in San Francisco. I thought at the time perhaps she was even Death itself, though I know better now.

I shut my eyes against her. The rain got even louder. I told myself I would open my eyes when I couldn't hear the rain anymore, and I must have fallen asleep with the storm still raging outside my window. It was still raining lightly, with a thin gray morning light doing its best to reach into the dark of our room, when I awoke.

It was on Friday morning, then, that my mother received the cable, which must have been sent Thursday night. It wasn't for my eyes, and my mother would likely have kept it from me, but she was distracted. The porter hadn't brought milk with her coffee. She wouldn't drink it without. So she'd stood up to ring for someone, looking around our hotel room for the bell, grumbling all the while.

As she turned her back on me, I snuck a look at the unfolded telegram on the tray. It was upside down, but I could read every word. At the end, I wished I hadn't.

```
Still delighted by your visit, hope you
will come again. Too quiet without you
and your lovely daughter. Terrible news—
her young bullfighter was gored in the
ring today, did not survive. How sad.
```

Immediately, I remembered the woman in white. Her appearance was foreboding, but she hadn't been clear. She hadn't spoken words like *Die like this* that I could take as a sign Death was near. She'd said nothing at all.

Perhaps she hadn't been clearer because that death was meant for Miguel—poor Miguel!—and not me.

Or perhaps she'd sent me a sign I missed.

I spent weeks turning it over in my mind, worried that I could have saved Miguel if I'd done something differently. Eventually, once we were squared away back in California, I decided I'd been helpless to prevent his death. Fate meant for him to die in the bullfighting ring, where he most belonged. A hundred women in white whispering in my dreams would have made no difference, not if that end was foreordained. I could no more change that fate than a single swimmer in the Pacific could turn the tide.

After leaving Spain as a foolish, lovestruck sixteen-year-old, I had no intention of ever returning. But life changes us. I had married a man I thought I loved, borne his child and been shunted aside for it, and lost both the husband and the daughter in different ways. After my experience with Bishop in Hawaii, unmoored, I remembered the contessa fondly and thought perhaps it was time to visit Spain again. In a sea of complicated, messy feelings, my gratitude to her had always been simple. I wanted her to know that.

Unfortunately, as I said, I was too late.

Then the Spanish mystic told me I would have thirteen husbands, the last of whom would bury me.

I'm still not sure whether receiving that message was the best thing that ever happened to me or the worst.

CHAPTER TEN

*My small but persistent common sense called on me in its
small voice and told me to return to America and accept the
compromise that the rich, solid, old California life, safe and
sure, was offering me. But one seldom listens to that whisper of
common sense.*

—**AC**

About six months after my second visit to Spain, I think it
was early 1889, I returned to the United States. It was then
I told someone—the least likely person, it turns out—the
truth about the prophecy.

I don't know why I told Jennie, the least mystical person I'd probably ever met. Maybe I wanted to hear her dismiss it as frivolous. It
would confirm that we were too different to ever agree on anything,
even if we'd been born of the same mother and raised in the same
house. It is truly remarkable how the same circumstances can produce
such different creatures. It was like mating an elephant with a teacup
poodle and producing one python and one pony.

I had come back to the States to look after business matters here
and there, visit friends and family on both coasts, see if I wanted to
return. That was the occasion to attempt a family dinner with Jennie,
to look for common ground I should have known we wouldn't find.

My sister and I had never been close. She'd been proper as a society
matron since birth, and upon her marriage in 1879, when she was
twenty and I was sixteen, she'd officially become one. Though she
didn't closely resemble our mother physically, the two were cut from

the same cloth: believing that women should only exercise the power given to them by society, staying out of the public sphere except to do good works, and stepping aside for men in all things. I stepped aside for no man, except to flutter my eyelashes at him if the spirit moved.

The man Jennie married, her first and only husband, was a perfectly standard specimen named Jacob Sloat Fassett. Jacob and Jennie married in Sacramento, then relocated to Germany, but it wasn't long before they returned to the States and Jacob was elected as a state senator in New York. So while the 1870s had scattered my mother, Jennie, and myself to the winds, somehow the 1880s found us all in New York, not far from one another.

I probably wouldn't have gone upstate at all if Darlene hadn't asked me to. I'd sent the note to Darlene after her wedding as I intended, and even with the slowness of the international mail, we had managed to reestablish contact. She'd become my steadiest correspondent. We hadn't seen each other for obvious reasons while I was traveling, but since I knew I was returning to the East Coast, I'd sent her a message. While she lived in Philadelphia, she had travel planned to upstate New York, and I offered to meet her there. My mother, in turn, offered a room at Jennie's to me, and I accepted, figuring that if I could camp on a Panamanian beach for one night, I could endure my sister's company just as long. But then Darlene had to cancel—her husband's business called them both away—so I was at Jennie's house by myself with no kindred soul to connect with, and I'm afraid it made me melancholy.

Unfortunately, the years apart had not made Jennie and me more compatible. Instead, the moment we found ourselves under the same roof for the first time as adults, my sister and I quickly discovered we could not stand each other.

The roof in question was Jennie's, or should I say her husband's. The couple was hosting an elegant dinner for some political contributors and other bigwigs. I was unsure whether my mother had known about the dinner when she encouraged me to stay. From my point of view, I was invited to the dinner only because it would have been a breach of etiquette for Jennie to exclude me. There were differences between doing a thing with enthusiasm and doing a thing out of obligation. I knew which this was.

I tried to fit in. I wore my most appropriate, modest, American-style gown instead of the more comfortable Chinese robes I preferred. During the predinner, I said almost nothing of my own exploits or interests, instead asking the other guests about their boring lives and doing my best to stay awake during their answers. I met four senators, all men with slicked-back dark hair and rounded shoulders, and if we'd played a parlor game where you mixed them all up and asked me which one had which name, I would've had no idea. I sipped champagne and nodded encouragingly, gave a winning smile, and moved on. I knew how to be a good guest. The only person I found memorable was a young woman named Miss Caryeaux, still in her teens, who had apparently been invited to balance out all the single men. She was clearly petrified of speaking to strangers. I kept her chatting for a solid quarter of an hour just to save her the trouble of having to introduce herself to someone new. She was quite knowledgeable about rhododendrons.

The trouble started when I insisted on bringing my champagne flute with me from the predinner in the parlor to the dining room itself. The footman reached out for the glass several times. The first time, I declined with good grace, but unfortunately my protests got louder as my patience wore thin.

"Ma'am," he repeated for the third or perhaps fourth time, his hand extended toward me.

"No," I told him firmly, pulling my flute back out of reach. "This is my glass. If I want you to carry it, I will hand it to you."

Jennie smoothly addressed the issue, playing the perfect hostess. Rather than inserting herself into the conversation, she made a chipper announcement to the room at large. "Now, we'll enjoy our wine with dinner, so if anyone still has a glass of champagne, you can leave it with the staff."

I raised my voice, making it merry. "Oh, but only a stick-in-the-mud follows all the old rules! I say if people like champagne, they should drink champagne. With everything! Even dessert! Don't you agree, Miss Caryeaux?"

Poor Miss Caryeaux froze, not sure where her loyalties lay.

Jennie stepped in graciously. "Mr. Fassett and I feel so fortunate to have every single one of you here with us tonight as honored guests. Thank you for coming. We're looking forward to both the food and drink, so let's all proceed to the enjoyment, yes?"

"Yes," said Miss Caryeaux eagerly and was the first through the door into the dining room. I quickly followed her, glass in hand, to cut off any further entanglement with Jennie's misguided footman.

The others made their way in, chattering as pleasantly warmed guests do, and we all found our seats. I had to admit Jennie set a handsome table. Not too ostentatious, and I wouldn't call it original, but it was certainly pleasing to the eye. Crystal, fine china, the best of everything. I realized I was looking at exactly the type of dinner I would have hosted, the life I could have led, if my first marriage hadn't been such a complete disaster. I wondered if it was too late to have that life. Then I hated myself for wondering. Everyone here probably knew the scandal attached to my name, though Jennie wouldn't have spoken of it. I never should have come back. I should have kept sailing toward the dawn.

Too late for that, though. So I drained the rest of my hard-fought champagne glass and called to a different footman to refill it.

"I'm sorry, ma'am," he whispered discreetly to me. "We don't pour champagne with dinner."

Quietly I removed one of my pearl bracelets, the heaviest and dearest, and pressed it into his hand. "Do your best."

The man was a hero. For the rest of our time at the table, my flute never fully emptied.

I quickly noticed that Miss Caryeaux, seated across from me, was looking miserable again. The men on her left and right talked straight past her, as if they'd been seated next to each other instead. Bad manners.

"Miss Caryeaux!" I called across to her. "How are you liking the"—I looked down at my plate, realized I had no idea what was set in front of me—"fare?"

Her head dipping up and down like a bird's, she said, barely loud enough for me to hear her, "Quite lovely, thank you. And you?"

"Looking forward to my first bite!" I said. I'd caught the attention of the man on her left, the more attractive of her neighbors, with my loud voice. I turned my gaze on him. "Young man! You have the best luck. The young woman next to you has not just her obvious beauty but a lovely mind. I'm sure you've heard that still waters run deep. Mind your manners and converse with her a while, won't you?"

He looked puzzled at first, but he turned to her and asked something in a quiet voice. When I looked up again later, they were still murmuring to each other. Helping manage her gave me a warm feeling. I might be unwelcome and uncouth, but I could do good when I chose, and their evening would be a better one because I'd intervened.

Alas, my shouting across the table had offended my sister, and the man on my right didn't seem pleased either. I heard him clear his throat.

"Hello, sir," I said to him. "Are you quite all right? Shall we call for more water?"

"I have enough water, thank you. Perhaps you should drink some of yours."

I noticed his wine was untouched and realized what trap I was in the process of falling into. "We haven't had the pleasure of meeting, but may I venture a guess as to your profession? Are you the local parson?"

"I am," he grumbled. I was downright impressed by how much disdain he could pack into two brief syllables.

I spent the rest of the dinner eating, drinking, and occasionally conversing with the man on my left, who was not a parson but whose wife glared daggers at me between every other sentence.

As dinner wrapped up and it was time for the men to adjourn for cigars and the women for sherry, the frequency of my sister's dark looks in my direction increased, and I knew the time had come for a reckoning.

"Amy," Jennie said, "before we join the others for sherry, would you come with me to the parlor? I have a little gift I want to show you."

"Happily," I lied and went with her.

We'd barely arrived in the parlor and I was still gripping the half-full champagne flute like a talisman when she wheeled on me.

"What is wrong with you?" she asked, her cheeks reddening, the angriest I'd ever seen her.

The possibilities were endless. I only blinked.

Jennie hissed, "These people matter. Their opinions matter. Haven't you ever thought of anyone but yourself, even once? Don't you go husband hunting here."

The idea that I would marry any one of these starched shirts, that I had even perceived them as actual men with blood running in their veins, was ludicrous. I blurted out the first argument against marriage I could think of.

"I saw a fortune teller in Spain," I told her. "He told me I'd marry thirteen times, and the thirteenth would bury me."

Though I hadn't meant to spill this secret, once it was in the air, I realized I wanted to hear her reaction. Knowing Jennie's conservative, orderly mind, she might help me probe what the fortune meant. Together, we could interrogate the use of "bury"—did the prediction mean that this husband would kill me himself and literally dig a grave in which to bury my remains, or did they simply mean that I would die still married to him? I was curious to know, and I couldn't tell another soul. Jennie hated people knowing our family's business. I knew she'd tell no one, not even her husband. Perhaps especially not him.

But just as I'd disappointed her over the years, she squarely disappointed me. "Well," she said, her voice tight. "You've already disgraced yourself with one divorce. It doesn't take a fortune teller to see your future holds more of the same."

"You're lucky," I answered. "You found the man you love at a young age. Not all of us have that good fortune."

Her voice was still tight as she disagreed. "It wasn't fortune. I took a measured approach. You didn't. And now see the differences between us."

"There have always been differences."

"That have grown wider." She folded her arms, radiating disapproval. "Purely because of your wild nature. I have a family, a good and solid one I love. And look at you. Divorced, disgraced. You couldn't even be trusted with your own child."

That one cut deep. I bristled, "You can't blame me for the actions of a terrible man I happened to be married to."

"Can't I?" she challenged me. "You made the choice to marry him."

I protested, "I didn't know. I couldn't have known."

"That first sentence is true," she said, frosty, "but not the second."

I took a moment to drain my flute of champagne, knowing it would further anger her. I desperately wanted to fling the empty glass against the wall and watch it shatter. I could almost see it already, the shards of clear crystal laid out on the floor in a pattern of damage, ruining the perfection she'd worked so hard to create.

Instead I struggled to master myself. I set down the empty glass on a side table, raised my chin, and said, "None of us ever truly knows another person."

"You say that," she answered, "because you've never tried. People stay mysteries to you because you don't put in the work. I know you to the bone."

"Do you?"

She made a kind of snorting sound, but she was already getting herself back under control. Her cheeks were back to pale perfection, her chest no longer heaving with caught breath.

"I know enough," said my sister. "I'd wager I know you better than you know yourself."

"Now that's a lie. You'd never wager."

She couldn't take her eyes off the empty flute on her side table. I could see her flexing her fingers, itching to put it away, to return the room to rights. She couldn't stand anything that wasn't just so. I had never been just so and never would be. And unlike a piece of glassware, I could not be sanitized and placed back in a cabinet to wait in silence.

Without looking at me, she said, "I won't throw you out of my house, because I'm not that kind of woman."

"I don't think you have any idea what kind of woman you really are," I said, hoping to wound her as she wounded me. "You followed the path Mama laid out. You never tried to be yourself."

"You're a fool," Jennie said sharply. "This is the path I wanted to follow. I'm exactly where I want to be."

I rolled my eyes. "You live an unoriginal life."

"So?" she said, sounding like her twelve-year-old self. "I'm happy. Are you?"

"Always," I lied. I was a good enough liar that even when she searched my face, she saw nothing but utter conviction.

"I won't throw you out," she repeated. "But you should go upstairs. I'll give your regrets. And in the morning, before breakfast, I think you should leave," she said.

I said, "I agree."

That moment in the parlor wasn't the last time I ever saw Jennie.

When the time came, we were both present at our mother's funeral. She wore the perfect black mourning gown and perfect air of sober consideration and glided around the room accepting condolences without ever once acknowledging my existence.

So ironically, those two words—*I agree*, when we never agreed on anything—were the last two words my sister ever heard me speak.

For the next decade, I never breathed a word of what the Spanish fortune teller had said. Not because of Jennie's outraged response and not because I thought people would care; I simply didn't think there was any chance he could be right. It was easy to write off the shiver he'd given me at the time. It was shock, I told myself, not recognition. Whether or not he was a complete charlatan, he had chosen an outsize claim. Thirteen husbands! Who could possibly get married thirteen times? Just once had nearly wrecked me. I couldn't see how I could possibly rack up a baker's dozen of spouses without collapsing of exhaustion.

Once I married my third official husband, I did tell the story on occasion at our Broadway parties, making it fun. I played up the idea that I would be so fatigued from wedding after wedding that any potential groom would have to bear me to the altar in his own arms. I laughed about needing to marry younger and younger and stronger and stronger men to make it so.

"Thirteen!" I trilled when I told the story. "Seven, perhaps, I could believe, but thirteen? Perhaps I could marry a handful of brothers at once for efficiency!"

People always laughed. Of course, I was their rich, effusive hostess. During those years, the gales of laughter my stories received had very little to do with whether they were funny. Their laughter was payment for my largesse, and they paid enthusiastically.

In private, years later, I've finally realized the story isn't funny at all. Thirteen felt like too many, but I didn't know I'd live this many years, and I never thought about how much it depends on who one counts as a husband. Or whether "husband" was really the right word at all for what the mystic meant to tell me.

Before I married a twelfth or thirteenth husband, though, I had to marry a second. As I left Jennie's house the next morning before breakfast, I couldn't see myself doing that. Who could tempt me? What reason could there be? I had everything I wanted, I told myself. Even if it wasn't strictly true, I didn't see a way that marrying a man would get me anything I was missing.

As with so many other things, getting married again felt impossible right up until it didn't.

CHAPTER ELEVEN

The longer I live the less I am surprised at how little we know of the real extent of human emotions and human weaknesses.

—AC

It takes a certain kind of person to find New York City restful, and somewhere along the way, I had become that person. It was full of noise and hubbub and chaos, but at least the people spoke English and I knew what currency to pay in. Besides, my mother was spending more time in New York City now, along with Gladys. And after all my wanderings around the world alone, there was something comforting about having family nearby. I wondered at myself. But people change over time, and I would not curse my own name for changing my mind about things every once in a while.

Besides, I felt sorry for my mother. She was not a natural lover of New York City but ended up there anyway after fleeing Sacramento in a bit of a dudgeon. There was a whole kerfuffle about a maid accused of stealing jewels, and my mother had testified against her, but the case had gone the maid's way. Offended her word hadn't been believed, my mother decided a change of scenery was in order, robbing California of its most generous benefactress once and for all.

She had everything of personal value in the Sacramento mansion boxed up and sent east to New York. She took up residence in the Larchmont house, where she and my father had lived briefly, long before any of my own exploits had reached the ears of any neighbors nearby. Once she was settled, I bought the house next door. My sister's house upstate might as well have been across the ocean; I never went there again.

Living in New York near my mother had all the advantages of moving back to San Francisco but with none of the disadvantages. The East Coast gossips weren't as attuned to me as the West Coast ones, and besides, there were so many other well-known, moneyed, public people in town, the papers had more news than they needed. Who would read about Amy Crocker Ashe, a minor heiress from elsewhere, when there were the doings of the Astors and Livingstons to report on? I felt boring by comparison. It was a feeling I relished.

My mother kept herself busy with charity, still every inch Lady Bountiful, and we saw each other frequently. I made good on my promise to join her committees and spent quite a bit of time working with the Ladies Museum Association. To make sure I was cultivating my own interests and not just following hers, I joined the kennel club and showed some of my dogs in competition, an interest I had borrowed from Porter once upon a time but chose to make my own.

And for the first time in a long time, I saw my daughter. She didn't call me Mother, of course. She called me Amy. At five years old, she was becoming a person. I saw nothing of me in her. Her eyes, hair, coloring, all belonged to Porter Ashe. But even to be in her presence without being rejected, without feeling like I was the worst mother in the world, that was reason enough to savor being near her. I bought her a doll she hated and another she seemed to like. I sang to her, intentionally off-key, comedic songs, and for the first time in both our lives, I made her laugh. It was enough.

But I wasn't her mother. I saw that so clearly. She had a mother who loved her, took care of her, provided stability. It would be dangerous and ungrateful to jeopardize that. I'd done foolish things, plenty of them, but I wasn't fool enough to jeopardize Gladys's happiness.

I spent time instead with Mama to begin trying to heal the rift between us. I'd seen firsthand how easily relationships could come and go. She would always be my mother, the only one I had, and I owed it to both of us to try to mend fences. We could focus on what we had in common, I decided. And in those days, in New York, that meant going to parties.

Mama had already done the work of figuring out which were worth going to and which weren't, so I was happy to accompany her whenever she asked.

Then one Saturday, at the last minute, she asked me to join her at a reception at the New York Yacht Club that evening. It was scheduled at an odd time, arrival at five in the afternoon, and she only told me about it at breakfast. There was barely time to get ready.

I left the house in a grumpy mood, annoyed that she hadn't given me more notice, which meant I had to wear a dress that some of the guests had likely already seen. I'd been in the city long enough to meet with a dressmaker to fashion a few more suitable gowns for the season, but none of them were ready yet. There was nothing wrong with the gown I wore, a royal purple fetchingly worked with gold to emphasize the sleeves and bodice, but I didn't like not having choices. I'd satisfied myself by having a hairdresser braid a plentiful number of ornaments into my hair. It would have to do. Still, I was on the back foot, and I didn't like it.

But when we alit from the carriage and I realized we were being left off at the docks, my curiosity was piqued.

"Do they hold their parties at a fish market?" I asked my mother, wrinkling my nose against the smell.

Luckily her mood was better than mine at that point, and she chose not to take offense. "Ah, didn't I tell you? The yacht club's headquarters are on an island in the harbor."

When I followed the sweep of her arm, I saw that a flat-bottomed boat was moored at the end of the nearest dock. A railing around its top deck was already lined with guests, women in gowns, men in evening dress. Even from the far end of the dock, I could hear their birdlike chattering, full of excitement. This was what I'd been missing.

Looking at them but addressing her, I said, "Well, that's logical, I suppose. The yacht crowd does love to sail."

We boarded the vessel and headed immediately for the top deck. I suspected I knew the reason for the odd scheduling now. I was delighted to find my suspicion confirmed as we crossed the harbor just as the sun began to set. Watching the sky shift into a gold-lit pattern of pinks and purples against the water's blue was riveting.

I'd been so busy watching the sky that I was taken by surprise when we bumped against the dock at our destination. When I turned, the sight of the headquarters building, lit up against the New York City night, took my breath away. Passengers who'd clearly been here before turned and began an extremely dignified shuffle toward the stairs that would take us down and off the boat. I dragged my feet, though, not ready to leave the comfort of the vessel. I supposed I had spent so much time on ships by now that I was more comfortable there than on land.

My mother, however, had little patience and nudged me toward the stairs. We were among the last to disembark.

When we finally stepped into the building, she turned and fixed me with a disapproving glare, then gestured at the merry crowd ahead of us. "Amy, look what you've done," she said. "Now it'll be ages before we get our champagne."

"I'm sorry," I said and genuinely meant it, at least where the champagne was concerned.

But instead of standing around waiting with the downstairs crowd, I headed for the upstairs railing I'd seen from the ship. Just like there had been an open-air place to observe the harbor from the ship, there was one to observe it from land. And as I hoped, I found a second bar there, less crowded than the first. I asked for and was given three drinks. That way, I could hastily down one to fortify myself for everything that came after.

Sliding two of the flutes along the bar toward my left hand, where I'd be able to sweep them up quickly, I grabbed the other with my right hand and began to empty it down my gullet. Even in my haste, I could taste that it was excellent champagne. I told myself I'd savor the next one, but in this case, speed was of the essence.

"Well, you haven't changed," said a voice.

I quickly swallowed the champagne in my mouth so I wouldn't spit it all over whoever was speaking to me, if in fact they were speaking to me at all. I could afford to take my time before turning. Either they knew me and would wait for me, or they didn't know me and there was no point in rushing the moment when we both realized we were strangers.

"I didn't know I'd be seeing you here tonight," the voice continued.

It sounded more familiar now, but I still couldn't immediately place it. It was a man's deep baritone. I had the vague feeling that his voice had deepened since I heard it, but that was all.

So I turned to look, keeping my hand on the bar near my remaining flutes to protect them, and looked into the face of a very, very handsome man.

He was impeccably dressed, standing out even in this highly capable crowd, the fabric of his tuxedo a luxurious weave with a subtle silken gleam. He appeared to be a few years older than me. Much taller. I looked up into his handsome, puzzling face. The nagging feeling was back. The warmth that spread through me at the sight of him said he was more than an acquaintance, but who was he, and where did I know him from? I chose to brazen it out, as was my way.

"I didn't know I'd be seeing you either," I answered, with the kind of mild warmth I'd learned was least likely to be misconstrued.

The handsome man tilted his head, and suspicion crept into his expression. "I thought you'd remember me, Amy." His warm voice had some urgency to it along with the slight annoyance. "Given that we could have been married for years by now. If the cards had landed a bit differently. Curse my luck, I suppose."

And then I knew. The face was more than familiar if I leaped back seven years in time, what now felt like a lifetime ago. When I'd only ever been Amy Crocker.

He'd always looked a bit older than he was, and his years had caught up to his maturity, so he wore his late twenties well.

"Hello, Harry," I said and gave him a genuine, fond smile.

The suspicion drained from his expression and was replaced with pure warmth. He moved as if to embrace me, thought better of it, and settled for cupping my shoulder with his broad palm and giving a tender, lingering squeeze. I widened my smile and savored the feeling.

Had I not been so busy with the terrible events of the past few years and then the experience of running to the other side of the world to forget about them, I would have wondered whatever had happened to Harry Gillig after he lost that fateful hand of cards to Porter Ashe.

Standing on the yacht club's island, years later, all decked out in our finery, I thought about how different things would have been had Porter's hand of cards come in second to Harry's. In one way, such a minor difference, a face card here, a flush there. But it would have changed everything.

Would a victorious Harry have asked me to marry him, as Porter had? Would I have said yes? Might we still have found ourselves standing here next to each other at this very event, years later, but having led an entwined life of married bliss in between?

After he dropped his hand from my shoulder, Harry tilted his head at me, still smiling. "It's such a pleasure to see you again, Amy. I can't quite believe it, to be honest."

My mind was absolutely buzzing, but it wouldn't have been

appropriate to say anything I was thinking. Instead, I said what was polite. "Mama will want to see you. Would you come downstairs?"

"I'd be delighted," he answered, and we descended together.

I handed off Mama's champagne to her and reintroduced her to Harry, and she exclaimed with excitement when she realized who he was. She was completely capable of feigning affection for people she disliked, but with Harry, she seemed genuinely pleased. I remembered, long ago, she had thought him suitable for me.

Harry, who knew the headquarters building well, found a slightly quieter nook off the main parlor so we could hear each other over the din. I left the talking to the two of them. Looking at Harry, I couldn't stop thinking about his younger self and mine, forming a triangle with Porter, back in that midnight hotel room over that hand of cards.

In terms of similarities, Porter and Harry were both well-off and well-known. The Gillig money was from silver mining, if I remembered right, and Harry had joined the family business, managing investments. But when I knew them both, they'd been very different men. Porter was a gambler through and through; Harry gambled on occasion, such as the poker game, but he had no passion for it. The trait inherent to Harry, the one I associated most with him, was his beautiful singing voice. Everyone said he could have gone on the stage, and I wasn't sure why he hadn't.

Harry said something I missed. My mother laughed wholeheartedly, not a polite laugh but one that seemed to leap from her, unbidden. The young Harry had not been much of an entertainer, except when he sang. I wondered how many other ways he had changed. I realized it was in my power to find out.

There'd been another important difference between Porter and Harry: how I'd felt in each one's presence. Porter had made my blood simmer in my veins. Harry never did. Harry was a hot water bottle: pleasant to keep around, comforting in cold weather. I felt better about my life just looking at his face. But the idea of going to bed with him felt, though not wrong, not exactly right.

There on the island in the harbor, my cheeks started to pink. Here I was, thinking about going to bed with Harry Gillig, who hadn't even shown the slightest interest in such things. All he'd touched was my shoulder, perhaps a gentle hand on the small of my back as we descended the stairs, but nothing more. I was making it up from nothing. Perhaps it was a sign I'd been alone too long. I cocked my head and watched Harry talk to my mother, his handsome face animated, that baritone voice soothing and lively all at once.

I could do worse than spend some time with Harry Gillig, I decided. If he wanted to spend some time with me, we could see where things led.

"Amy," intruded my mother's voice.

"Yes?" I'd missed something.

Mama said, with a faint undercurrent of impatience only a daughter's trained ear could hear, "Did you not hear Mr. Gillig's lovely invitation?"

"Please, Mrs. Crocker," Harry said. "Call me Harry."

"I'm too old-fashioned for that," she said, smiling. "But I'm sure Amy will be happy to."

Harry inclined his head toward me. "How about it? Will you come to the theater with me next Thursday?"

I turned the full force of my smile on him. "I'd absolutely love to, Mr. Gillig."

Harry's bark of answering laughter was so warm, so welcome. Then he leaned toward me and whispered conspiratorially, "Harry."

I whispered back, as if it were a password, "Harry."

Harry and I quickly became each other's preferred social companions. We enjoyed all the same things. We'd go to a Broadway show or opera one day, for a walk the next, enjoy dinner at my mother's house the third. Our conversation always sparkled; even when I saw him every day, I found myself looking forward to seeing him again, recounting stories I'd just recalled from our youth or wanting to ask his opinion on some matter. He seemed just as enthusiastic about me, and the smile that spread across his face each time we met felt irrepressible, genuine.

It wasn't quite a courtship, but I admit that every time I sat next to him in a darkened theater or my feet bumped his underneath the dinner table, I thought, *This man could be my husband.* It was partly the familiarity of him, the way I could see the young man he'd been and the one he was now, superimposed on one another like a pair of ghosts. He also represented what my mother wanted for me: the right man, the right choice, the right marriage, a second chance at respectability I probably didn't deserve.

He hadn't made any direct overture, but that didn't surprise me; Harry had always had something of the old-school gentleman about him. The other courtships I'd had, with Porter and the German prince and Spanish toreador before him, had been the unusual ones, all shadows and secrecy. Harry was only acting the way men of our class were supposed to act with women of our class. I was pondering the marriage proposal he hadn't yet made when I came to see Harry Gillig in an entirely new light.

Our social meetings up to that point had either been just the two of us or, including my mother, the three of us. But that Sunday, he asked me to take a walk in the park and mentioned we'd be likely to bump into a friend or two of his, and would that be all right? I answered that it would.

The day seemed special-ordered from a book of beautiful days, delivered and unwrapped for our perfect enjoyment. Only a few puffs of white cloud scudded across the bright blue sky. The grass of the park shone a gleaming green, and you could smell its freshness in the air. It was one of those spring days where winter is squarely in the past and summer only a dream of the future, a springtime perfectly itself. And as we drew alongside one of the park's loveliest fountains, where a spiral horn under a cherub's arm spilled water like an offering, the moment felt important. And it was.

"Harry Gillig!" I heard a musical voice call, and arm in arm, we turned.

"Frank!" Harry called in return. This must be one of the friends we were looking to meet, I realized. There was a warmth in Harry's voice he wasn't a good enough actor to fake.

Before I knew it, in front of us stood a young man almost as handsome as Harry, but with a slightly thinner mustache, dressed in a suit that, while perfectly nice, didn't quite meet Harry's high bar. But the new arrival's eyes were clear and bright in a way that suggested optimism, even before he said, "Such a beautiful day, isn't it? Just magnificent."

Harry said, "Amy Crocker Ashe, it is my distinct pleasure to present my good friend Frank Unger. Frank, you've heard me talk often of this lovely young lady."

"I have!" said Frank, extending a hand to shake. I enjoyed it when men shook hands with me instead of resorting to courtly hand kissing, which had always made me feel like a fussy doll destined for a dusty shelf.

I shook Frank's hand in return with a firm grip and said, "All good things, I hope."

His eyes cut quickly aside to Harry.

I hastened to add, "Oh, don't worry. I know that's not the case. You can't have heard of me and not heard some of the…less than flattering things the gossips say." Though the New York papers didn't trumpet my comings and goings in as much detail as the West Coast papers had, my sojourn in Hawaii had been reported locally, and reporters were starting to sniff around again.

"Ah, the gossips," said Harry dismissively. "We don't listen to them, do we, Frank?"

"Not unless they say something very, very entertaining," said Frank cheerfully. It made me laugh.

Harry said, "But they're more often than not harmful, and I..."

Frank waved a hand. "We know to ignore them, don't we, Mrs. Ashe?"

"I'd be honored if you'd call me Amy, please," I said. "Any friend of Harry's is a friend of mine."

"Well, that is flat-out delightful," answered Frank. "I was hoping we could be fast friends. From what I've heard of you from Harry— and in that case, it really is all good things, I swear—you and I should get along just splendidly."

We continued to chat and stroll, Harry moving to take my arm on the left so Frank could take my right. Frank and I covered the basic stories of our early lives, what had brought us to New York, all the things young people tell each other on first meeting. I didn't mention my ugly divorce or the fact that the daughter I'd given birth to wasn't mine anymore. I was equally sure there were things my new friend wasn't telling me. That wasn't what first meetings were for. Especially not on bright, sunny spring days when all of New York City is spread out in front of you like a waiting carpet.

We enjoyed our walk so much we decided to continue into the evening together, stopping by the Plaza at the bottom of the park for a fortifying drink while we discussed where we might dine.

As a woman, I was welcome in the room but not at the long wooden bar itself, so we settled into a small round table near the entrance. My companions gestured in unison for me to choose my seat first, which I did. Frank then sat to my left, mirroring the position he'd taken as we walked, and Harry was the only one left standing.

"Take a load off," I said, pointing to the remaining chair.

"I was thinking I'd order our drinks at the bar and bring them over. It'll be quicker than waiting for service. Champagne all around to start?"

"Always," I answered.

Then he walked away. I noticed the buckle on my shoe had come undone, so I bent down to adjust it, and as I lifted my head back up, my eyes alit on Frank's face. I thought he might be looking at me, expecting to continue the conversation, but he wasn't. His eyes were glued to the retreating Harry, lingering as if he were powerless to look away.

I couldn't unsee that expression once seen. It was a warm, hungry, rapt look, the kind I'd never seen on the face of a man looking at another man, yet one I instantly and fully recognized. It was how I'd looked at Porter, how Romeo had looked at Juliet. It was a bottomless hunger, and Frank was only lucky no one was looking in his direction but me.

I wouldn't say my heart sank, exactly, but the uncomfortable realization sat heavy in my stomach, even as we received our champagne and toasted to our afternoon's entertainment. Harry's lack of physical romantic attention toward me might not stem from old-school chivalry after all. It was a leap, yes, and I wasn't sure yet, in that moment. But it was the first time this other explanation had occurred to me, and I couldn't shake the feeling that I'd just been handed the answer to a question I hadn't even known to ask.

Harry snapped his fingers. "Amy! Where are you?"

"Oh, you know," I said breezily, leaning back in my chair. "Lost in thought."

"Are we so boring as all that?" quipped Frank.

"Not a whit," I said and meant it.

After two glasses of champagne each, a half hour of chat about nothing in particular, and a spirited debate on whether Keen's or Delmonico's offered the better piece of beef, the boys decided that Keen's would be our dinner destination. I looked back and forth between the two of them and realized I couldn't do it, not tonight. I needed to go home and think about this by myself. My good humor was already slipping.

Keeping my voice light, I piped, "I have to give you some bad news, my gents. Not so bad as all that, I promise! Don't look so grave! I think I'm too tired after all for dinner."

"Oh, I'm so sorry to hear that," said Frank, and I believed he genuinely was.

Harry said, "Can I see you to a hack?"

"It's only a few blocks," I said. "Don't worry about me. I'll just walk." I'd taken a Manhattan pied-à-terre so I didn't need to journey all the way back to Larchmont after excursions like this, off the east side of the park at Fifth Avenue.

"Are you sure?" Harry asked. "Tongues may wag."

"Let them," I said.

Frank leaned over in Harry's direction and said in an exaggerated stage whisper, "I knew I liked this one."

Harry, in the same spirit, whispered loudly, "I knew you would."

The mixed surge of pride and confusion that raced through my blood at their words was hard to quantify. Luckily, I was already on the verge of excusing myself. My cheeks burned and my head swam as I walked home alone.

The man I'd assumed was mine for the taking was, if I was reading the situation correctly, never mine at all. At least not in the way I'd imagined. And it wasn't the kind of situation easily sorted, nor was it something I could discuss with anyone else: not my mother, not my maid, no one. Darlene would understand, I told myself, but I couldn't share Harry's secret without permission, and to get permission, I would have to tell him I knew. That seemed impossible.

But it wasn't a crisis, I told myself. If I couldn't resolve the situation, I would wait for it to resolve some other way. Perhaps I would meet someone else and my feelings for Harry would resettle into friendship. Perhaps Harry would decide to spend less and less time with me until we drifted apart.

As it turned out, that was not what Harry decided.

The two of us were halfway through a viewing of *She's a Delicate Dish, Yes Sir* and had chosen to stay in our box during intermission instead of working our way downstairs to chat with our fellow patrons. It was an unusual choice for me, but I was enjoying having Harry all to myself for a change.

This performance was the first time we'd been alone in weeks. Once he'd introduced me to Frank, nearly every time I saw Harry, I saw them both. It was as if, once Harry had crossed that line, he wanted to dwell forever on the other side.

I enjoyed Frank immensely. Still, when Frank was around, I missed Harry. After catching that look on Frank's face, I discreetly watched Harry to see if Frank's affection was returned. It clearly was. They were comfortable enough around me to get closer than I suspected they did in any other company. It made me feel invisible, which I wasn't used to. It was funny, I thought, how you could miss someone even when you were in their presence.

And through all this, my heart was hurting, beset by questions. Was I in love with Harry? Or was he just familiar and friendly, a safe harbor when I had rarely known one of those in my life? I wanted to run to the nearest mystic and have them give me an otherworldly answer. It would have been easier to substitute someone else's judgment for my own. But again, it wasn't my secret to tell. The New York City gossips, avid and skilled, might learn anything I spoke aloud. I couldn't trust anyone, friend or stranger. In this case, there would be no intervention from the world beyond.

So as we waited for the second act to begin, Harry and I lounged in the box, talking about our plans for the upcoming summer. He looked so relaxed, so dapper, I was thinking that anyone else in the theater would have been thrilled to have him as their escort for the night. I was lucky he was with me, even with all the uncertainty running through my mind. He really was a good friend, I thought.

"Mrs. Astor's Parade of the Flowers is coming up at the end of July," Harry was saying, tapping his fingers lazily on the edge of the balcony. "I think I'll stay in town for that. Are you going?"

I rolled my eyes. "You know how she is as a host. I don't think a divorcée is welcome at that particular party," I said.

"But you want to go," he replied, as if it were obvious.

"Of course."

He tightened his mouth, then relaxed it. "Then go."

"Did you hear what I said about being a divorcée?"

"Yes. But you don't have to be a divorcée forever."

I shot him a look. "Believe me, I'd rather be Porter Ashe's widow than his ex-wife, but at this point, even the right events would be in the wrong order."

"I mean, if you didn't want to be known as a divorcée anymore. If you wanted to be a married woman instead, open those doors back up." Reading my mildly confused expression, Harry made his point more direct. "You could get married again."

I didn't understand why he was pressing at that moment, but it came clear soon enough. I shrugged as best I could in my gown, which was tight through the shoulders to emphasize my décolletage. To Harry, I said, "If someone asked, I suppose."

He leaned in my direction, spoke low. "What if I were asking?"

"What?" I couldn't help it, I laughed. Men of our class made formal proposals. They got permission from fathers or, if no father was in evidence, some other male family member. They made plans, brought out inherited rings. A proposal of marriage was an economic and familial proposition with far-reaching consequences. It wasn't idle chitchat for two friends during intermission, waiting for the second act to begin.

But Harry didn't take the exit I offered. He said, sotto voce, "I think we should get married."

"Harry, you're a dear," I began, not sure how to play my answer. I decided that lighthearted banter was the best way to begin. "But whatever makes you think I would ever want to get married again, after what happened the last time?"

"The institution of marriage didn't make Porter Ashe an ass," he said. His voice was earnest. "He did that all by himself."

I regarded Harry skeptically. "Yes, but being not married is working out well enough for me. And for you too, isn't it?"

He shrugged, and there was a world-weariness in that shrug I hadn't seen in him before. His voice stayed low. "There are good things in my life, yes, but I wouldn't say my life overall is good. It would be better if I were married."

"Why?"

Now his manner changed, and I was glad the two of us were alone in the box. Even with observers all over the theater, no one was close enough to hear us. He turned so his back was to the house. He faced me straight on. And there was an emotion on his face I couldn't remember ever seeing there before. It was suppressed, but it was there. I recognized it because I knew it for myself. Fear.

He said softly, "People look at bachelors askance. Think there's something wrong with a man if he's not a family man. You know it, Amy. You've heard whispers about men like that, haven't you?"

I had, of course, though none had reached my ears about Harry in particular. But I understood now that people were whispering about him. Maybe even about him and Frank together, if they'd guessed. Then I thought about how many times they'd invited me to spend time with the two of them, and something pinched in my chest. Had I just been window dressing? I'd genuinely thought they both enjoyed my company. And perhaps they did. But if I was completely honest, I knew deep down that they enjoyed each other's more.

To Harry, I said, "Just idle gossip."

"It isn't idle. Not if people latch onto it. And there's nothing stopping them if a man's a bachelor. I need a wife."

Then it came clear. I knew Harry Gillig wouldn't propose marriage to me without a very good reason, and I knew the reason wasn't love. At least not love for me, a woman he remembered fondly and liked well enough but barely knew.

I said carefully, "And you can't find another girl to fall in love with, one who will love you with her whole girl self?"

Harry looked straight at me then. "No. Believe me, Amy. There's no girl for me."

The house lights flickered once, twice. Intermission was ending; the next act was about to start. People below were taking their seats, murmuring, laughing, completely unaware of the tiny two-person drama playing out in our box high above.

As the lights went down, I said, "I'll think about it, Harry, all right?"

He reached over and squeezed my hand. It was already too dark to see his expression. "Thank you," he whispered.

We were married three weeks later.

The ceremony itself was small and brisk. There was no question of a larger one, of a church, a reception. Of course, no clergyman would have agreed to take us on due to my scandalous divorce, but more importantly than that, neither of us wanted to make a fuss. We agreed that both of our mothers would be furious to be denied the chance to make our wedding a high-stakes social occasion. We also agreed that that was reason enough to deny them. Harry wore my favorite of his suits, a deep charcoal gray, and I wore his favorite of my day dresses, a sprigged pink muslin with a curved collar that lent me a modern panache.

Our midday wedding at the courthouse was presided over by a judge with all the personality of a cord of firewood. He gave us our directions and we followed them. And in a handful of minutes, the deed was done. Harry Gillig and I were legally wedded husband and legally wedded wife. Harry had brought both of our witnesses, who signed the register with their full names: Ruby Morgan Fellows and Francis Chesterfield Unger.

Afterward, as agreed upon in advance, I climbed into the carriage and went back to my pied-à-terre to pick up my luggage. Harry and Frank, in a carriage of their own, went directly downtown.

We were all reunited on the ship for Amsterdam. The air was one of celebration, as was commonplace on these larger ships, with passengers thronging the deck as departure approached. Down on the docks, crowds of friends and strangers were there to wave us off, a sea of upturned faces so vast I had no idea whether any of them were familiar. Instead I focused on my fellow passengers, looking for my new husband and our companion.

Frank spotted me first and stuck his fingers in his mouth to draw my attention with a whistle, which he did very successfully. I greeted them both, trying to catch the festival mood with only medium success. I'd been lonely in a crowd before, but my second wedding day was the day I most remember wishing I didn't feel that way.

"Congratulations to the groom and best wishes to the bride," said Frank as we gathered. Of the three of us, he was always the best at remembering proper etiquette.

"Thank you," I said. "Are you ready for the journey of a lifetime?"

Harry broke in before Frank could answer. "Is anyone ever truly ready for anything?"

His tone was more melancholy than I expected, but I chose not to react. "Perhaps we can't be ready, but we can be more or less prepared. Frank, are you more or less prepared for the journey of a lifetime?"

Frank said gamely, "I'm looking forward to it, that's for sure."

We stood together at the railing, the three of us in a line, and waved down to the crowd on the dock for a bit. I still couldn't make out any of their faces. But their enthusiasm floated up toward us like a cloud, and I began to feel the spark of excitement I'd been hoping for.

But then Harry said, "Come on. I don't want to look at them anymore," and led us to a different spot on the railing, facing out toward the open sea.

It was quieter on the far side of the ship. We three weren't alone, but we weren't surrounded. I looked at Harry. Frank looked at Harry. Harry looked off into the distance, toward the horizon we would all sail toward, together.

I'd decided to go ahead with the marriage because Harry was right—my life would be better as a married woman than as a divorcée. My money could pry open plenty of doors, but in certain social circles, there was absolutely no substitute for a husband. It would be less of an issue during our European travels. The French in particular had always been much more accepting than America's puritanical sorts. But I planned to spend a good amount of time in New York, and for that, only a husband would do.

At least I liked Frank. I told myself that many times. He was charming, kind, amusing, and solicitous toward me in the extreme; some days I even liked him better than Harry. It was like having another husband, one I could wear on different days of the week. I always knew what he wanted, and he always knew what I wanted, and we both wanted each other to be happy. Would that all my relationships had been so simple.

The American press, of course, had a field day with my remarriage. I resisted the urge to read the papers myself during that honeymoon period, but my mother's letters, when they reached me, presented a summary. My divorce had been an outrageous scandal, went the argument in most papers, but my remarriage was a thousand times worse. Who did I think I was? Did I intend to live free of consequence?

The *New York Bugle* even managed to dig up the earlier reports of the midnight hotel poker game and somehow guessed, correctly, that Harry had been one of the players. I winced when I read the newspaper clipping my mother had thoughtfully included. She still hadn't forgiven me, and I wasn't sure she ever would, even though this time I'd married a man she would have chosen for me a thousand times over. She had no idea that her perfect man came with another man as a package deal.

Frank did surprise me once on that voyage. We were deep in our cups, and Harry had grumbled at both of us when we refused to go off to bed, preferring to stay up and watch the stars. Eventually Harry grumbled his way back to the room, leaving Frank and me alone, wrapped in warm blankets and staring upward, sipping too heavily from the whiskeys in our cupped hands.

"Do you ever regret not seeing your girl as she grows?" he asked, seemingly out of nowhere.

"I did see her. Still do. Somewhat."

"Oh. I thought you hadn't. Since she was taken away from you."

"She was, but since my mother has her..." I wasn't sure how to finish the sentence I'd begun.

Frank said, "But you weren't a mother to her."

"No. I wasn't," I said, my voice a little sharp. I was too drunk to remember to watch my tone.

He turned toward me. What I could see of his expression by moonlight seemed apologetic. "I didn't mean it that way. I only meant—it could be something else we have in common. Not seeing our girls grow up."

"Our girls?"

"I had a daughter," said Frank. "Still have, I suppose, though I don't think she'd even recognize me."

"A daughter? You?" Then I blurted, "How?"

"I was married, Amy," said Frank.

"But didn't you—didn't you *know*?" I asked. It was as close as we'd ever gotten to addressing the man between us. The secret we did what we did to guard from the rest of the world.

"I mostly knew. But I was young. And there were—well, you know as well as anyone, there are advantages to marrying."

"I do know that," I confirmed and took a long drink of whiskey I most certainly didn't need.

Frank was staring at the stars again. "And my wife, she… I mean, she entered into it expecting one thing and getting another."

"Most wives do," I said.

"That's why the choice you made with Harry is such a smart one," said Frank. "Most people aren't as levelheaded. I admire you, you know."

"I didn't know," I admitted. "But I'm glad I know now."

He reached over and patted my hand. "I'm grateful to you, Amy. We both are."

It was all getting too sincere. I flicked his hand away. "You better be," I said, as lightly as I could.

He seemed to realize I didn't want any more seriousness between us.

"The stars are so bright tonight," he said. "Don't you think?"

"So bright," I echoed, and that was all. I don't remember him ever mentioning his daughter to me again.

I never regretted marrying Harry, not really. I only regretted that my husband and I couldn't love each other in the way that we both needed to be loved. The difference was that he'd already found that love elsewhere. And me? I was still looking.

CHAPTER TWELVE

I think my true life began in Japan, and I almost wish it would end there.

—AC

Not long after Harry and Frank and I returned from our European honeymoon, Harry told me he intended to move to Japan for some time to supervise some investments his family had made there. Would I like to come with him? I didn't hesitate.

I'd always been entranced by the Eastern world, and Japan was not a country I knew well. Growing up in San Francisco, I knew the Chinese by their dress, decor, and cuisine, but not the Japanese. Japan felt like a ripe mystery. I wanted to throw myself into something foreign and unfamiliar. It had gone so well in Hawaii, except for the charlatan Bishop, who was certainly not Hawaii's fault.

It didn't hurt either to picture the frustration of the American reporters when they found out I'd gone to the other side of the world, beyond their reach.

Just as I'd immersed myself in Hawaii at first sight, I threw myself headfirst into appreciating the vivid colors and magnificent surroundings of Japan.

We began in Yokohama. My first experience on the crowded, lively streets was being pulled in the back of a kuruma, the Japanese name for a conveyance much like the Chinese rickshaw. Kurumas were pulled by men called kurumaya, their strong, bare legs pumping as they hauled the fortunate like me to our destinations.

As a child, it had never occurred to me to question that some people received service and others did the serving. We had domestics and cooks and butlers and such, and that was the way it was. But in my teen years, I'd become quite uncomfortable with the idea. My mother had noticed and sat me down to explain that yes, I was right, and only an accident of birth made the difference between rich and poor; our duty was not to make over the whole world so that inequity was no longer so but to use our privilege and money to improve the lives of those who weren't born with those advantages. So when I saw men pulling passenger carts in the streets of Yokohama, I didn't stomp off in outrage, nor did I refuse to be pulled and insist on walking under my own power. I smiled politely, chose the kuruma closest to hand, and rode in comfort. Once the kurumaya had delivered me to my destination, I thanked him sincerely, then paid him what he asked and more.

The first few months of 1890, Harry and I appreciated exploring the city together. Though he was often busy much of the day, we dined together in the evenings. We feasted on plentiful rice, soups, and noodle dishes, learning our way around unfamiliar words like *miso* and *udon* and the delicious tastes that went with them.

When there was time, we visited tourist destinations, seeing the botanical gardens, the promenade, and more. The wondrous beauty of Japan never seemed to end. The flowers seemed more colorful and fragrant, the air clearer, the people more interesting. Our residence was in the European district, called the Bund, which we explored on foot when we had less time for travel.

In those first months, Frank came to visit twice, and I welcomed him with open arms. I remembered when he'd shown something of himself to me. I wanted to answer his generosity with generosity of my own. We walked together, talked together, ate together, toasted late into the night together, and when the next day dawned, did it all over again. The three of us continued our explorations, and when it made sense, I made myself scarce. Frank still had a hungry look when he thought no one was watching. It only made me uncomfortable because I thought he should try harder to hide it. But no one here seemed to notice. I realized I needed to let it go, and I did. Neither that time nor any other did I say a single word to Frank about hiding his true feelings for my husband. That was their business, not mine.

All too soon, though, Frank's latest visit came to an end. I didn't go to the pier to see him off with Harry. Frank and I said our goodbyes at the house so I could leave them the space to say their own goodbyes privately.

A few days after Frank left, as Harry moped around our small house, I tried to cheer him up.

"Where else shall we explore?" I asked merrily. "I've heard wonderful things about Tokyo, and it isn't so far. We could weekend there. Perhaps all the way to Mount Fuji if your work doesn't keep you too busy?"

He blinked at me as if he hadn't quite absorbed what I was saying. I was getting ready to repeat myself when he said, "I'm so sorry, Amy. I won't have time to travel with you. I have to go on a trip of my own."

"Oh. To where? Maybe I could come."

"Not this time," he said. "I'm sorry."

"I'll be all right," I said. But I noticed he hadn't answered my question.

His planned trip of two months would ultimately turn into six, leaving me alone in Japan with the social freedom of a wife without the practical limitations of a husband. At least Harry was no hypocrite. I knew that whatever I got up to in his absence would earn no censure from him. I would do my best to be discreet, for both our sakes, but I had no intention of living as a nun just because I'd entered into a marriage contract. Men never seemed to be bound by these things. I wouldn't either.

My first attempt to travel to Tokyo was, in a way, ill-starred. I'd been warned that the road was rough, but the horse cart jounced so much I had to stop frequently, and that slowed my progress so much that I worried I'd arrive too late to take advantage of the plans I'd set up in the city. The friend who was supposed to accompany me had already turned back, but I forged on. I never did like to admit defeat.

All along the route, there were travelers' stations. These were hotels of a sort, though nothing a Westerner would recognize under that name; one private room was divided from another only by thin walls of bamboo or paper. Men's rooms were furnished only with a mat for sleeping. Women, like me, got a wooden headrest in addition to the mat to preserve our hairstyles while sleeping.

I had stopped at my third station, bone tired, and was lying on my mat in a forest-green kimono when I heard a voice. Obviously the paper walls did little to block sound, so I heard the man swear in English clear as day—he had the plummy accent of a toff and the vocabulary of a hardened South Seas sailor—as my only warning right before he came crashing through the wall.

It was obviously an accident and not an attack, as he had thrust his arms out to break his fall. This was only partly successful. I sat up in a rush to avoid him, scooting for the far wall, and he landed face down on the floor, narrowly missing my discarded headrest.

"Bugger and bother," he groaned, a mild oath compared to those that had preceded it.

I finished sitting up, tucking my knees to the side, giving him as much space as I could manage.

"Don't rush yourself," I said gently. "Take your time. You might have a concussion."

As he lay sprawled on his back, eyes closed, I took the opportunity to examine him. He was obviously an Englishman, pale-skinned and slightly sunburnt, but he didn't give off a tourist air. His hair was blond and tousled. His kimono was an elegant red as dark as wine, made of a thick brocade I knew from experience didn't come cheap. Because of his undignified position on the floor, I could see he'd chosen to wear drawers underneath, a decision that saved us both some embarrassment given the conditions.

After some time, I prodded, "So what's the verdict?"

He opened his eyes, which were a piercing blue. In his splendid accent, he said, "Would you like me to apologize? I feel an apology is in order."

Had we been in a salon or bar or any reasonable situation, I would have known what to do with my body. I would have crossed my legs and regarded him with cool detachment. But I could barely move without touching some part of him. So I held myself very still and said, "Really, I don't believe in apologies."

His rejoinder was quick. "Me neither. I just thought I'd offer."

Then, to my surprise, he reached into a hidden pocket of his kimono—not a usual feature of kimonos, so likely custom-made— and produced a packet of cigarettes and a matchbook. Still lying on his back, as if this were a thing he did every day, he withdrew a cigarette in one smooth motion, then extended the pack in my direction.

"Oh, I don't generally smoke," I said.

"Oh, make an exception for me, won't you? I'm worth it." There was a lightness in his voice, and that was when I knew. I recognized him as a fellow flirt. And flirtation was my very favorite pastime, one I'd gone too long without indulging.

I plucked a cigarette from the pack and put it between my lips. "I'll be the judge of that."

When he stuck his own cigarette in the corner of his mouth and withdrew a match to strike, I had a sudden realization.

"Say," I said, "are you in the habit of lighting open flame in a house of paper walls? I wonder if perhaps it's a bad idea."

He pulled himself up to a sitting position, cigarette still dangling, and said, "You know, I think you might be right. We'll simply have to find another occasion to smoke together. Sadly, I'm living in Yokohama."

"How interesting," I said. "I am also living in Yokohama."

"Then there's hope," he replied, and if I hadn't already known his intent, the way he held my gaze with those bright blue eyes left nothing to chance.

He introduced himself as Winston Huntingdon-Meer, known to friends as Hunny, though I could never bring myself to call him that. When I had occasion to refer to him, I called him Meer.

After soothing the owner of the travelers' station and compensating him for his damaged property, Meer suggested we accept the sign from the universe that my trip to Tokyo should be delayed to a later time, and I wholeheartedly agreed. We proceeded directly back to Yokohama and quickly made use of rooms with thicker walls.

The first month of our acquaintance went as well as anyone could have hoped. Our later conversations might not have lived up to the powerful charge of the first one, but we had mutual interests besides conversation. The passion I had with Meer wasn't as strong as what I'd felt with Porter, but I didn't want it to be. A craving like that meant losing one's head. With Meer, I could indulge in the most delicious of pleasures with him after luncheon and forget he existed by evening. We kept our connection discreet. When we were seated next to each other at an embassy dinner, no one hearing our conversation would have known we'd even met.

The beginning of the end came when I mentioned to Meer that I was still very interested in going to Tokyo.

"I've seen what I need to see there," he said dismissively. Then he thought a moment longer. "But I know a local man who would make a good guide. His name is Takamine. Some sort of baron, actually, an excellent chap. I'll send him your way."

"Please do," I murmured, with no idea of what was to come.

Three days later, one of my servants ushered the baron into my house, where I offered him tea and appraised him frankly over our steaming teacups.

I had never met anyone quite like Baron Takamine. His calm was so pronounced I felt like his mere presence lowered the temperature of the room by several degrees. He was unmistakably Japanese, his features fine and sharp, and a bit shorter and more slender than I. He wore Western dress of exceptionally high quality, a charcoal-gray suit with a weave so fine it looked butter soft from my close vantage.

In lightly accented English, he said, "It's a pleasure to meet you, Mrs. Gillig. I'm told you need a guide."

"Yes, that's right. I want to travel to Tokyo."

Pleasantly, he said, "But first you should see Yokohama."

I narrowed my brows at him. "Yokohama? No, you misunderstand. I'm so sorry. I've lived here in Yokohama for months."

"Yet you don't know the city. I assure you. You know the Bund."

"More than that!" I protested.

Still calm, he replied, "And the botanical garden and the promenade, am I correct?"

My cheeks began to heat. I took a sip of my tea to cover my embarrassment. I didn't like the idea that I would fit so easily into the predictable slot of Western tourist, a title I didn't care to claim even if earned it. I wanted to belong to the places I lived, no matter how long or short my stay.

I said, "You come recommended as a guide. But I don't know your fees or your services."

He waved a hand. "I charge no fees. And my services are whatever you require."

"That makes no sense," I said, though I kept my voice even. "Why would you provide services and not charge for them?"

His gaze was steady, implacable. "I see myself as an ambassador."

"For the West or the East?"

"Both," he said. "I represent my native country to the West, yes. I was a student at Yale and also the Sorbonne. So when in France and America, they see me as the embodiment of Japan."

"But here you are Japanese also. How could you not be?"

He seemed unruffled at being asked to explain. His voice was patient, measured. He reminded me of the etiquette tutor at our school in Dresden. "Here, I am a Japanese man who brings a little of the West with him wherever he goes. In this case, I would bring you."

"To Tokyo?"

"Elsewhere in Yokohama first. To places where Westerners rarely go. So my countrymen and countrywomen can see for themselves that a Westerner can conduct business or pleasure in polite, respectful ways."

I asked, "And you're just guessing that I am a Westerner who can do that?"

"I don't guess," he said, and though his voice was still as calm as ever, I heard the first hint of steel beneath it. "I would not be here if I didn't know you are the kind of person who knows how to conduct herself."

"Did Meer tell you so?"

"Yes," he said, picking up his teacup with a delicate touch. "But not just him."

His English was good enough that I felt comfortable using idioms. "So you asked around about me?"

He replied, "As you asked around about me, yes."

I smiled at that. Sauce for the goose, et cetera. I said, "But no one I asked had much to say. They wouldn't tell me anything about you, scandalous or otherwise."

"They knew I needed to make my own decision."

I bristled at the implication that the decision was all in his hands. "So what I think of you doesn't matter at all?"

"It does," he said. "And if you decide at any point you wish me to no longer act as your guide, we will part that moment, and we will part as friends. That is our agreement. I can also decide to terminate our relationship. But if I didn't trust you, I wouldn't be here. So we have firm ground to start from."

"Yes," I agreed, impressed even more by his savvy than by his tailoring. I thrust out my hand to shake, and he didn't hesitate to take it.

In the next few weeks, he reintroduced me to the city I already called home, taking me farther afield to meet groups of Japanese who'd only ever seen a white woman from a distance, translating as we discussed the foolish things our leaders had done and the things we as reasonable citizens most wanted to do. Meer had no interest in engaging in such activities, so the time I spent with him grew less and less as the time I spent with Takamine grew more and more.

Then, finally, Tokyo. Takamine accompanied me on the train—a far superior way to travel—and settled me in a suburban house with Japanese families on both sides, ignoring the city district where the other Americans huddled in a close cluster like newborn puppies and only ever talked to each other.

Once he confirmed that everything he had arranged for the house had been delivered, he rose to go. I reached out, then, and caught his hand.

"Stay," I said simply. Over all our time together, our walks and conversations and meals, I had felt our attraction growing. It was in the way his body oriented toward mine, the way he took great care not to stand too close, the way his breath caught when my hand brushed his. I'd never been wrong about such things. I knew I wasn't wrong this time either.

"I cannot," he said. "We will not endanger your reputation."

"I'm a married woman. My reputation is safe. You are only acting as my guide."

His eyes flicked toward the door, but he didn't move in that direction, and he didn't free his hand from mine. I understood what that meant.

"Baron," I said. "If you stay, you're worried someone will see you leave in the morning, yes?"

"Yes."

I tugged on his hand, drawing him closer. He took one more step toward me, then two. I had never leaned down to kiss a man before while standing face-to-face. I found the novelty of it thrilling.

I whispered, "Then we will have to make sure no one sees," just before my lips found his.

Two of the most powerful things on all of God's green earth are sex and religion, and my experiences with Takamine opened my eyes to new dimensions of both.

He introduced me to the Japanese religion called Shinto, which was unlike anything I'd ever known before. Instead of Western religions, which center on sin and punishment and put all their power in the hands of a chosen few, Shinto was an egalitarian, welcoming form of belief. If you purified yourself at the door of a temple, you could enter. Family, nature, and the spirits of the dead were all bound up in a circle of life and what lay beyond, and I found it fascinating. My firsthand exposure to the religions of the East helped me fully appreciate the dizzying possibilities of what a person could believe.

Takamine showed me too how a society's attitude toward sex could be the polar opposite of America's puritanical bent. One of the first events he escorted me to in Tokyo was the public opening of a new house of prostitution. I could barely comprehend what I was seeing. Speeches were made to a gathered crowd, everyone cheering as if it were the opening of any greengrocer, any bookshop. There was acknowledgment with no shame that every person's life should have room for sex if they wanted it. The American position, pardon the pun, was so very different.

Even with the openness of the Japanese toward sex, Takamine was meticulous in his discretion, rising before dawn to leave my house by the garden entrance so he wouldn't be seen. When we dined out in restaurants or attended public events like concerts, we acted as friends. Only in the confines of my suburban home did we reach for each other hungrily, shedding pretense along with clothing to utterly satisfy our hunger.

Except for one memorable time. He'd told me he had a surprise for me but refused to give even a single crumb of detail.

"But what should I wear?" I said.

With his usual calm, he told me, "Believe me when I say it doesn't matter."

The sense of mystery only increased from there. Next, when our driver arrived, I noticed he was a stranger, not the driver who had taken us everywhere from the opening of the house of prostitution to lunch at the garden and dinner by the river. Did the baron not want his usual contacts to know where we were going? I found this extremely curious.

We took a route through unfamiliar streets, and when I stepped down from the kurayama, the streetscape gave me no clues. The area was quiet. I didn't think it was the business district, but it didn't have the look of a residential street either. The buildings were a mix of old and new.

Takamine gestured for me to follow him to a small house where an old woman sat by the door. Engaging her in a quick, pointed conversation in Japanese, he said something I didn't follow. The woman opened the door, entered, and closed it behind her. He and I were left standing, just the two of us, no other person on the street to speak of.

"What did you say?" I asked him in a quiet voice.

"I said you are here for the experience," he said, an honor that was likely honest but not at all enlightening.

Once the old woman returned and shepherded us in, the three of us walked along narrow, dimly lit hallways. I remember that

Takamine took my hand, which he never did where someone else could see. We passed only one other person on our way, a young white woman wearing a black silken robe, her cheeks pink, her gaze vacant. I began to wonder exactly what I'd gotten myself into, especially when we entered a kind of waiting room and our escort handed me a black robe identical to the one the young woman in the hall had been wearing.

I looked to Takamine for advice wordlessly, and he indicated that I should shed my own clothes and don the robe. The old woman turned her back, and I did so.

"Won't you change?" I asked him, again quietly. I felt I had to speak in a hush; there was no other sound around us.

He answered, "It isn't for me."

But when the old woman showed us to yet another room, Takamine remained with me. He was there when she opened the door into a room lit by a single flickering lamp. He was there to lead me to a soft velvet couch, and though I could barely see in the darkness, he guided me with sure hands and seated me.

Then we waited. I tried to peer into the shadowed corners of the room, and I thought I could make out the outlines of other couches, but I couldn't be sure.

"Amy," said the baron in a soft voice right next to my ear. "It is only you and me."

But as soon as he said it, I saw another person in the room, a man dressed in pale yellow, startling in relief against the darkness. Where had he come from? He seemed a very old man. I was beginning to worry that I was somehow hallucinating though I hadn't been given any food or drink; could the mere air of the place be causing me to see things that weren't there?

The old man raised something to his shoulder—an instrument, I saw, some kind of violin?—and began to play. The music he coaxed from that instrument affected me in a way no music has before or since.

The very first note, tremulous and low, shot straight to my core. And when he drew his bow across the strings, I felt every bit of the music sing in me, zinging down my limbs until my fingertips and toes tingled almost to the point of pain.

I don't know how long the music went on, but it inhabited me somehow, and it drove me wild, pushing me ever closer to a peak, something sensual but not just sensual, building and building until I found my hands moving toward the front of my robe to relieve the tension.

That was when I felt the baron catch my hands. I moaned as he held my wrists, preventing me from giving myself relief. I couldn't bear it. The tension the strings had created in me was a pleasure beyond reckoning, a pressure that threatened to tear me apart.

The baron shifted in a quick, decisive motion, pinning both my wrists to one side with a single hand. He had not demonstrated such strength with me before, but I was too addled with sensation to fully understand what was happening. With his other hand, he swiftly parted the black robe, and as the violin reached a painfully beautiful crescendo, my lover touched me just once.

My release in that moment was mad, wild, unfathomable.

The next thing I knew, I lay aching and outstretched on a couch, though I could not have said whether it was the same one from earlier or a different one. The baron bent over me and cupped my cheek, looking down into my eyes with concern. I said the first thing that came to mind.

"I want to remember this," I told him, my eyes glazed. "Baron, help me remember."

His delicate lips curved in a satisfied smile. "Of course. I know just the way."

The next day, Takamine took me to a small, unmarked door in the business district. The space inside was clean and airy, with a faint scent I could not, at first, place. Then when I saw a small Japanese man step forward out of the shadows, his arms tattooed all over with intricate, beautiful patterns, I realized what I'd smelled. It was ink.

"Amy Gillig," Takamine said, "allow me to introduce the great artist Hori Chiyo."

The tattoo artist gave a graceful bow, which I returned.

Since Chiyo spoke no English and I no Japanese, Takamine translated for us both, helping us suss out how best I could carry a memory of Japan on my skin. We decided that two things were most appropriate: the snake, because it shed its skin, and the butterfly, because it left its old self behind to utterly transform. In the end, I decided that I would get both eventually, but for the first, I chose the butterfly.

Takamine sat close to me and held my hand as I asked the tattoo expert if other people like me had come to him for similar adornment.

"People like you? There is no one like you," came the translation.

I loved that answer but hastened to clarify. "People from America. Or Europe."

As Hori Chiyo hunched over my arm with the sharp needle poised for action, Takamine said, "He says Europeans, yes. Duke of York. Czar Nicholas of Russia."

"Before or after he became czar?" I asked, amused.

"Does that matter?" he replied, fingers still frozen in the air.

"Not in the least," I assured him. "Just making conversation."

Chiyo said something that Takamine translated as, "Well, less conversation."

"Very well," I said, nodding my approval, and a moment later, I felt the first pinprick pain of the tattoo needle. I held myself motionless, but it was still one of the most pleasurable physical sensations I can remember. Just that first moment, from no pain to pain, as the butterfly took shape.

The sensation of getting tattooed is hard to describe, and I'm barely tempted to try. Suffice it to say that there are a nearly infinite range of types of pain. Some are challenging to withstand, some are impossible, and some are indistinguishable from pleasure. While I squirmed under the needle, I hungered for the pain to end, but at the same time, I wanted it to last longer. Once it was over, I missed it. I hung on to the memory of that particular, exquisite torture for a long time.

Would my tattoo shock the narrow-minded Mrs. Grundys back in America? Yes, and that alone would have been reason enough to pursue it. But in truth, I didn't get my first tattoo for any reason having to do with the outside world. I did it for myself. Because I wanted it. And because I was a woman who could make her own choices. Wasn't that what I'd married Harry for? To move more easily through the world? If I couldn't do something truly wild with my freedom, one might not call it freedom at all.

In the end, the idea of sauce for the goose and sauce for the gander defined Takamine for me. My growing affection for him had pulled my attention away from Meer, who I neglected until he simply gave up attempting to contact me. Our affair faded away.

Two months after I'd become entangled with Takamine, long after we were both back in Yokohama, the baron and I attended an embassy event together, pretending, as usual, to be only friends. That night, we were fatefully introduced to a blond American woman named Penn Darnley. She was charming and vivacious, almost textbook in her Americanness, blue-eyed and icy blond. She was married, but that hardly mattered; so was I. When she laughed, she threw back her head and exposed her long throat, and I could tell immediately that the baron wanted to place his lips on that throat and lay claim to her. She was electric.

Almost right away, Takamine's visits grew less frequent. I had no claim on him and had never really asked one, but when I saw him watching Penn Darnley at another embassy event only a few weeks later, the hunger on his face showed me there was no getting him back.

Perhaps it was for the best, because the next day, Harry returned.

My husband didn't ask a word of what I'd been up to in my absence, though he must have heard the rumors, and I volunteered nothing. We were at our best when we lived only in the moment. It was as if the whole past six months, my affairs with Meer and then Takamine, had never happened. The only real reminder I had of either beyond memories was the delicate butterfly tattooed on my skin.

How do I describe the years of my marriage to Harry, how quickly they flew? We went to so many exotic places, then when they became familiar, we moved on. Two years in Japan were like a moment. The way I often remembered where I was in any given year was what I had bought Gladys for a birthday present.

I barely knew the girl, of course, and I certainly wouldn't get to know her from half a world away. But as spring approached, every year, she was on my mind. So in Japan, I bought her the most elegant tea set I could find, one not even intended for a child, and imagined her treating her dolls to a tea party that would make all the other girls green with jealousy. That was when she was six years old. We were still in Japan when she turned seven, and her gift was a length of silk she could order made into any garment she liked, whatever her current whim.

The years after that winged past like ravens in flight. I was in Borneo when Gladys turned ten, and I bought her a set of enormous handwoven baskets; in India the next year, for her eleventh birthday, I had the head of the hotel's housekeeping service procure and package an array of local sweets dizzying in their rainbow of colors and flavors. Perhaps my gifts could tell Gladys how I treasured her, even if I'd never been able to find the words.

CHAPTER THIRTEEN

Picture me, trying to free myself of this fear which made me cling to the things I knew and understood, and to throw myself instead into those other things I had come to find.

—AC

In these years, the call of the unexplained, the mystical, grew louder. Any time I docked in a new port, I made it a priority to find the local experts: fortune tellers, clairvoyants, and the like. The experience was always interesting. One can learn a lot about a culture by how they treat those with some connection to a world beyond. With each one, I waited for someone to repeat the prediction about my thirteen husbands, but none did. I was beginning to think that fortune teller had simply been a charlatan and that my second husband would be my last. Since Harry had never really fallen in love with me, it was a certainty that he wouldn't fall out.

I was married but not married, all that time. When Harry was present, we'd have meals together, and our time was always genial and comfortable. He was still a wonderful conversationalist, though I no longer itched to share a good story or silly anecdote with him, as I had in our early days. When we were apart from each other, we rarely reached out. I might go months without hearing from him and then get word he'd be arriving at our house the next day. He never burst in as if he wanted to surprise me or catch me out. There was a story about that published in some scandal rag back in California, but it was made up out of whole cloth. Even from the other side of the world, unfortunately, they still wrote about me. In the absence of facts, they simply published fiction.

Harry and I still had our moments. Soon after we moved to India in 1895, he took me to a glorious market to furnish the apartments we'd taken there. I piled a cart high with bright fabrics and carpets, feeling delighted to be embarking on this new adventure. But an odd feeling came over me, and I paused.

"Harry, what's the point of all this?" I asked him.

Seeming unbothered, handsome, and regal as ever, Harry took a moment to look over what I'd purchased. "To make where we live lovely. Is that enough reason?"

"That's not what I mean," I said. I couldn't account for the intensity of the emotion that had hit me. Suddenly, it just all seemed so futile. "We pile up things, and then we move elsewhere, leaving them behind. We just churn and churn. What's it for?"

To his credit, he seemed to understand I was wholly serious. He eyed me carefully. "Are you talking about the apartment or something else?"

"I don't even know."

"Here," he said. "I have an idea."

He spoke a few low words to someone off to the side, securing our new possessions, and then took my hand. Firmly, he led me a few stalls up and arranged me in front of a shelf.

"Beauty," he said simply. "We live our lives in pursuit of beauty."

The shelf was lined with gorgeous statues in gold and stone and everything in between. Perhaps any other day, I might have reached for a jade dolphin or a sterling snake, something without meaning, simply a beautiful object, as Harry's maxim suggested.

But that day, I raised my eyes to the top shelf. I saw there a gold statue of the Buddha, his pose cross-legged and steady, his face impassive, his fingers raised in a simple blessing. To his left and right, more

Buddhas, all along the row. So many different poses and materials, so many differences in expression and position, but all clearly meant to depict the same man. All seemed to be exactly what I was looking for.

Gazing into the Buddha's face, I felt peace come over me, a centered calm. As swiftly as I had felt unsettled just moments before, I now felt entirely right. I couldn't remember the last time I had felt so at ease with myself, like an oasis of perfect stillness in the center of a swirling storm.

"I'll take this one," I said.

As I said it, the feeling changed again: now, I felt a sense of being incomplete. I looked at the Buddha next to the one I had chosen, and as soon as my eyes lit on its face, the peace descended on me again. I looked away and back, testing the feeling, and found the same thing happening over and over.

The shopkeeper was still looking up at the first Buddha I'd selected and indicated it with an outstretched hand. "This one, ma'am?"

I nodded, then pointed to the rest of the row. "And this one and this one and this one."

Harry's laugh was a merry one, warm and encouraging, a genuine burst of delight I hadn't heard from him in a long time. To the shopkeeper, he said, "Well, you heard the lady!"

For the rest of my days, no matter where I was living or what I was doing, whether I was married or not, happy or not, lonely or not, I always had one room of my house dedicated to statues of the Buddha so I could retreat to that place and breathe my way back to a kind of centered calm. At one time, I had more than two hundred. I selected them based on whether they gave me the right feeling, and that feeling never steered me wrong.

I loved India with a passion. It spoke to me with a voice I hadn't heard since Hawaii. I'd enjoyed Japan, of course, and Borneo and all the rest. A rush of optimism always seized me when I sailed into a new port I'd never seen before, witnessed the landscape of a new country unfolding before me. Everywhere, I loved the unfamiliar. But India was more than that.

It wasn't just the landscape that felt like coming home. The ideas, the culture, the religion. India was the first place that I heard of the idea of *kaivalya*, or separateness. It's the achievement of realizing that your soul isn't the same as your body. No one is simply matter. It's a kind of liberation. That fit me like a glove.

Surrounded by my Buddhas, I realized it was important not to reduce them. The Buddha wasn't just a face to help me calm myself. He was a sage and a teacher, the founder of a religion followed by millions. He was an open door.

I passed through that door, throwing myself wholeheartedly into the study of Buddhism while Harry lived his own overlapping life, sometimes with me, sometimes gone. In India, Buddhism was my real homecoming. So much of what I learned seemed like it had been tailor-made for me. The idea of a middle way between sensuality and deprivation. The reminder not to cling to the impermanent things of life. Not everything slotted in perfectly—I'm sure my mother, had she been aware of my interest in Buddhism, would have suggested that giving away my fortune would be the best route to improving my karma—but there was so much there to unpack, to pursue, to savor.

Ever since my father's death, the world had judged me harshly. The press told everyone how to feel about me based on the hasty conclusions the press themselves had drawn from scant evidence. I found so much comfort in the idea that none of us should judge each other. I wished everyone could be a Buddhist, really.

The only sad thing that I recall ever happening to me in India was getting the news that I would be leaving it.

When Harry spoke the words "Our time here is over," I felt such a deep pang, as if something were being torn away from me.

I could have stayed, I know now. Perhaps I should have. I've wondered about it over the years, what might have happened. Would I have lived happily in India for the rest of my life?

I left India, but India never left me. Nor did Buddhism. And the core of my new beliefs would bring me happiness that I hadn't previously known. It took a while, and there were other things to sort out first, but I already knew that India had left its mark on me.

I prayed under my breath as we sailed away.

In the early years of my marriage, I'd felt married to both Harry and Frank, but that was no longer the case. I felt like a rock in the midst of a rushing stream, water always dividing around me, so much floating by, but my own substance untouched. In a way, it suited me. I wasn't exactly happy, but I wasn't unhappy. I thought perhaps, now that I was a woman instead of a child, this was how the rest of my life would simply be. Perhaps we all settle, in every sense of that word.

There were bright moments and dark ones. Sometimes one came on the other's heels. One year, I visited California and hosted a grand ball at the Palace Hotel to bring together old friends. I was delighted when King David Kalakaua, who happened to be on another one of his international tours, was able to attend. There were few people I'd known so long and none that I liked so much. Unfortunately, a week later, he suffered some sort of aneurysm or stroke, and a few days after that, he passed from this world. As if the news of a friend's death didn't cause me enough pain, some scandal-hungry *Chronicle* reporter decided I might be at fault, and the groundless story spread. It was a lousy but effective reminder to stay out of California.

After India, there were so many other places, but my husband and I no longer traveled to them together. Harry was in New York, and I was in Singapore. Harry was in England, and I was in New York. Harry—with, of course, Frank—stopped by Paris when I was already there, and I sailed for England that very day. The papers made a joke of it, but we viewed it as a game. The world was our playground. We both loved to explore. The idea that I could just up and leave any place at any time was charming to me. I had felt trapped before. And Harry had been right about our marriage freeing me up to do as I liked. My access to money was unfettered, which opened many doors both figurative and literal. I hadn't been sold a bill of goods. I went in with my eyes wide open. I would always thank Harry for that, even at the end.

I should have known that accepting less than my due wouldn't last forever. That wasn't the kind of woman I was or could be. I did my best. Harry and I did right by each other, as best we could.

But everyone hits their limit. I only had to discover where mine lay.

CHAPTER FOURTEEN

I returned to America with my husband, only to find that our life together was not advisable. We agreed to separate, and the divorce followed shortly. That is not an interesting story.

—AC

O f all the things that could have convinced me to make a change to my situation, the final straw was an unlikely one: a party I wasn't invited to.

It sounds petty. It probably was. I had become so accustomed to Harry doing as he liked because it gave me the freedom to do as I liked. I never begrudged him that.

Until in 1897, he and Frank went to Hawaii and threw a party so glorious, I heard about it on the other side of the world.

Harry knew how much I loved Hawaii. It had been my place before it was his. He must have known that I would willingly travel from anywhere to join a celebration on the beaches of what was still my favorite island. Why would Harry leave me out?

And oh, the time they had. The newspapers breathlessly recounted every detail. Flying in the face of formality, the party was called a "hop," everyone dressing in casual white clothes instead of the fancy frocks and suits required for a mainland affair. Each guest had a colorful lei of flowers draped around his or her neck, so the effect was one of bountiful color even though all the clothes were white. And the detail that everyone loved most was that the hosts took the stage and sang duet after duet, running through every kind of music the band could keep up with and more, their voices twining through the night. It seemed like a declaration of something, though none of the newspapers ginned up the nerve to say what. Several mentioned that Frank was engaged to an heiress named Helen Wilder, though they all stopped short of claiming Miss Wilder had been present at this party over which her fiancé presided with another man.

In a sense, it wasn't Harry and Frank's party I really wanted to go to. I knew that well enough, though it didn't soften my heart. What I wanted was to go back to my first trip to Hawaii, to be who I was back then. I wanted to be twenty-three years old, excited about the world, glamorous and confident, a friend of the king. But the king was dead, and I was rapidly aging, and I was finally feeling trapped in a marriage I had willingly signed up for, knowing it wouldn't give me everything I needed.

I didn't need anyone to tell me why I was feeling put out. What I needed was someone who would tell me what to do about it. I suppose most people would ask a friend for advice, but the only woman I'd consider asking, Darlene Venable née Messerschmidt, was half a world away.

So I sought a closer answer.

The local mystic seemed like such an obvious counterfeit, she had to be genuine. A charlatan who looks like a charlatan might be recommended by the tourist hotels but not the circles I traveled in, which were more discriminating. Everything about the woman reeked of a carnival put-on: from the dimly lit tent and its incense cloud to her heavy makeup and cheap spangled shawl. But her eyes within their thick kohl rings were bright, and she tilted her head when she looked at me, exactly like a crow would. She could have been twenty years old or sixty. She could have been Far Eastern, Mexican, Southern Italian, North African; she could have been wearing dusky makeup to mask a complexion as pale as mine. Hell, for all I could tell, she could have been a man. I decided to hold nothing back from her and see where our conversation led.

The first steps of her routine were exactly what I would have expected, either from a fake or genuine medium. The examination of my face, the gentle grunting under her breath. But then she turned that curious crow's gaze on me again and said, "You've heard it all before."

"I have."

"Then what can I do for you?"

"I've heard dozens of things from dozens of people. I don't know who to believe."

She shrugged, almost intimately. "That is your decision. I won't tell you how to sort through what you hear. Especially since I don't know the people who told it to you. I would tell you to be skeptical of what they say, but you already know that too, don't you?"

I nodded. "I do."

"So what we do here today, I doubt it will illuminate your life in a way you've never imagined. I think you've imagined it all."

"I have," I agreed. "But I'm still hoping you'll tell me something new."

"I may. But no guarantees."

"I don't come to mystics looking for guarantees. That's why I have lawyers."

She grinned, showing off teeth too straight and white for the beaten-down image she had chosen to project. She was a well-fed, well-cared-for woman. I knew the type, having been one myself all my life long.

"So," she said. "I do have a crystal ball if that's the type of thing you go in for. Or there's tarot, of course, though I will admit the cards are not my favorite."

The mere mention of tarot threatened to derail me—Bishop's face flashed in my mind, sneering, so clear I felt my whole body tense—but I forced myself to focus. "What is your favorite, then?"

She considered this question. It was unlikely she'd been asked it many times before.

While she was still considering, I said, "I assume most people come in here with an idea of what they want."

"Everyone does. Including you."

"I mean," I said, "they have a picture in their head. A romantic notion. They want a dramatic card reveal that tells them their lover's cheating or gazing into a hazy ball that reveals their future husband is right around the corner. They already know the answer they want to hear."

"And you're so different?" She wasn't being unkind, just prodding gently, challenging my assumption.

"I think I am. I'm genuinely open to anything. I really have no idea what you'll tell me, and I love the mystery of finding out." This was mostly true, though I was always holding back one thing: that mysterious prediction that my thirteenth husband would bury me. No one had repeated the dire prophecy. A little part of me was always waiting.

She spread her hands wide. "Well then. You asked what my favorite way to give answers is. All I want you to do is come up with the one question that matters most to you right now. The one question that runs as an undercurrent to everything else you do."

"Oh, that's easy enough," I remarked sarcastically.

She answered me by flashing that shiny grin.

"A single question," I said. "For what I'm paying?"

"If it's the most important question, I promise to deliver you an honest answer. To give you the key that unlocks what you yourself have decided you most need. And isn't that worth any price?"

"It is to you," I grumbled, but I didn't begrudge her. That was what money was for. The few dollars she was charging wouldn't matter at all to me and might matter plenty to her. And perhaps her answer to my question really would illuminate my future in a way I hadn't yet thought of. I could certainly use the guidance. Any guidance.

"Whether or not you give me any kind of meaningful answer,"

I admitted, "it's a useful exercise for me to wonder what it is in the world that most matters to me."

"That's why I like it."

I had an irrational burst of love for this woman, this completely unknown figure whose name I didn't even know, might never know. I recognized her as a kindred spirit. If I'd met her in San Francisco or New York, we would have been fast friends. And women like that were so few and far between, I felt melancholy at the recognition that I would almost certainly never see her again.

She gave me the time I needed for contemplation. I focused on my breathing, steadied it. Finally, I decided on my question. I said, "You promise an honest answer? Whatever I ask?"

She answered, "I assume you'll ask something about yourself, but yes. Your most important question, whatever matters to you. Is the question you're thinking of about your past or about your future?"

"Future."

"That's helpful. Plenty of people come in only asking to confirm their regrets."

"I have my question," I said.

"Very well. Ask it."

All in a rush, I blurted, "What should I change?"

Part of me expected the answer to be *everything*. Part of me expected the answer to be what my mother and sister told me for years: to give away the money, which I had no intention of doing, now or ever, since it was the only security I ever had. Part of me expected there to be no answer at all.

The uncertainty of it was intoxicating. She might say anything or nothing. But it wasn't a question I already knew the answer to. And she wasn't someone whose answer I could already predict.

I thought she would give me the ceremony I'd paid for, deliver the carnival routine that our surroundings promised. Instead, her response was straightforward.

"Your name," the woman rasped.

"My name?" In the depths of my surprise, I could only repeat her words.

There was no uncertainty in her voice, no coyness, as she spoke. "You can change your name without changing who you are. You can be even more yourself if you do."

She made it sound so easy. And I decided that it would be.

I'd changed my last name before, to Ashe for Porter, to Gillig for Harry. I didn't think changing my last name was what the mystic meant. At the same time, I didn't dislike my first name, and I was too old to train myself to turn around when someone called out Rose or Josephine or Claire.

You can be even more yourself, she'd said.

The answer came to me surprisingly quickly, carried on a memory.

Among my many flirtations in the dark gardens of Dresden, a young Frenchman had applied his lips to my hand and his intellect to my seduction.

"You are so lovely," he'd said to me, moonlight shining overhead. "And your name, it shows your destiny."

"My destiny?" I repeated, letting his lips brush over the back of my hand again, creating the space for him to linger.

"Aimée," he said, lengthening the syllables of my ordinary American name in a lavish and very French way. The beginning was the same, but instead of the flat *me* at the end, he pronounced the second half like the month of May. "It means *loved*."

Aimée Crocker, I whispered to myself. Yes. I would be more myself by changing. The mysterious fortune teller with the crow's gaze had indeed given me exactly the answer I was searching for. I felt better already.

On the boat back to New York, I was seated at the captain's table with two couples and a single woman I didn't know. Though Miss

Packard's trappings were those of a typical woman of our class, I could no more tell who she was at her core by looking than she could tell the same of me. I could only know by talking with her. So I began.

"I've decided to reinvent myself," I said. "Perhaps I'll travel to Africa this time, or South America."

"You could," she said and shrugged. "It sounds like a lot of work."

"I'm not afraid of work," I said.

Miss Packard eyed me carefully. "May I be honest?"

My experience with people asking this question was that they were about to say something unforgivable and thus were asking forgiveness in advance. But for whatever reason, I sensed that Miss Packard asked the question sincerely.

"Yes," I answered. "I'd very much like it if you were."

"Here's my opinion," she said, laying her hand on my arm for emphasis. "You live in the one place where you can completely reinvent yourself without even leaving town. New York City is the home of reinvention."

It hadn't occurred to me until she said it, that a change of scenery might not even be necessary. I was so used to moving on physically to move on emotionally. "Hm. Maybe."

Her manner became more animated, enthusiastic. "All it takes in New York to live a new life is to declare it. You can be whoever you want to be."

"If you have money, of course."

She said, "But that isn't a problem for you, is it, Mrs. Gillig?"

We both knew it wasn't.

More gently, reining herself in, she said, "Take a break before you decide. I know a retreat in upper New York State that would be perfect for you. Though, I suppose…"

The way she trailed off made me most curious. "Suppose what?"

"You might not like the crowd. Unless you're a Buddhist."

"I am!" I declared with joy.

"Well then." She smiled. "I think we've found where your reinvention will begin."

The retreat was everything Miss Packard had promised. Like-minded people, open-minded people, everyone here to rest and attune to ourselves. It was a small practice center upstate that opened itself to anyone who wanted to pursue their Buddhist principles, giving space either to commune with others or stay solitary. I found that at this point, I wanted quiet more than I wanted community, so I often meditated alone. Sometimes I chose my own stark chamber, sometimes finding a neglected corner indoors or a lovely outdoor scene. I meditated often by the side of the pond, and while others would find their own seats on the shore, we didn't speak to each other unless invited. I felt a connection with these like-minded people, but I was shy of revealing my identity. There was nothing wrong with Buddhist practice, and I wasn't ashamed of it in the least, but I didn't want my return to the United States to be heralded with headlines that twisted my truth into something ugly.

On the final afternoon, as I strolled through a beautiful set of woods communing with nature, I was trying to decide whether conversation with others would support or disrupt my goal. I was saved from the burden of decision by the young man who sidled up next to me and said, "These woods, ah. I'll miss this nature when we go back to Manhattan."

"Central Park not enough nature for you?" I asked.

"It's better than nothing."

"Far better," I said. "The last place I lived, there were no parks anywhere near our apartments."

"Where was that?"

"India," I said.

"India! Goodness!" He gestured at the trees around us. "Long way to come for this."

"I'm returning to my home in Larchmont," I said.

"Ah. Closer, then. Are you in Manhattan often? Or do you plan to be, now that you've returned?"

"Some weeks not at all, some weeks every day and night," I said. "Depends on the week. I keep an address in Manhattan as well."

"So you can have the quiet of the country or the bustle of the city. Choose just how much company you want on any given day."

"Company is overrated," I said with more emphasis than I intended.

He tilted his head at that, his bushy mustache bouncing slightly with the motion. "Present company included?"

"Not at all," I said. In the spirit of living as my most authentic self, I decided to be completely honest with the stranger. "I'm enjoying your company quite a bit. You're young and good-looking, well-spoken. I imagine you make friends quickly."

"I'm enjoying making friends with you," he said. "Perhaps we could arrange to cross paths when next you're in Manhattan?"

"Perhaps."

"What does it depend on?"

"What you'd want from such a meeting."

"Just to continue our conversation. Making friends, like we're doing. I don't know many Buddhists in the city either, so we could alert each other to events we might both enjoy."

That seemed fair enough. I'd satisfied myself that he wasn't striking up a conversation because he'd figured out who I was, angling for my money. I realized those suspicions weren't very Buddhist either. I was not doing a great job of being a Buddhist naturally, I decided, though there was no fault in that. I simply needed to work at it.

"Aren't you going to ask what I do?" he said.

"Such a stale icebreaker," I said. "I was going to go the whole weekend without letting that question pass my lips."

"Well, you're not the one who asked it, so your record's still spotless."

"In that case, please volunteer, if you'd like. And if you wouldn't like, that's fine with me." I meant it, though I had to admit I was curious.

"I'm a songwriter," he said.

"Really? For money?"

"Yes," he said dryly. "A decent amount of it, in fact. Do you know a lot of amateur songwriters?"

I considered the question. "I know a lot of amateur everythings."

"What are you an amateur at?" he asked.

"Oh, a great many things." It was the truth.

"What are you a professional at?"

"I suppose you could say I'm a professional heiress."

Chuckling, he said, "I suppose no one is an amateur one of those. It does pay handsomely."

I smiled. "So what sort of songs do you write?"

"Good ones."

"I suppose there's time enough for specifics when we meet in Manhattan," I responded.

His smile was broad, easy, lit from within. I wanted to see it again.

"Now that we know each other, I suppose I should introduce myself. My name is Jackson Gouraud," he said.

"Charmed," I said, and I was.

———

Before we met again, I asked around about Mr. Gouraud. My mother made a face, which was to be expected. Many of the higher society types hadn't heard of him at all. But my musician friends recognized the name immediately and reacted with pleasure: *so talented, such a keen fellow, such a sense of style*, they said. I must admit a secret, nurtured joy when none of them followed up their compliments with *And his wife too, so wonderful*. Jackson was not married. Jackson was young, yes, still in his twenties, which I had left behind, but Jackson wasn't a callow youth frittering away his songwriting monies on liquor and women and ponies.

So I rang him to say I'd be in the city soon, and was he interested in meeting for tea? He was.

"I'm eager to see you," he said.

Everything I had been taught as a woman was to remain coy, coquettish, holding myself back.

Instead I said, "I'm eager to see you too."

When we met for tea, our conversation was wide-ranging. He told me about the art of songwriting; I talked to him about my experience in Hawaii.

"How wild you were," he said, shaking his head, but not in a disapproving way.

"Was I so wild? It never felt that way."

"You know most women wouldn't go skidding off to the gateway to the East without companionship. And I'm sure you know almost no women would put on native dress and learn to dance the hula, as you describe it."

"Well, I think more women should," I said.

He grinned. "I think you're right about that."

"But in the meantime, I guess I have to settle for being unusual."

"I suspect you never settle at all."

I felt a blush creep up over my cheeks. I began to stammer something modest, saying, "Oh, I don't think that I'm all that..."

My right hand was lying on the table, and he clapped his own hand atop it, leaned in, and spoke to me with utter sincerity. "You're extraordinary. Never let anyone tell you different."

His earnestness was almost too much. I had to make a joke of it. "Well, they say what they say, you know. Would you have me stuff their mouths with cotton wool?"

But he didn't let me off that easily. His hand still lay atop mine, warm, insistent. "Sure. Let them talk. But don't you listen."

I demurred again, saying, "Mustn't I?"

He sang it then, in a voice like warm silk, "Aimée, darling, if they speak, tell 'em to paddle up a creek."

I laughed at that, his charming serenade.

"Promise me you won't make yourself smaller," he said, speaking plain.

"I won't," I promised, and he sat up straight again. But he didn't pull his hand away. He kept contact with me until he noticed the waiter heading our way, at which point he withdrew to avoid feeding the rumor mill. It was the reasonable thing to do.

After that, I saw Jackson twice a week at minimum. I made sure I wasn't hounding him. At each meeting, we specified whose turn it was to set the next meeting, and we alternated exactly, very modern. Perhaps because of his age or his lack of high-society breeding or both, Jackson didn't truck with the old way of doing things. He was perfectly happy to let me take the lead when I wanted to. I found that nearly as seductive as his other fine qualities. And he had plenty of those.

Above all, Jackson was easy, so easy, to talk to. Does that sound like a cliché? It is, I suppose, but for good reason. Some people can fall in love without talking to each other, but the older I got, the more I required it. Love without words opens everyone up to misunderstanding. It might feel the same in the moment—the pounding heart, the longing to close the space between—but lust burns just as bright if you never step back from it to take a good long look.

Words create that space. Talking at length, like we did in those early weeks, gives you endless opportunities to find common ground or opposition. What a person talks about most tells you what they believe. If Jackson had only ever spoken of the Broadway nightlife, if I had only ever spoken of shopping and jewels and society, we would have stayed friends, perhaps, but nothing more. It was the way we exposed ourselves to each other—my widespread travels, his emotional engagement with his art—that brought us together. Then closer together, and closer. From there, it was only a short hop to love.

And this all happened in public, perfectly proper. We'd done it over teacups and in theaters, not gambling palaces or cheap hotels. I didn't need to be alone with him to recognize and savor our attraction. When we spoke about it later, when we were both comfortable enough with each other to confess our feelings and our doubts, we realized we'd both fallen fast and hard. To have someone who listens actively to what you say, remembers the details of your stories, beams at you when you remember theirs? What could tell you more clearly that you're meant to be?

In many ways, my conversations with Jackson reminded me of those early days in New York with Harry, just after we'd been reunited at the New York Yacht Club party, before I married him and our relationship became a group affair. Jackson's wit was a little more barbed, his manner of speaking more performative, but he was always even-handed about making sure we both got a chance to share what was on our minds. And he was never unkind. I remember feeling warmed by that.

But Jackson wasn't Harry. And thank goodness for that. Most importantly, he wasn't in love with someone else. At that time, I wasn't sure whether Jackson was falling in love with me, but his attraction was obvious. When our hands brushed, I felt every hair on my arm stand up. When he leaned over to whisper something to me during a dinner and I felt the warmth of his breath stir the loose curls at the nape of my neck, I could barely stand it. I wanted to fling myself onto him. Only Porter had made my blood boil like this in our early days, and I'd been a mere teenager then. I felt young again with Jackson.

It was quickly becoming an affair.

Now, I was not completely opposed to an affair, and certainly I hadn't let my marriage hold me back overseas. But this time, I chose to be cautious. This wasn't Japan or Borneo or India. I couldn't pretend that what I did here in New York wouldn't be noticed. The gossips had gotten used to me now, and my name was gracing tabloid pages once more. There had been plenty of snide comments about how little time Harry and I spent together. When we were overseas, these had been easier to ignore, but now I was reading the papers every day. I worried that our marriage was starting to fail to accomplish one of its purposes. Entering into a full-blown affair with another man, especially a younger man, would ensure that the gossips took a closer look at Harry's life. It was all too easy to imagine what they would find.

On the other hand, didn't I deserve to be happy? I didn't dare ask a medium that question, as I worried they would tell me I didn't. For myself, I answered yes.

So when Jackson reached for my hand in the dark at the theater, I let him take it. And if we were in a box instead of a row, and no one else could see any lower than our shoulders, we might do a bit more. Hands could roam without betraying confidences as long as we kept our faces neutral. It became a bit of a game. As much as I wanted to, I never even kissed him, not while I was still married to Harry.

But it was becoming clear that something had to give. I hadn't told Jackson the truth about my marriage, mainly because it wasn't my truth to tell. But it was becoming clear to me that I didn't want a secret lover, not anymore. I didn't want a marriage to Harry with Jackson on the side. I wanted Jackson. Publicly. Properly. And there was only one way that would happen.

I was very fond of Harry, and he was fond of me, but fondness isn't always enough.

The end of my marriage to Harry Gillig was nothing like the end of my marriage to Porter Ashe. There were no fights, no lawsuits. No blood drawn, no tears shed, or at least not many.

I chose my moment. Frank was out of town on business, so I knew it would be just the two of us, which was important. Harry and Frank were so close that my husband sometimes substituted his friend's judgment for his own. I didn't want to take the chance that Frank might have an opinion running counter to my interests. My marriage to Harry had never been just the two of us. Ending it needed to be.

I didn't always choose the menu when we dined at home. I'd hired an excellent cook and trusted her to do the choosing. But this time, I wanted to serve Harry's favorite wine, hoping that a glass or two would make him a bit more amenable. I didn't want him falling-down drunk—not likely, as I'd only seen him that way two or three times our whole marriage—but wine made him cheerful and a bit slower, and that was exactly how I wanted him for this conversation.

So at my behest, the cook served Dover sole in butter sauce, new potatoes on the side, which would go well with the white burgundy my husband so enjoyed. I waited until his first glass was empty and the second had been poured. I had asked the servants to leave the room after serving the fish, told them we would help ourselves to dessert when the time came. No one asked any questions. They weren't paid for their curiosity.

"Harry," I began. "Remember why we got married?"

His eyes went hooded, an air of suspicion creeping into his features, just like it had back at the New York Yacht Club party when he knew I didn't quite remember him and was trying to hide that fact. "I do," he said, but nothing more.

"Our arrangement… I don't think I want to continue it."

"Oh." His voice stayed flat. "You want to…change the arrangement?"

"I want to end the arrangement."

He gave no visible sign of understanding, but he knew.

Gently, I went on, "The marriage part of it, I mean. I want a divorce, I guess I should say. Oh, Harry, I'm so sorry. You're such a good friend. And it's been…it's been the best marriage I ever had, that's for sure."

"Then why?" I'd never heard him so terse. There's nothing quite as chilling as silence from a talkative man. But I knew why his words wouldn't come. He was afraid.

I didn't want to hurt him, but it was inescapable. I wanted the hurt at least to be brief, so I wouldn't dance around it. I owed him complete honesty. "The reason isn't highly original, I'm afraid. I've met someone."

He looked down at his plate, gathering himself. But when he looked up again, his eyes were sharp. "Is it love?"

I considered this. Truthfully, I said, "It could be."

"Why don't you wait until you know for sure?"

"Harry," I said, "I can't wait. And I mean—I already know I love him. And I believe he loves me. It's just the physical expression… I want to be unencumbered before we take that step."

"You haven't expressed yourselves to each other physically? And you think he loves you?"

Finding the right words had seemed like a challenge. It was rapidly becoming impossible. I wish I'd had an extra glass of the white burgundy myself, to loosen my tongue. "The feeling is there. The urgency is even there. We've just been very careful."

Harry had no visible reaction, tapping his fork against his plate lightly, as if he were trying to do so without making a sound.

I said, my voice a bit tighter than it had been, "I'm doing the right thing here, Harry."

"Whatever you want to do with him," Harry said, still sounding obstinate, "I won't stand in your way. I never have. Why would I start now?"

"You won't mean to," I said. "But being married stands in my way, Harry. In being able to truly love someone out in the open for the world to see. You have to understand that."

His voice got sharper. I was glad I'd sent the servants away. "Do I? Do I 'have to,' Amy? It doesn't stand in my way, you know. Why can't you be more like me?"

"Believe me, I wish I could." Instead of lashing out, snapping at him, I tried my best. "I'm in awe of you, Harry. You're a wonderful man."

"But not wonderful enough to stay married to," he said, and there was bitterness there.

I couldn't let it shake my resolve. "Not when I'm in love with someone else," I said as gently as I could manage. "I'm sorry."

I could tell by the set of his shoulders that despite his anger, he was already beginning to resign himself to the need for this to happen, but still, he protested once more. "You know love isn't enough. You were in love with Porter, and look how that turned out."

Whether or not he meant offense by that, I didn't take any. "I was seventeen years old and stupid."

"You're not stupid anymore?"

"I may be, in some ways, but not this one. Believe me."

There was immense sadness in my husband's voice when he said, "Oh, I do."

"I'm sorry," I said again. "If I thought it was sustainable, I'd do it. If I thought I were capable of keeping how I feel about him under wraps. But I want—I want to love him without hiding."

Harry looked at me with wet eyes and said, "How lovely that you have that option, then."

My attempts at polite resolve fell away. I stood from the table and flung myself toward him, crying, "I'm so sorry, Harry, so sorry."

He caught me in his arms. We cried together.

The divorce was amicable and straightforward. The laws of New York were not so exacting as those of California, and if I said we had mutually decided we didn't want to be married to each other anymore, the State of New York was willing to take my word for it. Divorce was a completely different enterprise this time around. I almost didn't feel like anything had ended without the suffering.

But the papers came, all duly stamped, and the deed was done.

I was a divorcée once more. I shook my head in wonder, realizing that at one time, I would have considered a second divorce unthinkable, but then again, I had thought the same of a second marriage.

Perhaps I would be a married woman again and perhaps I wouldn't. But I was certainly a woman in love.

CHAPTER FIFTEEN

It is not the having of things or people or experiences that gives happiness. It is the magic moment when your hand just closes on the thing.

—AC

I'd intended to give Jackson the good news in private, but the universe had something different in mind. He'd been traveling on tour, a rare event, gone to California to meet with some fancy investor about mounting a new musical based on one of his songs. He'd been so delighted and proud of himself, I hadn't wanted to make our last meeting before he left about me, so he had no inkling of what was to come.

In his absence, of course, I could entertain myself. And there was a perfect occasion to do so. The ambassador of Japan was having a party, and I'd decided it was safe to go by myself given my attachment to the nation. My newly minted ex-husband Harry wouldn't be there; he'd left town the week before. The papers would probably say it was to soothe a broken heart, but the truth was he'd been planning the trip for months. He'd told me he was going to Germany for two weeks, asked if he should reconsider given our situation, and I'd said no. I hadn't asked him whether Frank would be accompanying him. That wasn't my business anymore, if it ever had been. I still had a pang of friendly feeling when I thought about Frank, whose company I had enjoyed, but I doubted I'd see much of him after my split from Harry.

I told myself there were plenty of potential friends in the world, men and women alike, and I had the rest of my life to meet every last one of them and find the ones I liked best.

It was a pleasure to sort through my cabinets and retrieve one of my best silk robes from my time in Japan. I caught a whiff of chrysanthemum in its silken folds, and for a moment, I was swept right back to that house outside Tokyo, all red lacquer and silk screens. Before Huntingdon-Meer fell through the wall, before Takamine stole me and then was stolen from me, I'd been happy there. It wasn't out of the question, I told myself as I dressed in a radiant display of color and grace, that I could be happy again.

As far as I knew, Jackson wasn't due back until the next Monday. When I arrived, fashionably late, I greeted our host with enthusiasm, then made a beeline for the refreshments. I intended to toast my new freedom with champagne. When I noticed the familiar set of shoulders, back turned to me, at the precise station I was heading for, I was taken aback. Could it be Jackson? He hadn't sent word he was coming back early, but then, there was no special reason for him to. It wasn't as if he was my husband.

But oh, I realized, how I wanted him to be.

He noted my presence and immediately grabbed a flute of champagne. He walked over and handed it to me. I took it without a word. He raised his glass to mine in a toast. I raised mine in response.

"Well, hello, Mrs. Gillig," he said.

"Hello, Mr. Gouraud," I said. Then I realized he'd provided the perfect opening for my news, which I couldn't keep to myself any longer. "And actually, about that Mrs. Gillig business. There's been an update."

His eyebrows didn't go up, but his gaze shifted, and I heard his breath catch. I doubted anyone else had noticed the difference in him, but I certainly did.

He said in what sounded like a barely interested voice, "An update?"

"I will no longer be using Mr. Gillig's last name, as Mr. Gillig is no longer my husband. The papers will be trumpeting the news tomorrow."

"I'm sorry," he said, glancing at the others around us, his voice entirely proper.

Softly, I replied, "I'm not."

That made his mouth quirk up at the corner.

I said, "I will of course be retreating to spend some time at home alone, as is appropriate."

"Well. We'll miss you on the scene."

"You needn't," I said, and this time, he didn't manage to cover his reaction. Luckily, it didn't seem like anyone was paying us much attention.

"Mrs....um, if you're not Mrs. Gillig, what do I call you?"

"You, Jackson, call me Aimée."

He smiled at that, not too wide, moving back to propriety. "Aimée. Yes. I suppose I'll call you that, if the wags don't think it's too familiar."

I shrugged but kept my voice low. "I don't particularly care what they think."

"The papers...what are they going to say the cause of the divorce is? If I may ask."

"We grew apart," I said airily. "Which shouldn't be hard for them to swallow. They've had fun pointing out how apart Harry and I have been for years. I'm sure at least one will make the oh-so-clever observation that as, some might say, we never seemed that married in the first place, it will be hard to tell the difference."

"Well. You may not be all that sorry, but take my condolences anyway."

I stepped closer to him, careful to remain outwardly proper. But I kept my voice low and husky, and I knew exactly how this tone affected Jackson. I'd used it in our box seats at the opera to great effect. "Jackson Gouraud, please understand condolences aren't what I want from you."

He swallowed. "No?"

"I could tell you. Or I could show you. Tomorrow evening? My place on Fifth?"

Words seemed to have deserted him. He only nodded. The look in his eyes at that moment will stay in my heart forever.

And when he came to my apartment the next night as commanded, neither of us needed many words to say what we wanted to say to each other now that I was finally free. Our bodies spoke for us, and they spoke loud and clear.

As the new century dawned, my life became a new thing once more. I traded in the pied-à-terre for a more spacious town house on Fifty-Seventh and continued to maintain my Larchmont residence as well, as I needed both for different reasons. Among other things, I'd become more serious about training and showing French bulldogs, and I couldn't simply pack a half-dozen animals in my overnight bag. Jackson tended to stay the night in Larchmont but not Manhattan. Of course he had his own house very nearby. I didn't stay overnight there, but I did sometimes visit late in the evenings, and he had to help me redo my hair before I could be seen outside afterward. He became quite an adept hairstylist. I might have hired him for the purpose if I hadn't already had a number of other, more unique uses I enjoyed putting him to.

I realized then that I was doing what the mystic had told me: my name was new and my life was new. Now I needed to hold my head up high. There was no shame in divorce, I told myself, not in this new era. If men and women found themselves unsuited, it would cause the least pain to anyone for them to go ahead and part. Any reasonable person had to see the logic in that. And I didn't have to associate with unreasonable people.

So it was time to see and be seen as my new self.

My first attempt to establish myself anew on the New York scene was a miserable failure, the exact type you might expect: I threw a party, and no one came. I invited all the highest of high society, up to and including Mrs. Astor, and though I knew she had no affection for "new money," I thought my transcontinental railroad money might be old enough to meet her standard. Turned out it wasn't. I won't dwell on the failure except to say that it provided me a fine opportunity to see Jackson Gouraud in a new light. When we were sipping coffee one morning and I complained to him about the poorly attended event, he said, "You should have asked me. I could have told you she'd never come."

"I didn't think she would. But I hoped."

"You invited all the wrong people."

"Wrong from whose perspective?"

"Wrong if you want to have fun. You want to have fun, don't you?"

"I absolutely do."

"Well then," Jackson said and grinned. "Next time, we'll work together on the guest list. And it'll be the best and most delightful and most ridiculous party this town has ever seen."

The party we threw together might not have merited all those superlatives, but it was head and shoulders above the party no one came to. After that, I never threw a party without consulting with Jackson. Then I did fewer and fewer things without Jackson at all. He had breakfast in my dining room in Larchmont so often that the cook added crumpets, Jackson's avowed favorite, to the regular menu. When I acquired a finicky new puppy and kept her in my lap all through breakfast one day, Jackson not only didn't complain, he offered to hold her for me and drip milk into her mouth while I ate my shirred eggs.

Jackson and I quickly became first-nighters, people who showed up for the first night of important Broadway shows and whose opinions mattered a great deal in that world. In a way, we were the perfect couple for the scene: me with my money and him with his friends.

The fact that he was so talented added to our cachet. I began to receive invitations to the openings of shows that hadn't even been fully written yet. I dutifully marked my calendar, ordered or refinished gowns, and piled on the pearls.

Was this the pinnacle of my happiness? Feeling like I'd been born for this moment, this life, this man? Having lost so much so far in my life, I realized I was afraid of being too happy. I was worried that what I had could and would be suddenly taken away.

I thought about that mystic in Spain, the one who had warned me one of my husbands would bury me. But he'd said it was the thirteenth. Keeping track, Jackson was only my third. Of course, I loved him so much I think that even if he'd been my thirteenth, I would have married him anyway. He could bury me if he liked. He could do absolutely anything. I was his. Luckily, he felt the same way about me—that he was utterly and completely mine—and we would never harm each other, never. The trust between us was absolute.

On my third try, I'd done what I'd wanted to do from the beginning: forge an alliance between partners, more equal and honest than the marriage between my mother and father moving in their separate circles. Jackson and I had separate circles of influence, yes, but they substantially overlapped. We could see his friends or mine, day or night, always together, and no one would bat an eye. We belonged in each other's spaces.

We belonged together.

———————

Jackson and I couldn't decide whether to make our wedding a huge social event or a quiet, private ceremony between the two of us. We talked about it for months, until I wondered if talking about marriage gave me more pleasure than actually being married. It also planted another seed in my head, one I had to share with Jackson the very day it occurred to me.

"Jackson," I said, "do you actually want to marry me?"

"Of course I do!"

"Then why haven't we done it already?"

"Speed isn't the measure of passion," he said. "I know you know that."

"I know. But it feels like you might be hesitating."

"I'm not hesitating any more than you are. We just need to agree on our plans." He paused, scratched his elbow, lowered his brow. "Wait. Aimée, are you asking me if I have doubts because you're afraid to tell me that you're the one who has doubts?"

"No! I have no doubts at all!" I meant it. I hid nothing from Jackson. I'd been intimate with many men in many ways, but never like this. That was what I understood love to be now: no veiled allusions, no games or bluffs, no looking past each other's faults, no walls between. It was my only chance of making this marriage work. And I was terrified it wouldn't.

Jackson wrapped me in his arms. "You're committed. I'm committed. Our marriage ceremony, whenever we have one and whatever it looks like, will simply confirm what already exists."

I snuggled closer. "I like thinking of it that way."

"So," he said. "What sort of party should we host next?"

"An excellent one."

I could see his mind whirring already, flipping through ideas one after the other. He had a particular look when he was concentrating intently like this. I found him especially beautiful in those moments.

"Ah, I know," he said, and I was almost disappointed to hear him speak, I'd been enjoying so much watching him thinking. "Here's the answer. The run of *Mr. Devil-May-Care* concludes at the end of next month. Shall we throw a shindig to celebrate?"

"Yes. With a theme."

"Of course with a theme!" he said, mock outraged. "What sort of party would it be if we didn't capitalize on a *theme*, Aimée?"

Then he started tickling me, and we didn't talk about the party for a while, but we both knew his idea was a perfect one.

I threw myself into planning an outsize celebration, with a "Devil May Care" theme to honor the musical and its cast. Costumes were encouraged, which meant no one would be turned away at the door for not sporting devil horns, but we'd keep a few pairs to hand out to those who appeared without them. Snacks would include deviled eggs, deviled crab, deviled ham. Of course dessert would have to be the delicious chocolate cake known as devil's food.

We invited three hundred, and Jackson and I built the list together, making sure it included all our nearest and dearest. It would be a party to end all parties.

When the night came, I donned my scarlet gown with excitement and laid on the maquillage with a trowel.

The room swirled with black and red, everyone having stepped up to the occasion of deviling down. Jackson and I greeted everyone as they entered, sending them off with a pleasant curse into the maelstrom of the party. A brooding harp played. What looked like live flames leapt in every room; those who investigated more closely found that these were ingenious little lamps that used fans and fabric to simulate fire.

After a few hours, champagne in hand, Jackson called me up to the performance area in the larger ballroom, where the evening's entertainment had been unfolding. I knew what we had planned, and the next performer on the docket was a children's choir, so I assumed I was being asked to introduce the act. But when I looked around, I saw no children. Instead, a woman at the front of the room wore the white raiment of an angel. I blinked at her.

For a moment, I thought I saw her, the woman in white, walking among the party guests and climbing up onto a piece of furniture so she could be seen. My heart was in my throat, and I staggered back, bumping into a horned demon who apologized politely. When I looked at the woman in white again, she was just an acquaintance in an angel costume, not the figure from my dreams. I placed my gloved hand on my chest to quiet my heart, strode forward with a smile, and took my place beside Jackson.

To the assembled crowd, Jackson called, "May I have your attention, please! Everyone! Your attention, just for a moment! We have a little surprise in store."

I almost asked, *We do?* But I let it ride. Jackson reached out for my hand, and I slid my fingers into his. He squeezed gently.

Then he turned outward and said loudly to the assembled crowd, "This isn't just a party."

I looked at him, quizzical, my face asking the question my lips did not.

He repeated, to me, "This isn't just a party."

The woman in the angel's garb put one hand on my shoulder and the other on Jackson's, smiled out at the crowd, and said, in an angel-sweet voice, "Dearly beloved."

Recognition dawned.

Hundreds of faces turned our way, expectant. They'd heard those words before, and though they weren't expecting to hear them in a room like this on a night like this, they quickly made the adjustment.

For my part, as soon as I understood what Jackson had done, I couldn't stop smiling.

"It's not just a party," I said softly, watching his face to make sure I'd gotten it right. "It's our wedding."

He tapped the end of my nose with a gentle finger. "Spot on, Mrs. Gouraud."

"Ah, my beloved," I said in a voice of utter wonder, "you are a devil indeed."

He grinned just like one. And I was sure, in that moment, I'd never loved anyone in the world more.

Though we didn't know it at the time, two of the guests at the party that turned into a wedding were destined for each other. One was a delightful young man of twenty years, an actor of some talent and one of our frequent dinner guests. He often sang along as Jackson played piano, and though other guests at our parties were often better singers, none was as enthusiastic or welcomed as Powers. He had a spark people loved, a way of reflecting light. The young woman was far less outgoing, even shy, and as far as I recalled, this was the first party of ours she ever attended, though she was always invited.

The young man was Jackson's brother Powers. The young woman was Gladys Ashe, who I'd given birth to during my marriage to Porter Ashe, legally not my daughter but my sister.

They began seeing each other in secret, not knowing whether we'd approve of them getting to know each other. Truth be told, I'm not sure whether I would have warned her away or not. It seemed a complicated situation. Who would get themselves into something complicated when they didn't need to? Weren't there dozens of young men who'd trip over their own toes to enjoy the company of the lovely Gladys?

But at the time, I knew none of it. After my surprise wedding, I was too wrapped up in a kind of newlywed life I'd never quite had. I'd been a passionate newlywed with Porter, indulging in naughty pastimes all over the Continent; with Harry, we'd sailed off to Europe and then Japan, where he and Frank seemed more like a married couple and I the beloved friend tagging along. I knew my honeymoon with Jackson wouldn't repeat that mistake, but nor did I want to trek to the places I'd visited with either previous husband. I remember thinking that this third husband would absolutely be the final one, that this was how I'd prove that Spanish fortune teller wrong. I'd made a misstep in choosing Porter and then again in saying yes to Harry. But I hadn't been such a fool with Jackson. Jackson would be forever.

So Jackson and I celebrated our marriage not with travel but with a new advancement in tattoo application called tattaugraphs. We'd mark ourselves with something that would, fittingly, endure. We came up with our own original design of two snakes, one twisted into the initials AG and the other the initials JG, which were permanently applied to my right arm and Jackson's left.

The tattaugraph process used an electric needle instead of the slower, more painstaking practice of inking and inserting the needle by hand. The soreness of my arm was more than I remembered from my previous inkings. Perhaps I had simply been in a sake haze in Japan when I'd had those patterns done. But Jackson tenderly dressed the sore area and painted the area with featherlight kisses. His lips against my skin stirred my blood, and I reached for him, and his nursing turned into something different altogether.

None of this is to say our lives were trouble-free. We were married in May 1901; disaster struck before the end of the year.

In December, we went a bit overboard on our first year decorating the Larchmont house for Christmas. I'd paid professionals to festoon the mantels with greenery and red ribbons, not to mention sleigh bells galore, but I felt a few things needed to be slightly adjusted. I was in the front parlor with both feet on the cushion of a chair and my hands retacking a crooked swag of evergreen when Jackson entered. I caught the blur of his shape moving but kept my eyes on the task in front of me.

"Oh good," I said. "You can give me your opinion."

"Aimée, would you get down from there?" he asked. I should have noticed the tone in his voice, but I was preoccupied.

Holding the swag higher, I said, "Does this look straight now?"

"It wasn't straight before?"

"The right side was too high. Now I think the left might be. Hard to tell from here. What do you think?" I held the greens up a couple of inches higher and squinted down at him.

He replied, "Just leave it for now, and come down."

"I can't. It'll break if I just let it put all the weight on one nail. Then we'll have to retack the whole thing on both sides, from scratch, and it'll double the trouble. So higher or lower?" I raised it an inch, paused, then lowered it an inch.

"It doesn't matter."

"Pick one!" I demanded with loving exasperation.

"Lower," he said. "Now get down here."

He said the last bit lovingly at least and stood next to my chair to fasten both hands around my waist and lower me down. I was glad he was there. I had climbed up without much thought for whether the dismount would be more of a challenge, and it helped to have him steady me.

Once my feet were on the floor, I said, "Next, the dining room."

But he put his hands on my shoulders, steadying me in a different way. "I need to give you some news."

"I hope it's good news," I said, wiping my hands on my skirt.

"I'm afraid not. It's about your mother," Jackson said.

"What about her? Is she inviting herself to dinner again? Cook told me after the last time she needs at least a day's notice or there might not be enough to go around. Trying to make two chops work for three people is just mayhem."

"Aimée," Jackson said insistently.

Then, by the tone of his voice, I knew.

I had the oddest sense that saying it aloud would make it true, and if I didn't say it, it might be something else. So instead, I ventured, "Is she…sick?"

Jackson's hands warmed me, but I still felt cold. He said slowly, "I'm sorry, Aimée. It must have been her heart. A problem no one knew about."

"Until it was too late," I said, still not wanting to say the word.

"Exactly."

Panic was starting to set in, but I fought it down. I said, "What else is there to know?"

"The housekeeper found her. Sometime after breakfast. She was fine this morning. But this afternoon…we lost her, Aimée."

For a moment, I felt I was floating above my body, watching it in motion. Watching myself reach out for Jackson, pressing myself into his arms. Watching myself swallow, over and over again, hoping to keep back the tears. Higher and higher I floated.

But then I slammed back into my body, and I felt everything. And it hurt. Good God, did it hurt.

"What about Gladys?" I said. In my mind, I saw a girl hunched over and sobbing, her small shoulders shaking with grief.

"Gladys?" repeated Jackson.

"Is there someone there to take care of her? Make sure she's fed, cared for?"

"We can invite her to stay with us. I don't know if she'll come, but if you want her to, we can ask."

"She can't stay by herself, can she? Poor girl."

Jackson said carefully, "Aimée, Gladys isn't a little girl. She's over eighteen. A woman."

My brain had been jarred so hard by the loss, I realized I hadn't actually been picturing Gladys, not as she was. The crying girl in my mind's eye was me. When I lost my father, I was ten years old. I was thinking Gladys would need what I had needed. But the situations were not the same.

To Jackson, I said, "I got confused."

He held me more tightly. "It will be a confusing time."

I had nothing in me to respond to that. He didn't seem to mind my silence.

Jackson sent telegrams to spread the news to family, thank goodness, and my mother's attorneys did a great deal of the work thereafter. They informed the newspapers so obituaries could be run; they opened the file that specified what to do in the case of her death, all about the funeral arrangements and the reading of the will. There was very little for me to do other than mourn, and I didn't know how to do that. Losing my mother at the not so tender age of thirty-seven was nothing like losing my father at ten. I was an adult now, a married woman. I hoped the newspapers would be more respectful this time.

My mother had been, at different points in my life, my most favorite and least favorite person; my feelings about her were no less complex once she was no longer living.

I would have liked the chance to say goodbye to her, though I don't know what I would have said. She'd died so suddenly. I was right next door. I could've easily been the one to find her, but I wasn't. I hadn't been the daughter she wanted. Had she died thinking I'd failed her? I would never be able to make that right.

I moved in a haze. Sitting across from Jackson at breakfast several days later, I blurted, "I should see if Gladys wants to travel together to the funeral."

Jackson looked up, then back down again. "She's already left."

"Ah." I couldn't tell whether I was disappointed or relieved.

The night before we left for the funeral, opening my eyes in bed long after dark but well before sunrise, I realized that the woman in white had not warned me of my mother's death. I felt oddly outraged by this, as if she had somehow let me down. Or maybe I just wanted someone else to blame. There was no point in trying to figure out what my supernatural visitor intended. I didn't even understand the living.

The trip across the country wasn't the worst of my life, but it was far from the best. The sound of metal scraping on metal, the chug of the engine, the blast of the horn, somehow they all sounded mournful. Jackson did his best to distract me, but I kept losing track of the thread of conversation, and in the end, I suggested he read a book while I stared out the window. I couldn't focus. I could think of little but my own flaws. I drank too much and slept fitfully and emerged on the far coast almost as much of a mess as I'd been when Porter kidnapped our daughter almost fifteen years before.

The funeral was glorious. Mama would have loved it. Which made sense, since she'd organized every detail. She'd even determined which mourners would sit where. My mother had kindly put Jennie and I in separate pews with our husbands and Gladys between us, though whether she'd done it for Jennie's sake or for mine, I didn't know.

After the somber funeral, at the festive reception, I sought out the daughter whose mother I had never really been.

"I'm so sorry for your loss," I said to Gladys, meaning every word.

"And I for yours," she said. Her voice was low and musical. She seemed like a stranger.

On a whim, I blurted, "When we get back to New York, maybe we can spend some more time together. More than we used to."

Her expression was skeptical, but her voice was not unkind as she said, "I'm old enough that I don't need a new mother."

"Whether you need me or not," I said, trying desperately to keep a grip on myself, "I'm here. We're both a little more alone than we were before. Perhaps you want that for yourself; perhaps you enjoy solitude. I don't know you well enough to say. But if you think you have room for someone in your life, I'd relish being that someone."

"We'll see," she said, which was about all I could hope for. After all that had passed between us, or more accurately what hadn't, I could expect very little. But there was still a kernel of hope that this time, in this one case, I might get more than I deserved.

Still, even though we took the same train back to New York, she didn't speak to me or seek me out. I sent a few notes to her house but received no replies. One day, I ginned up the courage to stop by unannounced and was told by the maid that she'd gone traveling. No more detail, no warning, just that. *Miss Ashe has gone traveling*, the young woman said and turned her face away as she closed the door.

It was sad to lose my mother, but it seemed that I had lost my daughter too, without ever really having known her.

CHAPTER SIXTEEN

Oh, the people, the human beings of this world! What a kaleidoscope they make with their changing colors, their twisting shapes, their constantly transmuting characters and variegated souls.

—AC

T he year 1903 proved highly eventful for us, not entirely by choice. We shut up the Larchmont house as usual in early summer and headed off to Germany for the season. In our absence, the Larchmont house burned down, everything in it completely lost, destroyed. The good news was that we were half a world away when it happened. Our lives were never in danger. Given that, the complete destruction of a house and its contents seemed minor. Physical treasures had been destroyed, and I did mourn the loss of so many souvenirs from my Eastern travels, but I liked to think of the burning as a purge of the unnecessary. It was a very Buddhist way to look at the loss. I was still trying to be a good Buddhist.

The American newspapers covered the fire, of course, most of them managing to restrain themselves from suggesting I'd brought the misfortune on myself with my wicked ways. Their tone toward me seemed to have mellowed after the initial scandal of my marriage to Jackson—a *third* marriage, and to a younger man!—had faded. They disapproved of our parties, but they disapproved of, say, Mrs. Vanderbilt in the exact same tone. Their columnists pointed and glared and then detailed every single outfit, decoration, and music choice down to the gnat's eyelash because they knew that if they didn't, the public would seek out the details from their competitors instead.

We rebuilt the Larchmont house bigger and better. We used the excuse to increase the size of the ballroom so we could invite more guests to our extravagant fetes. Our house was not our household. We could and did live anywhere. Most of my show dogs remained year-round in Larchmont—they'd been unharmed in the fire, thank goodness—but I'd brought a precious few pets with me. My favorite was my French bulldog Archimedes, who liked to lie by the fireplace and lick the tips of my fingers, then roll over and fall asleep on his back in the most undignified way. Jackson and I never failed to giggle at him when he did so.

We had just returned from a midday stroll when we noticed a card on the tray by the door. I opened it, barely paying attention, and then when I saw the words on it, I nearly squeaked with surprise. "Jackson!"

"Yes?"

In answer, I simply passed him the card. He was no less stunned.

"Mr. and Mrs. Powers Gouraud?" Jackson said in a disbelieving voice. "Since when was there a Mrs. Powers Gouraud? And who in the world is she?"

"Who in the world indeed?" I mused. I liked Powers well enough, but the relationship between a brother and sister-in-law is nothing compared to the bond between brothers who've known each other since childhood. If Jackson had no idea who his brother had married, I had less than no idea. Sometimes all that was required between spouses was a sympathetic echo.

Jackson was still reading the brief letter, searching its words over and over as if some clue hiding there might make it all make sense. To me, he said, "He says they got married in London. Do you think she's English?"

"Could be! Or could be Norwegian or American or from outer space for all we know."

"Hmm, I hope it isn't outer space, for all our sakes," he said, gaining back some of his good humor. "Though wouldn't that be a great tune?" He immediately starting humming. "Mm, hm-hm, my brother's wife is from Venus, mm, hm-hm, she must like his—"

"Jackson!" I shrilled, purely for the fun of it. We both fell out laughing.

I would've laughed less if I'd realized who he'd married, but they'd kept it from us on purpose, so I didn't blame myself one bit.

We had the table laid for a luncheon more American than German, as I didn't want to risk falling asleep on our guests in the early afternoon, which might happen if I stuffed myself with wurst and boiled potatoes. I was checking on the champagne to make sure it was properly chilled when the doorbell rang, and our German majordomo opened the door to Jackson and his mysterious bride.

You could have knocked me over with a feather when I realized that the dark-haired woman standing next to him, a shy smile on her face, wasn't a stranger at all.

"Gladys?" I asked in shock. She wore a more modest, formal costume than I was used to. It made her look quite grown-up. Or perhaps that was just the situation. Perhaps she looked more mature because she had shown up married, half a world away from where I'd ever expected to see her face.

"Otherwise known as Mrs. Powers Gouraud," said her bridegroom with a look of beaming pride on his face. Powers had a reputation as a prankster, but his expression made clear this was no joke.

"We've done something foolish," Powers said.

"Oh, it wasn't that foolish," said Gladys.

"I suppose for me it wasn't," he answered. "I'm not so sure about you."

She rolled her eyes at him, but with clear affection, and I understood that this was the dynamic they'd settled into.

"Powers!" exclaimed Jackson. "Did you go and get married on us?"

"I mean, you weren't foremost on our minds," said Powers, "but I suppose so, yes."

After a chorus of hearty congratulations, coupes were produced, and we toasted merrily to the happy couple.

I leaned over to Gladys and cupped her cheek in my hand. I had often searched her face for signs of resemblance and rarely seen any—she was all Porter—but today, on this occasion, I thought perhaps her eyes seemed a little like mine. I said, "Congratulations, dear. I'm so happy you found each other."

"We wouldn't have, if not for you," she said.

"You might have." I shrugged. "Fate has done stranger things."

Powers, who had overheard just the last bit of our exchange, said, "Aimée, are you calling me a stranger thing?"

I shook my head with a laugh.

"You know what the best thing about this marriage is," he said.

Jackson interjected, "Well, you can't talk about that at luncheon!" and the two brothers fell into boisterous laughter. Gladys and I exchanged an indulgent sigh.

Powers said, "What I meant was, because of the, let's say unique, nature of this family, I now get to introduce myself as my own cousin."

Jackson's expression was confused, so I said, "Because you married your brother's wife's daughter?"

"And her sister!" Powers crowed.

I glanced over at Gladys, but she wasn't meeting my eyes, and I suspected she had told her new husband that she didn't find this sort of thing funny. I certainly didn't. But I had a brand new brother-in-law who was very special to my dear, dear husband, and it was in my best interest to keep the peace. My feelings weren't so delicate as all that.

So I looked back to Powers and forced a laugh. "I'm not even sure I remember who I am to any of you!"

Jackson said, "I know you're the love of my life," and laid a showy kiss on my cheek with an audible smack of the lips.

The rest of the wedding story came out over champagne and chicken salad.

"We were sorry not to invite you," said Jackson, "but my wife insisted on inviting no one at all."

I thought fleetingly of my wedding to Harry, which had been only large enough to include two witnesses and a judge. Tactfully, I said, "That's her right."

Gladys, looking down at her napkin, said, "I didn't want anything large. I don't like crowds."

I'd known that about her, I realized. Gladys was a private person. She wouldn't have enjoyed a big formal wedding; it seemed a good sign that Powers had understood that and not given her one.

Jackson said, "So where do you go from here? Back to London?"

His brother answered. "We think Paris for a while. Right, my love?"

Pink touched his bride's cheeks as she said, "Yes, my love."

My husband was grinning widely. "Well, if you do, we'll try to join you there. Aimée, you don't dislike Paris, am I correct?"

I returned his grin. "Yes. You can certainly say I don't dislike it."

Gladys turned to me, and something shifted in her manner. "As Jackson said. We didn't want you to be offended that we didn't invite you to the wedding. Or let you know, before that, we'd begun to see each other."

"That's just logic," I told her, my heart speeding up at the intimacy of the conversation. She seemed to really be trying to connect with me for what I thought might be the very first time. "If you realized your attraction wouldn't last, you didn't want to disappoint us. Or something like that?"

She smiled shyly at me. "Something like that."

Jackson added, "But it has lasted."

They turned to each other. Powers said, "It certainly has."

All four of us, in two pairs, had arrived at wedded bliss.

That evening, in the privacy of our own rooms, Jackson said, "It's hard to believe she's your daughter."

"She isn't really," I said. "I mean, she is, but…well, you know the situation. She wasn't really raised as mine."

"Do you regret that?"

I took on an admonishing tone. "Jackson! Are we having a serious conversation after throwing back that much champagne? It seems ill-advised."

"Was it that much?" he mused. "Seemed modest to me."

"Remind me not to rely on you to define modesty."

"We both know you don't."

"True. In any case," I said, rolling down one stocking and shedding it briskly, "that's what happened, and there's no sense second-guessing it now. My mother raised her more than I did. Maybe that's what sent her looking for a partner after Mama died. The company."

"Powers is more than just company."

"Of course he is! And they'll be good for each other. She'll steady him. He'll liven her up a bit."

"And what about children?"

"What about them?"

Jackson hung his necktie on the doorknob, looking away from me. "The two of them together seem good, but there's always a chance they'll become more than two. I wonder if they'll have a big family. Do you know if Gladys wants one?"

"We never talked about it," I said, shedding my other stocking. I had a tendency to quickly make our second home as messy as our first, but we had a large household staff here. Even if I left both stockings on the floor, someone would deal with them in the morning. Sometimes I thought that was what my money primarily bought: the ability to neglect chickens I knew would never come home to roost.

"And what about you? Did you ever want a big family?"

I shot him a quizzical look.

He sat down next to me, putting his hands on my bare knees, and asked earnestly, "Do you think you'd want to have more children?"

"I'm not sure," I said, my voice cautious. I felt more naked than I was. "Is this something we should have discussed before we married?"

He said, "Perhaps," and my stomach dropped.

Maybe this was the thing I'd been dreading. The thing that would tear us apart. The hidden crack in what seemed like such a solid foundation.

But something told me not to lie, no matter what. "I hadn't thought that was something you wanted. It's not something I've been thinking about."

"I hadn't been," he said. "But the longer we're together, the more we share—I just feel like we could share that with children too."

"I'm not sure…" I wasn't sure how to say what came next.

"Aimée?" he said gently. He reached out for my hand and held it. As if I'd articulated my doubts aloud, he added, "You can say anything."

"I'm not sure I can still have children," I blurted. I rarely noticed or cared that I was a decade older than my husband, but now I felt every one of my thirty-nine years. I was terrified to look at his face. I gathered the strength to do so by looking down at our entwined hands. He hadn't pulled away. He'd heard what I'd said and not immediately rejected me. So I dared to meet his gaze.

I saw only love and concern there. He patted my hand, then said, "That doesn't matter to me. I'd prefer to adopt, even, if that's all right with you."

"Can I give it some thought?" I thought about the last time I'd asked a man for time to consider, back when Harry Gillig had asked me to marry him. This decision was no less momentous.

"Absolutely," Jackson assured me. "And maybe we can visit the foundling hospital together. So you can see what I've seen."

"When did you visit a foundling hospital?"

"I was writing a song. For that musical about the orphan. I needed to write from an orphan's perspective, so I wanted to see what it was like to grow up as one. Aimée, those children." There was pain in his eyes. "They have nothing. And then I come home to you, and we have everything, and I just…"

I understood. "You want to give some to them."

"Yes. But not just things. Love. We have love, Aimée, so much of it. Can you understand why I want to share?"

"I can," I said, and I did. So I agreed to visit the foundling hospital when we were back in New York in the fall.

Jackson was absolutely right. Seeing those children lacking every good thing, everything I'd taken for granted, made me want to gather all of them into my arms and make sure they never wanted for anything again.

I would never say so to another living soul, but the process of becoming a mother by adoption was far, far preferable to becoming one the old-fashioned way. Gladys had been thrust upon me in the most painful of ways, emotionally and physically, and the fog of birth had enveloped me for months afterward. In some ways, I never recovered. But adoption placed me firmly in control. I could choose how many children, their gender, their age. It was the opposite of forcing. And I blossomed in happiness, even as I felt a twinge of guilt for comparing the two situations. I kept that guilt entirely to myself. Not even Jackson knew.

We adopted Yvonne, two years old, and Reginald, just a baby, and added them to our merry household of dogs and parties and love. Gladys and Powers returned from their own European travels and took up residence at Mama's old address in Larchmont, close at hand. My circle seemed more expansive and love-filled than it ever had before.

And then the dreams began.

In my dreams, my poor children were beset from every direction. I hesitate to even think about the things that happened to them.

The blessing is that none of the bad ends they came to in my dreams would ever come to pass in real life, though of course I didn't know that at the time. I didn't know that Reggie wouldn't die in a fire or flood or falling from a window. Yvonne wouldn't be crushed by falling debris during an earthquake or swept out to sea in a rickety ship. Her tragedy was a different one. The worst disasters are the ones we fail to foresee.

So I'd awake panting and desperate, throw off the covers, and pad down the hallway in darkness. I knew the way by heart. I knew intimately how each step felt under my bare feet: first the plush carpet of my bedroom, then a section of bare wood as I approached the staircase, the thin weave of the runner on the stairs, more wood, then the rich texture of the upstairs hallway carpet, which during the day was a riot of multicolored flowers but only a dark, muddled pattern in the night. I never looked down anyway. Sometimes I went the whole way with my eyes closed.

No matter how many times I dreamed the danger and then confirmed to myself it hadn't happened, each time, the fear was completely fresh. Each time, I thought, *This is the time it means they're gone.* When I arrived at their bedroom door, I always paused on the threshold to see if I could tell whether they were breathing. Sometimes I could—Yvonne's soft snore was particularly welcome in those days—but more often, I had to walk slowly, ever so slowly, across the floor until I was within inches of the bed. I would bend lower, lower, lower still, both convinced that I would see a rising and falling chest or hear a faint whistling breath and equally convinced that I'd find the child cold and gone. More than once, I had to put my hand on Reggie's chest to convince myself that he was breathing, and sometimes I'd wake him by accident. There was something beautiful about his blinking, sleepy face, disturbed but not really disturbed by waking. As soon as he saw me, he'd sigh his way back to sleep, eyes closed.

And I would make my way back down the hall, feeling the floors under my bare feet, and climb back into my bed and pull the covers over myself, trembling and reassured.

If I'd gone in for head shrinking, I knew what the doctor would say. They'd say that I'd botched motherhood so badly the first time that I was petrified of messing it up again with my new children. On an unconscious level, I was absolutely certain of that. But on a conscious level, during the day, I had no worries about the children at all. I loved to see their sweet little faces. I enjoyed bringing them gifts, holding their tiny bodies, dressing them in fine gowns. At a memorable party, one with the theme of Founding Fathers, I had them dressed as a tiny George and Martha Washington and showed them around, laughing, to every single guest. They gave me no trouble and I gave them none. Perhaps that wasn't the model of motherhood that everyone wanted, but it fit perfectly into my life. Jackson's philosophy was the same. He was a loving father, but his identity as father didn't replace all the other identities I adored: the husband, the lover, the singer, the jokester, the first-nighter, the humble genius.

Was I a perfectly attentive, doting mother? I knew I was not. But was having me as a mother and Jackson as a father, growing up in fine homes on both sides of the Atlantic, better for Yvonne and Reggie than living in the foundling hospital would have been? Unquestionably. I often found that direct comparisons put everything more squarely into perspective.

For example, when Death next visited our household, it was a mild brush compared to what it could have been.

I'd never been one of those women who thought her pets as dear as her children. Men of that ilk existed too, but I found it was mostly women who doted so fully on their dogs that if their human child and their dog were drowning, I personally wouldn't trust them to save the right one. Still, I did consider our dogs part of the family. I grew attached to them. A loss is still a loss.

And four losses, in rapid succession, can feel like the world is against you. Or if not the world, perhaps something beyond the world, something beyond understanding. Call it luck if you must. Or call it fate. It has no name, honestly. We only make ourselves fools trying to give it one.

When my French bulldog Archimedes died, it didn't occur to me that it could have been for a reason. That a person could be responsible. No, I simply saw it as the ill luck sometimes dished out by the world. We had experienced the highest of highs with him—an excellent performance and high rating at the famous Westminster Dog Show—and his sudden death felt like an equivalent low. One day, he was healthy and lively, same as always. The next afternoon, we found him dead, lying in his usual nap position but unrousable, already growing cold.

It was after the second death I began to grow suspicious. For one dog to suffer a sudden death with no apparent cause was surprising; two felt like it couldn't be coincidence. My sweet-faced puppy Geppetto, who I'd never shown but had excellent promise, died less than two months after Archimedes. The children were especially attached to him of all the dogs. Many tears resulted. To them, I tried to show a brave face, but alone with my husband, I let the tears fall.

Two weeks after Geppetto died, just as suddenly and mysteriously as Archimedes, though I didn't feel any better, I forced myself to resume my calendar. I couldn't stay out of society forever. And when I briefly mentioned the recent losses of both dogs over savory crepes in Mornay sauce at luncheon with Doris and Grover Duquesne, Grover grew very quiet.

Doris turned to him and said, "We should tell her."

The air was suddenly electric. I wanted to leap in, to demand I be told whatever needed telling, but Grover was as skittish as a high-strung hound himself. Let any number of things be said about me, but never let them say I didn't know when to keep my mouth shut.

At first, Grover just shook his head at his wife, a quick shake, as if what she said could simply be dismissed.

But Doris pressed, saying, "She needs to know."

He waved a hand to indicate that it was okay that Doris speak but that he himself would not. His hands went to his lap, and his gaze went to his hands. It was almost as if he retreated to another world.

Doris lowered her chin and took a deep breath. "Last week, we lost our dear Bonnie Bright."

"No!" I gasped, hand to my chest. Bonnie Bright had won even more medals and ribbons than my own Archimedes. In fact, they'd come from the same sire, a tulip-eared gentleman named Nero Augustus, and were seen as each other's keenest competition. "What happened?"

"We can't be completely sure," she said, her voice low and strained, "but Grover thinks perhaps she was poisoned."

Again, I wanted to exclaim, but I was keenly aware others surrounded us. If Grover was hesitant to speak about the loss, he likely had his reasons. I merely nodded, suggesting that Doris go on.

Doris continued quietly, "She showed no signs of illness. And it was three hours after eating from a bowl that no other dog ate from that she began to fade."

"Could something have happened to the bowl?"

She nodded. "The groom fed her out by the stables. The other dogs were fed at the back kitchen that day."

"And you trust the groom?"

"Implicitly. But he was hardly the only person on the grounds. Our stables are close to the road, you know, and we have construction of a new gazebo underway in that area of the property. Anyone could have slipped into the area and slipped out again."

"And it couldn't have been an accident? Rat poison? Something from the barn?"

"It could have been," she said, "but it wasn't. We know how those poisons kill. This one was quiet."

I pushed away the remains of the dish in front of me. I had lost my appetite.

I arrived home still thinking about what Doris had told me. If these two dogs had been hurt by someone with ill intent, the rest were still vulnerable. We had security all around our estate, but it was hardly an impenetrable fortress. The number of people who come and go on an immense property, from maids to gardeners to deliverymen, would shock the unfamiliar. We kept the dogs inside to make sure they weren't wandering around, and I put additional security measures into place, but still, two more dogs died the following week. I took the rest of the dogs with me and shut myself in my bedroom. For the next several days, they didn't eat anything I didn't also taste. Jackson thought I was overreacting, and so did Yvonne, but Reggie joined me, testing small bites of chicken and beef prepared by the cook before hand-feeding the rest of the meat to our wiggling, squirming pets.

A week later, a man was arrested on suspicion of poisoning over half a dozen dogs, all of them French bulldogs who had been shown to great acclaim. He was a dog owner himself, but his dogs were the type with the rose ear, not the tulip ear, and he was enraged that his investment and effort had not paid off due to the new-fashioned dogs placing higher than his own.

I nearly wept with anger. How could a person who cared for creatures, who knew how much like love the affection of a dog could seem, do such a thing? But I would never understand murderers, whether it was humans or dogs who were murdered.

I did not have justice. I did not have closure. All I had was simmering anger and a sense that perhaps it was time for me to exit this particular stage, if people like this were the people I'd been associating with.

Perhaps you can see the pattern now. I couldn't see it then.

My luck was clearly turning for the worse.

Despite how happy I was with Jackson, despite the love and joy brought into our household by Reggie and Yvonne, a dark specter had gathered around me. Around us.

The signs were undeniable, yet I found a way to deny them.

That is what it means to be human. To persist despite the evidence. To live despite all the reasons not to live. I thought I understood, after all my youthful adventures—my father's death, my divorce, having my daughter stolen, the way everything seemed to slip through my fingers half a world away—what it was like to feel loss. I had no idea what loss was, not yet.

I would learn.

CHAPTER SEVENTEEN

Now I have none of the good, honest, Anglo-Saxon feeling of duty toward society. I care very little indeed about society and I find myself under no sort of obligation to that imaginary force.

—AC

Six years into our marriage, Jackson and I were just as much in love as we'd been the day he surprised me with a wedding. We were older but no wiser, and we liked it that way. We still threw rambunctious parties that ended well after midnight. One I was particularly proud of purported to be in honor of a Mr. Kaa, who was in fact brought out to witness all the guests who had gathered to fete him, though he didn't show proper appreciation for everyone who had turned out in his honor, as he was a snake. A twelve-foot python, to be specific. I was taking on a bit of Jackson's and his brother's prankster personalities, taking pleasure in watching my guests scatter and scream at the sight of the unexpected creature. I took even more pleasure in winding the snake around my body and strolling through the crowd, offering his coils for the brave to pet. A few guests took me up on it, but most turned green. Those of us who enjoyed Kaa's company had a few chuckles over it, and then I put him away for the night so the guests would have time to recover and enjoy themselves again.

So much of entertaining was not just about making the right impression but choosing a specific impression to leave the guests with at the end of the night. So I shocked them, yes, but I pleased them after, with a dessert buffet of jewel-toned pastries and endless bottles of champagne to wash them down. I recognized that champagne couldn't always make everything better, but I did feel it was generally worth a try.

Around this time, I realized that anyone who'd known me in the first year of my marriage to Porter Ashe wouldn't even recognize me now. I wasn't the same woman. There were only two things about my life that my first husband might have recognized: I'd retained his love of French bulldogs, and I still liked to read the newspaper over breakfast. Jackson had picked up the latter habit from me. He most enjoyed reading the artistic trades, but we took a few of the main papers from both New York and California to see how differently they treated the news of the day. Among our daily deliveries was the *San Francisco Call*, which was probably just as much of a gossip-mongering rag as the others but tended to include interesting shipping news of exchange with the East.

My detailed dreams plagued me, and I was beginning to consider seeking out a mystic to help me understand them. Every once in a great while, I thought I saw the woman in white among my dream figures, but there were so many other curlicues and furbelows in my dreams, I couldn't be sure of her presence.

Except there was one time, in the spring of 1909, when she spoke a word. She loomed exactly the way she had in her previous appearances, a blur of white against the white of the bedsheets, with a dark shadow cast behind her separating her shape from everything behind her. I had been experimenting with a technique for controlling what happened in my dreams, and I decided to try it with her. Could I get closer to her? See her face, when I never had before? In the dream, I moved nearer. As I shifted perspective, she kept shifting away. Her face was always just out of sight, the angle always just a bit askew. She kept herself a mystery.

I was still observing her, trying to close the gap, trying to solve her, when she spoke the word that stopped me. In the dream world, it made me shiver; in the real world, it startled me awake.

Husband.

Her shadow rose up and twisted around her like a boa. She didn't seem disturbed by it, though I never could see her face well enough to read her expression, so I wasn't sure how I associated calm with her even while the shadow boa's coils tightened.

Then I was awake and panting, checking to make sure Jackson still breathed beside me. The relief that washed over me was overwhelming. I woke him up just to tell him how much I loved him. He was still a bit cranky at being awoken, but when I explained why, he cradled me close.

The next day, I read in the paper that Harry Gillig had died.

It was an odd thing, to stumble across news of the death of one's husband in the newspaper, even an ex-husband, even one who'd been such an unconventional type of spouse. No one had thought to cable me about his death, though when I thought about it, I didn't know who would. I hadn't spoken to Frank in years. They'd been the most important men in the world to me in their time, and now one was dead, and one might as well have been.

It was all there in black and white. Dead at forty-nine years old after a two-day illness that had confined him to the Fremont Hotel. Apparently he'd been in ill health for some time, though his family—which family, I wondered?—had wanted it all kept quiet. Harry Gillig, celebrated commodore and member of the Bohemian Club, was no more.

When I first spotted his name in the headline, I was ashamed of what I thought. The first thing that ran through my mind, shameful as it was, was *thank goodness.* The dream of the night before was still vivid enough to shiver my blood. This was an answer to a question I hadn't let myself ask yet. But it was a good answer.

Because if she had been warning me about the death of my husband, the death of any husband who wasn't my current one was an acceptable outcome.

I debated whether to say anything to Jackson. But I decided that he'd find out soon enough, so I might as well be the one to tell him.

"Sad news, darling," I said. "The passing of someone who was once very close to me."

He raised an eyebrow at that. "Oh?"

"A husband."

"Ashe or Gillig?" he asked smoothly. "You seem sad, so my guess would be Gillig."

"Spot on," I said.

"I'm sorry, dear," he said. "He was young enough I take it that it was a shock."

"Apparently not to his family, who the paper says was trying to keep his ill health a secret. But to the rest of us, yes. Shocking."

"Do you want to hand it to me to read?"

I frowned down at the paper. "There isn't that much more to say. Only…hm, this is interesting. They mention me."

"I should think so," said Jackson, but not in a pointed way, simply agreeing.

"Oh, and you," I said.

"Well, that always makes it more interesting."

"Just briefly, though. Mentions that after him, I married you. That's all. But I come up again here, and…I'm not sure I like what they're implying." I held the paper in front of my face and began to quote from it. "'Gillig possessed a rich tenor voice, and had intended to go on the operatic stage, but after he married Miss Amy Crocker'—they spell Amy with a *y*, the old way. I should demand a correction."

"Probably not worth the trouble," Jackson weighed in. "Go on."

"'After he married Miss Amy Crocker, the divorced wife of Porter Ashe, he traveled extensively and neglected his voice.'" I put down the newspaper, somewhat harder than I meant to. "They're making me out to be a villainess! As if I crushed Harry's hopes and dreams."

"They don't say that."

"They certainly imply it. Besides, it was never my idea to travel. Harry loved it. He was the one who insisted on Japan."

"They're not interested in the truth," Jackson reminded me. "Only the story."

I frowned at the paper again. "I'd been thinking about traveling out there. I'm sure there will be some kind of funeral service, I could pay my respects. But if this is what everyone out there thinks of me, perhaps I shouldn't go after all."

Jackson said, "It's completely up to you, Aimée."

"Which means you agree it's a bad idea."

His face was uncertain. Kind but confused. "I think… I think you need to decide what you would get out of going. What would it accomplish?"

I pictured myself offering my condolences to Frank if he was there. I thought perhaps I was the only person who could understand a portion of what he must be feeling at this moment.

Then again, would Frank really want my condolences? It would look odd for me to offer them in public, nor did I have much reason to see him in private. It had been too long. If I'd stayed in touch with him all this time, it would make sense to reach out, but as it was, I should let sleeping dogs lie. I glanced over at my own sleeping dogs. They would have approved of the expression.

I said to Jackson, "You're right. It probably wouldn't accomplish much. Such a strange obituary anyway. They spend two paragraphs telling a story about a potato. I think someone wrote it in a rush." And I turned the page of the newspaper, moving past the obituary. It didn't stop troubling me, not for days, but I didn't read the words again. I didn't need to. They were burned into my mind.

I had no call to remember the visit of the woman in white until almost a year later, in early February 1910.

Jackson and I were still dedicated first-nighters, sitting in the front row of as many plays and musicals as we could practically get to on their opening nights. Jackson and I had tickets to the opening performance of a sweet little show called *Temporary Permanence*, a love story based on the lives of Marie and Pierre Curie. I knew how much Jackson had been looking forward to elbowing me during the most absurd rhymes, like "mainly hum" with "radium" or "mobile eyes" with "Nobel Prize." But two days before, Jackson had developed a bit of a cough, and the afternoon before the performance, his throat had begun to swell. I could tell by his cloudy eyes he was feeling ill.

I laid the back of my hand across his forehead. It was hard to tell whether he was feverish, he generally ran so warm, but I tried it anyway.

"Will I live?" he asked, teasing.

"You're warm-ish. Some life left in you yet, I suppose. How do you feel?"

"Like I swallowed sandpaper."

"Not the best luncheon of your life, I imagine. Is that all? The scratchy feeling?"

He looked aside. "I hate to disappoint you."

"You never could," I answered.

He swallowed, though I couldn't tell whether it was in preparation to give me bad news or simply because his throat plagued him. "I've got no energy at all, pet. I'm sorry. You'll have to go this one alone."

I removed my hand from his forehead, used it to cup his cheek. I could feel the beginning of stubble there. He hadn't shaved that day. Jackson always shaved. He was fastidious about his appearance. I told him, "No need. I'll stay here with you."

"First of all, no. Second of all, why would you? You might only catch what I have. Get up, actually. Step away from the bed."

I frowned at him, but seeing he was serious, I rose and took three steps back. "It wouldn't be so bad if I caught what you have, Jackson."

"For you, maybe! Think of the rest of us. You're terrible when you're sick. No stoicism at all."

"And you're the stoic model?"

"Never said I was." He gave a soft smile and kept teasing me. "But you get the tiniest sniffle and suddenly you're calling around for nose amputation specialists all up and down the Eastern Seaboard. Let's avoid it."

His points were all very logical, but I still didn't want to leave him. "But you'll be bored out of your skull. I could at least stay for company."

He shook his head. "This may be the only time I ever say this, Aimée my love, but tonight, I don't want your company. I want you to go out and have fun."

"I can't have fun while you're at home deathly ill! What if something happens to you while I'm gone?"

"Oh, hush," he said. "What could happen in a few hours? It's only my throat. I'll cough a while, and you'll frown at me, and in a week, I'll be right as rain."

I frowned at him.

He replied, with a crooked grin, "See?"

"I only frown because I don't like how it sounds."

"I'm not in love with my own coughing either," he replied cheerily, "but you staying home won't help with that. The money's already spent."

"The money's not important."

He chortled deep down, and even that had a rattle to it I didn't like. "Only people with endless amounts of money would say that. My sweet little heiress. You've had it so long you don't remember what it's like to do without."

"Why should I? I'll never have to do without, will I?"

He shook his head ruefully. "Take other reasons, then. I want you to go. Otherwise, you'll just be here moping around with me."

"You're my favorite person to mope with." I tried one more time to make light, but he shook his head at me. I was beginning to realize he wouldn't take no for an answer.

"Aimée. Go on. You don't have to stay out until daylight if you don't want to, but go, and show your face. Carry my regrets. Be the belle of the ball. This particular ball could really use one. Remember how grim Mrs. Elias's face is? Like a bulldog crossed with a dragon. You're sorely needed there."

"More than I'm needed here?" I batted my eyelashes at him.

"Now you're just flirting."

"Always."

"Then go flirt with someone besides your boring old husband. You can flirt with me when you get back."

"And the day after that and the day after that," I said.

"Don't forget the nights between," answered Jackson. His familiar voice sent a soft, welcome shiver down my spine.

I went out, as he asked. I sat through the whole play and knocked back two glasses of champagne at intermission between. I most regretted Jackson's absence when the tenor onstage begged the soprano to "swear you'll always love me as much as Becquerel's discovery." I even reached over toward the seat next to me to poke my husband and only remembered the seat was empty when the back of my hand brushed velvet.

When I got home, I padded into Jackson's room to check on him in the light of the dimmed bedside lamp. He was sound asleep, but the best I could tell in the near dark, his color looked good. I got as near the bed as I dared, listening to his breathing. I heard no rasp in his chest. With that knowledge, I made my way to my own bed and slept through the night.

Three days later, Jackson was coughing blood, complaining of searing pain in his throat day and night. His voice became muffled, as if someone had packed his throat with cotton, each word a labor. He pretended it wasn't as bad as it was, but I wasn't fooled. His eyes clouded with pain even as he attempted to force a smile.

A week after that, he was dead.

The dream I had the night Jackson died haunts me still. The confusing details of the dreams that had visited me for months were absent completely; instead of endless specifics, there were almost none. I wasn't even sure, in the dream, who or where I was. Instead I only saw her, the woman in white, casting a long shadow. The area around her might have been a thick bed with a plush white coverlet. It might have been a deep snowdrift. It might have been a bearskin rug or a loose canvas sail. All I could make out was her, white on white, with deep shadow between.

And there was a sound, louder than ever before. No spoken words. But the sound was what haunted me for days and weeks afterward, slamming into my dream consciousness without warning, an explosion of noise from nowhere. And it cracked me open like a fresh farm egg.

It might have been sad, the sound she made, a sob of pure agony. Yes. It would make sense if her sadness was my sadness, a connection between the two of us that ran deeper than anything the conscious world could explain.

But the longer I let that sound sit with me, replaying its tones in my head over and over, I wondered if it might have been a laugh.

CHAPTER EIGHTEEN

I felt so far away from everything and could see nothing definitely.

—AC

I'd lost a husband before, but not this way. First I got rid of one I hated, then I parted on good terms from one I liked. To have one I adored torn from my arms permanently was a whole new experience. I'd worn the title of divorcée like a stylish new shawl, testing it for fit and comfort. I found very quickly that widowhood did not suit me nearly as well as divorce.

I suppose the difference, first and foremost, was that I loved Jackson. And I'd lost him so suddenly, so completely, it didn't feel real. It felt like an awful dream I might wake up from at any moment. I couldn't make my mind catch up to reality.

The official word from the doctor was that the acute attack of tonsillitis had weakened his body enough to let the real murderer in: blood poisoning. Whatever had infected Jackson's tonsils, choking off his beautiful voice, took its time spreading from there to the soft tissues of his throat. From there, it descended into his chest, sending its nasty tendrils through his breathing passages and down into his lungs. That was the infection that proved fatal. His body worked hard to get the air it needed, but when there was no more air, there was no more life.

I had summoned the doctor for this accounting, and as he rattled off medical jargon, my eyes were dry. I had told the maid to show him into my bedroom, but he had refused to enter, informing me he considered it inappropriate to see me in that chamber unless I was myself ill. So I rose—in my nightgown and robe, which were plenty inappropriate no matter what room we'd be in, but I didn't particularly care—and met him on the house's large central staircase.

So I was standing on a carpeted stair and holding to the railing to keep from swooning, staring down half a flight to where the doctor stood on a landing, his face upturned. I asked several pointed questions about whether doing anything differently would have led to a different result. Had there been medicine Jackson didn't take? An operation he didn't have? Anything at all we could and should have done?

"We followed the established treatment protocol," the doctor said, which was not at all the same as saying nothing could have been done. He'd been the one who advised Jackson to wait out his illness at home instead of seeking more intensive treatment, so I doubted he would change his story at this point, but still.

I longed to hear someone say that we could have saved him. No one would say it, but it didn't matter. He was well past saving.

After I dismissed the doctor, I slowly mounted the stairs back to my room and lay down. I turned off the lamp. Then I lay there, alone and unmoving in the dark, for days.

It's easier for a rich woman than a poor one to be depressed, as there are servants to take care of what needs doing, but I would never have admitted it then.

I forgot about the children, forgot everything. It never even occurred to me to wonder who was taking care of them. When I opened my eyes, I couldn't focus; I made no sound, heard no sound. My world shrank to a tiny space, a hollow. I lost myself to depression and self-pity, letting the hours slide by and vanish without a trace. I can't even say I was in pain. I felt nothing. I had no conscious thought of trying to make myself invisible, but from this vantage, I can see that was what I was doing. I was disappearing.

Sometime into my stupor—I had of course lost track of what day it was—I heard a faint bell from far away. When I opened my eyes and saw light peeking around the edges of the heavy velvet curtains, I was unalarmed. It was a day like any other. Then the distant sound came again, and I realized it was the familiar three-note ring of our doorbell.

A thought flitted into my mind: *I wonder if they're delivering my gown for the party.*

Then, just after that: *I should have canceled that order.*

Finally, with such force it sent me sitting up for the first time in days: *I should have canceled the party.*

Jackson and I hosted parties more weekends than not, so it wasn't at all odd that we had one scheduled that Saturday. What was odd was that it hadn't occurred to me to cancel the party when Jackson got sick, and after he died, my head emptied like a shovel of dirt into a grave. So this Saturday—how far off was Saturday?—guests would be showing up at our home, this house of mourning, unless someone had told them not to.

A quick bellpull and a hasty, harried conversation with our housekeeper, Mrs. Graves, and it became apparent that no one had told them not to.

This, I realized, was where the type of high society that I had once enjoyed, the one earned out in Sacramento and San Francisco by railroad money and Crocker blood, would have taken care of things. The same would have been true here in New York of Mrs. Astor's world. They knew how to do things. They knew the rules. If a high-society house was in mourning, there were rules about who could visit and when and even what they could wear while doing so.

The world Jackson and I had chosen to live in, the world we'd helped create, prided itself on having no rules whatsoever.

So there had been no announcement of Jackson's death, no fleet of tiny white envelopes winging their way to the guests like so many elegant birds. The only person who might have thought to manage this process was my mother, if she'd still been around. My disoriented brain did misfire once, giving me *Just send a note to Mama*, before I remembered she'd been dead much longer than Jackson. Jackson hadn't been her favorite person, but she'd accepted him because she knew he made me happy. Had made me happy, until now.

I told the maid to get my bath ready, steaming hot, and lay out the dress that had arrived. I looked at it and thought of my mother again. She would have told me this was all deeply inappropriate, every last bit. Wearing a gaudy gown when my husband had just died. Welcoming guests to this house at such a terrible time. She would probably have been right. Only just now I didn't care. I would do as I pleased. I had hunkered down in silence and darkness for days. Now I wanted light, life, radiance, merriment.

I also wanted a whiskey, then another whiskey. Then I enjoyed several glasses of champagne, nursing one after the next as I prepared my toilette. After much deliberation, not aided by the lightheaded feeling that was starting to swamp me, I chose Jackson's most recent gift, a triple strand of enormous pearls, to set off the dark purplish blue of my gown. I was costumed for the evening as the empress of the night sky. No mystic had told me that I would lose my husband before I wore this dress, but it seemed fitting that I was taking on the mantle of someone who ruled over darkness. Ruling over darkness was exactly what I felt I needed to do.

There was hustle and bustle around as the rest of the household prepared. I couldn't remember what canapés I'd ordered to be served, but I could smell something rich and cheese-laden, and I figured there was no second-guessing any of it now. I was a different woman than I'd been when I drew up the menu for this event, but not so different that I couldn't appreciate the good taste of the woman I'd recently been.

I realized at that point I should have quit the champagne three glasses ago, but for moderation, it was also too late.

Swanning down the staircase that Jackson used to help me down, right past where the doctor had stood days earlier and refused to tell me we should have done something else to save him, I struggled to see this as a new place. I wanted to pretend that it was, to pretend that this wasn't the same carpet, the same walls, the same hallways that had echoed with his beautiful laugh. That he should have been standing right next to me, headed for the door to receive and welcome every guest as they entered our home.

Then the bell rang, the first guest arrived, and panic swamped me like a wave. The men we'd hired to hold the doors and the women we'd hired to take the coats were all in readiness in the foyer, waiting, and at the sound of the bell, they sprang into carefully choreographed action.

It was all wrong.

As soon as I caught sight of the blond head of our first guest, a giddy young tenor named Angus Cartwright, a sinking feeling hit me in the gut. Behind Angus stood another guest and another and another. I'd made a huge mistake. And it was too late to undo it.

Greeting the guests was a special kind of torture. I had smiled and gripped hands and laughed merrily in this exact spot so many times, next to Jackson. Now I was here without him. It was utter foolishness. I lost track of the number of times I introduced myself gaily and then paused, turning to my right for him to introduce himself, only to catch myself, cheeks flushing, when he wasn't there.

"Such a pleasure to see you!" crowed Ella Mintwind, a delicate-boned brunette currently starring in the most successful revue on Broadway. She'd been romantically linked with Angus the tenor, but given that they'd arrived separately, I assumed the romance was off. Ella kissed me in the vicinity of both cheeks in the Continental style, lay her delicate hands on my elbows, and asked, "But where is your delightful husband?"

"In the ground, I think," I said in a haze. "No, wait. I'm not sure. Maybe still the morgue? They haven't buried him yet as far as I know. Did you know he died? He died. It's been a few days. I think. No one asked me what I wanted done with him, so I don't know if nothing's been done or if someone else made the decision. We never talked about it. Who thinks they're going to die at our age? Or yours, I suppose? Certainly not at yours. My stars, you're basically a child."

The expressions on her nimble face morphed from amusement—she obviously thought I was joking at first—to confusion, then shock, then something that might have been sadness but, the longer I looked, seemed like it was probably just discomfort.

"Enjoy your evening," I said haltingly, then nodded to signal she could feel free to flee. She was off in an instant, swirling taffeta behind her like the wake of a fast ship.

Word made it through the party. I could hear it travel. Two of my favorite young men from the Broadway crowd, Arthur and Declan, came over and flung their arms around me.

"We're so sorry! We didn't know you'd lost him! So sorry."

"Likely not as sorry as I am."

"Likely not, you poor thing," said Declan and squeezed my arm. They seemed to keep touching me, soothing me, and I felt like a pampered pet. Probably I shouldn't have enjoyed the feeling. I did.

Arthur said, "Such a loss. He had so many songs in him yet."

"But I can't hear his music anymore," I said mournfully, and the whole evening, it was the closest I came to crying.

"We'll sing his songs," promised Declan. "Everyone will. Not tonight, though, if you don't want us to."

I considered this as seriously as I could possibly consider anything when I'd had a dozen drinks. To sing his words, his melodies, or not to sing them? We so often did at these parties, not a whole program of Jackson Gouraud standards but a song here and there, sprinkled through the night's musical selections like little treasures. The piano was right there, its gleaming keys freshly polished, the purest black and the purest white ready to resonate at the right touch. Who would play? Most of these people could. Jackson usually did. But Jackson wasn't here.

The gears of my brain stuck, churned, smoked. I felt like I considered the question of whether we should sing Jackson's music tonight longer than I considered my first marriage.

"Aimée?" Arthur prompted, hand on my elbow, brushing a lock of hair away from my eye. I could see no better with my view unimpeded. "What do you want us to do? Do you want us to sing his songs?"

"Not tonight," I said, firm in my decision. It would feel too much like memorializing him.

Instead, I let myself forget. Just for an hour or so. I pretended to myself that Jackson was right around the corner out of sight. That at any moment, he might appear again. Perhaps he was instructing Jenkins to call for more ice or visiting with an investor he hoped to work with for an upcoming show. That I might catch a wisp of his voice, or he might appear beside me and lay his hand on the small of my back. That across the room, I might see his smile.

It only worked as long as no one asked me about him. I was drunk but not stupid, and I didn't want to lie and seem insane. But for a while, I fooled myself. I imagined that at the end of the evening, I would take off my costume as empress of the night, and he would take me in his arms and tell me I was a thousand times more beautiful without the fripperies, and he would lay kiss after kiss on my bare flesh until I believed that he believed I was indeed that beautiful.

That hour was the happiest I'd been since Jackson's death and the happiest I'd be for weeks afterward. My only path to moving forward after loss was pretending that the loss hadn't happened.

With the obvious strange dynamic of the party, you'd think that we would have ended things early, but that wasn't how the night unfolded. Everyone, including me, seemed to want to stay for just one more drink. One more led to one more until after midnight. I was conscious enough of myself at that point to order the late supper brought out, sliced meats and peeled fruits piled high for partygoers to grab to refresh themselves and absorb the fizzing champagne from their bellies. I watched people overindulge and fall down. I watched the tenor and the Broadway star circle each other, flirt, argue about whatever had parted them, decide to stay parted. I watched the bohemian element throw caution to the wind and wrap themselves around each other in nearby corners, half-hidden in shadow. In this way, it was like nearly any other party we'd ever hosted. I let myself enjoy the illusion a little longer.

Phaedra Philips, whose millions had funded the scandalous revue *Miss Diamond's Misdeeds*, found me just as the guests had nearly finished stripping the long table of refreshments.

"You know I've never been one to mince words, Mrs. Gouraud," she said.

"Mince words. What an odd expression," I mused, deep in my cups. "Why mince? Why should we not slice or dice them? Grind them into paste? Who decided it should be mince, I wonder."

"Aimée. I want to say something to you."

I waved my mostly empty glass, a throwaway gesture. I couldn't stop her.

"I can't decide if this is the most appalling spectacle I've ever witnessed," she said in a voice of genuine concern, "or the most fitting memorial to Jackson you could have devised."

"Well, thank you for saying so!" I heaved my flute high in the air and toasted. We clinked glasses, so hard I thought mine might crack, but the glass held. I took another deep swig. It might have been a fitting memorial. People might have enjoyed themselves. If nothing else, they were thinking of him. He would hate to be forgotten.

But once everyone was gone and I'd climbed the stairs to my room again, my steps labored and slow, I felt foolish. If I hadn't appeared downstairs, even if all the entertainments and decorations had gone to waste, someone would have sorted it. Someone would have welcomed the guests or turned them away at the door. One way or another, it would have been fine. I didn't regret embarrassing myself—I'd long since gotten over feeling embarrassment—but I regretted the bone-chilling weariness that I knew would put me back in my bed for another week.

And so it did. Even once my hangover dissipated, the headache and queasiness fading, I had no desire or ability to rise. The movement of hours left me untouched. In the darkness, I saw small stars like the sparkles in the dress I'd worn. In the daylight, I stared at the wall. One of the nannies made an attempt to bring the children in to see me, but I couldn't help it: I growled at her like a wolf. Thank goodness the other nanny, who had clearly tried to prevent the ill-advised visit, was able to quickly whisk the tiny visitors away. They were young enough, I hoped, that they would barely remember their father. The less they remembered him, the less they would feel the loss. I would always remember him, like my father, too well.

Once the disruption had passed and my door was firmly shut to the world again, I turned my attention back to the wall. I had chosen an elegant golden wallpaper for the room, and in other moments, I had enjoyed looking at its pattern, but now it made me think of that short story about yellow wallpaper that had been published when I was younger. The whole conceit of the story is that the narrator, confined to a room, is going out of her mind. A shiver of recognition hit me when I made the connection. Was that what was now happening to me? Was I losing my grip on reality, and would I end like the story's narrator, fully unhinged?

This question absorbed me for a while. Body still, room dark, I engaged in a lively debate with only myself, inside my own mind. Was it possible to know that you were going insane, or was the mere ability to wonder about one's own sanity proof enough that you must be sane after all? I knew which option I preferred to see as true but had no idea what the real truth was.

My mind swooped and dove like a bird of prey. Some instinct told me not to rein myself in too soon. There are precious few feelings a woman is allowed to truly indulge without society's immediate censure. Grief is one that trumps all else.

So I would take my time with my grief. I'd earned it. I'd loved Jackson so wholly and thoroughly that I had trouble remembering what my life was like before him. If I let myself lie suspended in nothingness, I told myself, I wouldn't have to think about what came after him. If anything.

I have no idea how many more days I lay in that dark bedroom, letting my grief hollow me out. It would make a pretty story to say that caring for the children brought me back from the brink, snapped me into sense. That it was my instinct as a mother that made a phoenix of me.

That would be a lie.

I simply woke up one day, still stewing in my angry, lonely, regretful state of stasis, and thought to myself, *I'm bored*. After all that staring at the wallpaper, all the long hours of darkness and stale air, even though nothing around me had changed, I'd had enough. It was boredom that drove me back into the real world.

Whatever it was—and it was many, many things—my life among the living was never, ever boring.

I couldn't bear to stay in the house where I'd lost Jackson, of course. I knew that he would haunt me wherever I went—my love for him had never been bound to a particular place—but at least I could make an effort.

Where does a person go when they're sad and lost?

The answer was, as the answer so often is, Paris.

CHAPTER NINETEEN

It has been said of me that I collect people as others collect postage stamps. I used to resent it, but now I think it is probably true.

—AC

Being alone after so long with Jackson by my side was torture, but anything would have been. I left the children in capable hands and went ahead to Paris for a few weeks to make arrangements. While I looked for a house, I stayed at an artists' colony, the Hôtel Biron.

At any other time in my life, I would have been the life of the party, talking to the artists, living a vibrant life. Instead I walked like a ghost, haunting the halls. Only later did I realize who my neighbors at the hotel had been: artists like Henri Matisse and Auguste Rodin, the great dancing talent Isadora Duncan, taken from us too soon. Grief swamped me, but beauty helped me swim out of the dark.

The house I took was not far from the Eiffel Tower. I felt like if one were to go to the effort of living in Paris, one should be able to look out one's windows and see the landmarks for which the city was rightly famous. As money was no object, I only had to decide whether I'd prefer to see the tower or the Arc de Triomphe. The Tuileries were also lovely but best seen on foot. We could only see the tower from one window in the house, but there was none other available in the district. I quickly engaged it, made plans to move in, and sent for the children to join me.

Though I hoped their youth would make them resilient, Reginald and Yvonne were understandably devastated by the loss of the only father they knew. When I welcomed them to our new home in Paris, the three of us were still a bit like paper dolls. We moved around, took action, put on a good pretense of living, but our substance had been hollowed out. A hard wind might have blown us away.

Of the children, Yvonne recovered first. She had always been the more durable of the two. She had an angelic face, and even as it had thinned out from babyhood, her cheeks were still round, her face sunny. She looked buoyant even when she wasn't. So I knew we ran the risk of thinking she wasn't as upset about her father's death as she actually was. One was never in doubt on Reggie's feelings; he wore them on his sweet face like a banner.

But I knew Yvonne was starting to make her way out of grief when she began to pepper me with questions at all hours of the day. "Can we take a boat along the river, Mama? Are French fish like our fish? Is their water different? What about the air?" My heart lifted to know that she was curious about the world. It was indeed time for us to start living outside our own walls again.

I began to write things down. Nothing too taxing, mostly just scribbling down memories. With Jackson, I'd become the New York hostess, the first-nighter, the solid woman of middle age instead of the flashy young thing, but who was I now, without him? At first, I only wrote things exactly how I remembered them, but then I decided that since I was the one with the pen in hand, I could change details. Then I realized I could change more than that. I could create whole people, whole scenes, with only a seed of inspiration from reality, and then somehow, those creations seemed even more real. The act of creation felt godlike. Writing gave me a feeling of power when I sorely needed one. Whatever else writing became to me afterward, it started with that.

Once my daughter's requests and my writing helped me return to the world, I knew it was time to seek counsel on what to do next. I simply walked out my front door and headed toward the business district, and the first palm reader I saw advertised, I walked right in.

The woman who gave me the clue to my future had the curious name of Madame Adama, clearly not French, and I couldn't have begun to guess at her nation of origin. She was elegantly dressed, looking more like a businesswoman than someone who trafficked in the supernatural, though I had met enough mystics by then to understand that anyone could be both. The dark fabric of her high-collared dress had a rich sheen to it, contrasting with her pale face.

"Welcome," she said. "Palm fortune today?"

"Yes, please."

She indicated a place for me to sit. Unlike with other palm readers I'd seen, there was no small table between two chairs. There was only a high-backed couch in a lovely rose tint, big enough for two people to sit next to each other. Once I had sat down and arranged my skirts, she took up a position next to me, our knees turned toward each other, and reached for my hand.

A sudden impression took my breath. I'd had few female friends over the years, for various reasons, and this was such an ordinary thing, but I hadn't had the fortune of feeling it for myself, not that I remembered. A woman sitting next to me on a couch, reaching for my hand. It was a friendship that could have been. But she was a businesswoman, not a friend. I was here for something else. Still, I let myself relax into the feeling of friendship just for a moment.

"Now, madame," she said. "Have you had your lines read before?"

"I have," I told her, but no more than that. Palm reading was less interesting to me because it implied our lives were determined once and then never again, and I preferred to think of my life as changeable. I had certainly seen evidence that it could change for the worse. I hoped Madame Adama would show me a way that it might change for the better.

"I do not read lines like others," she told me, even as she cupped her hand under my hand, turning my open palm upward. "I will not tell you what your life line says, what your love line says."

"Good," I replied.

"I will tell you who you are. That will help you see what you must do."

I admired her confidence. I wondered how often it backfired. Some people had very decided opinions of themselves and didn't care to have those opinions contradicted. It was a risk. I enjoyed people who took risks.

Madame Adama brought my palm up closer to her face, looking closely without touching. This too was unusual for a palm reader. In my experience, they usually dragged fingertips down your various lines in a tickling motion that made you twitch, either to set you on edge or to prove they were really looking at the lines closely. I'd always found it unpleasant.

But instead this woman lay my palm out flat in front of her, close enough that I could feel her breath, supporting my hand from underneath with both of hers. I studied her face while she studied my palm. Her warm brown eyes were steady, with spidering lines at the corners from sun or laughter or life.

When her head came up at last, she smiled.

"You are a writer," she said.

I squinted at her, then moved to correct her misapprehension. "No, I'm not. I just write. There's a difference."

She leaned forward. "For some, there is. For some, the words are only words. For you, much more. You are a writer."

I pondered this announcement for some time. I looked down at my own hand to see if I saw what she'd seen. There were faint ink stains on my fingers that I hadn't noticed until now. Nothing else in my hand spoke to me one way or another.

"What else can you tell me?" I asked at last.

Her laughter was surprising, a bell-like sound as warm as her eyes. "Isn't that enough?"

As I considered, I realized it was.

But then she added, "Share your writing, madame. That isn't what makes you a writer, no. But you should. Share it."

When I left her dark alcove and emerged squinting into the sunlight, I reached down into my valise. I always had the book with me in order to scribble down notes on interesting things I saw or remembered, and just that morning, I had made a note on the final page.

I looked down at the book I'd filled, its leather cover stamped with gold. Could it become the kind of book people chose to read? Making its home on shelves hither and yon? I'd never seen myself as a writer before Madame Adama suggested it to me, so I'd certainly never thought about publishing. I'd heard enough horror stories from Jackson to shy away from creative fields that overlapped with business—art and money never seemed to mix as well as one would hope. But since I wasn't seeking money, perhaps my experience would be less frustrating. All I wanted was to know that my words were out in the world, bringing people joy. And I had to admit, I thought the work quite good, and perhaps it would raise the level of discourse in certain circles. People were too insular. Americans were particularly prone to thinking theirs was the greatest country bar none, but any person from any nation could benefit from encounters with the unlike. My stories could show some of those interactions. People might learn just by reading me.

The more I thought about publishing my writings, the more I wondered why I hadn't thought of this before. How many words about me had been chosen and distributed by other people? Hundreds of thousands? Millions? For so long, I had been a mere subject. Now I could be the author, choosing words to put out into the world. That felt intoxicating.

So I set about it as I would any other endeavor: I asked the experts I knew, which in Paris included some very charming and successful authors, and I followed their instructions to the letter.

A few weeks later, I found myself back in New York, lunching with a publisher. His name was Ephraim Russell, he published books on every topic from the history of money to the future of fashion, and he looked very much like a self-satisfied walrus in human form. I tucked that away as an idea for future stories—humans transformed to animals or animals transformed to humans? I took it as a good sign that even before I'd published my first book, I was planning my second. I found out later from fellow authors that looking ahead in such a way was not only usual but practically required. At the time, though, I was glad I had the boost of confidence just as I sat down to convince someone that my project was worth publishing.

"So, Mrs. Gouraud," said Russell shortly after our plates of roast chicken arrived. "Tell me more about your stories."

"They're not exactly stories," I said and gestured expansively.

"What would you say they are?"

"Picturesques," I said. "Fantasies."

"True or not true?"

I considered this. "It's too limiting to say either."

"Why will people want to read these…fantasies?"

"Isn't it obvious? Because I wrote them."

I gave him a big wink, displaying far more confidence than I felt. If the newspapers were going to make a character of me, I'd show them. I could make a character of myself better than they ever had.

"And what are they about?"

"The immense variety of people," I said. "Inspired by my many travels."

"So based on real people?"

"As much as any of us is real. Am I real? Are you?"

"I know I am," he said. "Not so sure about you, of course."

I grinned at that. I liked this man. I could tell he was full of bluster, the kind of man who bluffed his way through life but didn't have a fraction of the confidence he pretended to. He couldn't be taken at face value. But there was something easy about him, something I knew I could fit with.

"No one's sure," I said with great satisfaction. "Am I a goddess? A myth? A spoiled brat? A sad and lonely ghost of myself? These stories will feed the public imagination."

He pushed back from the table and regarded me. "Imagination might or might not pay, you know."

I could tell he was testing me. "Ah, but in this case, it does. Because I aim to feed curious minds. Since I was ten years old, people have been reading about me, wondering about me, forming their own opinions about me. They've been nurturing their grudges and doubts in the seeds of those fertile, expanding minds. Not just hundreds. Thousands. Maybe tens of thousands or more. And each and every one of those minds comes with a wallet attached."

I saw the change come over him as I spoke. Like a fish, he was well and truly hooked. He began to raise his glass. Then he paused. "Let's see your stories, then. You have a few written already, I hope? I reserve the right to say no, once I've seen—"

"You won't," I interrupted. "Either the math works or it doesn't. Don't tell me you have a certain literary standard you'd die to uphold. Do you?"

His glass stayed in the air while he pondered what I'd said. It was on the bold side, but I'd made my calculation, and I didn't waver.

I raised my own glass and touched it to his. "To the math."

He gave in. "To the math," he echoed, and we both drank.

We negotiated a price for *Moon Madness*—a decent one, in the end—and signed all the contracts that needed signing. Once that was done, all I had to do was write the thing.

Well, it sounded easy enough. But I experienced something else I later found out was common among authors—realizing you having a book in you becomes an exercise in the painful, withering process of learning how to get it out.

A glass of wine was usually necessary to calm my nerves enough to start writing, and if the writing was going well, I often treated myself to another glass, which unfortunately had a tendency to make me feel so comfortable and content that I wanted to leave off writing for the day. It was a careful dance to drink just exactly enough to be creative. Luckily, I got lots of practice.

Some days, the words poured out like water. Some days, they came hard, pulled one at a time with great pain and effort like abscessed teeth. For better or worse, the quality of the words seemed to have very little to do with how much work had been used to produce them. Some stories, I edited and revised so much that, as in the ship of Theseus, every single part was replaced over time. Some I considered ready for publishing exactly as they'd come from my pen the very first draft. But all the stories had one thing in common: they'd all been drawn from some experience I'd had or some person I'd met. Loosely inspired or nearly a transcription of real events, they all felt, in their own way, true and real.

I even started one about a woman with thirteen husbands, but I could never get it right. It was the only story that I destroyed, feeding every scrap to the fire. The prophecy that my thirteenth husband would bury me still haunted my thoughts. It would be like walking naked down the street to expose that story to anyone.

After several months of work, I was satisfied enough to send ten stories to Russell and confident enough to tell him that they could either be edited with a light hand or not at all.

Women had been writers before me. I was not so foolish as to think I was breaking new ground on that front. But no one with my experiences had chosen to share them in the way I had, and I knew I was still a curiosity. I had changed my name several times, but all my names were familiar to certain people. What we counted on was that there was some overlap between the people who responded to my notoriety and people who would pay good money for books.

So I became Aimée Crocker Ashe Gillig Gouraud, the writer.

And then I became a princess.

And then I got my heart broken and became something else entirely, but first things first.

First, the woman in white saved me.

In 1912, our second full year in Paris, the children and I were scheduled to sail back to America for a visit. This was unremarkable; Reggie once said that crossing the Atlantic sometimes felt like crossing the street. My children were becoming citizens of the world. I delighted in this. It was the childhood I wished I myself could have had—not just enjoying the finest luxuries that life had to offer but truly knowing and enjoying cultures everywhere. Learning that every person is a treasure, every society a gift.

But the night before our passage, I slept deeply. This was unusual for me. Usually the excitement of travel disrupted me, dizzied my mind so I slept only a fitful sleep, but for whatever reason, this night was different. I plunged deeply into sleep almost the moment I closed my eyes.

Then, she was there.

In white, as always. Shrouded by a dark shadow, as always. But this time, there was a flickering light, a cast of orange. It was only when I smelled a faint whiff of smoke that I recognized the orange for what it was: fire.

Then there was a blast of cold. I recognized—or thought I recognized—the cold of the grave.

Then I awoke and realized the scent of smoke was real. I leapt out of bed and ran for the door, not even stopping to put on a wrapper over my nightgown. In our kitchen, I found Reggie stamping on a burning towel, howling with rageful tears.

"I just wanted cocoa!" he yelled. "Cocoa! Cocoa!"

Luckily, I was able to stamp out the burning. I looked him over, every inch, to make sure he wasn't injured. He seemed unharmed, other than his bloodshot eyes and bright red face, both signs of his anger. I soothed him, stroking his hair, checking every inch of his skin once again. Only then did I notice the window was open.

"Reggie, did you open the window to make it cold?" I asked.

He shot me a disbelieving look. "Window?"

"Yes, the window. It's open."

He looked at it as if he'd never even seen a window before. "I didn't do it."

I decided it didn't really matter. All that mattered was that my child was all right. The whiff of smoke in the air was already growing fainter, though I suspected it would linger in my nose for days. To him, I said, "I'm glad you are all right."

"I didn't mean to make the fire, Mama." He seemed genuinely contrite.

I struggled with what to say but landed on, "Just next time, ask for help. Please."

I wouldn't have thought anything more about it, that unexplained open window, except that the woman in white had been present. She cast the whole dream in a different light.

So I changed our tickets for a later passage, and we didn't sail as planned. When curious friends asked, I told them it was because I was worried about Reggie, that I feared he'd set the fire on purpose, but I didn't really think he had. I thought a week's delay would be long enough to figure out whether or not the woman in white's warning had any immediate impact.

When I heard that the ship we had been set to board, the *Titanic*, had sunk, I immediately thought, *She was right.*

We would have been on that ship, the three of us. We could very well have died with John Jacob Astor and Ben Guggenheim, Isidor and Ida Straus, W. T. Stead and Henry Harris. We would have heard the orchestra playing "Nearer, My God, to Thee" as we descended into the icy waters, probably never to see shore again.

Instead, we lived. And it raised a question in my mind about the woman in white—did she mean to harm me or save me?

CHAPTER TWENTY

That is the way in which most of the legends about me started.
If only I could have lived up to them I would have had quite
a time.

—AC

Was I surprised when *Moon Madness and Other Fantasies* was a wild success? Of course I wasn't. I had decided from a young age to be confident, and more often than not, it had been the right choice. I was too old now—a ripe forty-seven—to change. I could change my name, my profession, my husband, my place of residence, but to change who I was deep down, that would never happen. People thought of me as fickle. That was what the newspapers told them to think. But in truth, I could change so many things because I trusted myself. Even when things turned out badly, I never got mired in second-guessing. I had seen others do this—my mother had been highly susceptible to it, God rest her soul—and it always made them miserable.

So when my French publisher bought out Maxim's for a night and threw an enormous soiree to fete my literary success, all the best people in the City of Light were there. I hadn't been allowed to set the guest list, so I had no idea who most of them were, but they were beautifully dressed, and they kept telling me what a talent I was, so I liked them all immensely. Even in a world under threat of war, we were able to shut out the outside world and disappear into the glitter and glamour of a good party.

One particularly eye-catching pair came in. Americans would say they were dressed to the nines; the French would have said they had on their thirty-one. I do not know what either number has to do with anything, but there was something about their high-cheekboned beauty that made them stand out even among the rich and beautiful. I found myself glancing their way repeatedly.

Finally I took the representative from my publisher aside and said, "Who is that lovely couple?"

He looked at the pair and turned back, shaking his head. "Not a couple. Brother and sister. They're Russian nobility."

"Nobility!" I exclaimed. I had reached the level of drunkenness that made every other sentence out of my mouth an exclamation. They instantly seemed even more interesting.

"Would you like to meet them?" he asked. "I'll introduce you."

I laid my hand on his arm for answer, and he walked me through the room directly toward them. I made sure to smile and greet others as I passed, slowing his pace, so that if the Russian nobles happened to glance over as I approached, they would see me being popular and gregarious. I found the power of a first impression to be enormous in these situations.

"Your highnesses!" he called genially as we approached. "Have you met our guest of honor?"

"I would certainly be delighted to," said the young woman in French, her Russian accent sharpening her consonants to diamond-hard points.

Then her brother turned. "As would I," he said.

He was even more striking up close. His skin was lovelier than I'd seen on many a pampered American lady, smooth as an eggshell. It contrasted beautifully against his fawn-colored mustache and beard, which had been trimmed with military precision. I had the faint feeling I'd seen him at Maxim's before, but we'd never been face-to-face like this, and I found I was liking the sensation.

"This is Madame Aimée Gouraud, the writer," said my representative. "Madame Gouraud, the Miskinoffs."

I had the feeling he had breached about thirty rules of etiquette by leaving off their titles and putting my name first, but my tipsy brain told me that it was my party after all, and what did manners matter anyway? My left hand was busy with a flute of champagne, but my right was free. I reached that hand out for the woman's first, since she'd been the first to speak.

"Elisabeta," she said, shaking my hand with a pleasantly firm grip, better than that of many an American businessman. "It's a true pleasure."

"Ah, the pleasure is mine," I said. Then I let her brother approach.

First he scooped my hand easily into his. With a dexterous flick of the wrist, he brought the back of my hand upward and his lips downward, brushing a kiss across my knuckles. Then, looking up at me through his lashes before he'd even stood up, he said, "Alexander, madame. Your servant."

I bestowed a smile on him and quipped, "Well, I could get used to this!"

We chatted easily about art and European capitals and all sorts of leisurely pursuits. The Maxim's crowd, familiar and unfamiliar faces, swirled around us while we anchored the universe. Elisabeta was apparently a talented equestrienne, so the subject turned to horses for a bit, and then to Alexander's upcoming trip to Japan. He'd never been, so I was able to steer him toward some of my favorite sites and events. The Bund, first of all. The cherry blossoms, if he'd be there through the spring. I left off the details of what I'd learned from Baron Takamine and gave him the broad strokes, recommending sashimi and ahi and the train to Mount Fuji without hinting at the depth of what else had happened to me there. We were strangers after all. There was no advantage in letting myself be known so fully, not just yet.

Elisabeta broke in, saying, "Really, all my brother needs to be a complete person is the right bride."

She looked directly at me as she said it.

Could she possibly mean that I would be a suitable wife for this handsome young noble? At my age? He couldn't be more than thirty years old, if that. I would see fifty before long. But her gaze, steady and insistent, held mine.

I said, "I certainly know what it is to marry the right person, but only after marrying the wrong one." This got me a laugh and redirected the conversation, though I couldn't stop thinking about what the young Russian woman had implied.

I found out later that Alexander Miskinoff was twenty-six, the same age Jackson had been when we married. All my legal husbands so far had been in their twenties. Porter had been barely twenty and Harry closer to twenty-nine, but they all qualified. I'd thought Jackson would change everything, but from this vantage, he was simply part of an obvious pattern. I had gotten older—no one would deny it, the signs were everywhere—but apparently my series of husbands had provided, in their own way, a fountain of eternal youth.

If I were to consider the notion of marriage again, what would be left to me? Something less than perfect love. And something more than simple lust, which I could satisfy without the bonds of matrimony to my everlasting content. Therefore, especially if I still harbored any worry about the Spanish prophecy, there would need to be some other advantage. I looked through my lashes at Alexander Miskinoff and thought about what he might be able to offer me.

The first answer was obvious: a title. I'd never had one of those before. Something in me had always wanted one.

He was powerful enough to increase my reach in life yet not so much so that he could overpower my wishes and will. My children would be safe. My true core would be undisturbed. He couldn't hurt me.

So I had decided on that first meeting that I'd be perfectly content to marry Alexander Miskinoff. I said not one word on the subject to him or anyone else. And in the end, it only took him a few months to come around to the idea on his own. His mind might not have been the thing that won me over on the merits, but it wasn't lacking, and that was enough.

Three months later, on the banks of the Seine, Miskinoff proposed marriage. It might have taken a younger woman by surprise, but by the time I'd reached my fortieth year, there was very little left in the world that surprised me. I saw the proposal coming. I had my response ready.

"That's a very flattering offer," I told the prince. "I'm prepared to enter into the contract, but I have some conditions."

He must have been shocked. He hadn't been kneeling, but we'd been side by side on a bench looking at the water, the picture of a perfect proposal, and his grandmother's ring was in his hands. To have a woman utter contractual language at such a moment I imagine took him entirely by surprise. He was much younger than I after all. Being born into royalty prepares one less, not more, for the vagaries of life.

Mildly, he said, "Oh. Conditions?"

"Yes."

"I will not be faithful to you," he said. It was clear he expected this to be a shock. He was not much used to American women, or at least those of my age and experience.

"Excellent," I answered merrily. "I have no plans to be faithful to you either."

This outraged him. He had been quite close to me on the bench, and at this revelation, he scooted away. "It is not the same!"

"It is in my marriages," I said, unruffled. I stared at the placid water and explained myself. "Perhaps you don't have the same expression in Russian. 'What's sauce for the goose is sauce for the gander.' Though the truth is it is the ganders who are usually using all their freedoms and leaving none for the geese they're married to."

His lovely brow furrowed, and I could tell I had spoken too quickly, too informally, for him to understand.

"Look," I said, keeping it as plain as possible. I put my hand on top of his to soften my words. "If you want faithfulness in a wife, that is your right. But you will not find it in me. So you may have one thing or the other—marriage to me or fidelity."

He got up and began to cross the bank of the river in long strides. I thought at first he was fleeing the scene without another word, and honestly, I wouldn't have minded. But then he spun on his heel and crossed back toward where he'd been sitting, and I realized he was pacing.

"Does it help you think?"

"Does what?"

I said, "Pacing. Walking back and forth. I find it helps clear my thinking. I assume that is why you're doing it. Because you need to make your decision."

He nodded, a bit reluctantly. I could tell he needed somewhere to put his anger, and he was made uncomfortable by the fact that I wasn't willing to act as a passive receptacle. I found this was often the case with men of the higher classes, though I had no real experience in how men of the nobility reacted to things, other than King David Kalakaua of Hawaii, who had been a different type of nobility altogether. I missed him, I realized in that moment. He had been a true friend.

"I have decided," said Miskinoff. "My decision is yes."

"Then so is mine," I said.

Miskinoff and I were married in Paris, the largest of my weddings by far. Yvonne was my attendant, her sweet teenage face a prettier adornment than even the finest silks we could buy her, and Reggie stood up with his new stepfather. I'd hoped Gladys might attend, but she sent vague regrets. I'd harbored hopes that as Yvonne approached adulthood, she and Gladys might establish a friendship of their own, but despite several attempts on my part to further their contact, neither showed much interest. I resigned myself to never having all my family in one place at one time. I had plenty of practice resigning myself to things by then.

The party afterward at Maxim's was one for the record books. I heard so many compliments about what a beautiful bride I made, and I knew better than to believe a single one of them. I was beginning to see myself as too old for beauty, wondering whether marrying a young, remarkably handsome man was really the best thing for me after all. But I only thought about that once it was too late, so I raised my glass and went on with the party.

Papa used to call me princess. And now, years later and soft in the face and older than he ever got to be, I chose to become one.

I had been and done many things. I had even been a princess before, an honorary one with her own Hawaiian island, though that had been entirely ceremonial. But I had never before worn a crown.

I should have chosen a better prince to lend me one, but at the time, Miskinoff seemed like a reasonable choice. How could I have known what was to come?

You were years off yet. I wasn't even thinking of you. And while you had taken so much from me already, what happened next had nothing to do with you at all.

There are an infinite number of ways a person can suffer or soar. The year 1915 showed me new ways I could do both.

CHAPTER TWENTY-ONE

I wonder how many thousands have passed through the fingers of my life. I wonder how astonished I myself would be if I could only remember them all.

—AC

Six months after acquiring a new husband, I still found myself struggling with the death of the previous one, in ways big and small. Add that to the bleak feeling of living in a world at war, and we all needed escape more than ever.

Unfortunately one of my chosen escapes was an unwise one, and it led to some interesting decisions.

Now, I had been a heavy social drinker all my life, beginning as a sixteen-year-old in Dresden and especially during my marriage to Porter, who rarely enjoyed an evening either out or at home without a whiskey in his hand. I also had a not-unearned reputation for going through cases of champagne at the wild times I hosted with Jackson. But I drank to be sociable, up until Paris. In Paris, I drank to forget. I drank to lose the connection that bound me to reality. I drank because when I drank enough, I could leave behind who I was and what had happened and exist in a strange in-between place where nothing hurt.

Of course the next morning, it hurt plenty. Each of those mornings, I swore I wouldn't drink again, I didn't need to drink again. Yet when I was offered a glass of wine at lunch, I generally accepted. One glass turned into two or three. I was far gone by evening.

I'd attempted to curb this pattern by swearing I would only drink when others were present, but finding company proved to be no real obstacle. My nearest neighbor, Madame Valentine, was almost always willing to oblige. Over an afternoon Chablis or pastis on her sunny balcony, we swapped stories and watched the world go by.

One day, she looked surprisingly serious. "Chere Aimée," she said, "I must ask you a question."

"Ooh, sounds grave," I said playfully. "*Must?*"

Her mood didn't lighten. "My friends have an upcoming production at the Folies Bergère. It is a burlesque, called *L'Enfer.*"

I knew the French word for hell when I heard it, and my curiosity was piqued. "Sounds like my kind of show. What's your question?"

"Your style of life has proved, let us say, inspiring. The writer has included a character based on you."

I was, for once in my life, speechless.

Madame Valentine took my silence for hesitation and rushed to soothe me. "You don't mind, I hope? They would be so disappointed. But if you disapprove, they will of course make changes."

"Disapprove?" I crowed. "This is delightful."

"Then I can tell them you will allow the character based on you?"

I raised my glass. "Actually, I have a much better idea."

That was how I ended up taking on the role of Princess Mamie Shocker myself. Had I been sober during the discussion with Madame Valentine, I would have asked more probing questions— What part of my life had the writer been inspired by? Was the portrayal flattering?—but in the end, it was a harmless lampoon and a bit of a romp. It was a small role, just a few lines. Princess Mamie, swathed in ropes of pearls, did nothing risqué. Mostly, she regarded the action of the show and made a few witty comments, which the writer had done such a good job with that no editing on my part was required. Princess Mamie shouted encouragement as the line of dancing girls shed their layers, and as the dancing boys did the same, she raised a glass and called loudly, "I approve!" Then she drained her glass.

The overall impression was of a bon vivant, larger than life, thumbing her nose at the polite. I had no objections, as I was all of these.

Of course I insisted that the flute I was drinking from onstage be filled with real champagne. Nor was it my first drink of the day. So as I made my mark on the opening night performance, I was at least a sheet and a half to the wind, maybe more.

What happened at the conclusion of the performance sobered me up.

As I emerged from the stage door, a man in dark clothes approached me. He had an oval face, soft around the edges, and only a few wisps of light hair on his head. His mouth was full and sensual, his brows knit in an expression of concern. When he spoke, his voice was warm despite its starched English accent. "Your spirit is crushed," he said.

I thought perhaps he was a mystic trying to promote his goods. He had that air to him, that whiff of the supernatural. "If it is, that's my business," I said.

While I considered brushing by him—I could have done so easily—he did the simplest, most powerful thing. He reached out and laid his hand on my arm.

It wasn't an attempt at restraint. I wouldn't even call it a grasp. Just a touch, a tender one. And I felt something inside me instantly soften.

Perhaps it was that I hadn't been touched the way I wanted to be touched in quite some time. Miskinoff was enthusiastic enough but poor at taking direction. A hundred men might have laid a hand on me in this way and gotten no response at all, but there was something different about this one, something magnetic. His touch both soothed and woke me.

In that warm voice, he said, "What I mean to say is I can feel the wound in your spirit. There's a bottomless darkness inside you. And the reason I can feel it is that I have one too."

"Oh, do you? What's yours from?" My question was sincere, though it might have sounded flippant. We seemed to have skipped ahead to an intimacy I couldn't explain.

His hand still on my arm, he said, "We don't know each other well enough for that yet. But I'd like to know you better. When I saw you on that stage, so debauched and confident and radiant, I absolutely had to meet you. Would you meet me at a salon tomorrow? You would take my social circle by storm."

The alcohol in my blood gave me a swimming feeling. My exhilaration from the crowd's applause mingled with the flattering way he looked at me. Coyly, I said, "I might."

Another man would have smiled, but this one didn't. He pressed his hand into my arm again softly, like one would stroke a skittish cat. Then he told me the address and said, "Very well."

"And what is your name? You didn't say."

There was still no smile on his face. I wondered if he ever smiled. But he looked gentle enough as he said, "My mistake, I should have said so. My name is Aleister Crowley."

He was…well, he was something. An interesting set of contradictions. He looked like a serious man, a banker or attorney. Yet the more I found out about him—he had founded his own religion, traveled the world, dedicated himself to the study of magic—the more his appearance was clearly at odds with who he was at his core.

We spent hours talking at the salon the next night, but he didn't touch me again, not for a long time. I believe now that it was part of a strategy, to get me hungry for his touch when it did come.

The salon was full of interesting people: artists and writers, thinkers and dreamers, people who seemed to have no purpose or identity in life other than discussing interesting things. I saw women draped in scarves, men in silken robes, people of no immediately identifiable gender smoking pipes and holding forth. I remember thinking when I walked into the room that this was the kind of scene I'd been looking for all my life.

Someone put a glass in my hand, and I began to sip from it. It tasted not quite like anything I'd ever had before. Clearly some kind of alcohol, sweet like mead but with the bite of good whiskey. I drank it all.

Crowley appeared at my elbow. "Aimée, I'm so glad you came."

"Of course. Thank you for inviting me."

"I would introduce you to our hostess," he said, that plummy accent rounding his words, filling them out, "but I don't want to share you just yet. Come and talk to me of your travels. Have you been anywhere interesting?"

Clearly he hadn't heard of me or at least hadn't followed the gossip, and that warmed me as much as the mysterious drink. "Oh, so many places. Japan, India, Hawaii…"

"Oh!" he exclaimed. "Me too."

"Which one?"

"All three."

"Really!" It was my turn to exclaim. "Few people have been so lucky to travel widely in the East. Which was your favorite?"

"Impossible to say. They're all extraordinary." His eyes lit up with excitement, his voice wholly sincere. "India has a special power over me, as it was where I discovered my affinity for the Buddhist religion."

Had I been less practiced, my jaw would have dropped. The alignment between his vantage and mine was so perfect that I started to wonder if it was a put-on. But I chose to take him at his word. "That was my favorite thing about India as well. Do you consider yourself a Buddhist?"

"No, not precisely. I am a student of many religions, but none of them gets it all quite right. So I created my own religion."

"I've never known anyone who made their own religion up," I said.

"That makes me sound frivolous," he said with a pout that was at least somewhat genuine. "But it isn't that way. Most people, even if they claim to believe a particular code, will disagree with it in the particulars. For example, what religion do you consider yourself?"

"Buddhist," I said without hesitation.

"And are you a perfect Buddhist? Do you follow every single principle it espouses, all the time?"

As much as I wanted to, I couldn't make that claim. "I try."

"Trying is not the same as succeeding."

"I'm aware," I said. "But is that the standard we hold people to? That they must be perfect?"

"I would never say that." He was shaking his head, looking serious. I'd intended it as a light joke, but I was beginning to realize Crowley took nothing lightly. "I've never achieved perfection in my own life. But I have combined the elements of all the religions I've studied into a religion called Thelema, and it does not require perfection of its practitioners. Perhaps we'll convert you to Thelema yet."

"Perhaps," I said, keeping my doubts to myself. "What is its most important precept?"

He spread his hands out, a gesture fit for the stage. In a tone of announcement, he said, "Do what thou wilt."

"Well," I said, sipping from my honeyed drink, "that seems simple enough."

"It is and it isn't," he answered. "You have a true will. Sometimes it can be occluded. Sometimes we don't really know what we want."

"True enough," I said. "So how do we know the difference?"

He leaned in closer. "Magic."

"In what sense?"

"We practice magic. To bring ourselves more into alignment with our true will. I sense from you that you have a great deal of potential for magic."

I drained the rest of my drink. "My late husband and I had an affinity for magic."

"Did you?" He looked surprised.

"Cards and coins mostly," I said.

"Oh. *Prestidigitation*." The sour note to his voice made it clear what he thought.

I tried not to feel insulted, but his intense condescension had annoyed me. We had seemed so clearly connected on the same wavelength. It unsettled me that he could be so derisive about something that had brought me so much pleasure. And I'd been thinking of Jackson. The wound was still tender.

I stood. "Excuse me, please. I believe I'll go in search of another drink."

Behind me, I expected to hear him sputtering, attempting to bring my attention back, but if he spoke, I heard nothing.

I lost myself in a knot of women circled on a group of settees beneath a large mirror, not far from a magnificent fireplace. Some were dressed properly enough that even my mother wouldn't have found fault with them; others were wearing things I found shocking even though I wasn't easily shocked. The woman on my left, who smiled as I sat down, wore only two patterned scarves, one wrapped around her chest and the other around her slim hips. Her shoulders, midriff, and legs were bare. Even the Hawaiians I knew would have found her immodest. Yet she sat there as if she were the same as any of us. She was the one who pressed another drink into my hand. And after a few minutes, I realized I barely noticed her garb—or lack of it—anymore. She was right, I thought. Clothes didn't matter. Nothing really mattered. As offended as I'd been by the end of my conversation with Crowley, maybe there was something to his religion after all: *Do what thou wilt.*

I felt a tap on my shoulder. I turned, expecting to see Crowley. I was thoroughly surprised when the person at my shoulder was one of the more formally dressed women, an elegant blond in an unusual shade somewhere between lavender and gray. She was seated on my right, a hair too close to be proper.

"May I speak with you?" she asked.

Perhaps I should have asked why, but it didn't occur to me. It was a salon after all. I turned more fully toward her, away from the woman in scarves, and said, "Yes?"

"The man who invited you here tonight. Do you know him?"

I played it off. "Who among us truly knows anyone else?"

Her stare remained flat, unamused. She said, "I suppose I mean to say, have you been acquainted with him long?"

"Not long," I admitted.

"His name isn't even Aleister," she said. "It's Edward."

"People change their names," I responded coolly. "I've done it myself."

That rocked her back for a moment, but she stayed intent. "I only mention it because it's a sign of how deceitful he is. And not just in that way. One woman to another, I would suggest you take care."

"Very kind of you to warn me when you don't know me," I said. I tried to keep the irritation out of my voice. But it seemed odd that she had taken this upon herself, and I wondered if her warning said more about her than it did about him.

"And his lovers," she blurted. "Not just women, you know."

I hadn't known that, but the tone in her voice, as if the very idea she hinted at was lurid, irritated me. Harry and Frank had loved each other as purely as anyone. I wouldn't judge. So I said to her in a sharp tone, "That's his business."

She deflated a bit. When she put her hand on my forearm, her fingers were cool. "I hesitated to say anything. But I wish someone would have warned me, so…" She trailed off. She withdrew her hand.

I felt a pang of regret. Something was driving her to talk so confrontationally, obviously against her nature. I asked the question as neutrally as I could. "What happened to you?"

From behind us, a voice said, "Hello, Alice. Having a nice conversation with our new friend?"

She shuddered when she heard him. It was Crowley.

Alice said to me, "I'll tell you what happened. This man pursued me, and unwisely, I gave in."

"That's about how long it took too," he said.

Alice's cheeks pinked at that. But she pushed ahead, saying, "It was my fault for giving in, yes. I wasn't blameless in our affair. But the affair wasn't how he ruined me."

"I ruined you? How could I?" he said with a cruel edge to his voice.

She ignored this. Instead, she said to me, "He wrote and published a book of poems about the affair."

"Oh?" I asked. It seemed to me that love affairs were commonly the meat of art, and any of us were well within our rights to write about our own experiences of love.

Crowley broke in, "I called it *Alice: An Adultery.*"

A chill went down my spine. This was something different altogether. For a man to do what he wanted, without regard for a woman's reputation or happiness, that felt unpleasantly familiar. I still remembered my first marriage. I knew what it was to have my name savaged for all to see.

Alice said to me, "So everyone knew."

I peered up at Crowley, who still hovered above us. Unsmilingly, he said, "My true will required that I do so. My happiness would have been compromised otherwise."

Alice growled out, "Do what thou wilt."

Crowley said, "Yes. Always."

"You didn't have to use her name," I said mildly.

But Crowley was still focused on Alice. "I memorialized you. It was an honor."

"It didn't feel like an honor," she responded. "I lost everything, my husband, my children, everything. You wrecked me."

"And yet you come to these evenings, where you know you'll see me, Alice," he said, arching an eyebrow.

The pain in her eyes was breathtaking. Because it was obvious he was right. As much as he'd hurt her, as betrayed as she felt, she'd been unable to stay away from seeing him again.

Alice had withdrawn her hand from my arm. It was my turn to reach out. "Thank you, Alice," I said. "I would rather know than not know."

Sadly, she said, "I doubt it will keep you from him." She looked up at Crowley's face. Her sigh was inaudible, but her whole posture had the tinge of regret.

I said, "That remains to be seen."

I considered what Alice had told me. I considered Crowley's history, his affairs. I considered the likelihood that whatever passed between us would be no secret. But my past was nearly as checkered as his, my romantic exploits nearly as numerous. And my reputation was already in tatters, had been for decades. As long as I guarded my heart, what my body did was almost irrelevant. What did I have to lose by letting myself be pursued?

I should have kept my eyes closer to home.

CHAPTER TWENTY-TWO

[Flirting] does not always end in love, nor in bed, nor in any of the conventional story-book ways. Thank God. Sometimes it gives you a real friend whom you respect. Sometimes it just peters out after you've had your fun. Sometimes it gets you into trouble. You never know. That, of course, is part of the thrill.

—AC

Time crept relentlessly forward, as time does. Before I knew it, I'd been married to Miskinoff two whole years. I still felt like a young woman if I avoided mirrors and didn't focus on my north-of-fifty-year-old face, but there was one piece of evidence I couldn't avoid: my children had reached their teenage years. Reggie was away at boarding school in the north of England—he'd begged to go—and Yvonne remained with me in Paris, beginning her studies at the Sorbonne. She was seventeen and beautiful. She reminded me of myself at that age, which should have been all the warning I needed.

Instead, I had no idea until I read it in the newspaper that my daughter Yvonne Gouraud and my husband Alexander Miskinoff had been seen leaving a hotel together, compromised.

It seemed both the most obvious and the most impossible thing, that she should seek to deceive me in this way. Unlike my own mother, I had encouraged my daughter to pursue her dreams. I had never boxed her in, never told her that her worth was in who she married. I had never spoken a single word to her about protecting her reputation.

Setting down the newspaper, I wondered if perhaps that had been a mistake.

I spent a good part of the day deciding how I would react to this. Confront him? Threaten her? Pay him to disappear, pack her off to school in another country, perhaps both? Ignore the whole issue and pretend I hadn't read the headlines that day? I almost went out in search of a clairvoyant, my old crutch, but decided only I could make this decision.

By the time Yvonne appeared in the early afternoon, I had a plan.

"I read about your affair with Miskinoff," I said, coming at it direct.

She paled but, to her credit, didn't try to dissemble. "I'm sorry you found out that way."

I shrugged. "There's no good way to find out something like this, Yvonne."

"You don't want him anyway," she said, lifting her chin in a posture of defiance I knew well. She'd never resembled me more. "You never did, did you? And he knows it. He and I are better suited for each other than you two ever were."

"You're going to find out whether that's true," I said, and I could tell that my degree of calm was unnerving her.

"What do you mean by that?"

"What I mean, dearest," I said, taking her hands in mine, "is that you should have the chance to explore whether this love is real without the prying eyes of the press on you."

"We should…what?"

I squeezed her hands, gave her a smile I didn't mean. "No one will approve of the two of you becoming involved, and that can go poorly in the press. I only warn you because I've been through it myself."

Her lovely eyes narrowed in suspicion, widened in confusion, a dozen fleeting expressions crossing her nimble face. "So you…"

"I've made arrangements for you," I told her firmly. "You'll spend a week together at a home in Portugal I've rented under an alias; no one will know either of you is there unless you are indiscreet. Can you assure me you will not be indiscreet?"

She nodded.

I went on, "If at the end of the week, you assure me you love no one but him and he loves no one but you, you will have my blessing. Perhaps he will want a divorce to marry you, perhaps not. That is for the two of you to sort. I won't stand in the way. But I do want you to take this time seriously. Most people do not have the ability or means to truly find out if they are suited before they commit to each other. You and Alexander will. Do you accept this gift?"

She still eyed me with suspicion, trying to understand whether I had some ulterior motive and what it might be.

I said gently, "Yvonne, I promise you, this is no trick. I only want you to be happy. Him, I don't care about, but you—you matter. I truly intend the gift of time. I hope things will be clear to you when the week is over."

She considered this for a long moment. Then, in a small voice, she said, "I hope so too, Mama."

The week was one of the longest of my life. I attempted to distract myself, but I spent every waking minute wondering what they each were feeling. At night, I stared up at the darkness and cursed myself for making a colossal mistake.

But at the end of the week, Yvonne returned to Paris alone. As soon as she arrived, she directed the maids to take her trunks to her room, then turned to me and said in a firm voice, "Mama, I don't want him."

First, I kissed my daughter's forehead and stroked her hair, told her I was proud of her maturity and thrilled she had come back home to me. I assured her that her—our—former lover wouldn't bother her again. I kissed her once more and sent her upstairs to her room, promising dinner for just the two of us at her favorite restaurant after she took the afternoon to rest. As she left the room, she gave me a tired but genuine smile.

I then went to my desk and put the letter I'd already written to my lawyer into an envelope, filing suit to divorce Miskinoff that day.

I'd learned my lesson from previous divorces, mine and others I'd heard about, and I knew lawyers were no longer enough. I hired an investigator to help dig up leverage I could use against Miskinoff either in or out of court, and it didn't take long for the truth to surface.

It turned out that Miskinoff wasn't even a prince.

The woman who had posed as Miskinoff's sister, the princess, on our first meeting wasn't even his sister. She was a cousin of some sort with a very distant claim on some sort of royalty in the Russian pantheon. His claim, however, was completely trumped up. He had simply been going around claiming to be a prince, and society had swallowed the bait. Once I instructed my lawyers to reveal to his lawyers that I was in possession of this secret and that I would happily make a public announcement on the subject if he fought the divorce, there was no further opposition to a quick division and dissolution of our ill-starred, ill-advised union.

I never had to see him again, and as glad as I was about that, I hoped he was gladder. Because he should realize how lucky he was that I was never in arm's reach of him again. If I were, I don't think I could have resisted the temptation to snap his neck. Of all the people who died of their association with me, either directly or indirectly, the faux Prince Miskinoff was the only one I would have willingly murdered.

Instead, I promised myself I would never get married again against my better judgment, and in fact, I kept that promise.

My better judgment, of course, was not always good. But in the meantime, I was happy to be a divorcée again. That seemed to be how the American papers liked me best. Announcements of my marriages always spent too much time listing all the other men I had previously been married to. I did not look forward to seeing Miskinoff's name anywhere near mine in the papers.

So as soon as the divorce was final, I swore I would give them nothing at all to write about. I would give up drink, stay in, be as boring as dirt. Which was easy to say and hard to do. I should've done what I wanted and ignored how they would react to it instead of shaping myself to fit them. I should have taken the advice I'd given my daughter upon the occasion of her narrow escape. You can only control how you feel about what they do, how you react. You can't actually control what they do.

As with all advice, it was always easier to give than to follow.

I had thought that Miskinoff would make me a princess. Instead he'd made me a fraud. I had compromised in order to marry him and regretted it. My relationship with Yvonne had barely escaped disaster. I hoped that as she became an adult, we might know each other as friends, as Gladys and I eventually had. Unfortunately, Gladys's marriage to Powers had not lasted. I was at least glad Jackson hadn't known how quickly they'd grown apart. They had seemed so in love when they surprised us with the news of their wedding. But I was not one to throw stones on matrimonial matters.

Whatever bonds of blood bind us to another person, they don't define the character or quality of our relationships. My sister, who had the same Crocker blood running in her veins as I did, had become nothing at all to me. The most important person in my life had been Jackson, with whom I shared no blood, only love. I did wonder if I eventually would have driven him away if he had lived. I seemed to do that with everyone else who mattered. It wasn't always my fault, though, I told myself. Jennie had judged me harshly. I had been willing to see her with clear eyes, for us to have a cordial relationship; she had been the one who decided we would be estranged. One person could not undo such a veto.

Only now, looking back, do I see how I followed the same patterns over and over again. Becoming attached and detached, living a life that overflowed, dealing with losses that I thought might crush me, searching for the ultimate connection.

I was, as I have always been, making my way toward you.

CHAPTER TWENTY-THREE

If I have often loved, I have at least loved well and fully.

—AC

The end of my marriage to Miskinoff was no reason to leave Paris. I'd been there before him, and it was my city more than his. All told, I lived more than two and a half decades in Paris, even though I was gone from the city for months at a time. The place couldn't claim me any more than a person could.

But after my fourth divorce, I did find myself drifting back into Crowley's orbit, and things between us changed. I'd sworn after Jackson's death never to take a man fully into my heart, but I'd made no such promise about who I might take into my bed, and I'd warned Miskinoff not to expect fidelity from me. But while I was married to Miskinoff, my relationship with Crowley was surface level, physical. Crowley didn't begin to confess his secrets to me until two years into our affair. I had seen him only as a distraction, an amusement. Crowley was not the only focus of my life, nor I of his. I had other projects. He took other lovers. We both did as we wanted, and it was far better than marriage, because neither of us pretended to have any claim on the other, so no feelings were hurt on either side. More than once during this period, I wondered why I hadn't chosen to simply have affair after affair without bothering with matrimony. That Spanish mystic hadn't known a thing.

At the same time, I knew I would never have behaved this way if my mother were still alive. I couldn't have borne to disappoint her so thoroughly. The lies that had once been printed about me were bad enough, but now they were nothing compared with the truth.

In 1917, in bed with Crowley, I learned why he had been so derisive when I'd mentioned that the "magic" I'd done with my husband was only stage effects, crafted illusions. Because the magic that Crowley pursued was real and true.

When he used those words, I propped myself up on my elbow and gazed right into his eyes. "Are you serious? Real magic?"

"Yes," he said, returning my fervor. "A connection with the spirit world. I imagine you've felt it before, yes? In passing? Perhaps in dreams?"

The woman in white sprang into my brain, her form stretched out on white sheets, accompanied as always by that ring of dark shadow. "Yes."

"Wouldn't you like to have a deeper connection? To know more about how the supernatural influences and supports us?"

I almost felt he could see inside my mind. He was speaking so simply of some of the greatest mysteries in the world, the tension between this world and other worlds that I had always felt but never been able to explain.

When he said, "The secret to magic is sex," I almost laughed aloud. But I could see he was deadly serious.

So I only said, "Tell me more."

He spoke for nearly half an hour uninterrupted. He explained how "sex magick"—he'd adjusted the spelling with an extra *k* himself to make it clear that this kind of magic was different from that practiced onstage by charlatans—was an art he and his circle had been perfecting. He made it clear that sex, the way he and I had practiced it, was not a form of magic. Sex magick required certain preparations, certain rituals, that he and I had never done. He explained that both heterosexual acts and homosexual acts carried tremendous power, and he had engaged in both in pursuit of knowledge and vision. I asked a few probing questions and found that he didn't believe there was any power in women engaging in sexual acts with women, only men with women and men with men. I assumed he had no real basis for this but was so self-centered he didn't want to acknowledge any path to power through sex that didn't have some chance of involving him personally.

And after he explained sex magick to me, he said, "You're a sexually powerful woman. I've known that ever since I saw you on stage in *L'Enfer*. I think you might even be the scarlet woman to my great beast."

"And what does that mean?" I had an inkling, as at least one previous candidate for the role had told me her experience of it, but I wanted to hear his version.

"The scarlet woman is empowered. A leader," he said with passion. "Instead of pretending virtue, she embraces vice. She is sacred in her profanity."

"I like the sound of it, I suppose," I said. "No promises."

"I ask none. But I do think you'd very much enjoy engaging in these rituals, and that could lead to a breakthrough. Would you consider giving sex magick a try?"

"When do we start?" I asked.

My body was not what it once had been. It had been so long since Porter and I had first christened our marriage bed with pure, lustful energy, the way our limbs seemed tireless. Even with Jackson, at the beginning of our love, my body was already beginning to slow. I desired him with a fervor that scared me, but when we lived side by side for years, there were plenty of nights when we decided that kisses would suffice and anything more entangling could wait a day or two. Why burn so bright if there's time?

But now, decades on, I knew I was no spring chicken. I had gained and then lost several stone over the course of my marriage to Jackson, and in Paris, I was neither fat nor thin. My body was a little more of a stranger to me. But I knew from what I'd heard whispered in salons and in intimate gatherings that to have any sexual desire as an American woman with her fiftieth birthday behind her was considered highly unusual. I didn't quiver with longing in between my irregular sessions with Crowley, yet when we undressed each other, that flame did leap up. He recognized the flame. And he seemed to be saying that it could serve my quest for knowledge as well as physical satisfaction.

How could I even think of turning down that opportunity?

Over the next year, though I did not neglect the other areas of my life like my social calendar, children, dogs, or promoting *Moon Madness*, I threw myself into the pursuit of a connection with the supernatural through sexual acts. Often these were with Crowley, but not always. The first time he suggested I engage in sex magick with another man while he managed the ritual, I blinked in surprise but found myself still game for the adventure.

I was a dutiful student. I followed instructions to the letter. And after a few months, more often than not, at the peak of pleasure, it was as if a curtain parted and I glimpsed another world.

The location of our spiritual adventures had always been fluid, moving from one circle member's house to another. That October, it happened to be my turn to host. I arranged the most private of my rooms upstairs for use.

Crowley's eyes were already glittering with excitement when he arrived. He was accompanied by a man I'd never seen before, but one so like him they could have been twins.

"Aimée," he said, "This is Barnabas."

"A pleasure," I answered. "Won't you come in?"

I gestured them upstairs—I'd given the household staff the entire day off to avoid any complications—and we set to work. Barnabas was a man of few words, and I was listening more than talking, but Crowley chattered enough for all three of us. He had recently begun examining the effects of the phase of the moon on sex magick, and the full moon on its way seemed to him a very good omen.

Even better, when he read the cards he'd brought for further auguries, his eyes went wide at what he saw.

"So auspicious," whispered Crowley, and I had never heard his voice so reverent.

"Shall we drink wine?" We often did, not for its magical properties but to relax the mind. I'd brought up several bottles to have them close at hand.

"Not just wine," Barnabas said, his first contribution to the conversation.

"But wine to start," Crowley said.

While I poured goblets for the three of us, I asked in a mildly curious voice, "And who will be participating, and who directing?"

Barnabas looked at Crowley and said, "As strong as the signs are today, why don't we all participate?"

It was unusual for anyone but Crowley to take the lead in these conversations; my interest was piqued. And I was further surprised when Crowley nodded simply and said, "Yes, that's good."

From that moment on, something had shifted. Barnabas was in charge. The way Crowley looked at him was fascinating; it reminded me a little of how Frank had looked at Harry, that sort of longing, but there was something else mixed up in it too. I wondered if it was narcissism. The man looked so much like Crowley that it would be like engaging in sexual acts with himself. Perhaps that was the whole point. I wasn't sure whether we'd all be participating simultaneously or taking turns, but I found that the answers to questions like that generally revealed themselves when the time was right. I raised my goblet to my lips for a fortifying sip.

But Barnabas stopped me. "Not just wine."

"And you mean…"

He produced a small white square from one pocket, gesturing for me to set my cup back down by the rest. While I did, he tore the corner off the packet. He poured a small amount of white powder in all three cups, then gestured for us to each take one.

"Barnabas," said Crowley, "are you sure?"

"I am."

"It may be too strong for you," Crowley warned me.

"I may be too strong for it. So I guess we'll see."

Raising the glass to my lips, I noticed that neither of the men had yet drunk their portion. My eyes met those of Barnabas over the rim. I asked, "And what will it do?"

"Relax you."

"And if I'm already relaxed?"

He seemed unbothered by my curiosity. He looked at Aleister, who raised the cup and began to drink like a good boy under his tutor's eye. Then he said, "To receive what the dark wants to tell us, we must be open. In all ways. It will open you."

I had a moment's hesitation, but I had been accepting drinks from people in this circle from the very first day I joined them. There was no reason to act the prude now. It would be the height of hypocrisy.

"Sip or drink down?" I asked.

"It's a little bitter," he said approvingly. "Drink down."

One gulp was enough to dispatch it, and I barely had enough time to set the cup down before his hands were around my waist. In an instant, he'd lifted me onto the arm of the nearest couch and stepped between my parted legs to embrace me. Our lips met, so hard it hurt, but the hurt was part of the pleasure, and I was stunned to find myself instantly ready.

I thought I heard a swift intake of breath from Crowley but couldn't be sure. My blood was pounding in my ears, rushing. Because though the swiftness of the man's motions surprised me, I wasn't scared by his urgency. I felt it myself, immediately.

This was unlike any of my other experiences with sex magick, which had been highly choreographed. Whether with Crowley or another, each step had been prescribed. The ritual was what made it magick. But this time, there was no ritual, or very little; Barnabas was chanting under his breath when his mouth wasn't busy elsewhere or sometimes even when it was, but without direction, I simply went where instinct took me, and every motion felt right and good and, above all, powerful.

To surrender myself without surrendering, to dominate from submission, I learned an entirely new way of achieving pleasure. And pleasure would open the doorway to the beyond.

No conscious thoughts whirred through my brain, no regrets, no choices, only instinct, as the near stranger's tongue plumbed the depths of my mouth and my fingers quickly untied the string at his waist.

"Open," he chanted, "open."

From behind me, I heard Crowley chant, "Open, open."

Clothes littered the floor. Skin met skin. One man was between my legs, the other's chest pressing against my back, more than one pair of lips on my neck, and I joined their chant, "Open. Open."

The delicious sensation was crawling through my body like an entity unto itself. I had learned what it felt like when my body responded, how to nurture that flame into a full-blown fire. What I'd done with my husbands was out of love and lust. This was different. A means to an end. I treated my body almost like an animal—not in the same way that I'd inhabited my animal body when giving birth but watching its skittishness and reaction, keeping an eye on its behavior and making changes to compensate.

The tight sensation was building within me. This was the moment.

"Open," someone groaned into my neck, and I opened myself in every way possible, ready for whatever came next.

I reached into the darkness within myself, the way Crowley had taught me, but further than I had ever reached before.

Was it the full moon that made the difference? The odd mirroring feeling of having a man behind me and a man in front of me, their gestures and caresses echoing each other? Or was it the drug that had been placed in my drink? I would never know. It doesn't matter. It only matters what I saw.

First I saw a glowing white shape. Not an orb, not a sphere, nothing regular. It came clearer as I approached. A woman's back, I realized. The shape of her dress. I hadn't recognized the shape as human because she was curled in on herself, arms wrapped around her stomach, head down, but now I could tell. And my heart began to beat quicker. Because there was something deeply familiar about that dress. Even more so as the woman unfolded herself, long sleeves trailing, and turned to face me.

It was her. The woman in white. The one I dreamed about for years. The one who always seemed to appear in times of trial, when death was near. I felt the same way seeing her this time as I had every time before: confused, knocked back, fearful. But this time, I saw that she was doing nothing to make me feel that way. She was simply there. I was the one who attached fear to her.

As she completed unfolding herself, her face looking into mine, my fear and wonder turned to something else entirely. Shock ran so deeply through my body, I felt I'd become solid rock.

Finally, I saw her face.

It was my own.

CHAPTER TWENTY-FOUR

My curiosity had grown into passion like a sudden flowering.
But there remained the fear of that beautiful vision which
would foretell the end of my life.

—AC

I awoke alone, abandoned by the men who had drugged and pleasured me into a state of explosive revelation, and I have never been so grateful. I never wanted to see them again. It was counterintuitive, I know—having achieved a new level of consciousness, a new connection with the supernatural, shouldn't I have been eager to find my way there again? To at least keep open that possibility? But what I had learned terrified me.

For decades, I had believed that this woman in white was the dark force that kept leading me toward disaster. Now I knew that I myself was the specter I'd been running from. If I'd been mistaken about this, what else had I gotten wrong?

First, I took time to recover. Whatever drugs they'd fed me left me weak and hazy, not so much disoriented as detached. Nothing was worth making an effort for. Not food, not drink, not the prospect of fresh air. Paris lay right outside my window, and I couldn't bestir to set foot on its streets. The bed was my world, the sheets my shroud. In a way, this kind of torpor reminded me of how I'd fallen apart when my grief for Jackson was new. I was lucky the walls of my apartment were covered in green paint instead of yellow wallpaper or I might have fallen back into that particular darkness, even though it had been years.

When my mind was my own again, my body reminding me of its more prosaic needs, I rose. I was told that Crowley had sent messages; I refused them unread. I instructed the doorman to turn him or anyone from our acquaintance away. Something about the loss of control had soured me on exactly what I'd always loved about my time with Crowley: the feeling of shadows around every corner, endless mystical knowledge ready to seduce us into darkness. I was done with darkness. I wanted light.

I wanted to know why I had, it seemed, been haunting my own dreams for decades in a way that couldn't possibly be real.

So I undertook my travels again, but this time, my visits to mystics and mediums and clairvoyants weren't just a convenient sideline. Speaking with guides to the supernatural was the whole point.

I began back in Madrid, searching for the medium who had once told me my thirteenth husband would bury me. I practically hunted him. But every lead turned into a dead end, and I had to admit that too many years had passed to find someone whose name I had never even known.

So the search continued. As far as anyone else knew, I was simply kicking up my heels, touring some of my favorite world capitals for sport. But I threw myself into the search for answers, trusting only my own instincts and networks, asking pointed questions to every psychic, spiritualist, and telepath I could find.

They gave me unsatisfying answer after unsatisfying answer. The woman was Death itself, said a supposed clairvoyant in London's seediest district. A leather-skinned guru living in Amsterdam said the woman was my mother; a Bohemian channeler with red hair the color of a copper penny said she was my daughter. In Trieste, high on the hillside facing the ocean because the mystic said she saw visions in the salt spray that scattered when angry waves struck the base of the cliffs, I was told the woman was an amalgam of every woman I'd ever known, that the "mystic feminine" was trying to get in touch with me, and that I wouldn't understand her messages until I "owned my womanhood entire," whatever that meant.

None of their pronouncements would explain why the woman who haunted me had my own face. I didn't explain that part to them, of course. I was holding it back to use as a test. Every single one failed.

Returning to Paris in resigned frustration, I sent my luggage on ahead and searched out a mystic I'd met but hadn't seen in years. I thought that perhaps it would be just like the universe to deny me what I searched far and wide for but provide it within a short distance of home. In my exhausted, unsatisfied state, I had to drag myself to his parlor, figuring even if our meeting was useless, I wasn't likely to feel any worse than I already did.

The mystic in question had a magnificent mustache and a velvet eye patch, a bit moth-eaten but still impressive. I was introduced to him through the artist's circle that included Auguste Rodin, who had been a fellow resident of the same hotel when I'd stayed in Paris years before. Our stars had both risen a great deal in the meantime. Monsieur Rodin and I had happened to bump into each other in the dining room at the Ritz and drained a bottle of delicious claret between us over the course of a short half hour. I mentioned that I was always interested in having my fortune told, and he recommended a man in the Marigny, a mystic going by the name of Monsieur Chuchoter, which translated to Mister Whisper. Even though the name was slightly laughable—I kept thinking that Jackson would have loved to use it for a Broadway revue, something with a jaunty tune behind the words—I decided it was worth pursuing. If nothing else, perhaps a visit to Mister Whisper would make for a good story to tell at parties in the future. I could always use more stories to tell at parties. The old ones were going a bit gray at the temples, as we all were.

And it started out like a good story too. The elegant little painter had given me directions to where the medium held court, which involved going down a dark alleyway until I reached a blue light, a promising beginning. Even the weather was cooperating, chilly but not cold, an atmospheric amount of fog lingering in the city's low-lying areas. The alleyway didn't have fog in it. I decided that for the purposes of the story, I would give it some. The flickering blue light did cast some appropriately long, wavering shadows. If somber music were playing underneath the scene, it would have made as fine a film as any I'd seen, all tension and dread and dark promise.

The door beyond the blue light had a disappointing lack of iron scrollwork, but it was right where the painter had said it would be. I knew I'd reached my destination. I had no idea what I'd find behind the ordinary-looking door—a speakeasy? a storeroom?—but it turned out to be a nicely furnished little parlor, not so different from what one might find in the higher class of whorchouse anywhere on the Continent.

Two substantial chairs, upholstered in a lovely hunter-green velvet, flanked a small round table draped with a scarf that shimmered in the flickering light. The drape appeared to have precious metal, silver or gold, woven into its design. The soft lamps added to the atmosphere. Books lined one wall, the kind with dignified, gilded spines, which I suppose was the one detail that set this decor apart from that of an elegant bordello. None of the paintings on the remaining walls had a recognizable subject, but they all used the colors and tones of melancholy, a deep wine red, a midnight blue.

In one of the velvet chairs perched a young woman dressed in black from her long skirts to her high collar, skin so pale I wouldn't be surprised if she'd never encountered the sun. Again, perfect for my future telling of the tale. She could almost have been a vampire from Mr. Stoker's novel *Dracula*. I hadn't read it myself but had been subjected to a tiresome number of acquaintances at parties who felt the need to recount its plot at length, back when it was all the rage. The presence of a real live vampire would certainly make this story a better one.

I said to her in my best schoolgirl French, "Excuse me, if you please. I'm in search of Mister Whisper?"

She replied in perfect English, "Of course."

From nowhere I could see, she produced a small silver tray in the shape of an oval with a rectangular card in its center. The card appeared to be blank. She gestured for me to sit in the other velvet chair, and I did. She laid the tray on the small table between us.

"The reverse of the card shows the rate for Monsieur Chuchoter's time." Her slight accent became apparent in the longer speech, but still, her English surpassed that of some native speakers I knew. "If you agree, we will proceed. You may place the payment on the tray, and I will summon him."

"Summon? Like a demon, from another dimension?"

She didn't even crack a smile to acknowledge the joke. "No, miss, from another room. He does not meet with clients until payment has been provided."

"A good rule," I admitted and flipped over the card on the tray. The amount was exorbitant. I paid it in paper francs, counting them out one after another with possibly excessive ceremony, then slid the tray back in her direction. I folded my hands in my lap to wait.

True to her word, the young maybe vampire made no move to bring her master into the room until I had paid. She didn't count the payment herself but seemed satisfied with my counting. Then she rose with a swish of her taffeta skirts. I expected the ring of a bell or some other flourish, commensurate with the payment, but what happened next was straightforward. She crossed the room and opened a door that I hadn't previously noticed, as its edge was perfectly aligned with the edge of a bookcase. Actually, I thought, a secret bookcase door would fit nicely into the Mister Whisper story

I would eventually use to entertain friends and acquaintances. The young woman in black stepped through the half-open doorway into darkness.

I considered following her, though it was obvious I was supposed to wait. I even shifted in my seat to rise. But in the next moment after her black-clad back disappeared, through the gap came a man in dark garb. The aforementioned mustache and eye patch were his most distinguishing features, but his uncovered eye was also a most pleasant shade of brown, and his face was all elegant angles. His answers might or might not be worth what I'd paid for them, but he played the part well, and I always appreciated a bit of show.

His steps were unhurried as he closed the space between us, then seated himself in the velvet chair the maybe vampire had vacated.

"Are you comfortable, miss?" he asked, his tone not quite honey sweet but more tender than I would have expected from a stranger. His accent was heavier than hers. It also wasn't French. I would have to listen to it longer to place it, and I had other things to focus on. This man might be the one. He probably wasn't, but I hoped he was.

"Yes, quite," I answered. "My name is…"

He flipped an open palm in my direction. "I do not need your name. I find it only interferes with the reading."

"As you like it. What do you need to know?"

He pondered this a bit, his single eye dancing. "Need? Nothing. I can read cold, if you prefer. Much of tonight will depend on what your preferences and interests are."

I had so many things I wanted to say. I held back. My purpose was not to entertain myself or him; it was to get the answer I sought. "I'm interested in the truth," I said.

"Are you certain?"

"Do you not believe me?"

"I believe that you believe yourself," he said, and it seemed to me his accent came from Eastern Europe. "But many people are mistaken. They believe they want the truth, when in fact they want what is…palatable." He stumbled a bit over the long word. It made me like him more.

"I'm not interested in what I want to hear, if that helps. I'm ready to hear anything. Even if I don't like it. Especially if I don't like it."

He nodded in approval.

With a speed that surprised me given his previous stillness, he slid his hands over the gleaming scarf that covered the table between us and pulled the fabric toward him with one swift yank. It slithered off, like a discarded woman's dress. He nodded at the bare wood of the table, which was raw and pale, with no varnish or polish to make it fit this room.

"Place your hands on the table," he said. "Palms down."

I was beginning to feel seduced, though his tone wasn't seductive, at least not overtly so; the way he directed me was halfway between a physician and a lover.

As he asked, I lifted both hands from my lap and rested them lightly on the table. I wasn't wearing gloves, so I could feel each fingertip pressing into the cool, rough wood. This wasn't like any reading I'd ever had before. Most mediums, when they used a person's hands in the reading, examined the palms to read each line—the life line, the love line, and so on—but that didn't seem to be Mister Whisper's intent.

He began to work with the scarf he still held, first unfolding it fully. I had an odd moment's panic that he was going to throw it over my head, blotting out the light, but the impression came from nowhere; he simply continued to work the fabric, coiling it into a long roll. I steadied my breathing. He then looped the scarf loosely over one of my wrists, then the other. He neither covered my hands nor restrained me. I sat there, alternating between looking down at my hands and up at his face, wondering what was about to happen. There was one flick of his eye that made me think that what he was doing wasn't preparation for the reading but the reading itself. He was close enough to me to hear when my breath changed. It was possible that a person's reaction to this odd ceremony would tell a man like this what he needed to know.

Finishing to his apparent satisfaction, he leaned back in his velvet chair. His eye swept me from head to hands, my wrists draped in beauty, my hands bare and exposed. When I looked down at them, my hands felt like a landscape, the knuckles someone's idea of mountains, the veins like rivers. They looked like they didn't belong to a body at all.

I thought I was ready for anything, but when his first words came, they were a complete surprise.

"A man," he said.

I shook my head, protesting, and one hand shifted. "I came to ask about a woman. From my dreams."

"Shh," he said, and there was nothing at all of the lover in his manner now; it was a harsh sound, a hiss of command. He laid a fingertip on the back of my hand to still it but then immediately withdrew. His back was against the chairback again. "I will find your truth. If you knew how, you would have found it already."

I couldn't argue with that.

His eye closed, his head bowed, he repeated, "A man."

I resisted the urge to ask questions. It was a very powerful urge.

Mister Whisper opened his eye but didn't look at me. He was looking down at my hands, these foreign, separate objects that lay between us. I wondered what he saw there. "He ensnared you. Like no man before or since."

That could have been any man in my life, I wanted to tell him. They'd done it in different ways, but they'd all done it. Porter had snared me with lust, Harry with convenience, Jackson with that pure bright love I'd forever lost. Takamine had snared me with mystery and, more recently, Crowley with the promise of forbidden knowledge. If you wanted to go all the way back, even my father had trapped me in his way, though it had been a gilded cage of love and money. It was harder to think of men who hadn't tried to trap me than men who had.

"At first, you were willing," he said in the tender version of his voice, his accent squeezing the words, "but then, it turned. He changed what you thought was happening. He took something from you."

I wanted to crack the tension with a joke, but it mattered too much. Besides, I was beginning to suspect I knew who he meant.

Mister Whisper moved his hands then, but not to touch mine. He cupped them in front of him as if he were carrying something. Water or sand or something precious. His eye met mine, sharp.

"He held your soul," he said.

Then it was utterly clear. He could only be talking about one man: Washington Irving Bishop. Mister Whisper's lone brown eye looked at me expectantly, for confirmation.

"Yes," I breathed.

Still holding my gaze, seemingly unblinking, he said, "You took it back."

"I did?"

"You thought you did."

That startled me, and I blinked, breaking our connection. "What?"

"He didn't give it back to you. At the end. You took it."

Those days and nights in Hawaii rushed back into my memory in full force, and it even felt like I smelled the perfume of salt on the wind. We'd fought on the driver's seat of the horse cart. He'd pushed, I'd pulled back. I'd felt that strain, that ache, in my chest. Somehow I'd snapped his spell. Now it began to make sense. "Yes. I took it."

The man said, "You did not get it all."

The thought dizzied me. "My soul?"

"Yes."

I sat with that for a minute. It wasn't the wildest thing I'd ever heard in my life, but I'd never considered the possibility. To clarify, I said, "So he still has some of my soul?"

"He does not have it, no. He is dead."

Of course he was. I'd heard the story, and it was awful. It would have been much worse if I'd liked him.

"So where is it?"

He winged a hand upward, graceful. "Loose."

Mister Whisper's price had been outrageous, but I never regretted paying it. And after all my rehearsal in the moment, all my stage directions to myself about the maybe vampire and the fog and the blue light and the secret bookcase door, I never did end up telling that story at parties after all. He'd told me the truth that I didn't want to hear, as he'd promised. A wondrous and terrible revelation. It felt far too important to recount over deviled crab and champagne cocktails, to trivialize with waved hands and widened eyes. In the end, I kept Mister Whisper for myself.

CHAPTER TWENTY-FIVE

And if I could live it again, this very long life of mine, I would love to do so. And the only difference would be that I would try to crowd in still more...more places, more things, more women, more men, more love, more excitement.

—AC

Now I had a new question to ask, a new truth to pursue. Part of my soul was loose in the world. How could I get it back?

The natural choice, again, would have been to turn back to Crowley. He and his circle had the deepest connection to the otherworld that I knew of. But after some time away from them and their nocturnal habits, I was even more fixed on never falling back into that man's orbit again.

I didn't want anyone to know what I'd discovered. It seemed dangerous, to be severed from part of your soul. I hadn't lost that piece of soul until well after some of my misfortune, but was it possible that a soul, once loosed, wasn't bound by time or space? I decided to throw myself into finding out. But I refused to use the methods I'd already used. Instead, I would shed my bad habits like a snakeskin and emerge into the sunlight.

I was reminded of what I'd learned in India, the idea of *kaivalya*, a kind of separation between soul and body. I had known that the body and the soul weren't always together, but for whatever reason, it hadn't occurred to me that the soul itself could separate. All these years later, my anger toward Bishop should have dissipated, but I still found it lodged under my ribs like a hot coal. He'd done this to me. And he wasn't around to pay for it.

Of course no punishment I could have devised for him could have been worse than the actual end of his life, the nearly unbelievable truth: he'd been killed by autopsy.

Back during our intimate days and nights in Hawaii, he'd told me about his particular, strange affliction. In a rumpled bed, ocean breeze wafting in through the open window, he stroked my bare arm and said, "Now, Amy, I have to tell you something important. If at any point I appear dead, I need you to know I'm still alive."

I couldn't help it; I laughed. "That's absurd! How can you promise not to be dead? What if I watch you drown? What if, I don't know, you stab yourself with your dinner knife? You can't ever be so certain."

He looked a bit hurt at my laughter. As soon as I registered the look on his face, he smoothed it away, then reached out and laid his fingers on my chest gently. I felt that surge of connection, the link between us. I immediately began apologizing with excessive emotion, finding myself suddenly close to tears.

"There, there," he said, stroking my arm again. "The fault is partly mine. I have not found a good way to approach this topic, and I see the way I stated it was confusing. But it isn't a joke. I'm as serious as can be. Life and death are at stake."

"Tell me."

So he did. "I have a particular catalepsy. A problem with my heart and how it circulates my blood. On occasion, the pressure inside my body drops remarkably low, and I faint."

Fainting didn't sound like such a dramatic problem, just an inconvenient one, but I didn't want to risk hurting him again. I blinked and waited for him to go on.

"This isn't a normal faint," he said. His voice was level, matter-of-fact. "Not a swoon, not the kind of thing that smelling salts can cure. When I go into these faints, I can't be revived. I have no pulse, no breath. I appear, to the outside world, completely devoid of life."

I was shocked. "How can that be? No pulse, no breath?"

He shook his head. "It is simply how I'm built. Believe me, all the best doctors have poked and prodded me. When I am in this space, sometimes I can even perceive what's happening around me, but I can't move or speak. I am present but not present."

"It sounds terrifying."

"It's unpleasant, but I've come to accept it as the price of my gift. Perhaps it helps explain how I tap into magic. Perhaps I'm already half on the other side of the veil. But the reason I tell you isn't to worry you. Only to enlist you in defending me should I fall victim to one of these spells."

"Defend you? Against what?"

"Doctors," he said. "I carry a card that warns medical professionals of my condition, but it's important also that those near me know the truth. So if you wake next to me and I appear dead, do not call authorities. Do you understand?"

"I do," I said and swore myself his protector. I was rewarded with a kiss.

For the duration of our strange relationship in Hawaii, I never saw evidence of Bishop's catalepsy. We parted ways before he experienced such a spell. The terms we parted on ensured that I never wanted to see him again.

But when I heard several years later that he had collapsed in New York and that his mother claimed that the autopsy meant to identify the cause of death had actually killed him, I wasn't entirely shocked. I wondered if it had really happened, the thing he'd feared most, having his head cut open while he lay there motionless on the slab. Most of all, I wondered where the card had been, why the doctors hadn't known to leave him be. Even with my dedication to Buddhism, my decision not to judge others, I had never been able to forgive

Bishop. If he really did suffer at the moment of his death with the full knowledge that he was about to die horribly and needlessly, I still didn't feel even a bit sorry for him.

But now, knowing that the piece of soul he'd taken from me was loose in the world, I wondered if it was time to confront that old memory. I couldn't see Bishop, but I knew where his body was. His grave had been there for years, mere miles from my New York homes, and I had never visited.

It was time.

———————

Green-Wood Cemetery was the permanent home to many of New York's most celebrated citizens. Had it been the front row of a Broadway show, it could hardly have boasted more famous names. For all that, from the moment I stepped onto its paths, I felt a calm and clarity that made me think I'd chosen right. I didn't presume that I'd been reunited with my soul so quickly; that wasn't the feeling I had. But the urge that had pushed me in this direction cooled a bit, and I took that as a good sign. I wondered if I'd dream of the woman in white or if those dreams had ended now that I knew the truth.

I had made sure to learn the site of Bishop's grave before traipsing hither and yon—the cemetery was large enough that I didn't want to spend hours in search of his final resting place. Though to be honest, it wasn't as if I had more urgent business elsewhere. This journey would take the time that it took. My children were old enough that they didn't need my attention. I had no husband at home waiting. This cemetery was the only place, for now, I needed to be.

I'd pictured his grave shaded and quiet, but when I reached it, the patch in which Bishop's body was interred lay in full sunlight. In many ways, his grave was just like those all around it, a meager marking out of a small plot. No matter how far we wander in our lives, how many thousands or millions of miles, in the end, we only need six feet of land for our final rest.

But Bishop had been memorialized by a woman who loved him. When I looked at his tombstone, I immediately felt the immensity of his mother's grief. Outraged at what had happened to her son, she'd published an angry book on the subject, hounding the doctors who, in her mind, had murdered him.

His pale, towering tombstone read "THE MARTYR" in enormous letters. It showed his year of birth, 1856, and death, 1889. Where had I been that year? I asked myself. It was hard to even keep track. Thirty years ago already. They'd passed in a blink.

I was baking in the sunshine, flipping back through my memories as if they were printed photographs, when I heard a voice behind me.

"Are you a devotee?" she asked.

You might wonder if I felt haunted; I didn't. I immediately recognized the voice of a living woman, and when I turned to look at her, even though I had never met her, I knew exactly who she was.

"I am not," I told her as I turned around.

When she saw my face, she knew. "Aimée Crocker Gouraud," she breathed. "I know you have other names, but I don't remember them."

"I barely remember them myself," I said, intending to be gentle. She looked like a woman who could use some kindness. The hem of her dress was frayed; by the dark shadows under her eyes, I guessed her patience was too. "I suppose I should say I'm sorry for your loss."

"Think nothing of it. I know you're not sorry," she answered, neither smug nor outraged, simply matter-of-fact. It seemed to me that if we'd met under different circumstances, she and I might have gotten along swimmingly. But we stood next to the grave of a man I'd hated, a man she'd loved enough to marry. The chasm between us could not be crossed.

I said, "In any case, I know what it is to be a widow, and I wouldn't wish that on any woman. So you have an ally in me."

"I don't need allies," she said. "But I do need to know why you're here."

"Do you?"

She considered this, then answered, "I would like to know. Please. I'm fully aware you and my husband had your involvement, and he told me it ended badly."

I felt a strange pang. I'd never known how he saw the end of our relationship; when you banish someone from your life, you forfeit the right to know such things. To hear this now was news from the dead. It wasn't the supernatural kind, but it still twisted something in my chest.

Mrs. Bishop—I realized I couldn't remember her first name, if I'd ever known it—fidgeted with her sleeve. Then she looked up with a bold gaze, her eyes meeting mine. "So the question naturally comes to mind, especially after all these years, why are you here?"

I could have lied, but I was old and rich, and unless this woman had a secret position as a columnist for the *New York Tribune*, I had no reason to fear her. She could bring no consequences to bear. "I recently found out he took even more from me than I thought. And I'll have no peace until I get it back."

"An item?" she asked. She looked completely unsurprised at my allegation.

"Of a sort."

She tugged on her cuff again and sighed. "I suppose, then, you should come to my house. I still have many of his things, or things he claimed were his. If you find your item, feel free to take it with you."

"That's awfully generous," I said.

"It isn't," she said crisply. "I would've gotten rid of every single thing years ago if I could. His mother keeps the place like a museum. Keeps me like a museum too. If I even speak with another man, I get an earful from her about how her poor son would be destroyed if he knew of my lack of fidelity."

I was flabbergasted. "Her poor son has been dead for decades."

"Well," said the woman dryly, "in her opinion, his death seems to have changed very little about our marriage."

"I'm sorry," I said, and I genuinely was.

"Let's go," she answered. "We can take my carriage to the house. You can stay for lunch and peruse the museum."

"And if his mother is there?"

"She doesn't come on Tuesdays, thank the Lord," she said. "Luck is with you."

I certainly agreed with that.

Exactly as Mrs. Bishop had said, the house resembled nothing as much as a museum. It even had that curiously airless, dusty quality, though no dust was visible. When she settled into the corner of the room as I began to make a slow circle, she went motionless, closing her eyes. In the dim light, she looked like a waxwork, just another collectible object Bishop had left behind.

Items were piled on every surface with no discernable order or ranking, just as if he'd piled things up and meant to come back to sort them later. What looked like a sterling silver candlestick sat atop a precariously uneven pile of books; stacks of notebooks, perhaps once neat, had slid sideways and covered up half of some reed instrument that somewhat resembled a pan flute.

With interest and care, I circled the room once, then twice. I knew I wouldn't get another chance. If I didn't find what I was looking for... But what *was* I looking for? I had no idea.

Then, there it was. Peeking out from under a haphazard collection of brightly colored scarves, I saw a familiar pattern: the swarm of line-drawn bees that decorated Bishop's tarot deck.

It was, without question, the one he'd used to do my readings back in Hawaii. The precious, one-of-a-kind deck that belonged to him and him alone. Under the bee-patterned backs, I knew every card in that deck by heart, from the Fool to the World, images leaping up inside my eyelids when I closed my eyes. The force of memory hit me—salt wind off the ocean, sun, sweat—and I knew I'd found what I was looking for. A kind of warmth rose off it, calling to me.

"Mrs. Bishop? I'll take this," I said, pointing at the deck of cards.

"All yours," she replied without even turning to look.

CHAPTER TWENTY-SIX

There was something I wanted. I did not understand but I wanted it fervently.

—AC

So I sailed back to Paris, as close to a real home as I'd ever had, with the tarot deck burning against my skin. Before I boarded the ship, I tucked it inside my corset, flat under the hollow of my ribs. There it would be safe from thieves. It was the one thing my money could not replace.

Even if no one else knew how much the deck mattered to me—hardly anyone would even know it wasn't just a deck of playing cards, let alone assign the pack value—I was irrationally terrified it might disappear. In my uncertain moments, as I crossed the ocean once more, I wondered whether it really had any import or whether it was just the force of memory that convinced me the tarot deck was the key to everything. It just *felt* important.

But I made it back to Paris with the cards still secret, and the first thing I did upon arriving home was to dismiss the maid and undress in solitude, peeling away layer after layer until I wore only a chemise and pantalettes, the skin-warmed deck of cards clasped in one hand. I pulled on a thin white dressing gown over my underthings to chase away the chill and considered what to do next.

Primarily, I considered whether I should wait for an auspicious day.

The idea of the full moon sprang to mind, bringing a fiery memory of the way I'd achieved the knowledge of the woman in white's real identity. I had ended my association with Crowley's circle, but there had been immense power in the magic we'd made, and the temptation to return to them had never been stronger.

Instead, I decided to sit down in my Buddha room. As always, seeing the peaceful faces all around me brought me closer to my own feeling of peace. There were more than a hundred Buddhas surrounding me, from the plump and delightful to the elegant and disapproving. They reminded me that life is impermanent; we cannot get caught up in the stream. We need to know when to let go.

A feeling of rightness flooded me. I had crossed the world and come back. No one could hurt me here.

On a whim, I decided to go ahead and draw cards. I didn't want to do a reading the way Bishop had. I wanted to do things my own way. That had been the theme of my life so far after all.

So I sat on the floor at the edge of a patterned rug in my skivvies, took a deep breath, cleared my mind of every single thing, and turned a card face up on the bare floor in front of me.

First card, the Emperor.

It's almost impossible to describe what happens next. Time snaps; the world vanishes. And I am in the hallway of my family's mansion in San Francisco, standing outside my father's room. My father, alive. My father, a powerful man, commanding, supreme.

My father, a kind of emperor.

In the hallway, the spirit I've become hears him gasping for air. At the same time, I hear my younger self, the ten-year-old down the hall, awake. She considers calling for her parents. But I can't let that happen. I whisper to my younger self, *I don't want you to see him die like this.*

Time snaps again, and light goes dark. Back to my real life, my real body.

I was sitting on the rug in Paris, surrounded by Buddhas on every side, the Emperor card laid out in front of me.

I reached out with trembling fingers and turned the card face down. It felt momentous, that I had connected with my own past. I could never tell anyone. But deep inside me, something felt changed. Better.

My fingers turned the next card as if I had no say in the matter, as if it were a foregone conclusion.

The card: the Tower.

A card of change, disruption, transformation.

Then time snaps again, that same disorienting feeling of weightlessness, that same sense that the world has vanished from around me.

And I'm in a hotel room, my eighteen-year-old body stretched out on the bed next to Porter's. Dark outside the windows, dimly lit here in the room. Bare limbs, tangled. Sheets rucked up, tossed aside. If I were real, my breath would catch at how beautiful and young we were, we are, in this moment. The night before we leave for our honeymoon.

I look down at my younger self, and I don't know what to say. She is bound for so much pain. Is it a greater gift to say nothing at all?

I'm unsure whether I can change anything. I'm even less certain whether I should try. Because what if changing my life changes too much? If I save my younger self from the tragedy of the train wreck, could something else even more disastrous happen? If I warn her about Porter, will she divorce him before Gladys can be born, and would that be the same as killing my own daughter, ensuring that she'll never live?

I whisper it softly, so softly, *I can't tell you not to go*. I fade away.

Back in my room in Paris, I turned the card face down. Goodbye to the Tower, goodbye to transformation. The still, silent faces of Buddhas all around me bore witness. I thought I could see approval in their eyes.

Next? As quickly as I could ask myself whether I should, I did. Another card, turned face upward.

The card: the Empress.

It's becoming familiar, even reassuring, the way time collapses or explodes or disintegrates around me. I lean into it.

The house in Larchmont. I see my thirtysomething-year-old self with Jackson, and I don't immediately recognize the setting. It isn't nighttime. That's different. It isn't the same as appearing to myself in a vision, those dreams, like the night my father died or the night before my honeymoon. I'm tempted to linger. I see myself happy here with Jackson. Loving. Alive. The feeling of missing him is like a bottomless well.

But instead, I gather my white dressing gown around me and turn away from this self of mine. Because if the Emperor card took me to my father at the moment of his death, it isn't hard to guess what moment this is. The death of the empress. The shadow pools around my feet, and we travel together, through walls and air and walls again, into the house next door.

My mother looks out the window, her breath stuttering. I can tell right away she's in distress. As my living self giggles over breakfast next door, my mother is dying.

My mother's eyes are wide as she sees my pale self approaching. I wonder what she sees. Am I translucent like a ghost? Do I look as real to her as she does to me? It doesn't matter. She is alone and dying, and now I am here with her, shadow wrapped around me, to keep her company.

I lay my hand atop hers. I don't know if she can feel it.

"I'm here," I say to her, over and over. "I'm here."

Something like a smile spreads over her face, even as her panting breath becomes fainter, even as the strain makes looking into her eyes painful. And I am there when her panting ceases. I'm there at the moment I wasn't able to be there in life.

But the moment doesn't last, and it isn't my choice this time, how time snaps and ricochets and flings me back to a quiet room in Paris where the tarot cards lay in front of me, the Empress face up, staring in my direction.

This time, I hesitated. My fingers hovered over the card, looking at that face, the face that did not at all resemble my mother but was her all the same.

I turned the Empress card face down.

I'd begun to tire. The effort of this magic, or whatever it was, was taking a toll on me. I could feel ache spreading into my limbs. My heart felt wrung out—I'd witnessed the deaths of both my parents in a way that wasn't possible by the rules of the world yet felt more real than life. Time to stop, I told myself. I could come back another day. When I felt stronger. I got as far as tucking my feet under me, rising to my knees, bracing both hands on the floor. I felt every one of my fifty-plus years in the ripples of pain and tension through every joint.

But then I realized, what if this was it? My only chance? I had to admit that some times were more auspicious for revelation than others. What if right now, right here, some conditions were occurring that might not come again for days, weeks, years?

Creaking, pain pulsing in my knees and hips, I lowered myself to sit on the rug again. This time, I saw no approval in the eyes of the Buddhas surrounding me, but neither did I see any sign of disapproval. They gave me nothing. I knew what that meant. This decision was mine alone.

Whatever this connection was, whatever these meetings meant, I could take the rest of my life to figure out. But if today was the only day I could ever meet these selves, I had to keep going. Connecting. Turning cards.

So I steeled myself, took a deep breath, and turned the next card in the deck face up to witness what Bishop's tarot wanted to tell me.

The card: the Lovers.

I had both anticipated and dreaded this possibility, knowing there was only one moment it could take me back to, the one word she'd given me—I'd given myself?—that foretold the death that had nearly destroyed me.

Time snaps.

The Larchmont house again, later. The stain on the carpet from where Reggie had spilled a can of paint, the mirror over the mantel I hadn't bought until 1906. I lie next to Jackson, sated. Though we often part in the evenings to sleep in our own separate beds, this is a night I stay by his side all night long. Drowsy, I drift off.

I stand in the room, a vision of white wrapped in darkness, and I say to her what I most feel. *I wish you could hold on to this husband.*

My body on the bed stirs and flutters, then seems to drift back into slumber. I know what I said, and I know what I heard, and they aren't the same. In the morning, my past self will only remember hearing the word *husband.* When Harry dies, she'll be glad. But a few months later, she'll lose Jackson. My floating self can't prevent the tragedy. What happened will happen.

But I feel the fresh pain in my chest as the moment expands, soars, explodes.

It hurt, still, when I opened my eyes in the quiet room in Paris.

I turned the Lovers card face down without hesitation. I didn't want to spend another breath in that moment. The pain had spread further, a feeling of exhaustion settling into my bones. Yet I was afraid to stop. Each of these connections was utterly priceless. Could I have one more? Two? What would happen if I pushed myself too far? I thought about the shadow that wrapped itself around me when I traveled. It had not just a color but a temperature. It was colder than the air. Yet there was something comforting about the familiarity of it. I realized that when I traveled through time, when I was the woman in white, that shadow was always with me. There was nothing in the real world of which I could say the same.

I settled and sighed, gathering my strength, before I turned the next card.

The card: Judgment.

Time snaps and throws me back, but I know where I'm going. It makes so much sense now. The Judgment card is a reminder that we will die, an encouragement to take stock of where we are and whether, at the end, we'll be found wanting.

I open my eyes in another room of the same house where my traveling self sits. I feel a queasy doubleness, separated by time but not space. I know that if I go upstairs, I won't see my body seated on the carpet in the Buddha room, but at the same time, I feel a strong aversion to opening that door.

No matter. That isn't why I'm here. The card pulled me here because this is a decision point, one where the wrong decision would cost me and my children our lives through no fault of our own. Who knows what decision I would have made without the warning I'm here to deliver? But that already happened. I'm just closing the circle.

I move upstairs to where I know this Aimée, the 1912 Aimée, will be. I open the door to her bedroom and step inside. She's stretched out on the bed in her nightclothes, sheets rumpled around her, a deep crease of worry between her closed eyes. Just as I'm deciding whether to indicate my presence, her eyes open and fix directly on me.

I don't need to say a word. She sees me, and she knows.

Task complete, time flings me back into my body in the quiet room, more jarring this time.

I opened my eyes to focus on the Buddhas around me, drawing on their peace, reaching for calm. My heart hammered. At the time, I had downplayed our decision to change our plans to sail on the *Titanic*. So many others had the same story of a near miss. But this time, I felt it, how real it was, the danger. How everything could have simply ended. The feeling of loss that swam through me was almost more than I could bear. Almost.

The Judgment card challenged me. Had I been ready then to stand at the pearly gates? Was I now? The idea of it all being over was simply unacceptable. I would live as long as I could, as madly and passionately as I could, and never take no for an answer.

Boldly, I turned the Judgment card face down and flipped the next card up, smacking it down on the wooden floor with an audible slap.

I looked at the upturned card: the World.

I reached inside myself, as deeply as I had in the days of sex magick, turning all my attention and energy inward.

The World.

I expect the moment to blink and snap, for the world to change, but nothing outward changes. I'm not in a hotel room or the Larchmont house or anywhere at all, not even the room in Paris. I see nothing, feel nothing but the coolness of my shadow companion. I am in the void. I am everywhere and nowhere.

Exactly where I need to be.

The World is completeness. It is consciousness expanding to connect with all that is and has ever been. It is union, and I lean into that union, binding myself to everything and everyone, the land and seas, the stars, myself. The welling of emotion overwhelms me, a powerful elixir of relief and love and eternity like a wave, and if I were in my body, I would sob with it.

And I feel something snap into place in my chest, filling a space I hadn't realized was empty. I am, finally, whole.

When time releases me, it does so tenderly, propelling me through nothingness to nothingness until I feel myself gently land.

I opened my eyes. I was back in the world, in the quiet room in Paris. The light seemed brighter, colors more vivid. The rug underneath me was almost too vivid to look at, a riot of greens and blues, and the pain in my body was stronger but somehow more bearable. Pain can remind us that we are.

I could smell a faint scent of lilacs drifting in from the street through the slightly opened window. Had it been open before? When a person dies, in some cultures, they make sure to open a window to let out the soul. But in my case, the soul has come not out but in.

Struggling to my feet, wrapping the dressing gown more tightly over my trembling limbs, I felt one more thing: an absence.

At my feet lay the cards, the World still showing its face, the others their bee-patterned backs. In a way, it was like seeing the dead body of a friend, knowing their spirit was no longer there. But the spirit that had animated them was mine. That piece of soul. Which now lay within me, where it should have been all along.

I left the dead cards on the floor of the Buddha room for the space of a day. Then I gathered them up, took them to the drawing room where a fire roared in the hearth, and burned every last one of them to ash.

As I walked the streets of Paris, feeling whole and peaceful, I wondered if the feeling would last. Now that I had my soul back, I felt lighter and larger, taking up all the space in the world I could desire. I made a vow to savor it as long as I could.

Then I had a thought that stopped me in my tracks.

Was I meant to die now? Now that I'd not only done so many outrageous things but raised my children, connected with my past selves, and reunited my soul?

The Parisians around me must have thought I was mad, though as always, they were too well-mannered to say so. They simply flowed around me like water as I stood there dumbfounded.

You'll think it's silly—perhaps anyone would, but especially you—but that was my thought. Having achieved peace in life, did that mean it was time to die?

I thought of consulting a medium to ask the question, but this one time, with the sun overhead and the Eiffel Tower in the distance spearing the sky, I decided this wasn't a question to ask others. I'd ask myself.

Is there anything left for you to do, Aimée Crocker Ashe Gillig Gouraud Miskinoff?

When I began laughing, I'm sure those around me became even more certain I was mad. But they let me be mad. I was glad of it. My laughter reached out to the top of the Eiffel Tower and among the flowers of the Bois de Boulogne and over the tables at Maxim's and all along the banks of the Seine.

There was only one thing I could think of. This time, I would get it right.

CHAPTER TWENTY-SEVEN

I think the ruling passion of my life has been my love of contrasts.

—AC

In 1925, I married Prince Mstislav Galitzine, Count Ostermann. He was a gorgeous young man, dark and slender, with a magnificent dark mustache than lent him a dignified air. I had recently turned sixty. The prince was, like the two husbands before him, twenty-six years old. Marrying him was a thumb in the eye of society, of expectation, of the Spanish mystic who couldn't possibly have seen this particular one coming. More than four decades before, inexperienced and impetuous, I'd been engaged to a prince. Eleven years before, blinkered and susceptible, I thought I was marrying one. This time—after a thorough investigation—I finally did.

I became Princess Galitzine, Countess Ostermann, and the party we threw to celebrate was the last great party of my life. Our home was thronged with Russian expatriates, an entire horde of beautiful young people with shabby coats and heavy jewels. The noise was thrilling at first, then overwhelming, then painful. I couldn't blame the young Russians themselves. It seemed I was at fault. Parties, after decades, had finally begun to lose their luster.

Surrounded by all the noise and merriment that I'd loved so long,

I thought to myself that perhaps I had seen all there was to see in the world after all.

The story of my fifth marriage is a short one. My fifth husband wasn't a wretch like Porter, a friend like Harry, a true love like Jackson, or a fraud like Miskinoff. He was only a young man who had accepted the promise of money in exchange for a title, chasing a golden lure. But like any fish that finds itself wriggling on the end of the fisherman's line, he realized he'd made a bad bargain. In the end, though he thought all he lacked was money, getting it wasn't enough to make him happy. If he'd asked me, I would have told him that.

Money lets you acquire the things that you believe will make you happy, but that's no guarantee that you'll actually be happy once you have them. I did better than most, enjoying my wealth, enjoying my life. Galitzine wasn't wise enough to know himself, and what he thought he wanted didn't satisfy him. A common enough affliction, as we all know, in the young. He was a nice enough young man and a good friend to Reggie. I might not have loved him, but I would never find it in myself to hate him, no matter what terrible things he said about me in anger.

I set him free, though that wasn't how he saw it. He sued me for a divorce settlement that would keep the money coming. But by now, I had all the best lawyers, knew all the best arguments, and in the end, he not only didn't win an allowance but was forced to pay the court fees for his unsuccessful suit.

But besides my title, he gave me one other essential thing.

He didn't mean to, I don't think. We were having the type of argument we'd started to have all too often once he realized he was unhappy and needed someone to blame. Again, in the young, more common than not. Galitzine made a smart remark about me not knowing what it meant to be a wife, and I reminded him that I had plenty of experience.

"You've only been a husband once," I said. "Remember I've had five husbands, so I've been a wife five times."

"At least," he said dryly.

For whatever reason, this irritated me, and I began to needle him. "What do you mean? You think I don't know how many husbands I've had?"

Galitzine glared at me above his plump mustache, saying, "Well, my very experienced wife, I imagine the number of men you have loved has been much higher." He probably hoped the glare might intimidate me, but I'd seen far more fearsome faces.

More amused than intimidated, I asked, "Love. Is that what makes a husband?"

"All I mean is that a ring and a piece of paper are well and good." He crossed his arms, petulant as a child. "But am I a true husband to you?"

The more he talked, the less I understood his point. "What do you mean by true?"

"That's it exactly," he said, slapping the table between us. "We are in a legal union."

Coolly, I said, "Yes. I'm glad you noticed."

He ignored the barb, eyes glowing with excitement over his idea. "But that is the extent of it. I am sure you have been involved with other men, men who perhaps did not put a ring on your finger but who meant a great deal to you. More than I do."

This, at least, made sense. "Perhaps."

"Be truthful with me this once," he said. "You have been with far more than five men."

"Yes." From someone else, it might have sounded like an accusation, but we were simply confirming facts. I wasn't ashamed.

He went on, his voice unexpectedly brimming with emotion. "And almost all of them were more important to you than I am. I feel no shame at that. I just want to make you see. There are many, many kinds of union."

And I began to think of those unions, the men I felt bonded to, whether or not we'd been legally married. Galitzine was right. He was among the least treasured of the men I might have reasonably considered to have been my husbands.

"You're absolutely correct, Slava," I said. What I said next was probably unnecessarily harsh, but I wanted to be alone with my thoughts, to turn over this new idea and examine it from every angle like a glittering gem. "Now leave me."

His response was quick, cruel, and clever. "I'll hardly be the first."

As the door shut behind him, I poured myself a finger of whiskey and reflected.

I thought a long, long way back, all the way back to the German prince and the bullfighter. Then Porter, then Harry, but not just Harry—I'd felt bonded in a way to Frank and also Baron Takamine in Japan, another man with whom I'd had no legally recognized relationship but an undeniable, powerful bond.

Then I began to count them on upturned fingers. Alexander, Miguel, Porter, Harry, Frank, Huntingdon-Meer: that was already six. Takamine made seven.

I continued my tally, adding three more legal husbands—Jackson, Miskinoff, the prince himself—and that made ten. Then there was Crowley, I thought. My entanglement with him spanned a decade, more years than four out of five marriages. Then I remembered Bishop—as much as I'd hated him, how miserable he'd made me, I couldn't deny how inextricably linked we were. That horrible man carried around a piece of my soul, changed the course of my life. It was his tarot deck that had enabled me to connect with my past selves across the barriers of the natural world. I hated him, but he counted.

Rings didn't make husbands. In a way, I had fused with so many other men, some sexual and romantic, some one or the other, some with a different kind of bond entirely.

And when I counted up those men, the ones who had made a

difference in my life, touched me deeply in ways that went beyond the physical, I realized it all.

There had been twelve.

Perhaps, after all, the Spanish mystic's prediction was not out of the realm of possibility.

Your thirteenth husband will bury you.

So who would he be?

———

It was time, I decided, to go back to New York. I was done marrying princes. I was done marrying, period, because I'd been warned not to take a thirteenth husband. How impossible that number had seemed once. How foolish I could still be, my advanced age notwithstanding.

Mystics were harder to find on the Upper East Side than they'd once been, but my doorman at the Savoy-Plaza was a helpful man of my acquaintance, and he steered me in the right direction. The woman was a new kind of mystic, one who encouraged people to look more within themselves for their answers, believing everyone knew their actual truth deep down but needed guidance to find it.

So this mystic handed me a piece of paper and told me to draw what scared me.

I began sketching, as commanded, but without a clear sense of what I meant to draw. What could scare me, a woman who was old and rich and hardly loved anyone? What was left?

But when I looked down, I saw what had taken shape.

It was me, I saw. The woman in white. As I'd seen her that first time, when my father died. My young self had assigned fear to my older self's appearance, confused, lost. The drawing itself showed me more as I had been, not an apparition, merely a woman on her own.

The mystic frowned down at the drawing, ran her finger along its edge, then drew her finger back. She tilted her head to scrutinize the drawing from different directions. She looked so long I was starting to feel she might be a charlatan. If she was, I told myself, my doorman and I were going to have words.

After a long silence, she asked pointedly, "How long has he been visiting you?"

I was confused. "Him? There is no him. Only her."

"Oh." She looked oddly cross. Then her expression shifted into some kind of recognition. "Oh, you look but you don't see."

"I know what I saw," I insisted stubbornly.

She pointed at the picture I'd drawn. "Him."

"Her!" I said, stabbing at the paper with my finger, right on my own blurred face, the face that I'd drawn just as I remembered it, too soft-edged to recognize as myself until I knew the truth. "There is no him. Only her."

Mirroring my frustration, she jabbed a finger hard, right on the drawing, so hard she almost tore the paper. "There! Right there he is."

She was pointing at the shadow.

I'd drawn it just as faithfully as the woman in white, showing how the shadow outlined her, clung to her every curve. I opened my mouth to tell the mystic it was just a shadow, but then, when I looked right at the tip of her fingernail, I saw it.

In the swirl of shadow I'd drawn, there were darker smears. And if I looked closely, at the right angle, what leapt from the shadow wasn't just more shadow.

Eyes. A mouth. A faint curve that could be a nose.

A face.

It was Death.

It was, I finally recognized, *you*.

CHAPTER TWENTY-EIGHT

*Not that I am afraid to die, but rather afraid of the great
mystery of death, afraid of what I do not understand, of things
that I have seen strange vague glimpses of during this curious
life of mine.*

—AC

I wonder that you have any time for me just now, with a war on, bombs raining from the skies in beautiful London and the whole of Europe mired. Thousands will die today. Is it indulgent of me to cling to these last hours of life, to hold you captive with stories about all the heartbreaks and mysteries and stunning reversals that came before?

Perhaps. But you and I both know you're not the one who's captive here, and there has always been something extraordinary between you and me. If you wanted to get on with it, you would.

On one hand, I'm more than a collection of moments. We humans all are. But at the same time, each of these moments has led me to the next, then the next, through the days and over the years, finally arriving at this particular moment, here, with you.

In a sense, I've been trying to outrun you for years, ever since that first visit, which I didn't recognize for what it was. The vision of light and shadow. Me, visiting my younger self, and you, always nearby. After you took my father, I ran and ran, but no matter how many miles one sails or people one loves or dollars one spends, Death always comes. You always come. I happen to be particularly fortunate.

Is anyone else lucky like this? To have lived a life so full and satisfying that they're not just ready for you but eager?

I suppose, though, that's the way I've embraced most of my adventures. Eagerly. In a way, going with you is the natural next step in the adventures to come.

You understand, don't you, how I was distracted? In the visions, I saw only myself, the woman in white, not knowing you were always her steadfast companion. You were so faithful to me, and I didn't even realize you were there. And I was distracted by life. All the noise and light and excitement and love, always love. It's hard to say whether that's a distraction, I suppose, or the whole point.

Last year, when I voyaged to Paris with my grandson, Reggie's boy, I felt in my bones it would be my last real journey. He'd urged me to postpone because of the threat of a German invasion, but I insisted. In a way, we were both right. Our visit wasn't disrupted, but only two weeks after we sailed for home, the Germans besieged Amiens. Surrender followed a month thereafter. So I was glad I strolled those familiar streets one last time. Perhaps, somehow, I knew. But I suppose it's easy to say that now. Does looking back ever provide true clarity? I think today it has. I think today, I can face everything. I'm facing you. I know what the rattle in my lungs means, and I have no false hope of survival.

And last night, I dreamed of us for the first time as we really are. Not the woman in white, the ghost with my face, who haunted me, with just a sliver of shadow around her. That's how it started, of course. In life and in the dream. But last night, you uncoiled yourself, growing in shape and form. We stood next to each other, the woman in white and Death himself, her shadow. Equally important. Equally present.

And the way they stood next to each other, hand in hand, was what made me realize.

Partners. Equals. The marriage I had always wanted. The ideal husband and wife.

My thirteenth husband.

I don't hold a grudge against you for what you took from me. I'm tempted to say I don't think anyone should, but I don't tell others how to feel; I've lived my life in a spirit of tolerance and openness, and now isn't the time to change that. Everyone deserves to have their own opinion about death, just as they can have their opinion about anything. What matters most to me is how I feel about you, and in this moment, I know.

I'm ready for you.

You're here with me, in the same form I've always seen you. As a shadow. As the other half of me, balancing dark with light. You are part of me in a way that I didn't recognize for years. I recognize it now.

You reach out your hand. I reach back.

"You won't bury me," I say out loud. It feels very important, just now, to speak. "He was wrong."

You say, *In a way, yes, in a way, no. After I take you, they will bury what's left.*

"That won't be me," I reply.

I get the best of you.

I tell the absolute truth now. Why lie at the end? "You always have."

Together, we evanesce.

AUTHOR'S NOTE

It is the oldest of saws that truth is stranger than fiction, but here's the truth about Aimée Crocker: she jam-packed far more exploits into her life than I could possibly fit into this novel.

Some of the wildest stories in these pages were either drawn directly from or inspired by the historical record. Aimée did in fact report seeing visions of a ghostly woman in her bed beginning when she was ten years old, though the vision wasn't linked to her father's death. She also reported being warned by a fortune teller not to take a thirteenth husband. During her marriage to Galitzine, she was quoted in the *Oakland Tribune* as saying the prince was her "twelfth husband if I include in my matrimonial list seven Oriental husbands, not registered under the laws of the Occident." So the numbers actually work, more or less.

The honeymoon train wreck at Tehachapi Pass is historical fact, as was Aimée and Porter's scandalous divorce and custody battle, including its final resolution of the judge awarding custody of their daughter to Aimée's mother, Margaret. During the marriage, San Francisco newspapers did report that Porter Ashe both shot a bear near Lake Tahoe and killed a shark with a champagne bottle while swimming off Santa Cruz. Aimée did meet King David Kalakaua and accept his invitation to visit Hawaii, where she did have a run-in with missionaries from the Society of Cousins and fall under the spell of Washington Irving Bishop, who did later die gruesomely from being autopsied while he was apparently still alive. See? Wild!

I've dramatically streamlined most of Aimée's self-reported Asian adventures, relocating the violin episode from Shanghai to Japan and skipping entirely over her stories about living in a maharajah's harem in India, falling in with a Chinese gangster named Huan Kai who tried to have her killed, and being kidnapped for the purposes of marriage in Borneo, among other implausible tales. You can read these and equally outlandish stories set all over the world in Aimée's 1936 memoir, *And I'd Do It Again*.

In 1897, Aimée's third husband, Harry Gillig, and his longtime friend Frank Unger did throw a lavish beach party in Hawaii as described here, though said party was not likely the catalyst of Aimée's divorce from Harry. They divorced in 1900 after Aimée met Jackson Gouraud, the love of her life, who did, again in what seems outlandish to us today, die of tonsillitis in 1910.

Other borderline unbelievable, documented events: Aimée's daughter/sister Gladys married Jackson Gouraud's brother Powers, causing Powers to joke publicly that he was his own first cousin. Aimée's adopted daughter Yvonne was caught in a compromising position with Aimée's fourth husband, Miskinoff, and Aimée responded by directing them to live together to test the relationship. The occultist Aleister Crowley, inventor of sex magick with a *k*, had an on-and-off love affair with Aimée for at least a decade.

In other cases, this piece of historical fiction may be more fiction and less history. Stories about Porter Ashe gambling for Aimée's hand in marriage show up in multiple sources, though the method morphs from "poker dice" to an actual hand of poker, and Harry Gillig only sometimes appears as a competitor. The details of the poker game as I've spelled them out here (the wedding, the hotel) are completely fictional. Similarly, Aimée and her friends may or may not have been abandoned by a chaperone while at finishing school in

Dresden, but that is one of her many claims, as are her involvements with the German prince Alexander of Saxe-Weimar-Eisenach (who she refers to as Saxe-Coburg) and a toreador named Miguel during that period. Washington Irving Bishop's mother did mount a crusade to punish the medical establishment she believed responsible for her son's death, but she had already died by the time I depict Bishop's widow complaining about her to Aimée (at a meeting which is, you guessed it, fictional).

I also changed details to fit the demands of the story in these pages, nearly always to simplify. For example, Aimée and Jennie had two other sisters, Nellie and Kate, both of whom died in the 1870s, and a cousin named Elwood who the family had adopted. Some sources indicate that Aimée and Porter's daughter was initially named Alma and that Margaret changed the girl's name to Gladys upon adopting her, but I eliminated this change to reduce reader confusion. Gladys's kidnapping at the hands of her father and uncle took place in Los Angeles, not San Francisco, but again, that story was complicated enough without additional logistics. I also left out two more adopted children, Dolores and Yolanda, relocated Margaret Crocker's funeral from Buffalo to Sacramento, and kept Jackson and Aimée at the Larchmont house when they actually relocated to Long Island (where the real-life house fire and dog poisonings happened). I also fudged Gladys's age slightly at the time of her mother's death and opened the Plaza Hotel in New York City a year early for my own convenience. Aimée's performance as herself in the burlesque called *Hell* took place in New York City in 1911, not Paris in 1915. The Countess of Salvatierra is a character of my own invention, as are Darlene Messerschmidt, the lawyer Everleigh, the publisher Ephraim Russell, and each of the mediums and mystics Aimée consults, including Mister Whisper.

If you want to read more about Aimée, I highly recommend Kevin Taylor's extensively researched book *Aimée Crocker, Queen of Bohemia*, which was invaluable in my own research about the heiress's wild life. You can also enjoy his work at aimeecrocker.com.

The opening quotations from each chapter appear in *And I'd Do It Again*.

READING GROUP GUIDE

1. Often throughout her life, Aimée finds herself in a foreign country where she knows no one and where money and time are no object. If you were in this kind of situation, what would you do?

2. What do you think of palm readings, mystics, tarot? Do you believe they can be accurate?

3. Have you ever experienced something you couldn't explain, such as a vision or a miracle?

4. Aimée, especially in her younger years, acts mainly on impulse. Do you tend to act impulsively, or do you prefer to plan everything out?

5. What is the key to a good marriage? Does it matter how much time you spend together before you marry?

6. Aimée's life is often used for gossip in the newspapers, both to her amusement and frustration. How do the tabloids affect her marriages? What does something like constant scrutiny from the press do to a relationship?

7. Aimée finds it difficult to balance being a parent and being a partner. How hard is it to find time for your partner after having children? How do you find a balance?

8. Both Aimée and Harry, as a woman and as a gay man, are trying to cope with being lower in society, and they decide to marry for convenience. What do you make of this decision? How do societal pressures affect one's decision to be in or leave a relationship?

9. Do you believe dreams mean something to our waking lives? When you dream, are you able to control the events, or are you more of a passive participant?

10. Why do you think Aimée is so interested in mystics? What do they offer her?

11. Do you believe Aimée had thirteen husbands in the end, as the mystic claimed? What constitutes a husband, a partner, or a lover?

A CONVERSATION WITH
THE AUTHOR

How did you first hear about Aimée Crocker? What made you want to write a novel about her?

One thing I find so wonderful about writing historical fiction is that in the process of researching one book, I'm constantly stumbling across stories and people that I tuck away for future books. In this case, I had a little help. During the research process for *The Arctic Fury*, I decided I wanted as many women as possible in my fictional Arctic exploration party to be inspired by real women of the 1840s and 1850s. My husband is great at research, so I asked him to send me links to some relevant names. He found, among others, Aimée Crocker. We both realized right away that Aimée didn't quite fit with the brief of what I was looking for to build *The Arctic Fury*, but she was too interesting to forget about entirely. She deserved her own book.

How did you choose what to add to the novel and what to omit?

That was definitely a tricky part of the process. When I was researching my only other biographical historical novel, *Girl in Disguise*, there was so little information about Kate Warne to hold on to. I had to do a lot of extrapolation and invention around Kate. I have friends who write about much more well-known figures, some who left behind letters and diaries, and in those cases, there's a lot more information to feed into the hopper. Aimée is somewhere in between. There's a decent amount of information, but not all of it is factual. The problem with her is knowing what to believe. Especially in her memoir, *And I'd Do It Again*, she just isn't a reliable narrator. So my choices couldn't be about sticking to the "truth," since that would imply a single correct account. Instead, I chose the stories that helped shape a cohesive narrative for *my* Aimée.

How do you go about researching someone like Aimée Crocker?

Much of it involved the usual sources for people of this time period, like newspaper articles. But reading her memoirs was nonnegotiable too. I cross-referenced a lot of sources to build a timeline of her life and looked for more information to fill in the gaps. Aimée was written about so frequently that there was a decent amount to draw from. I enjoyed the experience.

We don't find out to whom Aimée is speaking until the end of the book. Tell us about creating that structure.

I'm so glad to be asked this question! My decision to have Aimée speaking directly to Death was a lightning bolt of inspiration that struck partway through the drafting process. A little earlier than this, I had read Rebecca Makkai's wonderful novel *I Have Some Questions for You*, which also uses a narrative voice that sounds like second person but turns out to be direct address. The moment when you as a reader realize that there really is a "you" is so powerful, and then when you find out who that "you" is—it adds a whole new layer to the book. I had done something similar in a short story years ago, but I wanted to see if I could pull it off in a novel. And I think it makes the book far richer.

What do you hope readers take away from Aimée's story?

When we look back at history, it's easy to see it as a monolith, to assume all the people of a certain time thought a certain way. But if you look around today, there's no consensus in society about who people should be and how they should act—there's tremendous disagreement. Why would the past be any different? So when we say that society in the nineteenth century valued a certain "ideal woman" who focused on nurturing her family and taking care of her home, that's not untrue. But it doesn't mean that every woman was the "ideal woman" or that certain segments of society wouldn't much rather be interesting than proper. Aimée demanded divorces and chartered ships and got tattoos, not because she was ahead of her time but because she had the money and influence to do what she wanted regardless of what other people thought. She got to be the woman she wanted to be. We get plenty of stories about women from history who were held back from doing that by their circumstances. So I like sharing Aimée's story as a counterpoint. We can't all live her globetrotting life, but could we all take a stab at pursuing happiness with a little more passion, a little more fervor? I bet we could.

ACKNOWLEDGMENTS

It's quite a process, growing a book from the mere kernel of an idea to a finished product readers can enjoy. Often, it feels like a miracle. The miracle of this particular book involved countless great minds and willing hands. I'll name as many as I have space for and apologize to those I've inadvertently left off the list—I think each successive book, as much as I enjoy writing them, shaves just a bit more horsepower off my brain.

My editor, Shana Drehs, at Sourcebooks continues to set the standard for keen editorial guidance and a knack for knowing what books and authors need. Nicole Cunningham at The Book Group has been a powerhouse partner; our first time working together won't be our last. It's been a joy working on this book with both familiar and less-familiar faces at Sourcebooks, a tremendous home for authors: thanks so much to Dominique Raccah, Chelsea McGuckin, Heather VenHuizen, Stephanie Rocha, Margaret Coffee, Valerie Pierce, and Molly Waxman for all their hard work. Particular thanks to Sabrina Baskey and Jessica Thelander for their eagle eyes, and Cristina Arreola and Anna Venckus for making sure that readers who are going to love this book know, first of all, that it exists. I'm also grateful to Jenny Meyer for handling foreign rights, Michelle Weiner and the team at CAA on the film and TV front, and DJ Kim, Elisabeth Weed, and the rest of the squad at The Book Group.

I am incredibly lucky to count so many fellow authors in the historical fiction world as colleagues and friends. Kris Waldherr did heroic work saving me from my own ignorance in the field of tarot; Kerri Maher has been my local hero for brainstorming, long walks, strategy sessions, and other forms of much-needed author support. I asked Fiona Davis, Noelle Salazar, Marie Benedict, and Heather Webb for blurbs at a singularly bad time of year with a short turnaround, and they all came through like champions. I was blown away. Therese Walsh and the Writer Unboxed community continue to provide inspiration, information, and general warm fuzzies like nowhere else, both online and at UnCon.

Readers, I wouldn't be here without you. Booksellers and librarians, your energy and enthusiasm astound me. Jonathan, let's do this again sometime.

Thank you.

ABOUT THE AUTHOR

Bestselling author Greer Macallister's historical novels, including *The Magician's Lie*, *Woman 99*, and *The Arctic Fury*, have been named Indie Next, LibraryReads, Target Book Club, and Amazon Best Book of the Month picks and optioned for film and television. As G. R. Macallister, she is the author of the Five Queendoms series, which *Paste Magazine* called "the best feminist fantasy series you probably haven't read yet." A regular contributor to Writer Unboxed and the *Chicago Review of Books*, she lives with her family in Boston.

THE ARCTIC FURY

"I suspect there is nothing, literally nothing,
of which women are not capable."

—Lady Franklin

Eccentric Lady Jane Franklin makes an outlandish offer to adventurer Virginia
Reeve: take a dozen women, trek into the Arctic, and find her husband's lost expedition. Four parties have failed to find him, and Lady Franklin wants a radical new
approach: put the women in charge.

A year later, Virginia stands trial for murder. Survivors of the expedition willing
to publicly support her sit in the front row. There are only five. What happened out
there on the ice?

Set against the unforgiving backdrop of one of the world's most inhospitable
locations, *USA Today* bestselling author Greer Macallister uses the true story of
Lady Jane Franklin's tireless attempts to find her husband's lost expedition as a
jumping-off point to spin a tale of bravery, intrigue, perseverance, and hope.

**"Equal parts courtroom drama and literary thriller, *The
Arctic Fury* bears all the twists and turns of a runaway
train... A remarkably unique and mesmerizing tale."**

—Kristina McMorris, *New York Times* bestselling
author of *Sold on a Monday*

For more Greer Macallister, visit:
sourcebooks.com

THE MAGICIAN'S LIE

An immersive story of a notorious illusionist
whose troubles have become all too real.

The Amazing Arden saws a man in half on stage every night, and the country loves her for it. But, one night, when she switches her saw for a fire ax, the crowds are left wondering if it was a new trick or a very real murder. When her husband is found dead beneath the stage, the answer seems clear.

Despite her best attempts to flee, Arden finds herself in a one-room police station with a young officer desperate to know the truth. Even handcuffed and alone, Arden is far from powerless—and what she reveals is spellbinding. Over the course of one eerie night, the magician will have to pull off one final act—this time with her own life at stake.

**"A spellbinding tale... Macallister, like the Amazing
Arden, mesmerizes her audience."**

—*Washington Post*

For more Greer Macallister, visit:
sourcebooks.com

GIRL IN DISGUISE

For the first female Pinkerton detective, respect is
hard to come by, but danger is everywhere.

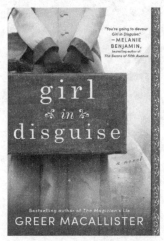

In the tumultuous years of the Civil War, the streets of Chicago offer a widow mostly
danger and ruin—unless that widow is Kate Warne. As an undercover Pinkerton
detective, Kate is able to infiltrate the seedy side of the city in disguises that her
fellow spies just can't manage. She's a seductress, an exotic foreign medium, a rich
train passenger—all depending on the day and the robber, thief, or murderer she's
been assigned to nab.

But is it only her detective work that makes her a daring spy and a clever liar?
Or is the real disguise the good girl she always thought she was? As the Civil War
marches closer, Kate takes on her most pressing job ever. The nation's future is
at risk, and she's no longer sure where her disguise ends and the very real danger
begins.

**"A fast-paced, lively tale of intrigue and deception, with a heroine at
its center so appealingly complicated that she leaps off the page"**

—Christina Baker Kline, #1 *New York Times*
bestselling author of *Orphan Train*

For more Greer Macallister, visit:

sourcebooks.com

WOMAN 99

A vivid story about a young woman whose quest to save
her sister risks her sanity, her safety, and her life.

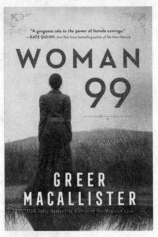

When Charlotte Smith's wealthy parents commit her beloved sister, Phoebe, to the
infamous Goldengrove Asylum, Charlotte knows there's more to the story than
madness. She surrenders herself to the insane asylum, surrendering her real identity
as a privileged young lady of San Francisco society to become a nameless inmate,
Woman 99.

The longer she stays, the more she realizes that many of the women of
Goldengrove Asylum aren't insane, merely inconvenient—and her search for the
truth threatens to dig up secrets that some very powerful people would do anything
to keep.

"*Woman 99* is a gorgeous ode to the power of female courage."

—Kate Quinn, *New York Times* bestselling author of *The Alice Network*

For more Greer Macallister, visit:
sourcebooks.com